PRAISE
EDGE OF THE K

T0267808

"The skillful writing makes the book a worthy read. . . . A complicated dystopian political thriller enhanced by lively prose."
—*Kirkus Reviews*

"Author Sheri T. Joseph has crafted a riveting novel . . . a brilliantly original concept that captures you right from the start."
—*Readers' Favorite*, 5-star review

"Via pristine details, intriguing characters, and such timely themes as technology ethics and societal collapse, Joseph's broad, bold tale of an any-day-now dystopia never strays from the intimacy of a father and daughter's mutual love."
—Anita Gail Jones, finalist for the PEN/Bellwether Prize for Socially Engaged Fiction and author of *The Peach Seed*

"Like all great dystopian fiction writers, Joseph holds a magic mirror to our world in a compelling, complex story."
—Lori Duff, INDIE Awards Gold Medalist and author of *Devil's Defense*

"*Edge of the Known World* is a compelling story about technology, identity, and privacy that illuminates some of the most pressing questions facing society today."
—Corie Adjmi, Best Book Award and American Fiction Award–winning author of *The Marriage Box*

"Joseph's wild, far-flung, and intrigue-filled adventures offer much for future diplomats, as well as scientists, to ponder."
—Mary Carlin Yates, Ambassador of the United States and former deputy commander of the US Africa Command

EDGE
OF THE
KNOWN
WORLD

EDGE OF THE KNOWN WORLD

A novel

SHERI T. JOSEPH

Copyright © 2024 Sheri T. Joseph

All rights reserved. No part of this publication may be reproduced, distributed, or transmitted in any form or by any means, including photocopying, recording, digital scanning, or other electronic or mechanical methods, without the prior written permission of the publisher, except in the case of brief quotations embodied in critical reviews and certain other noncommercial uses permitted by copyright law. For permission requests, please address SparkPress.

Published by SparkPress, a BookSparks imprint,
A division of SparkPoint Studio, LLC
Phoenix, Arizona, USA, 85007
www.gosparkpress.com

Published 2024
Printed in the United States of America
Print ISBN: 978-1-68463-262-6
E-ISBN: 978-1-68463-263-3
Library of Congress Control Number: 2024906895

Interior design by Tabitha Lahr

All company and/or product names may be trade names, logos, trademarks, and/or registered trademarks and are the property of their respective owners.

This is a work of fiction. Names, characters, places, and incidents either are the product of the author's imagination or are used fictitiously. Any resemblance to actual persons, living or dead, is entirely coincidental.

'S WONDERFUL
Music and Lyrics by GEORGE GERSHWIN and IRA GERSHWIN
© 1927 (Renewed) WC MUSIC CORP. and IRA GERSHWIN MUSIC
All Rights Administered by WC MUSIC CORP. All Rights Reserved
Used by Permission of ALFRED MUSIC
FOR OUR 100% CONTROL IN THE WORLD

NO AI TRAINING: Without in any way limiting the author's [and publisher's] exclusive rights under copyright, any use of this publication to "train" generative artificial intelligence (AI) technologies to generate text is expressly prohibited. The author reserves all rights to license uses of this work for generative AI training and development of machine learning language models.

To DJ, Kev, Adam, and Jess,
the eighth wonders of the world

refusé

noun /ri-ˈfyüz-se/ [English, derivation of *to refuse*, from Latin *refusare*, to pour back]

1. a person refused permission to emigrate from their land of origin, who upon fleeing to avoid persecution or danger is refused entry or sanctuary by other lands

2. a person subject to return under international treaty

3. *slang usage*: a person considered unwelcome due to geographic origins; a connotation of human debris

I. THE OLD WORLD

1

Alex poised at the roof's edge listening to the foghorn. She had long ago identified the distant boom as the mating call of a ghost ship trapped inside the Golden Gate. It was a perfect evening for a frustrated ghost, if not a tipsy twenty-three-year-old postdoc atop a rickety three-story fire escape ladder. The August fog howled with gale force, maddening the bay and sinking the city in premature night. Alex eyed the dumpster and alley far below. Not the ideal way to exit a graduation party, but her magic-act disappearances were the stuff of Institute legend, and her soon-to-be ex-boyfriend guarded the flat's only door. He wanted to talk about their future.

Her choices were to face the future, sprout wings, or take the ladder. Alex did some mental math. A missed grip meant hitting concrete at thirty miles per hour. Her father's voice echoed in her head: *Stop, rag mop. Think!*

A waft of brine and tar came from the shrouded piers. The flat was on Polk Street, behind the VA shelter of Ghirardelli Square, and belonged to her soon-to-be ex, a Global Security Adjunct with the exquisite name of Michelangelo Giancarlo Valenti. It was typical junior faculty housing, with wharf rats scritch-scratching inside the walls and stealing bait from traps, the steady *zing-zing* of Guizi Hunter video games, stained denim slipcovers, and fingerless gloves for when the heat went out. This being a bon voyage for newly minted PhDs, red plastic cups littered the warped floor, while squeaking springs from the bedrooms made rhythmic last-fling music.

The mood sang of freedom and possibility. There were no senior faculty here to bemoan a war ended twenty-five years ago—their loss of liberties, the humiliations of the Austerity or the repressive cynicism of youth culture—as if her generation had requested an intractable economic depression and psychosis of life under the constant threat of war. The TaskForce Institutes were the training ground of the Allied Nations' civilian leadership. The days of unfettered travel were a memory, and their coveted TaskForce officer cards the gift of an international life.

Alex was the youngest of the cohort, the youngest PhD the Institute ever awarded, and the only one not leaving the backwater San Francisco campus. No one could understand why she refused field work, never mind the Fellowship at dazzling Headquarters in Shanghai. *Always lie by telling another truth*, a rule of omission that helped to keep her story straight. "If y'all grew up in West Texas," she had told the others in her most entertaining drawl, "you'd find it mighty purty right here." She was glad for the other Fellows, but also bitter, ashamed, sick with wanderlust, and if forced to happy-drawl one more time she would have ignited the flat like a rocket launch.

A chill gust of wind laughed in her face. Alex's dark waist-length hair and pleated skirt sailed crazy around her. *Stop!* She clambered to the ladder in reckless defiance.

Every emotion had a certain half-life. Ten rungs down and she was orange with rust, a level arm's length from Michelangelo's illuminated bay window, and watching her warm geek friends debate neo-capitalism and play beer pong without her. Her anger at the faceless world cooled to the loneliness of the ghost ship. Now she was freezing, her stiffening fingers making for a precarious grip. She had lived in the city for seven years yet still had forgotten her coat, hopeful as a tourist, to be schooled again by the devious summer weather.

Michelangelo came into the bay window, and Alex flattened to the ladder. Her tattered pink madras book bag *varoomed* with his gunning-the-Ferrari ringtone. She hooked an arm and fished madly for her phone. "Hey, you," she answered, bird-perched in shadow. "Great party!"

"*La mia bellezza del Texas!*" His Italian accent rose and fell like a sine wave, free of consonants. Tomorrow he posted back to Rome, ending her first experiment in using men.

"Where are you?" he asked.

"I'm hanging out."

He sighed in relief—so sweet, so simple. He was a fantastic if wet kisser, with a wealth of brown curls kept in perfect disarray thanks to a shelf of expensive hair products. After a few bottles of Umbrian wine, he was her prime source of classified High Council intel.

People always confided in Alex, a cursed kind of gift, as if the secret she had learned on her sixteenth birthday—the great divide of her before, and after—were a pheromone attractant for private things. So she knew Michelangelo was slumming it. His family was wealthy, nasty, and as politically connected as the Borgias. Like everyone at an ultra-elite institution, he was terrified he was destined for something great and would die before finding out what.

"Come to Rome with me, Texas," he said. "We will be the spaghetti western."

"I wish," she said, watching a wharf rat the size of a pug scuttle across the alley. It stared back up at her, bold and toasty in its little fur coat. "But I'm teaching seminar. I'm trapped here." True, with no need to add that she dare not risk the ubiquitous security g-screens across the Nations, which took Europe, Asia, and most of North America off her personal map. Peel away the ever-shifting Regional Organizations in Africa and South America, the Federation's satellite states, the toxic red zones, and her globe became vanishingly small.

San Francisco remained one of the few places with a conservative distaste for random screens. Her father's first rule was *You stay put.* No chancing fate at airports, train stations, even toll plazas. The city was a jewel compared to the Plainview Penal Ranch where she lived her first sixteen years, but the spans of the scenic bay bridges were still bars.

"What about us?" asked Michelangelo.

"Let's burn that bridge when we get to it."

Michelangelo drooped in the window like a sunflower at dusk. Alex thought of her father's second rule: *Do not get attached. They cannot help you, and you can only do them harm.* It had a corollary: *Intimacy increases the temptation to confide. Keep your britches on.* That was fine in practice, as her professors joked, but what about in theory? She really liked Michelangelo. He was kind and respected limits—no squeaky springs for her. She wanted to give him something, and she had only one currency.

"Can I tell you a secret?" she said, picking one he'd like. His profile perked up. "Everyone assumes I had a hard childhood. Mom died in childbirth, I grew up in a prison, et cetera, et cetera. But Plainview was an honor farm, just an electric perimeter, with crops and livestock. Patrick, my dad, was an inmate, but also the prison doctor. He was an ex–A&M linebacker, a hyper-moral gentle giant. Everyone adored me and let me get away with murder."

Michelangelo nodded sagely. "Sì, sì, a loving childhood always shows."

"Sundays were holy," she continued, transported from frigid perch to happy feral days of beating sun and scrubby plain. "We'd build tumbleweed ships from my dad's Greek myths and have pickup football games. He always had a razzle-dazzle play. Then, when I was nine, the Creationist preacher lady started coming from Lubbock for services. She was married to Warden, so we had to go. She preached that the War had been God's Flood, the Diasporas the new Babel. Our Chinese Allies were granted purgatory with the Baptists; our Federation enemies were going straight to hell with the Methodists. My father despised her as an amoral hypocrite. Then one Sunday, I hid under the exam table to see why preacher lady needed a *very* private checkup every visit."

Michelangelo laughed, poor bambino, and it was worth reliving those horrifying minutes scrunched beneath the exam table with her hands clapped over her ears. She had kept her father's adulterous hypocrisy in her back pocket to brood over through the years, unable to explain his insane risk. If Warden had found out, her father would be buried in Plainview.

Tonight though, through the lens of young adulthood, she could appreciate the power of his need and loneliness. Prison was endured through a series of essential fictions. Denial allowed the sunlit moments, the small joys and anticipation that carried you through the desert nights.

Alex resumed an awkward one-armed monkey descent trying to hold the phone to her ear while Michelangelo chattered about *amore*. The ladder ended five feet above a stinking trash bin. She hesitated, caught on the crux of her own story. The Rule demanded another desert night alone in her twin bed piled with stuffed animals, her hands moving over her restless body. Or—she could embrace denial and climb back up to a man's warm arms, a journey to an imagined land if only until dawn.

The foghorn brayed her location like a ghostly snitch. As Alex fumbled to muffle her speaker, a beam of flashlight hit her eyes. "Alex *Tashen*!" came an imperious female voice from the street. "Are you fucking high? Get down this instant!"

"Is that the Kommandant?" asked Michelangelo. "Oh, Texas, this is how you say goodbye?"

It was like being trapped between two advancing armies. The fumble cost Alex's frozen grip, and she toppled into the dumpster.

Alex didn't have long to ponder the mysterious slimy things that cushioned her fall.

"Out of the trash," came Kommandant Burton's crisp alto, an expression of zero concern that said *don't even try for a sympathy play*. Alex climbed out to face the woman who, at five foot one, was the most intimidating person she knew.

Suzanne Dias Burton was a fifty-two-year-old Allied general and West Point alum with a doctorate in biological sciences, a member of the Nations Science Academy, a special adviser to the secretary general, and the founding ruler of the TaskForce Institutes. She wore a camo field jacket, her crown of short black ringlets blowing above skeptical eyes and mahogany skin. Her entire personality was distilled in her planted hand-on-hips stance. She made regular visits to the old vets in Ghirardelli. Still, her appearance fit with a psychic-seeming propensity for ambush at the guiltiest moments.

"I see you're hard at work on my brief," said the Kommandant, the excuse Alex had given to skip their monthly status dinner that evening. It would have been their seventy-fifth dinner since Alex arrived from the ranch as a bewildered sixteen-year-old prodigy — the Kommandant took keen personal interest in her rare Special Admits. "Walk with me, Alex." The Kommandant peeled a slice of cold anchovy pizza from Alex's blouse. "And stay downwind."

They both lived near the Presidio campus a dozen blocks away, so Alex prepared for a forced march and harangue. The overdue brief was for a Commission departing in a few days, and there were other sins to cover. The past week alone, she had tripped and caused a domino fall of faculty at Convocation, pranked a blowhard emeritus into lambasting his own research, and performed a wicked imitation of the Kommandant that had unfortunately gone viral.

On the other side of the equation, her publications in prestigious journals brought glory to the Institute. Her Diaspora 101 was the most popular freshman course across the international campuses. When she sat with major donors at fundraising dinners, they wrote enormous checks.

So her punishment was scathing rather than terminal. "Time to grow up," began the Kommandant. Alex made her usual escape to daydream, surfacing every few blocks to pick up the Kommandant's last sentence and express appropriate contrition. The barred windows and shops of Union Street turned into a trek through the Himalayas, sun-haloed peaks and plumes of ice crystals streaming at hurricane force to vanish in a perfect sky. The view barely stretched her imagination — no snowcap could be colder than the corner of Fillmore and Union.

The gang of shelter kids ran to greet her. Judging by their reaction, she looked ghoulish, her lips corpse-blue with cold, the tomato sauce on her blouse giving a good impression of blood. Alex handed out the fun-size Snickers she always pinched for them from the Institute Commons, adding petty larceny to her list of sins.

The Kommandant's ire, though, was fixed on the corner by Alex's building, where a stout US Homeland general in a greatcoat was reprimanding a young Metro cop with a pinched, sullen face. The cop held a neon-orange baton with a black rubber handle.

Alex jolted backward as if touched by a live wire. Metro police checked ID with retinal and facial recognition apps on their phones. She welcomed such biometric scans, which confirmed she was her true self: Alex Tashen, an overeducated, underpaid TaskForce Academic who belonged here. But this cop's neon baton was a field genetic screener, capable of spotting a certain invisible freckle.

Patrick gave her a one-in-ten chance of being detected at any g-screen, a probability he had drilled into her brain with lectures on dependent and independent conditions and images of a revolver at her temple. Alex tried to melt among the shelter kids and stay calm. The g-screens were still cumbersome, with a cheek swab inserted into the tube and, depending on connectivity, a twenty-second wait for ID confirmation to display. TaskForce officers, with their stratospheric clearance, typically got courtesy fast-tracked with a quick biometric.

"Did you not get orders?" the general was telling the cop. "Everyone gets screened, even me. And especially those TaskForce bastards."

The Kommandant charged forward, and Alex was dragged along. The night turned into a bombardment of useless detail—the taste of bay fog in her mouth, salty as tears, the sickly yellow orb of a streetlight. Panic and revulsion surged to an overwhelming urge to run. Patrick's steady voice returned with the rule of three Ds: *Distract, Divert, Delay. Keep your wits and find an out.*

Kommandant and general saluted each other in cool and familiar contempt. Alex wondered if they had served together in the US Army during the War, both being equally ancient middle-aged. The Kommandant's subsequent transfer to Allied Service would explain the native hostility.

"What the hell?" demanded the Kommandant. Alex and the cop could have been little red ants on the sidewalk. "A random g-screen in my city?"

"It's a pilot with *your* TaskForce Bureau of Solidarity," said the general. The news seemed like a squirt of vinegar in the Kommandant's eye. "Join the Guizi Control Program and get the tech free. It's called domestic safety."

"It's called political bullshit." The Kommandant turned to the cop to prove her point. "Tell us, soldier, what do you know about guizis? Speak freely, we're not your Command."

The cop needed no prodding. "The guizis started the War, ma'am. Their diseases killed a billion. My mom and dad lost their whole families. The Federation is a guizi state, and they're still sending human bio-bombs to attack us. But they all got the mark of Cain, so we can catch them with this." He pulled the swab from the g-screener. The orange tube lit ready-green. "The Treaty makes us send guizis back to the Federation, but better to shoot them right here."

"Bah," the Kommandant told the general. "See the impact of junk science on weak minds? Guizis under every rock. Mass g-screens are expensive, inefficient, and breed hysteria that undermines the Treaty."

"I don't give a rat's ass," said the general. "It's about time Homeland got a slice of TaskForce pie. Have you been to Burlingame lately? Why does that cesspool get less resources than your Protectorate?"

"Great question, sir!" cried Alex, seizing the diversion. As long as she was speaking, the swab could not go in her mouth. "Burlingame is a hundred fifty-seven thousand domestic displaced, with static growth. The Protectorates are safe havens for international War displaced, and exhibit exponential growth. The Nepali Protectorate alone has twenty-four million, three hundred fifty thousand in a depopulated Indigenous province of twelve thousand square miles. More hornet's nest than cesspool, I'd say, with the Independence unrest. But you are correct. Allied defenses must be robust across all zones. Sir!"

"Who the hell?" sputtered the general.

Alex worked her frozen fingers into a crabbed salute. "Dr. Alex Tashen, sir. My doctorate is in economics, sub in geography, with a focus on empirical microeconomics. Theoretical is fine, but we work in the real world, right? I do development modeling for Diaspora populations."

"Your *doctorate*? How old can you be, child? Is the Institute handing out PhDs in kindergarten?"

"A five-year-old would be less trouble," said the Kommandant.

"Where'd you get those eyes?" demanded the general, as if Alex had shoplifted the set of aquamarines from a boutique.

"Indian-Swedish ancestry," she replied, the honest answer to the incessant question about her striking high-contrast coloring. "And all Texan. Now, y'all be busy, so I'll be—" The surly cop raised the screener. Alex switched from educator to instigator. "I'll be thinking about the untold cost of terrorism on domestic GNP. G-screeners are a deterrent, and TaskForce tech must be fairly apportioned. Sir!"

"From the mouths of babes!" the general told the Kommandant. "You American turncoat."

"Isolationist fool," said the Kommandant. "Since that worked so well last time." Their ensuing firefight exceeded Alex's hopes of delay. She threw in the occasional statistic for fuel. The ends of her hair flew like needles in her eyes, her nose streamed. Shivers progressed to shudders of cold.

"Can't you see under your noses?" the cop yelled at the elders. He pointed the screener at Alex, and her legs went weak in terror. "Look! The girl is freezing to death."

They blinked at him. "Where in hell's your coat?" the Kommandant demanded of Alex.

"Shoo, child," said the general. "Shoo. Get on home."

Her fifth-story studio was baking hot from the broken thermostat and smelled of cigarette smoke from the vent. Alex went straight to the half gallon of Smirnoff in her freezer. She downed her usual three slugs, but her trembling only increased. If the Solidarity pilot program were implemented here, her globe would shrink to the stifling confines of her room. Three more slugs, and warmth spread in a delicious rush from chest to toes, her fear floating just offshore. The great lesson of her bereavement, no surprise, was that she could anesthetize like a Slav. The vodka jug went *ca-chink* atop a trash can of empties.

She changed into her purple DON'T MESS WITH TEXAS nightie, then kicked through the ankle-deep carpet of dirty clothes, crumpled shut-off notices, books, stuffed animals, drafts of her dissertation, and candy wrappers. Patrick's *Bulfinch's Mythology* hid under her forgotten coat. The worn leather binding smelled of him. She flipped the gold-rimmed pages, thinking about the cop's humane lapse and the mysterious multidimensions at play in every human mind.

It was no mystery, though, how the night would have gone if the screener had blinked red for detected. She tried to imagine Michelangelo's reaction if her luck had run out tonight.

If they come for you, would he stand by you? Patrick once asked about a boy she liked. The answer remained no. Michelangelo would back away, as any man would.

The foghorn sounded, the call now tinged with despair, and Alex spiraled back to the ranch seven years ago, during the broiling summer of the great divide. She had applied to the TaskForce Institute without telling Patrick, knowing it was a fantasy. An inmate's daughter had as much chance of admission as Cyclops, their one-eyed rooster. When her miracle acceptance arrived on her sixteenth birthday, she was too jubilant to notice Patrick's distress. She danced about their Quonset hut, then took the Jeep for a victory tour, spinning donuts in the scrub and whooping at the top of her lungs. The inmates bedecked the Jeep with banners: GIG 'EM, ALEX! LOOK OUT FOR THEM WEIRDOS IN SAN FRANCISCO!

Patrick had been practically living in his clinic lab, racing to finish a paper on a blood disorder before his parole. He emerged for a hug when she returned, but an emergency medical call had sent him off in the Jeep. Alex waited until he was out of sight—against that landscape, even the armadillos stood in high relief—and bolted into the lab for a sneak peek at the birthday present he always hid on the top shelf of the locked cabinet with the narcotics and old lab notebooks. One notebook lay propped open, as if to dry. Alex caught the faint lemon scent of the clear reagent used to count cells with the diode laser, her most boring chore. Curious, she shined the hand laser on a page. To her astonishment, her father's tight cursive had appeared like magic in the blank spaces between the lines of neat penciled equations.

Confession of Patrick Tashen

Welcome, future jury, to the Plainview Penal Ranch, north of old Lubbock and a thousand miles from nowhere. I'm a MD/PhD in computational biology, serving a seventeen-year sentence of medical labor. But I'm a father first. So I'll begin with a day of bad parenting any of you parents will understand. When my Alex was eight—

She dropped the laser with an alarmed laugh, and the words vanished. Her cyber-whiz father had an anachronistic attachment to paper, but this was nuts—unless he judged it more secure than the Net, where any encryption raised AI flags. It was wrong to invade privacy, she knew, but also wrong to have a story written about you in disappearing ink. She picked up the laser.

—Alex was eight. I spent the afternoon raging at my ugly data. I live at the interface of cyberscience and genomics. I am singularly qualified to overcome a singular problem of genetic editing. Yet every result I modeled killed my virtual patients with fevers or exploding hemoglobin.

I surfaced to a suspicious quiet from Alex. She moves in clouds of happy chaos. Silences were the lull before the big uh-oh. I found her in the tumbleweed Argo ship we had built, armed with a month's ration of chocolate and a forbidden toy gun. With her dark wavy hair, golden skin, and big doe eyes, she looked like a chocolate-smeared outlaw princess of the Raj. But the color of those eyes is from a Nordic sky, the blue of glacial pools and winter. Sometimes she is funny-looking to me, and sometimes she takes my breath away. She will be noticed. Anywhere. It strikes me as an unfair complication.

Back to the gun. "It's for guizis!" she said. "They bring plagues like killed Mommy. Shoot 'em in the head, the ugly monsters!"

I grabbed her, this child who is my very reason for living, and yelled that guizi is a mean word, don't ever use it. I'm an ex-linebacker from a state where they grow 'em big. Alex was shocked to tears.

Guizi. The world intruded, even here. I hugged Alex until she was back to twirling my beard around her finger, her habit since infancy. "You were the deadly death of doom!" she said. Everything with Alex is high drama, but she can't hold a grudge.

"Don't call them guizis," I told her. "They are refusés. They're regular folk, just like us. Words matter. They make people angry and afraid."

Alex, of course, had nonstop questions. I knew it was a disservice to wrap her in marshmallows. But how to explain the truth to an eight-year-old?

The lab had gone dark but for the spotlight laser Alex held to the page. A frightened yammering in her head said stop, this notebook was Pandora's box. But she had to know what was inside.

The truth has a very short half-life, future jury. So this is for you too. We sat in that Argo, drawing maps in the dirt and talking "how." How the dirty bombs that began the War caused the Russian and Euro stampedes into Central Asia, and how the new Federation Regime trapped them there. How overcrowding and starvation bred disease, and how the Regime used flu victims as primitive germ warfare. How the Regime sealed its borders after the Treaty, and gave everyone living within those borders a gene therapy to prevent cancers from drifting radiation.

The therapy didn't work, but it did have an unintended consequence. Gene therapies get delivered with special viruses, called vectors. This vector left behind a harmless snippet of its DNA in each recipient's genome, meaning all their cells. Germ line, meaning the snippet is inherited. I kissed the spread of sun freckles on my daughter's nose. "It's like an invisible freckle," I told her, "passed from parent to child. But this freckle shows up on a g-screen."

The truth is that simple, future jury. The truth was snuggled on my lap, cracking herself up with knock-knock jokes and trying to feed me her candy. How could I tell her the rest of the truth? It felt like murdering my child.

I opened my mouth. No words came. Parenthood, it seems, turns otherwise bold and forthright men into freaking cowards.

I tried again at story time, with a variant telling of the Golden Fleece. In not so ancient times, Jason lived on a scrubby island with his pregnant wife. When the sickness came, he had no medicine. Everyone on the island died but him. One day the grief-stricken Jason found a baby on the shore. She had the invisible freckle. The island was a sneaky place to hide her. Jason went on a quest to remove the freckle. She grew up to travel the world and have many grand adventures.

Alex's frown shifted to a connection made, and my heart accelerated to painful thuds. "Well," she announced, "that baby could never be me."

I dared to ask why not. Alex rolled her eyes, a hint of teen years to come.

"That baby was adopted, Poppa," said Alex. "But I look just like you!"

She doesn't look anything like me.

As the years flew past, endless red-eyed nights at my lab research, I convinced myself it was kinder to wait until the therapy was ready before telling her the truth. I was hoping today, her sixteenth birthday, to give her the gift of a safe life. But my final results show that her freckle will not be removed but rather hidden in most of her cells. Every g-screen will be Russian roulette. She's tearing about the ranch in my Jeep, celebrating her Institute admission, out of her mind with the freedom ahead. What do I tell her now?

A blast of foggy gale brought Alex to the now, popping her studio window ajar and fretting the paper maps on the wall. Borderless blue-green prints of the physical world lay in rebuke against the red-yellow chop shop of the political maps. Sepia antique maps displayed terra incognita, with dog-headed men devouring unhappy Christian sailors. Every place was incognita to her.

She had run away that night, as if she were still any normal sixteen-year-old, wandering the moonlit brush and sobbing through cycles of grief and shame, knowing her rage at her poor father was misplaced but unable to help it. The absurdity of her flight had finally circled her back to her father's arms: Where did she think she could go?

As it turned out, she had unknowingly provided the answer. Patrick turned her improbable Institute acceptance into a razzle-dazzle play. The San Francisco location, plus the TaskForce officer privileges, were worth risking the genetic array required for admission. With her settled, Patrick rejoined the Red Cross in the hazardous Nepali Protectorate, where he had served during the War. *You stay put, rag mop, and wait for the world to change.*

She never did get all his lies straight. Some things he told her. The blood disorder was a cover for his years of g-marker research, meant, quite literally, to be read between the lines. He knew of no other refusés in the Nations. He had delivered his research notebooks and Confession to a confidant in the Protectorate for safekeeping.

Other things he refused to tell, or claimed not to know: How she had been smuggled to the ranch as an infant, who her biological parents were, what future jury he wrote to, who was the confidant with his notebooks.

The secrets might be necessary, she knew, but they poisoned his precious visits to San Francisco. She was desperate for answers, and to go with him, and was always angry when he left.

Alex hit play on Patrick's Gershwin songbook, *'s wonderful, 's marvelous*, and did a slow waltz to the maps. Centered on the wall was a topographical map of the Himalayas. She traced the dark plastic bumps of the Annapurna range where, eighteen months ago,

Patrick's medevac plane had disappeared. Everyone aboard was presumed dead, the remains swallowed by an avalanche.

The wildness of her grief had been complicated by an unfathomable sense of abandonment. No astronaut adrift in space could feel more alone. A craving for risky humanitarian work was not the same as courage; where was his compassion for the one who really needed him?

Her stubborn heart insisted his death was another lie. The Nepali Protectorate was a hotbed of dissent; perhaps he'd violated his parole and had to go underground. Why he would fake his death without a word to her, knowing how she would suffer, was a mystery she shied away from exploring.

"Hi, Poppa," she said to the map, trying to summon his voice. "Everyone's leaving tomorrow. And I almost got screened tonight. I miss you so much." The many griefs of the day compressed into one. Alex clutched the book and wept in bitter, gasping sobs.

Her phone interrupted with a sharp ship-whistle alert that she'd never heard before. The screen flashed repeatedly with the clasped-hands logo of the Allied Media Service, official news site for the billions of Nations' citizens. The cyber-secure media fortress was clearly being hacked.

The screen settled to a text: *Asylum Netcast #1. Occasion: The Fall of Warsaw Safe Area, twenty-fifth anniversary.*

Alex felt goose bumps rise. The Safe Areas were an ugly, shameful chapter of the War the Allies tried to forget, enclave tent camps that had collected hundreds of thousands of desperate Federation refugees under promise of Allied protection. One by one, the Safe Areas were allowed to be overrun by Regime forces, who carried out systematic mass executions and atrocities.

Netcast #1 continued to scroll. *The shame continues to this day. Allied patrols recently intercepted a Federate family escaping the Regime. We sent them back. They were taken to Jablsynk gulag, where this recording was made.* The video showed a woman, a man, and three children in a concrete room. The preteen girl had the mother's fair hair. The Federate guards were young, unremarkable. One guard ran his hands over the girl's chest. The father lunged forward, and another guard shot him in the back of the head.

Don't call them guizis, read the text. *They are refusés. Asylum now.*

Alex fell against the map wall, knocked breathless with shock—not at the heart-ripping images, but because she had seen this video before. It was the same horrific, stolen footage that Patrick had shown her on his last visit to San Francisco.

When refusés escaped the Regime, he had told her, they often brought smuggled evidence of the danger they faced if returned. The Nations tossed them back, per the Treaty, but archived their evidence. His years of biologic research had translated into novel tools in cyber-immunity, allowing him to exploit a vulnerability in the archive and hack into the videos. He had made this copy to show her, to dispel any illusions about a removal. Now he showed the Nations.

Faith, fact, need—she no longer wondered at those borders. Her heart was a physical world of unbounded conviction. This Netcast, a genius middle finger to TaskForce security, was Patrick's creation and her proof of life. He was fighting for her, as he always had, in hiding as he had once hidden her.

His timing of the Netcasts to the historic falls of the Safe Areas was a brilliant strategy to heighten sympathy and outrage. And to build buzz. If Asylum Netcast #1 was Warsaw, then Netcast #2 would correspond to the Fall of Riga. That anniversary was only eight weeks away.

Alex's elation wavered. Patrick did not know that Netcast #2 would be his last. One of the classified security files she had hacked from Michelangelo—her own foray into the black arts, playing on the human vulnerabilities of trust and affection that could breach any system—reported a new geo-locator code, a so-called Hallows virus, that nullified the anonymity of the Dark Net and closed in on the true source signal with each new attack. TaskForce security would see the pattern of the Safe Areas, too, and be ready for Netcast #2, with coordinated raids and eyes in the sky directing the dragnet forces to Patrick's location. They would pump him with interrogation drugs and force every secret, including hers.

Her phone was back to showing the time. Not an hour ago she was climbing down a fire escape. She was a plaything for some vicious gods, and nothing about this life was her choice.

The foghorn called her to the window. Five stories, sixty miles per hour at the ground, no ladder. Alex leaned out to the void of pinprick rain, precariously balanced at the edge of despair.

Familiar voices rose from the street, and Alex jerked back to safety. The Kommandant and the general stood in the circle of yellow streetlight, sharing a smoke, too engaged to have checked their phones. The incline of their bodies suggested they weren't going home alone tonight.

Alex's first reaction was queasy surprise that people that age still wanted it. It was followed by the mournful realization that the Kommandant was getting more action than she was.

Still—the chill night felt different, fresh with change. The wind tasted of towering mountains and snow. She thought of her overdue brief, the Commission headed to the Nepali Protectorate on the strength of her expertise. She couldn't travel because of the g-screens. But now screens had traveled to her. Safety was an illusion. If she didn't find and warn Patrick before his next Asylum Netcast, they were dead anyway. She had eight weeks to save them both.

The thought electrified every atom of her being. She did have a choice: either stay put as she had promised, a powerless victim, or use her gift of brains to fight back.

Patrick's voice in her head thundered, *Stop. Think*. An occasional g-screen here was not the exponential risk of constant screens in Asia. But a search plan was coming to view, like a laser held to invisible ink. It was time to live as her father lived, and not by what he said.

The surprise couple below lit up another smoke. It was probably best to let the Kommandant finish her hookup, but Alex had read that sex for old people took a long time, and she had none to waste.

"Kommandant!" Alex yelled down. The two soldiers ducked as if shot at. "The Commission doesn't need my brief. They need *me*."

The Kommandant squinted up against the streetlight. Her petite upturned face worked from irate to calculating, as if this one new variable might cure her multiple headaches. "Maybe," answered Kommandant Burton. "But I'm not the one you need to convince."

2

It was a lucky man, Eric Burton once believed, who knew where he belonged. He knew. It was sixty-three hundred miles due west of his current position in San Francisco, back in Shanghai's Allied Headquarters Tower, leading his CyberIntel team through the prize complex cases. Eric prized every aspect—the pinnacle intellectual challenge, the gratifying responsibility for public safety, the recognition of merit as represented by the eightieth-floor view from his rosewood-paneled Director's office.

But there was a downside to knowing where you belonged, and it, too, was represented by an office, this one in a storage area behind the San Francisco Legion of Honor cafeteria. Eric ducked his head through the area doorway, cracked his skull on an exposed pipe, collected his temper, and knocked at the exact second for his scheduled meeting. A peevish voice told him to wait. The space reeked of frying beef. Eric contemplated the decapitated Thinker that once graced the courtyard. The bent figure looked embattled and ashamed, and Eric knew just how he felt.

The meeting was with the museum Security Admin, and the rudeness was no surprise. Turf wars and jurisdictional grabs were the stuff that powered the universe. No local wanted a twenty-nine-year-old TaskForce Security Operations Director up in their business, even a disgraced one sent home to grow his beard, let out his belt, and mull over his excruciating court-martial. But the upcoming Directors' conference opened at the Legion, and the Kommandant had ordered him to get his pathetic ass off her couch and check security. His colleagues were arriving from Shanghai. They left messages he did not return: "Come on, drinks at Perry's, grow a sac and call us back." He could see them shaking their heads, saying, "Damn shame about Burton," as they carved up the new Asylum Netcast case and helped themselves to his slice.

Eric checked his phone. Still no word from his brother, Strav. Eric channeled his concern into observation of the slipshod security—unplugged metal detectors, the ugly white mold on the Thinker, the security door propped open to the primordial soup of morning fog.

"Enough," said Eric.

The Admin was not prepared for the forcible entry of a shaggy, redheaded, six-foot-nine, two-hundred-seventy-pounder in jeans and a flannel shirt, bearing no outward badges of authority yet conveying an expectation of absolute obedience. Five minutes later, Eric left with his uploads, a sullen headache, and a life-or-death need for a supersized chili cheeseburger with monster fries.

His cafeteria spree was interrupted by the Kommandant's *hup!* ringtone, the sound of know all and see all. Eric hit audio only. "Remember, no junk food," came Suzanne Burton's voice. "You're getting fat. Be home for lunch?"

"Yup," he said between bites, careful to avoid telltale drips on his shirt. He and Suzanne were first cousins on the paternal side, their twenty-two-year age gap an ineffable relationship flux of parent–child, siblings, and commanding officer. Eric could envision her standing full height, which hit his third rib, an impatient little bird with her head cocked, her kitchen walls a retrospective of his framed sketches.

"I've got an analyst for your Commission," said Suzanne. "Alex Tashen. My top postdoc." Tashen's CV and photo popped up on Eric's screen. She looked about twelve.

"Nope," said Eric.

"Listen up, soldier. I know you promised Strav it'd be the two of you. But this is a High Council mission, not a bromance road trip." The Commission was, in fact, Eric's shot at redemption; a probationary assignment arranged by Suzanne that, if performed to the satisfaction of his Disciplinary Tribunal, offered reinstatement to his directorship. Eric had overridden her advice and appointed Strav, a TaskForce Diplomat, as his Commission expert. Strav, on extended leave in China's northern Khanate, had yet to respond.

"The expert must produce top work," Suzanne continued, "and your brother can't get his shit together to even accept the position. Like a blackout zone could shut him up. No, he's probably violating orders again and—what's that sound? Are you chewing?"

Eric swallowed fast and headed out. The Legion had been retrofitted for security after the War, but the frosty Ionic columns were bullet-chipped, the stained glass boarded with plywood, and every third display was a yellowing poster stamped *RETURNING SOON!* Still, the place had a grand feel of put-upon nobility and, like him, still required some respect.

"Strav's fine," Eric told his cousin, defensive because she was right. As always. "The trauma counselors cleared him for duty."

"Bah. The boy could talk a snake into growing hair." That was irrefutable, as was Strav's growing collection of Diplomatic reprimands. Reckless. Unfocused. Unreliable. "Diplomatic is out of patience," Suzanne continued. "This Commission can't be his strike three. Alex's dissertation was on the Protectorate. She can cover Strav's work, hell, write the whole report. It's a great solution."

"To a problem set we don't have. Or is this an order?"

The scientist in his cousin knew when to shift methodology. "A faculty favorite, our Alex. A true polymath. I'm very fond of the girl."

Eric suspected that would be news to Alex. He braced for a low blow.

"Alex's dad was a bioengineering star, before he was convicted of assault on a policeman. He lost it all." Eric's screen lit with a syllabus of one of Patrick Tashen's early papers, ensuring that the uncomfortable parallel with his own plight sank in. "The dad died a few years back," Suzanne continued. "Alex is on her own. Zero family. She needs the field work for tenure track."

A school group mobbed the Rodin Gallery, giggling at great marble buttocks and filling the halls with cacophonous life. Eric waded gingerly through, the kids gaping up at him in delicious terror—at least children were open about staring, and yeah, kid, he did play basketball.

"She's a book-smart kid," Eric told Suzanne. "I'm not babysitting in the Protectorate."

"You're afraid," she said, a limited patience exceeded. "Afraid Strav will see an analyst as a vote of no confidence. Time for tough love, Eric. Or he is going to fuck this up for both of you."

A gaggle of girls in the long skirts and white blouses of the Creationist High School entered the gallery, shepherded by a blonde with a head mistress robe and the build of a champion swimmer. She gave Eric a once-over, and his head almost swiveled off to keep watching her. She was everything that attracted him—direct, an athlete's grace, and a frame big enough to take his weight. But the aggravation with the Admin still gnawed. Instead of flash-fantasies, he got a lukewarm blip, like a shot of Novocain in the balls, and happening too often since his court-martial.

A tall, super-slim schoolgirl with a windblown ponytail and untucked shirttails trailed behind her mistress, intent on a tracking map on her screen. She progressed by pure Brownian motion, oblivious to people swerving around her. A collision with the marble Prodigal Son sent her skittering on all fours. She popped up with a self-conscious toss of her head that proclaimed, *I meant to do that*. Eric felt a rumble of amused cheer he hadn't known in a very long time.

It lasted until he recognized the face from the CV. Eric hung up on his cousin. So Suzanne had sent Tashen his GPS coordinates to plead her case in person. Eric hated the slimy feel of conspiracy; he refused to be taken down by two women who, combined, weighed less than he did.

The stairway down to the Old World offered ignoble retreat from the gawky postdoc. Eric had spent many hours of his youth in the warren of lower galleries, sketching the masters in a haven of loner seclusion. First, to the Da Vinci Studies for Military Equipment, fine distraction while the would-be analyst hunted him down. *Wooden Machine for Hurling Stones and Bombs*—clean lines, definitive measurements, a practical if deadly purpose. *Spinning*

Wheel Design for Sixteen Crossbows. People who yearned for the good old days were delusional.

"Love you, cuz," texted Suzanne. "Love you too," Eric texted back by rote, though it was true. Eric could not stay mad at her. Suzanne Burton might disdain politics, but no one attained her sphere of influence without being very good at it, and she was fighting for their little family with the weapons she knew.

On to the anatomical drawings. Spread-eagled *Vitruvian Man*, trapped with his wrinkled ball sac exposed over the centuries. Sepia flayed torsos provided a visceral view of *The Sexual Act in Vertical Section*, as if he needed more discouragement. Next up, Da Vinci's quick sketch *Study of a Young Woman*, wistful eyes and a life force he never could capture in his own drawings.

Zero family. So what? The modern world was built on a shaky platform of orphans and widowers, fatherless sons and sole survivors.

Eric sat heavily on a bench. He'd give a year's salary to see Strav round the corner—the old Strav, an aristocratic charmer in a bespoke suit, his eyes lit in his half-mocking grin. "Really, brother," Strav would say, "such murky miasmas of misery!" He would clap Eric's back to dislodge the stubborn melancholy, and make him play hoops until his misery dissolved.

The downside of knowing where you belonged was knowing you could lose it forever.

Eric's childhood memories were blanketed by a layer of protective fog, so it was hard to discern between recollection and later stories. The Burton line was a stern military legacy of service. Suzanne's father, the older brother, married a tiny Brazilian doctor. Eric's father married a statuesque Norwegian mathematician. The results were the Chihuahua and Great Dane of cousinhood, a triumph of range in a single generation that inspired Suzanne's studies in genetics.

Eric's mother had abandoned the family after his birth, and his father, a brooding physicist, had little interest in the human realm, including his son. Fortunately, "big cuz" Lieutenant Suzanne, at UCSF for her doctorate, lived nearby to be his moon and stars.

She'd walked him to the first day of kindergarten with his new Superman lunch box. Much later, he learned that she had deployed that afternoon, with the declaration of war and the first wave of the Guizi Flu. His father, away at a conference, died in a safe camp, and his nanny died in a Safeway food riot. Their house and much of the city burned in the Terror fires. He never did learn how he survived alone on the streets for a year. Suzanne had returned sick and starved from a POW camp and found him in the overflow orphanage in the old Neiman Marcus. He remembered being scared by her sunken eyes, and how hard she cried. They were the last of their family.

His next seven years were in a series of local boarding schools while Suzanne turned traveling fixer for the fledgling Allied Nations, driven by a mission of Never Again. Eric managed between her visits. His disconcerting size for his age helped maintain the essential solitude he craved. Words stuck like gum in his head, anyway. By his fourteenth birthday, he stopped bothering with conversation, and Suzanne woke up to the small world that needed fixing too. A week later, in trademark no-compromise fashion, she assumed command of the new San Francisco TaskForce Institute, moved Eric into her two-bedroom apartment, and enrolled him in Institute Prep.

Eric had known only barracks-style living, so having his own room was luxury beyond dream. Left alone to unpack, he enjoyed a shower with a door that closed. He went to the living room dripping naked, looking for towels, to find a skinny, prepubescent Eurasian boy dressed as for a costume epic. He wore embroidered felt boots, a coarse belted tunic, and, judging by the smell, had arrived by pack animal.

The boy stared at Eric's crotch in horror. Prep was a bastion of traditional Chinese, Muslim, and Christian values, with modest dress strictly enforced. Eric found the prudery hilarious.

"What's the matter, runt?" said Eric, animated by the joy of his private space. He hit a Superman pose. "Never seen a pecker before?"

Never a circumcised pecker, as Eric learned. "Do you mock me?" cried the boy, jumping to a boxing stance. He spoke with the lofty accent of a British lord. "Thou great siz'd coward!"

"Huh?"

"*Troilus and Cressida*," the boy offered, his fists high.

The front door flew open. "Bah, cuz," Suzanne told Eric. "You'll make me snow-blind." He gave a snarl of affronted adolescence and grabbed a cushion. Suzanne waved, unsurprised, at the strange boy.

"Congratulations," she told Eric, like she was gifting him a pony. "I got you a brother."

"You are a Moor!" the boy told Suzanne in delight.

"He's not staying in my room!" yelled Eric.

Suzanne's hands went to her hips, and she stared him down.

"Though she be little, she is fierce," noted Strav, and Eric had to give him that one.

A debrief over grilled cheese produced the most astonishing flow of language Eric ever heard from a human being, much less another kid. Strav Beki, son of Beki, head of the nomadic Beki Clan, was "almost" twelve, before this trip had never been in a permanent building or used electronics, spoke Mongolian, "British," Mandarin, French, and some Latin "of course," had four sisters, five uncles, and eighteen cousins. He had come with the clothes on his back and a battered *Pelican Complete Works of William Shakespeare*.

"You are one wackadoodle package," said Suzanne. "What migratory forces produced you?" She gave him a geneticist's scrutiny. "Do I spy some Slav in Strav?"

That opened another floodgate. Strav's grandfather was a Brit who posted to Ulaanbaatar for the Foreign Office, and married a ballerina of Russian-Mongolian heritage. Later, during the War and Chinese Claim, the extended family was delegated to the Khanate. His grandfather went too. "*Mea familia curo primum*," explained Strav. "I care for my family first.

"When I was born," he concluded, "Grandmother said I made more noise than Stravinsky. The shaman found the name propitious." He grinned at Suzanne, brows shooting up with a devilish wag. It was a high wattage beam of trust and inside jokes, and transformed an otherwise unremarkable face into one of irresistible magnetism. To Eric's shock, Suzanne smiled back. Strav aimed his stun-gun grin at him, clearly accustomed to charming people at will.

"Nope," said Eric.

The Khanate, Suzanne later explained, was the most restrictive of China's postwar Cultural Preserves, the traditional herders, hunters, and horsemen glorified as a reminder of world-conquering hordes. In subtext, the region was kept to medieval times to repress rebellion. Resistance remained. Beijing stomped too hard on a protest, and Strav was sent to the Institute, in Suzanne's personal keeping, as a negotiated token of human rights reform.

"If he's successful," she told Eric, "it sets a dangerous example for the other preserves. Kid is going to get hammered. Your mission, soldier, is to keep him here."

It wasn't easy. Strav wouldn't hit his growth until he was seventeen, when he shot up a painful inch a month to six foot two in his Brit grandfather's rangy frame. At twelve, though, he was the smallest boy in Prep's jade-hued halls. The Chinese Nationals constantly goaded him to pick a fight, which would be grounds for dismissal. Worse than the surreptitious shoves and vulgar whistles were the insults to Strav's honor—he was a half-breed barbarian, a pretty boy for man sex, his sisters were whores, his parents did unnatural things with their sheep.

Eric's problem was Strav's eagerness to take on the Nationals. Teaching the runt Western sports was a grudging pleasure; Strav was the finest natural athlete Eric would ever know, on his way to Institute soccer star, a born daredevil with a ruthless streak that kept coaches on nervous edge and thumbing their rule books. He'd inflict real damage on his tormentors before getting returned to the Khanate in a body cast. So Eric kept the bantam warrior close.

Suzanne fell first. Strav bought her a flower every day, even a dandelion, and made her laugh again. It occurred to Eric that big cuz carried wounds he could not see. She seemed to know the nights that Strav quietly cried himself to sleep out of homesickness, and returned his unguarded affection with Mongol cooking, even making *airag*, fermented mare's milk, which fouled the apartment for a week.

Victorious, Strav turned his siege to Fort Eric. At dinners, he told stories from the Mongols' Secret History—the rise of the Great

Khan from outcast and slave, the kidnapping and rescue of his wife, Börte, the alliances of families and *andas*, or sworn brothers, a bond stronger than blood ties because it was freely chosen.

"Nope," said Eric.

Still, they were fine roommates, both neatnik perfectionists focused on school, sports, and superheroes. Eric was fluent in science, but English induced paralysis. Strav, with language skills as effortless as a hawk in flight, had algebra meltdowns that left kick holes in their walls. They tutored each other. Their conversation ranged from Superman versus Batman to Patton versus Genghis, and back to the Beki Clan being of imperial caste, the direct descendants of the Great Khan and tasked with preserving his bloodline.

"The Khan had the amber eyes of a wolf," Strav boasted one night over third helpings of lasagna. He held his eyelids open for Eric to admire the slivers of yellow in the black-coffee irises. "*This noble king called Genghis Khan / Who in his time was —*"

"Fuck your Shakespeare!"

"Chaucer. Not up to Yuan poetry, but adequate. The point is, we few descendants —"

It was a mistake to fight Eric with numbers. "Few descendants of Genghis? Ha. You and sixteen million other people."

"Preposterous." But after Suzanne explained signature male Y chromosomes, Strav was red-eyed, and the imperious lift of his chin was a thing of the past. The Beki blood carried no special purpose. His family, as mocked, were mere destitute herders at the fringe of civilization. Eric felt like he had run over someone's dog.

The next morning, Strav left for class looking anxious and ashamed. Eric realized he had destroyed the one article of faith that let Strav cope with the hazing.

By lunchtime, however, Strav's arrogant bounce was back. "Think about it," Strav enthused. "My ancestor had five hundred wives. Sired one thousand children. Ten thousand grandchildren. Sixteen *million* modern descendants. Now *that's* what I call a *man*!"

Looking back, Eric supposed that moment changed his life. The War had destroyed most cloud files, but he had a photo of his father. The dour face matched his single memory: "Leave me alone, boy, I'm having greater thoughts." At fourteen, Eric saw the beginning of the same vertical furrow on his own brow. It frightened him. Perhaps there was a difference between being a loner and loneliness. Maybe you had to be born with Strav's resiliency. Or maybe you could let that force pull you in and shape you like gravity.

The next time a National whistled at the runt—*his* runt—Eric went berserk with a liberating animal rage, and he beat the offender bloody until Strav dragged him off. The National's loss of face kept the matter from being reported. The hazing stopped.

Life eased into a string of contented busy days, with little family routines giving an aura of stability. On May 15, Allied Remembrance Day, two men came to visit. They were cultured and gracious, with visible war wounds—one missing his left arm at the elbow, the other with glassy white radiation-burn scars on his face. They brought red bikes as gifts for "our boys," and joined family dinner in the tidy yellow kitchen. Eric heard them talking with Suzanne all night, the three voices pitched low in the private language of seasoned coconspirators. The next day, Suzanne resumed her indefinite greater-good travels.

With Eric in charge, the boys went on a pizza-fueled tear of unfettered young males. Eric hacked them into eye-popping hours of porn. They scavenged abandoned neighborhoods for old laptops for Eric to repair and Strav to upsell to upperclassmen. Eric got devirginated by the women's volleyball coach and then hung around the gym, hoping she'd use him again. Strav spent evenings at Yang Racetrack riding in some banned event called a Dirty Naadam, returning exhilarated but so battered that Eric forbade the trips.

Eric knew he should be glad for summer, when everyone else would go home and he'd have the campus and apartment to himself. Instead, a week before finals, the gray returned.

He thought he had outgrown this secret shame, so the episode brought extra misery. The gray began, as always, with a siren call to sleep, like a bear growing sluggish at winter's approach. On normal nights, Strav read while Eric filled his sketch pad with geometric designs. Now Eric was dead by nightfall and sleeping through breakfast. Homework went undone. His coaches benched him.

Strav's baffled concern faded to background static. As his world shrank to the nub of himself, Eric focused on the lifeline of daily routine. He managed.

The morning of his physics final, he gave up and stayed in bed. He woke to violent shaking.

"Get up!" Strav howled. Eric pushed him away, and Strav threw himself on the bed to lie mummy-like beside him. "If you won't take finals," said Strav, "neither will I."

Eric pulled a punch. He could flunk out and return to public school. Strav would return to the Khanate and never go to school again.

"I fought to come here," Strav said through hot tears of frustration. "The Elders said I would bring shame. They *want* a closed Khanate. Everyone expects me to fail. Wants me to fail. They didn't count on you. We stand or fall together."

Eric sat up. His mind was still sludge, but the gray a shade lighter. "Do you miss your father?" he asked.

"He says I'm impossible. But of course I miss him."

"I wish I missed mine. He sounded like a real jackass."

Strav nodded. "That's why you are coming home with me to the Khanate next week."

"What?"

"To meet your family. Our sisters are a pain, so be prepared, *anda*."

"Who?"

Strav sprang up. "I found a restriction loophole in the Preservation Code. I bribed the official to file papers that you are my anda. It's a legal adoption by the Beki Clan." He flipped Eric a yellow card like a throwing star. "Here's your family visa. We'll be going home a lot now."

Eric felt a wormhole gathering over his head, forces beyond his control. "How—"

"Did I pay the bribe?" Strav shrugged at the simplicity of it all. "That's why I did the Dirty Naadams. To place bets on myself."

The language center of Eric's brain slammed to lockdown mode.

"You are not alone, anda." Strav tossed him his clothes for finals. "*A man of few words is the best man.* Everyone will love you." He considered Eric's bulk. "Everyone except your horse."

The schoolkids ran screeching into the Da Vinci Gallery, playing tag around Eric's viewing bench. Their laughter was the sound of that first summer in the Khanate, when his real life began. Little sisters clung like burrs to his legs, uncles taught him to hunt and read the awesome night sky, and parents warmed him back to life when he got lost in an August snowstorm. The Mongols knew a thing or two about hypothermia.

This was the first summer he had missed in fifteen years, due to his probation. He was there when Strav was betrothed to the beautiful daughter of a powerful clan. He was there at the Beijing Office of Ethnic Affairs when, with a smack of perfunctory red stamp, Strav was made a proud married man, albeit with his bride a thousand miles—in some ways, a thousand years—away.

He was there when Envoy Beki was pulled from the explosion in Croatia one year ago. Rational atheist or not, he had spent hours outside the surgery bargaining with God, or the devil, or any other deity listening, offering anything he possessed for his brother's life. It had seemed a deal was struck; the price was his court-martial. *Mea familia curo primum.* Lately, though, it felt like a different version of his brother had been returned, an erratic Strav 2.1.

Eric moved to the Greek and Roman sculptures, part of his brain noting the Fibonacci sequence in the carved stone spirals of hair and pubes, the other part pondering his Commission problem. How did his and Strav's future come to hinge on one fucking report?

The Khanate's summer Naadam tournament began in a week. Strav was likely staying in order to compete, a reckless violation of his Diplomatic orders and his promise to respect his recently healed body. In truth, Eric had no idea how Strav would perform in the Protectorate.

That left the heartburn postdoc, Alex Tashen. The girl reminded Eric of his youngest Beki sister, a real handful, always needing to be fished from a river or trying to sneak out of camp. Eric groaned aloud at the instant transfer of vexed affection and protectiveness. It was hard enough to establish command with Academics, who viewed every order as the opening round of a debate.

Yet if Suzanne was right, and she always was, Tashen was the analyst to cover Strav's work. The injury to his brother's stiff-necked pride was trouble for another day.

The book-smart solution passed right by Eric, her eyes still on her tracking map. "Seriously," said Eric. He tugged on her messy ponytail, and the hunt was over.

3

Alex and Eric stepped back from each other, flanked by the rows of white marble gods.

"Director Burton?" cried Alex, a belated recovery. "What are the odds!"

"Don't even," said Eric.

Alex had pulled an all-nighter on her Commission pitch, and the world had a punch-drunk topspin, or she would not have beamed up at him. She knew from his CV that he shared Patrick's math brain. But here was Patrick's furrowed brow as when catching her out, the same fearsome oversized authority, and though the two men looked nothing alike—the diorama would have been freckled young Viking versus grizzled Ottoman corsair—the scowl was a trip back to Plainview. She could not understand how it took so long to find him. It was like missing the Sphinx in the desert.

"Listen up," ordered Eric, a heroic attempt at control, but Alex was caught by the life-size alabaster statue beside him. The pedestal tag read, *The Farnese Hercules*. Alex gave a strangled laugh.

Eric followed her gaze to the statue. His scowl shifted to a squint of recognition, as when meeting someone you knew, but out of context. Alex, shaking with repressed mirth, watched the revelation come. The someone was him. His height, tight-curled beard and features, same weight-of-the-world expression, abs that had him reflexively suck in his gut. The epic display of genitalia was a bad dream of being caught naked in public.

There was no hiding a flush with Eric's coloring. Alex could feel his brain churn, his mouth opening and closing with the effort at a commanding retort.

"Well fuck a yellow duck," said Eric.

That was the end of Alex's control. Her laugh went on and on, rising to silvery whoops that had everyone in the gallery grinning. Eric watched with his arms crossed, shaking his head. "Sorry," she gasped, wiping her tears. "This comes of too much *Bulfinch*."

Eric flipped through her publications on his phone. "You study the impacts of terrorism," he said. "Doesn't excuse your covert decrypts and searches. Can't hit classified intel for research."

Alex stopped hiccupping to gape in awe and trepidation. Sixty seconds on his *phone*, and he'd pierced her cleverest hacks like they were cotton candy. Never had she so appreciated Patrick's attachment to invisible ink and paper.

"This is a Security Ops Commission," said Eric. "I am your commanding officer. Misappropriate research? You're out. Don't follow orders? Out."

"Yes, sir!" This was no Michelangelo to be played for information. "Wait. I'm going?" Alex started to throw her arms around him, hopped to an awkward bow, and finished with a salute.

"I am doomed," muttered Eric. Yet she saw him bite back a smile, a contagion of happiness, and his massive frame seemed lighter somehow.

The Creationist schoolgirls came gabbling into the gallery. Their big blonde mistress strolled over to stand by the Hercules statue.

"Dismissed," Eric told Alex.

"Hello, old one-eye!" exclaimed Alex, and wondered at Eric's violent start. She pointed to the illustrated antique map behind the mistress, where Cyclops devoured a hairy human leg. "It's the Hereford Mappa Mundi, vellum reproduction. That's where the Protectorate would be!"

"Go. Away."

"Medieval mapmakers abhorred an empty space," said Alex, intent on repaying his kindness with the inestimable gift of geography. "They filled the voids with embellishments from the Solinus repertoire of mythical beasts. Here's the one-legged *monocol*, not to be confused with our friend the one-eyed *monoculi*. Cannibals galore. Soulless mermaids to the north. The mappa mundi disregards classical knowledge and actual reports to create a visual panorama of the world where fantasy outweighs reality."

She frowned at the unfamiliar ice cap in the leather North Sea. Close up, the ice was a white powder blowing from a ceiling vent. "Weird," she said. "When I was a kid, Major Ash used to drill me on saboteur devices. There are microbes that eat metal and leave a white residue like that." She laughed self-consciously. "As if the Legion were a target, ha."

To her surprise and some alarm, Eric turned a laser-like attention to the vent. He told his phone to call Li Chow, priority TaskForce Forensics alert.

"Hey, fuckhead," came an amiable response over background bar noise. "How's the sac?" Eric described the situation, and a similar powder he'd seen on the Thinker. He asked Chow to check the security uploads he'd taken from the Legion Admin, specifically a twitch in the sensor system that tested as a harmless anomaly.

Eric handed the phone to Alex. "Hey there," said Chow. "Talk to me."

"Just—Major Ash talked about microbes that weaken a structural framework. That maximizes the impact of smaller explosives that are easier to plant. Silly, right?"

"Iron Balls Ash?" Chow chuckled. "He wrote the book on disposal ordnance. Spent the last twenty years in a Texas hellhole for rigging government contracts. How do you know him?"

"He was my babysitter."

The crimp in the conversation lasted until the results arrived. "Got a live one," said Chow.

More Security Ops officers joined the call, and Alex struggled to follow the jargon. The anomaly was actually a systems attack implicating multiple city landmarks. Each site was presumed weakened in structural integrity and planted with explosives. The detonations were likely timed for the upcoming Directors' conference.

The immediate concern, she gathered, was that hidden explosives might be programmed to detonate early if detected or disturbed. Each site needed to be evacuated without triggering alarm systems. Local law enforcement would be stretched thin.

"On it here," said Eric. "Don't let this dick Admin blow me up." Chow called the Legion Admin with the new TaskForce command and safety protocols. Eric called orders for the few museum guards to clear the main floor, leave the lower galleries to him.

"Report to your pal the Kommandant," he told Alex. "Scram. And—I'm—sorry—about your dad. I saw some of his papers. He had a great mind. It's not fair."

Alex looked up at Eric through a surprised sting of tears, and realized she wasn't going anywhere. The best of men, the invincible giants, only thought they were invincible; they set sail on their fragile ships, promising to return, and never did. She was done watching from that shore.

"I'm a TaskForce officer," said Alex. "Sworn to Serve the Nations ya-de-ya." She pulled up the map of the labyrinth galleries. "I do wish we had a ball of string."

Together they cleared the lower floor. Eric stood on the stairs, checking the upper-level reports, while Alex made a second sweep for any kids playing hide-and-seek.

The fire alarm went off in an ear-splitting siren. "No alarms!" she heard Eric roar into his phone between the shrills. "Off, off, turn it off!"

Thunder sounded around the Legion, a cascade of triggered bombs. The world exploded.

Eric was sprinting through the galleries to Alex when the bomb went off overhead. The shock wave blew him away from the collapse of beams and plaster. He staggered up, choking on billows of dust. The gallery was pitch-black, a cacophony of metallic shrieks and groans. An exit light blinked on, creating an eerie green haze of smoke. The gallery looked as if a giant hand had clawed the ceiling to dangling pipes and joints. Water poured from severed fire sprinklers.

Eric spun about in the cold torrential rainstorm, the dust streaming in rivulets down his face. "Alex!" he yelled. This was his fault for
letting her stay. "Alex!" A sodden skirt protruded from a fallen beam.
Eric attacked the debris in terror, but Alex was not inside. The beam
must have missed her legs by inches, and she had squirmed free.

He found her by a jam of girders and drywall, her white blouse
and long shirttails plastered to her body, her face caked white with dust.

"I think there's a kid in there," said Alex. They knelt with a splash,
and she pointed to a small hand about five feet back in the girders.

They went to work in wordless communication. Eric straddled
the end of the beam, bracing and heaving until the muscles in his back
began to tear, while Alex pushed anything solid she could find under
the metal. A narrow tunnel opened. Alex crawled inside with Eric
planted in support, both knowing he could not hold the structure if
it slipped.

An eternity later, she wriggled back out. Eric let the beam crash
down, and they fell gasping to the floor. Alex held up a stiff detached
hand. She tapped it against the parquet.

Clack-clack. The hand was marble.

"Fuck a yellow duck," said Alex.

Their phones were dead. They did a slogging perimeter search
for openings, hoping to capitalize on Alex's weasel-like ability to
navigate tight spaces. The gallery was sealed like a tomb.

Exhaustion deposited them on a bench that had landed upright
in a clearing, as if awaiting the next Da Vinci fans. Eric considered
the bleak array of scenarios. The fire alarms were connected to the
biohazard system, which might respond to those metal-weakening
microbes with the release of fumigants. That program was only
activated once a building was cleared of occupants; the fumigants
were highly caustic on skin, laced with neurotoxins that could block
nerve impulses, paralyze muscles, cause seizures and dementia. They
were fatal at concentration.

He could only hope the program was paused pending search
and rescue—no guarantee, considering the Admin's ineptitude so
far bordered on malevolence. Alex began shivering with cold and
aftershock. Eric checked her for injuries, and found only a scrape

on her thigh. If anything worse happened to her, the Admin was a dead man.

Alex gave a weak laugh of discovery. "Look," she said, tracing the boot-shaped scrape. "It's Italy."

"Who feeds you? You look like one of those stick-bug things with the eyes."

"You mean stick *insect.*" She waved her gangly arms like antennae.

Eric was accustomed to being corrected by family. "Come here, bug." He pulled her onto his lap and put warm arms around her. Alex nestled against him as from memory. The sprinkler rain dwindled. Drops ran down the beams and plopped in measured, peaceful rhythm.

The air system thudded, its compressor turned high, and Eric caught the sickly sweet smell of fumigant. A fan of yellow mist sprayed from a hole in one of the exposed air ducts.

"New plan," said Eric, his mind racing. Alex's low body mass meant she would be most affected by the saturating air in the small gallery. Eric tied his shirt over her face as a mask, and pulled off his soaking jeans to tie off the duct. At this rate he'd be as naked as his statue, not that it mattered. The only way to leave now was after a Hazmat crew cut off their clothes and decontaminated their bodies. He intended to keep Alex alive for that humiliation.

"It's a good look," said Alex at the exhibit of white boxers printed with red sailboats, and black socks. "And so much of it."

Eric climbed a mound of drywall to reach the duct. Working carefully from the opposite side of the fissure, he knotted the jeans legs around the hole. The air system thudded again. A new fissure blew open on his side of the duct, and fumigant hit his chest like from a can of spray paint.

He skidded to the ground in flailing agony, engulfed in invisible flames. Alex grabbed his wrists, and in a panic surge of adrenaline managed to drag him into the waterfall of a broken pipe. The pain receded as she washed and scrubbed his body with his shirt. Eric's eyes streamed, and up came his chili cheeseburger and monster fries.

"Sorry," he rasped, and her quavering smile was about the bravest thing he thought he'd ever seen. He looked up. Yellow mist now sprayed from a dozen pipes.

He tried to smile. "So. You want to marry me?"

"Don't be ridiculous," said Alex. "Who else would I marry?"

Eric took a deep breath to answer. Nothing moved. He tried again, a moment of *now what?* and then slowly keeled over as the muscles in his chest refused to obey, the paralytic chemicals enacting a very personal lockdown. Bitterness overwhelmed him; for them to die by friendly fire, in an administrative bungle, was the most pointless death. He had a moment to worry about Suzanne blaming herself, and about abandoning Strav when he needed him most. His thoughts collapsed into primal terror, a wide-eyed suffocation in the open air. Alex's face came close, and blurred.

Alex, leaning over Eric, saw his eyes bulge and lips turn purple, and her years at the clinic kicked in. She tested his airway, checked his motionless chest, put her mouth over his and blew hard. His chest rose and his normal color returned. She kept breathing for him, establishing a rhythm, and could not understand why she grew tired, so tired she dozed off between breaths and jerked awake to find his mouth again. White pricks of light flashed deep in her skull.

"Hey, rag mop." Patrick sat on a pile of drywall. He wore his plaid flannel shirt and was young, from the days of tumbleweed ships. He looked so chipper that Alex's reaction was irritation.

"I could use a little help," she said crossly. "Plus, I'm freezing and everything hurts."

"His tongue has fallen back," said her father. "Tilt his head to clear the passage. That's it."

"He tastes like barf, and I think he's dead."

"Not yet," Patrick admonished. "See his eyes following you? The poor bastard is trapped in there. Keep breathing and don't whine about it. Medicine isn't pretty. Sick people vomit and shit and stink. You, for example, are about to lose your bladder." He aged as he spoke, growing silver in his beard. A foghorn sounded, and Alex felt like there was something important to tell him about a Netcast, but she couldn't remember what.

Patrick opened the *Bulfinch* on his lap. "Where are we?"

"Golden Fleece!" she replied between gulps of air.

"Jason sent his invitation to the adventurous young men of Greece, and found himself at the head of a band of bold youths. Hercules, Theseus, and Orpheus among them." Snow began to fall, thick heavy flakes that tickled her face. The book finally shut.

"You can stop now, rag mop." Patrick faded into the fall of white. "You tried."

The flakes swirled and stung, rising to a blizzard, and Eric was stretched beneath her on a glacial mountaintop, his open eyes speckled with ice, his skin white with ancient frostbite.

A giant white crow with no eyes hopped up and pecked at his frozen chest. The rest of the eyeless flock descended.

"Leave him alone!" Alex screamed. She grabbed a splintered pipe and slashed at the crow. The bird gave an awful human scream, and crimson blood poured from its beak. The crows joined in a macabre dance around her. Alex swung and sobbed and the snow fell heavy, a blinding white veil into nothing.

4

He was not yet a monster, and this race would prove it.

The thirteen Naadam horses splashed through the frog-song of marsh, reached solid grassland, and hit a run as a single fluid creature, an earth-shuddering gallop that sent billows of dust to the blue Khanate sky. Strav held back his horse and bided his time. The ruins of Ulaanbaatar loomed behind a dusky ridge of mountains; this was home, the center of the earth, and he knew every cluster of marmot holes where a horse might break a leg. It was still ten miles to the screaming thousands in the stands, and he had a plan.

The race turned into a projectile force of hooves, crops, and cursing riders garbed in their traditional warrior claims: Kyrgyz, Tatar, Turik, Uighur, and Mongol clans from the broiling Gobi to the dark Siberian larch forests. Naadam celebrated the three traditional games of archery, wrestling, and horse racing. The Chinese usurpation changed the race from tough ponies ridden thirty kilometers by even tougher flyweight children, to Chinese syndicate thoroughbreds and ruthless sponsored horsemen. Strav's horse, a firecracker chestnut colt named Fast Talker, belonged to the Shanghai International Track where Strav trained, and only felt like his.

The new Naadam allowed an impossible sweep of events for the title of Invincible Leader and Father of Wolves—the Wolf Khan, as translated. Hard training and insane luck had delivered Strav two upset wins. First, his red-fletched arrows from a horn bow at seventy-five meters, then toppling a sumo-sized wrestler with a speed move perfected on poor Eric. Now for the final.

Strav pressed his face to the horse's streaming mane, the drum shock of hoof to ground reverberating through his thighs into his recently healed spine. If Eric could see, he would straitjacket him. But the monster demanded this race. Naadam might be a traditional test of manhood, but there was a gut truth in the old ways that cut through the modern dross. He needed to know that force of willpower could beat any odds, reverse the darkness and cure the distorted thing inside him.

The path funneled between two rocky outcrops, pressing the horses into a dangerously crowded mass. The leading rider, a Tatar in green silk, slashed his crop at the Turik's horse behind him, striking the animal's eyes. The horse stumbled and the rider flew off. Horses twisted double as their riders tried to pull aside, sickening thuds as the body jerked and danced beneath the hooves, then a chain reaction pileup of thrashing animals and men.

Strav was slammed from the saddle. He took a glancing blow to the head and sat up in a daze, thinking he was about to speak at the World Bank Conference in Brussels; it seemed very important to get to the dry cleaner before it closed, or he wouldn't have a shirt for his new pinstripe.

A horse trumpeted, the fog cleared, and Strav saw he was going to lose.

The Turik was dead, his back snapped into a *V*. Another rider had an ankle caught in the stirrup and was dragged away at a gallop. Groaning riders crawled to their injured horses.

Strav's mouth tasted of blood and dirt. He whistled, and Fast Talker trotted over with his ears flat back, an equine "I did not sign up for this shit." The inevitable specks appeared in the Eternal Blue Sky, bearded vultures and black kites already wheeling above the dead. Strav fought an inner skirmish; the bloodshed added revenge to the race, and the monster was shaking its bars.

He tried to think what Eric would say, but the noise inside grew louder. He lunged back in the saddle with a *Chu! Chu!* in full flight pursuit of the Tatar.

The race had no set course, but everyone followed the fast safe path that had been ground into the steppe over eons. Strav veered off to go hazardous cross-country. The Tatar could not risk the local rider taking a hidden shortcut. He had to follow, and he did.

Fast Talker hurdled a series of barbed-wire fences to Strav's hoarse cries of encouragement. Within a mile, the riders were passing the scars of dead empires and foreign occupations. The signpost read "Taboo" in Mandarin, but everyone in the Khanate knew this was a forbidden place, once used by the Soviets to store armaments. The emerald grass and pink flowers disappeared among corroded trucks and leaking drums stamped with skulls and crossbones. Rows of Russian crosses marked the soldiers dead by a bullet or Mongolian winter, fair-haired boys in ill-fitting uniforms who were never going home.

The Tatar hesitated at the graveyard scene and, as anticipated, decided Strav was bluffing. Strav tore through the field where he and Eric had spent teenage days mapping buried shells and devising catapults to make things blow up. It was suicidal to take at a breakneck gallop, but the monster didn't care. He wove Fast Talker around the remembered points of danger revealed by artificial disturbances to the earth—that gravel too even a furrow, a surface too smooth. The Tatar matched every swerve just ten lengths behind.

Strav headed toward the exit gap in the wooden fence, then slowed as if Fast Talker had pulled up lame. The Tatar whipped past them in furious relief, dead on target to the largest buried ordnance. The fireball explosion sent Fast Talker into a runaway bolt through a rain of earth, horse, and Tatar. Strav gave Fast Talker his head, and they careened over the fence.

As Strav approached the finish line, the remaining riders were a clot of dust a mile back. He passed the bell-ringing Taoist priests in black caps and magenta robes, and lines of spirit banners. He leaned forward to speak the traditional thanks to his horse in untraditional words.

"*I will not change my horse with any that treads,*" Strav whispered, and Fast Talker's ear pricked back to hear. "*When I bestride him, I soar, I am a hawk: he trots the air, the earth sings when he touches it.*"

A brigade of mounted warriors in Hun helmets and armor fell in at the hundred-meter mark. A great rising "Huzzah!" and the brigade stood on their saddles to canter in escort. A pack of Beki children rode screaming out to "Uncle Strav!" with their short legs bouncing off beribboned ponies. Strav winked and held up a hand to let his nieces and nephews lead him in. The brigade halted at the observation platform of dignitaries and oligarchs. The province general bowed, the soldiers fired a salute, and it was over.

The brigade was overwhelmed by the rushing crowd. Fans touched the horse's sweat for good luck and grabbed at Strav's deel coat, pulling him down to a pile-on of exultant young men. It was a suffocating crush, and Strav snapped. He screamed, punching and kicking, and when the nightmare cleared, he was at the center of a stunned crowd, his arms hooking a fan's shoulders and twisting his jaw so any movement would snap his neck. The man lay rigid with fear.

Strav released him, hyperventilating, and made a show of a good-sport slap. The crowd roared at the glorious joke and hoisted the Wolf Khan on high.

The next night, a north wind swept the Beki summer encampment, carrying the chill of the never distant winter. Strav lay awake in the *ger*, feeding wood to the central iron stove. Everything of home, Cossack hats to painted rafters, smelled permanently of wood smoke. The low flames flicked shadows over the lacquered furniture and plush rugs—Outsiders were surprised at the comfort inside a felt tent—and across his parents and youngest sister on their cots. Eric's long cot was turned against the wall. A cabinet by the altar held his mother's college diploma from before the Resettlement, the medals of his father, a lifelong herder and champion archer, and the smuggled photos of his and Eric's trophies and graduations. The photos were removed for visiting Elders, who viewed Strav's dual existence as a dangerous example and destabilizing force.

They had no idea.

One year earlier, he had awoken in an ICU, immobilized by casts and frantic with heavily drugged pain. Then Eric's steady "I got you, bud. You're okay." The concussion had stolen his recall of the previous weeks. Between surgeries, he learned he'd been sent in to negotiate for hostages in Croatia—a heady assignment for a twenty-six-year-old—and had disappeared for ten days. When local police stumbled on the hidden site, the firefight had exploded a munitions cache and demolished the building, killing hostages, kidnappers, and police alike. He was dug from the rubble, the miracle every rescue worker dreams of.

As the sole surviving witness, he was unable to illuminate the tragic events. The disappointed investigators closed the case with an order to contact them with any recovered memories.

His nightmares started soon after. At first they were fantastical—thousands of eyes judging him in the dark. Then vivid fragments. A gasping thing dangling from a ceiling. Eighteen squares of light. Hunched human forms too upsetting to relate to anyone, even Eric. He would never tell the psychotherapists. There was no such thing as confidential records. Night terrors were a typical manifestation of survivor's guilt, no more. But the eyes began appearing in daylight, grinding away at the fine line between dream and recollection.

He had pored over the investigative and medical reports. There was no evidence of what had transpired during captivity. No evidence of prisoner abuse, only a footnote that "catastrophic injuries from the explosion and collapse complicate the findings." He questioned Eric with every trick he knew. Eric was a terrible liar, with a long pause of a tell. But there was no hesitation in his "Sorry, bud, no one knows."

One day in physical rehab, the therapist strapped Strav's wrist to a rope pulley. Strav struck him without thinking. The vivid fragments snapped into an arc of true memory.

The night sky lightened to translucent pearl gray. Strav laced his smuggled running shoes and wrapped his deel over the highways of keloid scar that traversed his torso. The field surgeons had saved his life, but it looked like they had operated with machetes. At least the scars read as honorable wounds.

There lay the great irony: his catastrophic injuries were a gift that masked the truth. He understood the banality of what his captors had done to him. *Politics of Torture* was mandatory reading for the Diplomatic degree. The practice was as ancient and endemic as war and disease. So what if he'd been hurt, reduced, humiliated? It had been endured by millions before him, in versions limited only by human imagination. It would be endured by millions yet unborn. Armed with such perspective, overcoming the trauma should be as straightforward as reconditioning an injured muscle, a matter of commitment and discipline. Private work. No loved ones would suffer more worry or pain on his account. And he would die before seeing his family dishonored.

Strav made his obeisance to the altar. The new parchment above the shrine proclaimed him the Leader of Ten Thousands. Wolf Khan. Somehow the cure had turned to another hell.

The Tatar's death had been judged an accident in a high-risk game. Strav searched what was left of his soul for a sliver of remorse, if not for the Tatar, then at least for the horse. His revenge was misplaced here. He could never reach those who had ruined him and killed his charges. Yet he felt only the dark thrill of power, a semblance of control regained; destruction as a drug, and just as addicting.

He belted his hunting knife and ducked out the short blue door to a world bleached silver by moonlight. The wind carried the scent of sweet summer grass and the lingering howl of a wolf. The sheep milled in their corrals; the guard dogs whined and paced. He glanced with a pang at Fast Talker's empty pen. The thoroughbreds were on the train south, bred for show and flash instead of winter on the steppe. Strav supposed the same was said about him.

A piteous bleating arose from the goat corral. A young upstart male had rammed the king into the fence and broken its leg. Strav sighed. It would be old goat for dinner tonight. He dragged the animal out by the horns.

His sister, Batgerel, appeared in a fine stealth escape of her own. She helped flip the goat and pin it with her elbows. It peered at them with terrified devilish goat eyes.

"I haven't forgotten," Strav told his sister. They called her "The Bat" because Eric used to carry her around upside down by the feet. Now she was twenty-three, a tribal medic, and determined on Outside medical school. "You need an organic biology book." Strav grabbed the goat's warm ear and inserted his knife behind the jaw, a quick, deep draw across the throat to sever jugular and carotid.

"Jeez," said Bat. Blood gushed and the goat went still. "It's organic *chemistry*, you moron."

"Seven languages here. Nine, with dialects." Strav slit the back tendons and hung the goat upside down to drain while Batgerel chattered about transfer credits. Strav wanted to turn the carcass into a punching bag. He had promised his sister a study visa, but Beijing's quotas were tighter than ever. He did not have the political capital to press the application and had to be very careful. The last traveler to anger Beijing had seen his family's removal from the steppes to one of the prison-like agriculture collectives.

"I saw Eric's letter," said Bat. "About the Commission. Not fair you get Eric to yourself for a month."

"Why are you in my stuff?" he yelled, the angry call of brothers everywhere. He looked around for anything else that needed killing. No such luck. "Maybe I'm not going back."

Strange how saying something aloud gave it power. People warned he would have to choose between two disparate lives, but he never felt a disconnect in moving from glinting chandelier conference to bulldogging errant sheep. Now a deep intuition told him it was safer for everyone if he remained in the simpler life.

His sister stared as if an impostor were in his trainers. Right— quit TaskForce and lose any voice over visas. Never bring Suzanne flowers again. And Eric—his brother, his shelter. No more daily workouts, the plotting over finances and careers, the careless, once- in-a-lifetime synchrony of teamwork and trust.

A gold brick of sun burst on the horizon. An explosion was building in him too. It was either run or rain down in chunks like the Tatar. He threw off his deel.

The Bat folded the coat, a mute sign of love that nearly brought him to tears. She said, "At least you'd make your own wedding this time."

Strav ran. Despair clipped his heels like his morning shadow, his sister's words a rhythmic track: *make it, make it, make your own wedding.*

He had been happy to honor their families' long pledge, less about Sochigel perhaps than the acknowledgment of his rightful place in the community. The marriage was official by Chinese law, but his injuries had delayed the Mongol ceremony, which required blessings and consummation on sacred ground. The Croatian building collapse had resulted in severe spinal injuries, but, to his endlessly mortified gratitude, the doctors worked their miracles to restore measurably solid erections and fertility. Once the nightmares started, though, children became a moot point. He could have the potent sperm count of the Great Khan himself and still recoil from his wife. To crave a woman's skin on his, to welcome a sister's kiss, a friend's embrace, were purely remembered joys. Touch was the most profound of his losses, and the most isolating.

A new auspicious date would soon be chosen. Failure to consummate would be grist for gossip throughout the Khanate, every busybody Aunt Tita whispering advice and folk remedies for making a man stiff. He'd rather kill himself in the Taboo.

The run worked its pacification. When a Chinese army truck rumbled to a stop, an obscene metallic din in the prairie stillness, the diesel smelled of opportunity. The driver, a smuggler nicknamed Cash Flow, owed him *guanxi* favors for a cousin's job with a hedge fund.

"Envoy Wolf Khan!" said Cash, climbing out for a deep bow. He was young, with a pencil-thin mustache. Like any ambitious smuggler, he practiced his English whenever possible. Formalities complete, Strav requested the chemistry book for his sister, and to send a message to his brother, Eric.

Cash's smile froze under the mustache. "Please accept condolences." To Strav's blank expression, he added, "For your big white anda." Cash explained that the *Asian Times* had listed the victims of an explosion in a museum in San Francisco.

"That's not possible," said Strav. It was like being told Mount Bengar had vanished.

"A week ago," Cash answered.

Strav's mind went into flailing denial. Eric could not be gone because he had yet to hear about Naadam. Suzanne would have called, but maybe she did; his phone was in a locker at the distant border. Could he have been riding and playing games while his brother lay cold on a shelf? Monstrous as the world could be, this made no sense.

Strav grabbed Cash and shook him. "Did you translate the English yourself? Was the word *fatalities*? Or *casualties*?"

Cash twisted away. Strav jumped into the truck's driver seat and left the smuggler in a cloud of diesel. The border train departed at sunset. If he drove like a demon, dying inside, he could make it.

5

The Kommandant Mansion sat at the top of San Francisco's Presidio Avenue, high among the charred foundations of the old embassies. Tonight, the closing reception of the TaskForce Directors' Conference, the Mansion was the last island poking above the sea of August fog. Ten days had passed since the Legion bombing, and Suzanne was intent on a show of TaskForce spirit. Officers and guests wandered her manicured rose gardens and crowded the ivy-garlanded bars, making toasts to the Nations and loosening up for the real parties later that night.

Suzanne had built the Mansion seven years earlier, when the boys graduated the Institute and posted to Shanghai International, so they would have no excuse not to stay with her on visits. Their rooms and the guest rooms were crammed on the third floor, with the entire second floor her master suite and library. Suzanne stood in the library's bay window, staring out to where the bay should have been, lost in days past. Windsurfers skittering across the Gate like water bugs, sailboats so numerous you could hop deck-to-deck to Alcatraz. The thud of a basketball in her driveway and the boys' trash-talk laughter before they raced into her kitchen. Ordinary days. She should have sewn them like jewels in her hem.

"It's a big ask, old girl," said the first man on her library wall screen. At fifty-three, Pieter Handel, Allied Nations Secretary General, was silver-maned, his face unfairly ennobled by wrinkles. He refused to wear a prosthetic for the arm he lost in the War, and kept his left suit sleeve pinned up as a public reminder of Never Again. "He may find the Directive disturbing. But the Asylum Netcast has—"

"—changed everything," finished the second man on the screen, Chief of Staff Ari Martin. The men were calling from Ari's hospital room in International. Ari lay emaciated in a bed looped with IVs, only his compassionate smile undiminished. He and Pieter were both of mixed Persian descent, and native German speakers; Ari had often been mistaken for Pieter's better-looking brother, before the radiation burns left his face a patchwork of glassy white scars.

"The Regime sent a formal complaint today," said Pieter. "They claim the Asylum Netcast is Allied-sponsored propaganda. That we are building public support to alter the Return provision, to offer asylum to Federation defectors."

"It says another Netcast will constitute a breach of the Treaty," said Ari. "This is a threat of war."

Suzanne turned from the invisible bay and tried to reenter the groupthink. The three of them had met thirty-three years earlier as interns at the United Nations in Geneva, and bonded into immediate family. In those days, when she and Pieter were lovers, he had told her he would become secretary general—accurate, though they could have never guessed of what. She had never doubted him, even when she found him in bed with Ari. Such were the complications of love, only slightly less messy than politics.

She and Ari had welded into the stable base of Pieter's triangle, his consiglieres, conscience, and the only people he trusted. Pieter married, led Europe through the War, willed the Allied Nations into existence and steered it clear through the regressive decades of bigotry and fear, all while keeping Ari as his lover. Genius, she learned, was a complicated creature. Even a rumor of the true relationship could destroy the leadership that maintained a fragile civilization.

"This Asylum Hacker must be stopped," said Pieter. "It makes no sense to keep our prime asset benched. What do we think, old girl?"

"We think the asset is not so prime." The screen camera followed her to the young invalid sleeping on her chaise lounge, his size 18 feet dangling in the air. Pieter and Ari looked stricken; they had been frequent family guests over the years, and considered the boys their protégés. The nurses had done a hack job shaving off Eric's wiry beard, and his sickly yellow jaundice was emphasized by the raw pale skin. Now that the antidotes had purged his system of the toxin, claimed the doctors, his heart irregularities would end, his lung capacity and strength returning in a rapid curve. He looked comatose, though Suzanne suspected he was feigning sleep to avoid the party, the conspiracy, or both.

"How is our Alex?" asked Ari. "What a debt we owe her! Are you still keeping her in your guest room? I don't know, old girl. It sounds like you've got a third."

Suzanne saw Eric turn his head to listen about Alex. The big faker. She walked out of earshot to punish him.

"Alex is here, all right. Spends her days searching for my caches of chocolate. She looks fine. She didn't get the lungful Eric did, and it hit a different part of her nervous system. Her problem is seizures. When Hazmat found them in the Legion . . ."

The memory made her too upset to continue. Pieter had flown in to hold her hand in the emergency waiting room, or she might have lost her mind. Eric's heart had stopped twice. The next days in the ICU were a lesser nightmare. Alex kept screaming about giant white crows—the poor white-clad Hazmat rescue team she slashed up—while Eric kept pulling out his tubes to search for Alex. Now it seemed to Suzanne that, psychologically at least, they had recovered, and settled like a mated pair, while she was still a gibbering wreck. Ah, youth.

"The doctors keep adjusting Alex's seizure meds," said Suzanne. "It's tricky because she fights the blood work, who knows why?"

Suzanne cranked opened the leaded pane window facing Presidio Avenue and leaned out for some chill, composing breaths. Pieter and Ari followed her view on the camera. Together they watched the best of TaskForce stream through her spiked entry gate and into the reception.

"Eric will hate the Directive," she told the men. "But he won't refuse. The doctors cleared him for the Protectorate next week. That's insane, but Eric insists. I want him settled there first."

"He'll be fine, old girl," said Pieter, legendary peacemaker for a reason. "He'll have Alex and Strav to help him."

"Not if Strav gets suspended for dereliction," she said. Strav had surfaced at the Gobi Border Station yesterday, having just heard about Eric. It was not a calm call. "Diplomatic ordered him to proceed directly to the Protectorate."

"I'm sure he'll arrive there tonight," said Ari. "Even Strav wouldn't flat out—"

"Disobey?" Suzanne pointed their view to the elegant young man striding up the front walk.

Strav bowed to Suzanne in the window, then grinned up at her, a night-slicing beam of masculine charm. A bouquet of Suzanne's favorite calla lilies emerged from behind his back.

"That boy is going to be secretary general someday," said Pieter.

"Or the Destroyer of Worlds," said Suzanne. "Could easily go either way."

"Wow," said Eric from his chaise lounge, watching Strav's agitated pacing. "I must really look like shit." Suzanne had ushered Strav into the library and bailed. Eric wanted to give his anda a few shots of her hidden bourbon to calm down. But Strav didn't touch liquor, a statement against the pervasive alcoholism in the forced settlements.

"Who did this to you?" Strav burst out.

Eric swung into tech talk, the surest way to lull Strav into a stupor. "No group has claimed responsibility. Solidarity thinks it was a Protectorate terrorist cell. But the sophistication of the cyberattack is at odds with the primitive bombs. The q-signal dropped and—"

"I should have been here."

Eric saw the quivering jaw, and he moved to crisis management. "Yeah, fuckhead, gone, and win the one Naadam I miss in fifteen years." That got a shaky grin. Soon Strav was in play-by-play of the elimination rounds, the virtues and flaws of the horses, and the death of a malicious Tatar, a worrisome story that Eric decided was best not to pursue.

"Wolf Khan," marveled Eric. "Beijing won't like this, bud. You're going to be a celebrity."

Strav frowned at a nonexistent smudge on his cuff link and polished it with his sleeve.

Eric sighed. "Okay then. Did you do your wife?"

Hearing was magically restored. "Not yet. There's a new auspicious date after your Tribunal. You can be home for the ceremony." Strav's voice dropped deep with emotion. "Thank you, anda, for trusting me with your Commission. I will make a report to win your reinstatement. Your faith in me means everything."

Eric shrank into his pillow. He had intended to deliver the insult of the analyst after they met up in the Protectorate, fait accompli. Now, Strav's headstrong arrival demanded a new plan.

"Suzanne told me a girl saved your life at the Legion," said Strav. "What luck she happened to be there!"

"Yeah, luck," Eric said vaguely. "She stood in the water like that—*Venus de Milo.*"

"You mean Botticelli's *Birth of Venus.* Presumably she had arms."

"Yeah, arms, and amazing eyes. You could blow her over, but she dragged my heavy ass across the room." Eric's meds were wearing off, making him groggy and fretful. "I had time to think. All regrets. Like when I wrecked your red bike. I never paid you back."

Strav sat by his side. "It would be a strange thing if debt existed between us."

"About leaving you. Didn't think you'd forgive me." His eyes closed.

"Sleep now," Strav said quietly. "Sleep, brother. What wouldn't I forgive you?"

Alex turned in front of her guest bedroom mirror, trying for the right look for the reception downstairs—professional yet attractive, modest yet worldly. She put on eye shadow and lipstick, worried that Eric might find it too heavy, and scrubbed her face clean; she arranged her hair in an elaborate updo of pins and bows, and decided she looked like a cockatoo.

"What do you think?" she asked.

"You are *not* thinking," said Patrick. The guest room was nautically themed, and he was sitting on a sea chest. He was in his late thirties, with hay stuck to his overalls. "The Kommandant takes you into her home, and you sneak in a bottle of vodka. You eavesdrop on the Burtons' private family conversations. You will risk dozens of g-screens in the Protectorate. Your search plan is suspect and dangerous. And wear your hair down."

Alex shook her hair loose and ignored the rest. Here was one symptom she did not tell the doctors; the hallucinations in the Legion had not gone away. Patrick's voice, once an echo in her head, now sounded real. She smelled his wool sweater and saw his calloused palms, although when she tried to touch him, he was always somewhere else. Her questions about how to find and warn the real non-ghosty Patrick about the Hallows geotag were met with a stern "This is about you, young lady," which made her feel like a guizi Cassandra. Analyzing the phenomenon in a rational way, she supposed his presence was a continuing effect of the neurotoxins or anti-seizure meds. But she didn't want to suppose too much, because he might stop coming.

"Guess what I overheard?" she said, a more appealing term for her ear pressed to the library door. The wooden panel had muffled the words, but she got the gist of Eric and the Kommandant's argument. "I'm supposed to cover a Commission member we're meeting in the Protectorate. They're really worried. He sounds like a total whack job." The diversion failed.

"About Eric," said Patrick. "You will be tempted to share your guizi secret, especially if you get—intimate. He is sworn to turn you in. If he did not, and you got caught, which you inevitably will, he's guilty of aiding and abetting. Do you want to be the reason he hangs for treason?"

"Eric is my commanding officer. There's no—intimate." Not after the mortifying lecture from the Kommandant: Security Ops was quasi-military, and Eric could not risk a fraternization charge at his Tribunal. The new couple was to keep it in their pants until after the Commission.

But it was no fun arguing with a father who read your mind. Patrick was right. Even if Eric wanted to help, there was only one option. She could not be left hiding in the open, as now, risking detection, a walking threat to the Treaty. She would have to leave public life, return to a Plainview, or worse, a Black Ops site—preferrable to a Regime gulag, in absolutes, yet still at the cost of her freedom. And that was the best outcome.

"No fraternization?" said Patrick. "Talk about a rule honored in the breach! So why did you get that birth control booster this morning?"

Alex tried for nonchalance. "Just being responsible, per your third corollary."

She took three pulls on the bottle. Patrick turned translucent with anger, and she could see through him to the antique sea chart on the wall. Sea serpents curled around masts, cherubs blew the four corner winds, the seas thundered down into inkless voids. In a few weeks, she would either be back here grading papers or over the edge to that great unknown.

"You said to find the small joys," she said as her father shimmered away. "I can handle it."

The reception was an overheated roil of TaskForce uniforms and no escape from parental lectures.

"You look terrible," Suzanne told Alex. She put her inner wrist to Alex's forehead and pinched her flushed cheeks. The anti-seizure meds caused fever, and Alex was under orders to rest, but Suzanne knew there was no keeping the escape artist from a party.

"Listen up, Dr. Tashen. There's a new Commission member. Envoy Strav Beki. You'll report to him." Suzanne was stopped by the suspiciously wide-eyed show of surprise. Alex was spared another lecture by the two identical, ridiculously pretty little girls of kindergarten age who ran to Suzanne, their golden hair bound in fluttering pink ribbons. The girls were crying about the moose head mounted over the mantel. Suzanne explained it had belonged to her and Eric's grandfather, a great admiral. The girls said the moose winked at them, and they wanted Daddy.

"Whoa," Alex murmured at the approach of a strapping olive-skinned man with the twins' blazing gold hair. "It's Apollo from Olympus."

"Try Jacob from Calgary," said Suzanne. "Eric's cadet partner. Jacob Kotas, Greek descent. Fantastic recessives on the hair, eh? God, I love genetics."

Jacob knelt to comfort his daughters. Pressed together, the three platinum heads seemed to radiate light, not reflect it. Suzanne refused to hold Jacob's looks against him—it was no fairer to be prejudiced against great beauty than homeliness or deformity. He was a devoted single dad, and traveled with his girls. She had insisted he bring them tonight.

A good Kommandant knew the rumors, so Suzanne knew that freshman year, Jacob's hot girlfriend had a quickie with a drunk Eric. The Burton libido had a way of clubbing fine brains into oblivion. Eric had salvaged the friendship, but it was not a proud moment in Burton history.

"It's a scary old moose head," Alex told the twins. "First time I saw it, I almost ran back to Texas. Texas has moose. You ride them with a moose saddle, and they give chocolate milk."

The girls demanded a moose ride. Alex stomped about with a delighted child on each foot while they all laughed. Jacob praised Alex's action in Legion, offering thanks and concern. Suzanne, in turn, congratulated Jacob on his promotion to Solidarity Director of Guizi Control.

Alex went quiet and stopped mid-ride.

"The program is a team effort," Jacob said with genuine Canadian modesty.

"How often does Solidarity catch a guizi?" asked Suzanne.

"That's not the question, Kommandant. Detection numbers are low because the program is a deterrent. Can we be assured the Regime does not use guizis as bio-weapons?"

"We cannot." Suzanne detested rhetorical questions. "Yet I see a paradox. The Asylum Netcast proves the Regime is a brutal enemy. Isn't that what you want?"

"The Netcast is a lie." Jacob's outrage was real, and Suzanne felt its sway. "The worst kind of lie, that the Nations have the resources and responsibility to cure the world's ills. We barely feed and secure our own people. This Hacker manipulates old unverified images into sentimentalist propaganda to inflame the public and push us into another war. What kind of monster would kill millions again for a few individuals? I think we can bear a bit of paradox."

The twins pulled on Alex's skirt, begging her to visit them in International.

"Here's the question I ask every morning," said Jacob. "What can I do today to make the world safer for my children?" He excused himself to take the girls to the sundae cart.

"He's gone evangelist," Suzanne marveled. "What a great unmuddled take on life."

Alex gave her a spacey, muddled smile. Suzanne checked again for fever, and ordered her back upstairs to rest. To her surprise, Alex obeyed.

The word started with the Chinese Nationals at the reception, and Suzanne watched it move with the velocity of a pandemic, triggering excitement even in those with no idea what the hell a Naadam was: that this year's triple champion, the Wolf Khan, symbol of ancient warrior pride that no Outside person would ever meet, was a TaskForce Diplomat here at the party.

When Strav emerged from the library, people stared and applauded. Strav went white, and Suzanne went to feel his forehead too. She was surprised by the guests' fan-girl behavior, yet baffled by his tension—Strav was at his best when playing to a crowd.

"Are you upset about the Commission analyst?" asked Suzanne. Her heart sank at Strav's puzzled look. Clearly, Eric had punted on the awkward news. "New suit?" she asked as a distraction. Strav cared deeply about pleats and linings, and could speak at length about lapels. No luck. "Okay, Envoy, listen up. We got an analyst to help with the report. Dr. Alex Tashen. An expert in Protectorate politics and governance."

"Who needs help? I certainly do not."

"Of course not." Suzanne could almost see the little demon of shame on Strav's shoulder. She was glad Eric wasn't there for I-told-you-so. "Alex is ah—another Special Admissions. Grew up on a penal ranch. It's an opportunity—"

"—to cover my subject area. Fine. He may take my place on the Commission. I have better things to do."

"Oh do you? Don't be a sardonic jet-lagged ass. And Alex isn't a—where are you going?"

"To sleep, perchance to dream. Sardonic asses need their beauty rest." Strav stalked off, a bitter one-two-three waltz through the staring crowd.

They are real, Strav told himself, but that the staring eyes were not a paranoid nightmare for once was little comfort. His escape was interrupted by an anxious attaché, who begged him to stop a diplomatic cockfight between the China and India trade ministers at the reception. It was gratifying to be asked for help instead of being told he needed it. Strav greeted the ministers in Mandarin and Hindi, using their congratulations to establish his position as neutral arbiter. But as he moved to phase two, establishing common ground, more people joined to watch. Strav's pulse raced and he was drenched in sweat, his words throttled by a helpless constriction of chest and throat. He bowed—*gào bié, vida ke samaya, au revoir*—and bolted, the confused gazes heating his back.

Merde.

So his career was to join his catalog of losses. He could converse with individuals, but an audience was the eyes in the dark. They stole his voice, and what was an Envoy without a voice?

Strav sped up the staircase like a diver needing air. His bedroom had a sliding glass door to the deck. His image in the black glass showed pits for eyes, an uncanny projection of a Yama death mask. He stepped outside to a gauzy night of fog and foghorn. The deck off his room was partitioned by a six-foot trellis of gnarled ancient honeysuckle—ancient, at least, by San Francisco standards. No one could see him.

He fell into a wicker chair. The patio table had a book of matches. He lit one to watch the dancing flame. The monster whispered to light the deck on fire. The wind gusted in alarm and blew out the match.

"Bloody hell," Strav said, repeating his grandfather's grumble about steppe winds. "Absolutely beastly weather in these parts."

"A foggy day," warbled a soprano from the other side of the trellis partition, and Strav almost jumped from his skin, "in London *Tooown*." A gurgle laugh, and the voice added, "I should think this weather would make a Brit feel at home."

Strav peered through the wall of woven honeysuckle and made out a slip of a seated figure. Bloody hell again. She must have been resting in the guest room.

"Beg your pardon for disturbing your solitude," he said in a British accent. He hadn't trotted it out in a while, and it was a good day to be someone else.

"No, I'm leaving," she answered. "I've run out of antifreeze." A glass chinked, ice cubes rattling in disorder. "Though it is a fantastic night, isn't it? Absolutely nothing exists beyond this railing. It's a void to Alpha Centauri, and we are the only survivors on the last ship in the universe."

That was fine by Strav. He automatically analyzed the traits revealed by speech— articulation clear and sophisticated, a fair amount of drink fueling the sentiment, the lilting confidence of someone accustomed to being the center of attention. Probably an undergrad sneaking off to drink alone, indicative of alcohol dependency. Yet there was something fantastic about the night, the floating disassociation from the world and dreamlike anonymity.

"Are you an Academic here?" he asked.

"What an insulting suggestion. Academics are as exciting as demented cabbages."

Strav grinned and lit another match. "What is it you do?"

"I'm a—philanthropist," she said grandly.

So he was not the only one who found it a good day to be someone else. "Is your filthy lucre an inheritance, or are you a singular entrepreneur?"

"Oh, I'm singular. One genuine frickin' miracle of science. Cheers." Her glass chinked in a solo toast to singular creatures. "What do you do?"

"Oh, I'm a bit of a nomad." The match light danced in his

cupped hand. "How do you entertain yourself when you're not giving away your money?"

"I like to read."

"Brilliant. Reports from your foundation? Or fiction?"

"Fiction? Never! That's supporting the drug trade. A fiction writer prostitutes human suffering for profit. Why invent trouble, when one of the great cataclysms of history was twenty-five years ago? Fiction is parasitical to reality. And with nonfiction, you don't have the added irritant of deciphering what's true or created for special effect. No, I'm for biography."

Strav gave a long whistle. "Far be it for me to defend literary types and other professional fornicators. Still, it's a rather lugubrious view."

"Lord. Those British schools do work the vocabulary."

"You can't trust historical accounts. The human mind processes reality in a very predictable way. Every witness, not to mention every politician, becomes genuinely convinced of their personal version. Listening to their righteous truth is hardly worth the noise."

The long whistle was returned. "Talk about righteous! Listening can be a very useful art. Especially for professions involving negotiation and persuasion. If you are ever looking for a career, nomad, I would not advise diplomacy."

Strav burst out laughing, deep and spontaneous, and was surprised he still knew how. It felt wonderful.

"You have a great laugh," she said dreamily. "A dark harmonic between a cello and an oboe." Her chair scraped back. "Well, it's cold, and I'm meeting someone—"

"Here." Strav peeled off his jacket and tossed it over the trellis wall. He'd throw his whole suit over if it would keep her there. After an excruciating wait, he heard a small sigh as her arms slid through sleeves still warm from his body.

The next words through the trellis, however, were a darker spell of night. "So everyone lies," she said. "Tell me, nomad. That Asylum Netcast. Is it a lie too?"

"Unclear." He was surprised by the question. "Such images are typically doctored. The propaganda is so thick on both sides, it's near impossible to discern who is manipulating information and to what end. Multiple players may even be unintentionally working at political cross-purposes."

Another sigh through the trellis; clearly, complex abstraction was not what she sought. "You wouldn't know," she said, "but guizi is what the Chinese Allies called the first Euro refugees during the War. It means white foreign devil. It's Mandarin."

"Mandarin," said Strav. "Fancy that."

"It came to mean everyone in the Federation. Think how different now if the ones who escape were called refusés, like the Netcast said. Guizi is a devil, and refusé a sepia-toned immigrant in Ellis Island."

"A name would not change the Treaty mandate of return. After all, a—"

"—rose by any other name would smell as sweet," she said, leaving Strav blinking in the dark. "I never bought that line. The name changes everything. Refusé is an affirmative term. Refused permission to emigrate, then refused asylum—see, the two negatives make a positive. It trips off the tongue so lightly: *ref–us–ééé*."

"If you are trying to channel Nabokov," said Strav, "the three lilting syllables are *Lo–li–taaa*. And look at the trouble she caused."

"It wasn't her fault!"

"But I take your point. There is honor in a good name. And you can be stripped of it quickly." The fog gained a shared bitterness. "Why did the Netcast disturb you so?"

"In the old days," she said in a faraway voice, "all they needed to pass were new papers. Can you imagine looking like everyone else, but marked as different inside?"

Strav didn't have to imagine; it was a hard business, trying to pass as your former self.

"You can tell their lives were going fine," she said, "and bang, everything changes."

"Yes," Strav said. "You are who you are, until you're not." His next words were a statement, not a question. "What happened to you."

"Oh, just—something bad when I was sixteen. The person I most trusted was a liar. The world was a lie. I keep reliving it."

Strav assumed an implicit child abuse. "I understand," he said, lost in the spell of mist and dark. "There is faith in the world, and you're not even aware of it until the break. I had never run into a situation I could not talk my way out of before. The cell was cold at night, concrete walls and a steel door, very cold. There was a barred window up high. The light through the bars made a shadow of eighteen squares. Exactly eighteen."

"Are you all right, nomad?" she asked, a real fear in her voice that moved Strav deeply.

"Can we talk somewhere—"

A gang of officers in great tequila cheer came out to the yard below. The noise woke Strav as if from a trance. The fog infused with electro-beat and cigar smoke. It took him a minute of the shouts and music to realize she was gone, had slipped away without a goodbye.

He understood; the spell was broken, and each knew they had said too much. How could he have admitted remembering his captivity, risking a reopened investigation? It beggared belief. And she had to be equally disconcerted. Exposing herself as a guizi sympathizer at a TaskForce function was a career-ending slip. They needed to remain strangers. They would pass right by each other, without recognition, and hold their secrets ever tighter.

"No," said Strav, startling the revelers in the yard. "No!" he said in defiance, a sense that life depended on seeing her again. He ran downstairs back to the reception, searching through the guests and waiters. But he didn't know her face or name, her job or age. He cursed every game and lie between them. And if he did find her, what could he say—that he was off to a distant Commission and then home to consummate his marriage?

People stared, and Strav got a sense of how wild he appeared, spinning in his shirtsleeves. *Shirtsleeves.* He pumped his fists, knowing how to find her.

He spotted her across the crowded living room, a slender figure made slighter by wearing his suit jacket. She carried a ridiculous pink madras satchel. A group of professors waved her over, and Strav watched her toggle to a fine actress smile. Although she walked with confidence, she had the funny *sproing* of a colt finding its legs. Her wave of greeting knocked a waiter's tray of champagne into a cascade of bubbly. The professors mopped up, apparently resigned to her frequent calamity.

Her skin was the same golden cast as his, her hair as dark, but her big round eyes were violently light, a juxtaposition of strange and familiar that was positively alarming. Her hair fell to her waist in a riot of waves, like a creature with its own idea of fun. She was striking, certainly, with every man in the room eyeing her. But to Strav, she was not beautiful.

It did not matter. Minutes earlier, he could not have imagined wanting to be touched again, but now his body played a wicked trick, compressing every missed desire of the year into one blast of need. It recalled the rushes of adolescence when it first occurred to him that women were always naked beneath their clothes, making it a solid week before he was good for anything. He was there again, transfixed and so alive it hurt.

Forget Naadam: she was the talisman that was going to save him. Already he felt the old empathy stirring under the coals, and a suffusion of optimism. She, too, lived behind a mask to guard a secret wound. They would save each other.

His jacket rode light on her shoulders as she laughed. The idea of her wearing his clothes just slayed him. He closed his eyes, and she was walking toward him wearing nothing under the jacket. She understood his disfiguring scars, that he was a beginner again, he might come too fast and that was fine; she took his hand and grazed it over her bare thigh, up inside the silk-lined coat, and he became frantic, moving his mouth over her neck and breasts, lifting her up to wrap her legs around him. She tugged open his belt, reached down to guide him . . . and there was a hard tap on his shoulder followed by Jacob Kotas's "Hey bro, you okay?"

Strav gawked at Jacob. "A cramp," Strav croaked, bending over. The French attaché was hitting on her, braving the professors to bring her a drink, and Strav considered breaking his wrist with a perfunctory twist. She was his now.

Even though she did not know his face, it seemed to Strav they were already lovers, so he was not surprised when she lit up at his approach. The transformation was remarkable—there was no faking the mix of affection and pride, the touch of shyness, the glow of mutual trust and wordless understanding. No woman had ever looked at him like this before, but now it was essential as air. He had not known a smile could create a before-and-after, but there it was.

He grinned back like a fool, even as it sank in that she wasn't making eye contact with him but rather with a point above and behind his head.

"Hey, bug," said Eric.

Eric leaned heavily on a cane, a great quiet dignity, and as always people slid out of his way. He came around Strav and held out his hand. The girl took it. They smiled at each other, oblivious to everyone else.

She was the girl from the Legion. He should have known her from Eric's fumbling description, her presence on the family deck. His anda's woman, as sacred and untouchable as a sister. An inner howl of loss and betrayal started low and kept rising. Knowing it was irrational only made it louder.

"Hey, bud," said Eric, gone strangely nervous. The girl turned to Strav without a shred of interest. "Yup," Eric told her, "this here is—is—" until Strav realized, oh final indignity, that Eric was too distracted to recall his anda's name.

"Bother," Strav said in a British accent, "I must have left my jacket somewhere. Trials of a nomad, you know." The whole god-awful evening was almost worth it to watch her face.

"What's happening?" Eric asked in bewilderment.

Strav dropped the accent, letting her know she'd been played, and turned his anger on Eric. "Good of you to tell me about the Commission analyst," he said. "Dr. Alex Tashen, convict spawn! Once again, special admissions trumps credentials. Good luck with your charity case."

It was insider sarcasm, him being the first special admit, but gasps from the professors told Strav he had seriously violated the social contract. Eric froze in dumb paralytic denial.

"This is what you tell people about me?" the girl asked Eric, her eyes welling with tears.

"Ah," said Strav. It was like being in a slow-motion fall, watching the ground race up with time to register that this was really, really going to hurt.

Her self-possession returned with a glittering smile. "Good luck, indeed," she told Eric. "You'll need it with a disturbed egomaniac of such towering incompetence that you ask a postdoc to cover his work." Strav felt his own eyes well up; Eric made a horrible choking noise.

"But where are everyone's manners?" said the girl. She extended her hand to Strav. "I'm Dr. Alexandra Tashen, the charity case. You must be Envoy Beki. The basket case."

II. THE MOUNTAINS

6

The monsoon gods yawned and took a breather, letting a pale wash of morning sun filter through the Himalayan mist to brighten Prosperity, the teeming capital city of the Nepali Protectorate. The sunshine glistened off the fish scales in Bhadrakali Market, spread over the ancient stone temples and modern gun batteries, brightened the concrete expanse of the TaskForce Compound and shot through the shutters of Alex's dim room in the Peace and Love Hotel. Alex flung open her door to the exterior corridor, her mouth full of toothpaste, and gave a foamy chirp of joy. She, Eric, and Strav had arrived a week earlier in an opaque downpour, and it felt like the entire water cycle of Southern Asia had followed her ever since.

Alex bounced to the bamboo railing with her hands outstretched to catch the light. Ghost wisps of steam rose and evaporated on the sport court below, a vanishing act that reminded her of Patrick, and why she was here. Her phone gave a lion roar, Eric's futile attempt to enforce punctuality. Alex tore downstairs through the TaskForce bustle, each person dressed in the insignia of their service: Diplomats sleek as killer whales in their dark suits, fellow Academics in wrinkled khakis or her own cheap skirt and white blouse, NGO folk in trekking shoes, the rival Security Ops agencies—CyberIntel, Forensics, and Solidarity—indistinguishable in taupe uniforms but for Solidarity's old-school dash of military berets.

"Hey, bug," said Eric, sitting in the café behind his usual six-stack of waffles and bacon. Alex ordered her rice congee. As every morning, Eric inspected her for missed buttons, and she checked that his inhaler was breast-pocket ready. And if the third place setting remained conspicuously empty, as every morning, Alex refused to give a damn.

At 8:30 a.m. precisely, Eric called for the briefing. "No theories. No geography tutorials."

"But it's *interesting*!" Alex protested to the tiny dried fish in her congee. They gave her the briny fisheye back. "This place is a sociology experiment run amok."

Twenty-five years earlier, stung by the fiascos of the Safe Areas in the West, the Allied Nations had transported a million Diaspora refugees at the Sino-Indian border to the safe isolation of Nepal's Pokhara Valley. The native Gurung and Magar peoples were soon displaced. Now, twenty million second-generation refugees knew home as an inaccessible mountainous territory of imported languages, religions, and enmities, governed by a corrupt Protectorate Authority Viceroy.

Patrick had served in the region as an Army doctor during the War. Alex had attributed her father's interest in the Protectorate Independence Movement to his passion for high-moral/low-hope causes, starting with hers. But she now understood the attraction, and how the crackling air of rebellion would inspire his scientific brain to produce the Asylum Netcasts.

She also understood why the Kommandant had chosen the Protectorate Commission as Eric's vehicle for reinstatement. In seven weeks—the same mind-blowing time frame as Netcast #2—the Allied High Council would vote to renew the Authority's jurisdiction. The Commission's security assessment was a hot-button topic that would spotlight Eric's value.

Alex intended to make Eric look superhuman. Yet he was remarkably single-minded about his cyber and policing sections, with little patience for the economic and welfare assessments, and none for rhapsodic overviews of Independence in the grand cosmic scheme.

"Did you know Independence is a misnomer?" Alex informed the briny fish. "The entity would be a self-regulating Common-wealth of Nepal, an economic—"

"Briefing calendar!"

"Director Burton, meeting with the Solidarity captain. Envoy Beki, meeting with the Viceroy. Dr. Tashen, analyze the IMF report and pick up the Wolf Khan's laundry." All true, with one very critical omission from her day.

"Dismissed," said Eric. He squeezed her knee, and her entire body sang out in longing. How she wanted to sleep with him. It was not just for the sex, though she was aching and troubled for it, but real sleep, curled up against his back snug as a cub, to stretch long and drowsy in the morning light, play idly with his chest hair as they talked about the coming day.

"How's the big ticker?" She pressed her hand to his chest, willing a strong, steady beat.

"Ticker's good," he said, and called after her, "You be good too."

The Compound walls were a fortress tale of iron pike fencing and fixed defenses, with concrete blocks and gargantuan steel balls littered about like titan toys. Alex approached the exit gate to Provna Boulevard in a pitch of anxiety-laced excitement. Eric had her under strict orders to never leave the Compound alone, though attacks against the TaskForce had abated with the imposition of martial law. It bothered her, this perverse correlation between a police state and violent crime. The greater her chance of getting nabbed in a g-screen, the less likely she was to get blown up or mugged. What kind of rotten choice was that?

Today began Plan A. Her heart said Patrick was running his Netcasts from the Protectorate, though he could be anywhere. But one person was definitely here—the mysterious local confidant he had entrusted with his g-marker research lab notebooks and Confession, five long years ago.

Patrick had told her they remained in contact, in case the notebooks were needed. She had spent years sleuthing the confidant's identity—she was no master hacker, though Patrick had taught her well—searching her father's private records, asking him trick questions, and, more recently, accessing regional security and surveillance records from Michelangelo. Her short list was ready to go.

The five candidates were men of Patrick's age. A monk, a War College colonel, two businessmen, and a doctor up in hinterland Abad. There could be no revelations of hacker fathers and classified geotags, no digital trails. She needed to approach each one in person and speak with protective ambiguity. *I think you knew my father. He would want to know I'm here.*

If one was the confidant, her message would speed to Patrick. Patrick would surface from whatever murky underworld he inhabited, demanding to know what extinction-level crisis necessitated her forbidden travel. They would hold each other, cry, laugh, and forgive.

It was time to hit the streets and speak a name to strangers. Today was monk day.

"Morning, y'all!" Alex greeted the Compound sentries. She invested time each day flirting, ensuring that upon reentry they would wave her past the long line of the g-screen for a quick biometric. She had currency everyone wanted—inside information about the Wolf Khan.

"Important night for you-know-who," she told the sentries, working an angel-faced innocence particular to big blue eyes. "The crescent moon ceremony. He draws ancient symbols on his naked body and howls at midnight." Let the Envoy assign her demeaning chores, find the prime moment to cut her from discussions by switching to a different language, belittle her as "the intern." He wanted her gone. Well, this convict spawn wasn't going anywhere for seven weeks, and the trip was about fighting back.

In the meantime, his treatment of her as his personal servant increased her credibility with his fans. "No escort today," she told the jostling sentries. "I'm on a confidential pharmacy errand for the Wolf Khan. Y'all won't tell anyone, will you? Men develop problems down there from too much pounding in the saddle. It's called wet noodle syndrome, he can't get a—"

"Alex *Tashen*!" Alex almost fell over; the Kommandant was supposed to be in San Francisco, not here on another ambush. The Kommandant wore a demure brown dress instead of her blue uniform, as if to look undercover. Yet her single snap of "Posts!" sent the sentries running.

"Envoy Beki is your superior officer," said the Kommandant. "Do not think I won't yank that visa, missy. I will." The Kommandant had delivered her a lecture before the Commission departure, excusing Envoy Beki's behavior—how the Envoy was a complicated guy who had suffered grievous injury in the line of duty, from a very conservative culture, a devoted brother and husband. The Kommandant had tried to retract that last factoid; Strav's marriage, she had told Alex, was private family business, not to be mentioned.

So the man she had bared her soul to on that foggy deck was married. The snake. And how did any of the litany excuse a cruel and malicious streak?

Being good, it seemed to Alex, was a matter of perspective. The Envoy was good at fighting dirty. She was good at learning fast. Beneath the Envoy's expensive draped suits lurked a self-conscious, first-class prude with a hair-trigger sensitivity to insult and a conservative-culture thing about his manhood. Brilliant, as he said.

For a complicated guy, he sure was easy to torment. A pitcher of iced tea spilled in his lap at a conference—lucky for him it wasn't the hot coffee he told her to fetch. Fun little hacks, like the personalized ad for treatment of erectile dysfunction that popped up in his deck at an Authority meeting. And last night's reception, when she hacked the translation program so the tribute screen read, "Congratulations, Wolf Khan! The Nations celebrate your splendid tight ass," instead of "tight seat on a horse."

Provna Boulevard was calling, a sensory overload of traffic roar, diesel fumes, and sauna heat. "I'll be good," Alex promised the Kommandant, speaking the universal Burton pacifier.

The Kommandant felt her forehead, and said the last thing Alex expected. "Listen carefully. Do not provoke Strav. Do not underestimate him. Strav gets what he wants. And Eric will always choose his brother."

The Kommandant strode into the Compound before Alex could ask why she was here.

You are not blameless in this, said Patrick in her head. *Why can't you let it go?*

Why? Because she could not forget the magical connection with a faceless nomad on that foggy deck. Because the Envoy represented every illusion turned to shame and loss. He didn't need to know the truth of her life to make her feel like a guizi.

Alex bolted out to Provna Boulevard and hailed a three-wheeled tuk-tuk. "The monastery at Bhadrakali Market, please," she told the elderly driver. She clutched the fringed struts as they careened through rusted yellow cabs, trucks, and oxcarts, past a Mormon tabernacle built like an ivory drip-drop castle, the gold onion domes of Russian Orthodox churches, the blue spirals and minarets of mosques, a drab Creationist box. Government billboards urged: MORE CHILDREN! LIFE WOULD BE EMPTY WITHOUT THEM!

"Foocking kids!" the driver screamed at the street urchins lobbing rocks into the roadway.

Alex tumbled windblown into the Bhadrakali Market. The din was skull-crushing, the warren of stalls reeking of garlic, fish, and stale sweat. The scraps of the world were on sale here, bolts of dark ethnic cloth, racks of stolen phones, Guizi Invasion comic books, cannibalized car parts, white wedding gowns, and porcelain crematory urns. Fire-eaters spat blue flames into the air.

"Excuse me, sir, where's the monastery?" Alex asked a piroshki vendor. She could imagine Patrick standing here, grease dripping through the paper napkin as he talked subversion with a saffron-robed monk. The vendor responded in Russian, or perhaps it was Ukrainian or Lithuanian or Polish. Why had Patrick never made her study languages? English is enough, he had maintained, the lingua franca. Though perhaps that was his own refusal to accept that his Texas bluebonnet might end her days in a foreign land.

Eric's face appeared on her phone. "Get back here," he roared. "If you have a seizure—"

"Sorry, terrible reception!" Alex yelled, holding the speaker to the hiss and sizzle of piroshki on the iron stove. She turned the phone off.

The street urchins swarmed the stall. The vendor collared an elfin, towheaded boy with his hand in Alex's madras bag. The boy snarled, and with an admirable flex of entrepreneurial spirit gave

Alex a gap-toothed grin. "Pretty lady have dolla for the Independence?" he yelled in the local pidgin, as if volume would clarify any confusion of pronunciation. Small, filthy hands pawed her skirt. "For the Independence!"

"Rats on two legs." The vendor had sudden English. "The Mafias bus them in from Abad."

Alex looked at the pinched faces and matted hair, a girl's wrist you could break with a sneeze. They resembled the fair-haired kids in the Netcast video. But instead of fear and hopelessness, she saw sly defiance and proud refusal to look at the food.

"I'll take them all." Alex pointed to the tray of piroshki. The vendor snorted at her naivete but accepted her money. She handed out the warm dough balls to the shoving children. The elfin leader thanked her with a reverse pickpocket, slipping a choice dumpling into her bag.

Black-helmeted police walked past the stall, rifles cradled in their arms, g-screeners bouncing at their ammo clips. Alex slipped out the back of the stall.

She soon discovered her map of the market was pure mappa mundi, more imagined than real. The monastery was a flower mart. People thought the monks were dead. Worse, she was seeing Patrick everywhere. A glimpse of a broad back and shaggy dark head disappearing around a corner, and she was off, breathless with anticipation, racing after a man who turned to her, startled or amused, but always a stranger.

Her last shot was a temple up in the old forest. She set off heartsick and wilted from the heat. The path climbed through lost-world stretches of fragrant pine and alder. A few rhesus macaques, the surviving remnants of the sacred monkey tribes that had once covered the hills, hooted and ran along branches beside her. Her spirits rose with the altitude. In winter or spring, this path would provide a dazzling panorama of the Annapurna range, peaks set as sharp as dragon teeth. For now, the mountains remained shrouded by monsoon; she had to accept their existence as an act of faith, the way she accepted that those peaks were studded with fossil seashells, or that twenty-five years ago this polluted valley was a tourist Shangri-La.

The temple was long abandoned. A circle of bronze prayer wheels stood silent under a crumbling pagoda roof, the footstones worn to a channel by fifty generations circling clockwise in their devotions. Alex's disappointment turned to curiosity about the bug-eyed demon heads carved into the wooden beams. The elaborate carvings bore traces of crimson paint and earthy life. Very earth; many of the figures sported erect phalluses the length of a forearm beneath protruding bellies. After a guilty glance around, Alex petted the monstrous organ on a smug-looking demon, amused and disturbed by the flush of warmth between her legs. And wasn't that what fertility figures were about, to make people focus on reproduction, arousal, drum-banging sex, and why did Eric insist on waiting—

The daydream ended with the thirty-pound rhesus macaque that dropped from the eaves onto Alex's back, going for the piroshki. The tactic clearly got humans to drop the goods, but the madras strap caught on Alex's shoulder, and the monkey weight sent her flying backward into the knee-deep pond of rainwater in the courtyard. Alex and the monkey sat up to face each other in astonishment, Alex's skirt floating around her ribs, the monkey looking the picture of a disgruntled little old man.

The monkey got possession and took off at a splashing gallop with the bag. The monkey tribe watched from the trees, screaming raucous *hoo-hoos* of approval.

The bag held the TaskForce ID required to get a biometric instead of a g-screen. "Bad monkey!" yelled Alex, splashing in pursuit. "*Bad monkey!*" She snagged the strap and locked in a tug-of-war. The angry primate bared yellow teeth. Patrick's voice rose in her head, *It's more afraid of you than you are of it*, but Alex could not agree.

The Greek chorus of monkey chatter stopped, and Alex fell back with the bag. Envoy Beki leaned against a temple column, crisp and cool in an impeccable white linen shirt.

Eric must have tracked her and sent the Envoy to bring her back like a runaway child. Alex tried to imagine the Envoy had not watched her play with a demonic penis, or tangle with a monkey, that she was not on her butt in a mud pond. No. She would not give him this satisfaction.

"What a pleasant surprise," she said, as though he had popped by for tea. "I thought you were busy pandering to the Viceroy."

"Most mornings," he said. "But I'm not needlessly shackled by consistency. This was not a show to miss. You give meaning to the Descent of Man."

The monkey faces swiveled back to her scummy pool of humiliation. "Really, Envoy. Darwin? If you studied anything besides rhetoric, you'd know the Descent of Man concerns evolutionary theory and sexual selection. Complicated stuff. Better stick to playing fetch for your master. Now trot on back and tell Eric I'm fine. He'll give you a nice treat."

His face went to stone. The Envoy was so often at Eric's side that she did not think of him as big, but everyone was dwarfed in Eric's presence. Now she was acutely aware the man in the ruins was a large and powerful figure in his own right. Something very wrong was gathering here. The isolation of the place sank over her, leering demons in their rotted posts, the dark yaw of surrounding forest. The stone man made an almost imperceptible lunge that sent her scrabbling back crab-like through the water.

He stopped, and her fright dissolved to an absurd sense of relief. Had she thought a TaskForce Envoy would drown her in twenty inches of filthy water?

The Envoy disappeared down the wooded path, his fists dug into his pockets, his pants unintentionally stretched across the seat. Alex had to grin; it really was splendid. *'Tis a pity he's an ass* came to mind, though the quote seemed off. How sad that the man to correct her should be the one person she would never ask.

The monkey settled on a piled stone wall, his hairy little shoulders in a dejected hunch. Alex sat nearby in the same posture.

I've survived the day from hell, she thought, then realized it wasn't even noon. Alex looked at the abandoned temple and thought how the monkey's life should have been, his family protected by saffron-robed monks, gobbling up the sweet offerings left by worshippers.

The monkey held out a crooked little hand. She handed him the waterlogged piroshki. He bolted it down without the least thanks, to avoid sharing with his kin.

"No more begging," she told the monkey. "Without our pride, we're nothing."

Eric checked that Alex was back on the Provna and pulled out his sketch pad, determined to avoid her distraction. His hand traced unthinking strokes of black line on white paper, while his mind turned to the 3D sculpture of colored ribbons rotating on his wall screen. The overheated office and cramped desk faded away. Each ribbon represented a weakness in the Authority's cybersecurity wall, a highly personalized mental modeling that helped with intuitive leaps. Eric pulled the green ribbon, and the sculpture collapsed. Junk design. A child could breach that wall.

A hunger pang returned him to daylight. His assigned office was a statement in self-importance—velvet sofas, ceremonial swords on the wall, steel chairs to discourage sitting. Eric glanced at his sketch pad. The drawings from his musing periods yielded architectural doodles. But here was an eye, a mouth, a sweep of cheekbone, instantly recognizable as Alex's face.

"Seriously," said Eric, amazed.

He jumped at a knock, expecting Alex. His cousin barged in instead.

"Congratulations, soldier," said Suzanne. "You've got a Top-Secret Directive."

She tossed him a red-rimmed Level-Five Classification screen, an exceptional clearance that transcended TaskForce territorial quibbles. Eric's surprise at his cousin's appearance turned to extreme wariness. She would only be here if the contents were inflammatory. And they were.

"Me, spy?" he said in flat disbelief. "On another Security Ops agency?"

Suzanne assumed battle mode of hands-on-hips. "This Asylum Netcast changed the rules, Eric. This Hacker must be caught. The Treaty is at stake. The Netcast touches Guizi Control, so Solidarity is lead on the investigation. But it's all hands on deck. Solidarity refuses to share critical evidence and programs with the other agencies. That compromises the hunt. We need you to pull a copy of Solidarity's geo-locator program for the other agencies. In return, your own Chief assures your reinstatement. And it is a great service to Pieter."

Now Eric could see the shape of things, a clandestine power battle between Handel and the ambitious Solidarity Chief, who was challenging Handel in the upcoming secretary general election. Eric had no great love for Solidarity. He'd always been leery of the emotionalism and religious fervor of their anti-subversion mission and often admired the white-hat activists they hunted. Yet they were all Security Ops, same team.

The Netcast was Jacob Kotas's investigation. He had tested that friendship enough.

"It has to be you," said Suzanne, as Eric knew she would. Their brains were too alike to not anticipate every objection. "You have the rare skills. You are a free agent, thanks to probation. Pieter trusts you with a Level Five."

"And if I refuse, I start a war?" said Eric. "This is total bullshit."

"Your Commission is still real. In fact, it's excellent cover. Solidarity has gone renegade, Eric. They turned the Protectorate into a fiefdom and will do anything to oppose Independence. Use that for entry to their protocols." Suzanne gave a huge jet-lag yawn. "First thing, though. Get control of your goddamn team, before your brother and your girlfriend kill each other."

Easier said than done. The moment Suzanne left his office, Eric tapped into Compound security. The entry cam showed sentries clustered around a soaking-wet Alex, instead of minding their posts. How, wondered Eric, had she managed to get drenched the first dry day in Prosperity? Eric barked a few choice words over the speakers that made the sentries back off in a fright and Alex hightail it to his office. She burst in, to stand muddy and dripping on the expensive rug.

"It wasn't my fault!" she said hotly. "The monkey started it!"

"I don't care," he replied, though he was dying to ask about the monkey. "*Never* turn off your phone. Jesus Christ, you think

I can't tell that from a jammed signal? I swear I'll chip you—" He stopped at the mischief lighting her eyes; as if she wouldn't love to mess with a tracking chip.

"Who jams signals?" she asked.

Eric bolstered his forces. No weapon was harder to defend against than sincerity. "We jam signals, to prevent insurgents from using them to detonate bombs."

"Oh, Eric, I am sorry." The *sorry* was sincere, too, acknowledging the frustration of his weakened state, and inability to run after her himself. Alex turned her magpie eye to the polished weapons on the wall. She popped in several times a day to play with the swords—she had smashed what he dearly hoped was only an imitation Ming vase—and to nap on the cushy sofa. Still, he was touched by her conviction that a fine office was his due; the restoration of his professional status before her eyes brought a pleasure he'd never imagined.

"Did you like my report on Solidarity arming the militias?" she asked, wrestling down a Hussein's silver-and-gold blade.

"Yup." If only she used her intelligence for the forces of good. "Listen up. You've been telling stories about Strav."

"Women ask about the Wolf Khan. Does he have a girlfriend? Does he wear boxers, briefs, or boxer briefs? Do they think I *wash* his laundry too?" She swung the blade in a furious arc. "And you," she said, preempting his lecture. "You've no idea what women ask about *you*."

Eric had a pretty good idea, and admired her play to male vanity. "This is about Strav."

She stomped into a fencing lunge, her left hand poised like a scorpion stinger above her head. "I merely offered a few facts about Naadam."

Offered nonsense, as Eric heard it, a breathless detail of naked wrestlers smeared with sheep fat, and goat carcass polo. "Bullshit," Eric said. Alex was entitled to tease his own ugly mug, but no one got to ridicule Strav. "Goat polo is Kyrgyzstan. No one from the Khanate—"

"Kyrgyzstan, Mongolia. Close enough."

"Close enough? You've got a PhD in geography!"

Alex handed him the heavy sword to hold at extension, check-ing on the tremor that had plagued him since the hospital. Two days ago, the blade quivered like a seismic reading. Now the metal was steady in his hand. They both gave a humph of satisfaction.

"En garde!" Eric growled, cutting the air like a pirate. Why she always lightened his heart was a mystery. He slashed and dodged, remembering what it felt like to be twenty-nine, a man in his physical prime. Alex spied his open sketchbook and pounced.

"It's me," she said in wonder, holding the sketch like a mirror. She turned the pages to the Golden Gate Bridge, a bristling gunship in Shanghai harbor. "Oh, Eric, you did these?" She hopped on the sofa and struck the pose of Hercules from the Legion. "I am Eric Burton!" she boomed in a fake bass, her chest out, with a forbidding scowl. "Artist Extraordinaire! Cyber-God Deluxe! Protector of the Innocent and Defender of the Realm!"

This is what comes from too much familiarity, Eric thought sourly. When you start out seeing each other in a hospital bed, tubes snaking out of every orifice, when you've wiped each other's tears and drool and worse, where is a new relationship supposed to go? They had almost died for each other, seen each other at their worst and, perhaps, their best.

"Eternal Team Captain!" Alex proclaimed. "Blue Whale among Cetaceans! Olympian among Mortals!" She threw a thunderbolt, and Eric did feel hit by lightning, a euphoria of being alive. He also wanted to shut her up. He grabbed her and kissed her with every-thing he had.

Authority regained, he let her go, and Alex pulled him back. Eric opened one eye to make sure the door was shut, and his hand wandered over her damp back. Her tangled hair smelled of rain hitting the earth, sweet and musky, her body straining against his with a desperation both thrilling and alarming, as if she was trying to crawl inside him. His hand slid to a breast, her nipple hard to his touch, and her little sounds came faster, her hips in a rhythmic pulse against him. Eric smiled. Finally, a mystery he understood.

He pulled up her sodden skirt, and she went rigid with antici-pation. His hand brushed up and down the cool skin of her legs to her inner thigh, playing with her underwear, until his fingers slipped inside to the little shock of warmth between her legs. She rocked and shuddered in release, her cry muffled against his shoulder.

They kissed again, and Alex's hand began a search, exploring the fence post in his uniform pants. "Do it," Eric muttered, his stomach drawn in to let her hand slide inside his waistband.

Footsteps thudded in the corridor, a dismal reminder of the world outside the door. Eric groaned and moved her hand away.

"I know," she said in a low rush, "we have to wait, but what if it's too late? Bad things happen, people learn things about each other, and maybe you wouldn't want me anymore."

"What's this?" Eric lifted her chin. It seemed impossible she was the same rambunctious girl with the sword. "Are you a secret axe murderer or something?"

Her mouth turned up a touch, emphasizing the misery in her eyes. Attention was required here, Eric knew. The door had a lock, and yet . . . He still could deny fraternization because what had happened here—some teenage petting, no more—did not count as sex. Not really.

"Look, bug. You're my girl, right? It's just a few weeks. I'll make it worth your while." He set her down from her perch. She had an orgasmic afterglow he doubted any man could miss, so he waited until the footsteps disappeared before propelling her out the door. "And no more walkabouts!" he said, remembering why he'd been mad at her.

Order was restored, the sword back on the wall, but even an urgent jack-off in the bathroom failed to settle Eric's mind, a sense of having chosen the wrong colored pathway with Alex. She was right about bad things. Beyond the danger of encroaching war, you could get blown up in an art museum or hit by a bus, and never get that shot at happiness again. Therein lay the ultimate tangle— how to live as if tomorrow might not come, versus building for a tomorrow that might.

How, indeed. Eric shut the sketch pad and turned to problems he could solve.

———————

The Kommandant was still at the Peace and Love a week later, for no good reason Alex could see. It finally occurred to Alex that, just maybe, the tough old soldier was struggling after the Legion scare and didn't want to be alone.

"Who's running the Institute?" Alex asked the Kommandant.

"You do know I run seven Institutes," was the snapped reply.

Alex did not know, but it gave her an idea. She had five weeks until Netcast #2. Now Eric kept an eagle eye on her whereabouts, complicating her face-to-face with the contact candidates. She had managed quick forays to the two businessmen on her list, but their blank ignorance seemed genuine. That left one candidate in Prosperity—Colonel Yuri Bulgakov. Bulgakov was Allied Military, but had spent the past two decades turning the local War College into the Protectorate's only public university. His office would not return her calls, and she could not sneak the long trip across town. But the colonel could not refuse a visit from Kommandant General Burton.

"We should visit the War College," Alex told the Kommandant. "It could be your eighth Institute." The Kommandant kept reading the news. Alex thought about the Kommandant's hookup with the Homeland general. "Colonel Bulgakov is a founder of the Independence movement. His work is seminal. He's revered by his faculty and students. Plus, he's a widower."

The Kommandant put down her screen. "Are you trying to set me up, you creature?" She made a flicking "whatever" motion. "Fine, if it's for the Commission Report."

The War College office got right back to her.

Patrick's incarnation was waiting for Alex in her room that night. She had strolled about the Compound koi ponds with Eric and was humming a Gershwin medley. The air was swampy with heat and moisture, the evening begging for the release of rain.

"We need to talk, young lady," he said, a non sequitur, since he was in his Aggies football uniform, and her age. He removed his helmet and wiped his unlined brow. "You were baiting the

Envoy again. Calling him Eric's comic sidekick at the dinner. It is dangerous."

"You never let me have any fun." She danced about doing a flamenco with her clamshell hair clips. Still, the warning recalled the Envoy's face at the Monkey Temple, her primal fear as she floundered backward through the water.

"Latent propensity for violence is a universal male trait, varying only in degree. Take me. A life devoted to healing, yet I crippled a policeman who shoved my wife at a rally. Take Eric. A guardian of the Nations, yet court-martialed for breaking a man's jaw over a petty disagreement."

Alex nodded. She was learning that Eric was a lot better at protecting other people than at protecting himself. His account of his assault likely held a secret story. She respected that.

"The Envoy is different," continued Patrick. "There is active malice. And it brings out an unnerving potential in you. This is no game. He knows your weak spot about guizis. You know he recalls his captivity. Those eighteen squares on the floor."

"Are you defending the malicious bastard?"

"He is fighting something bigger than you. *Every man hath a good and a bad angel attending on him in particular, all his life long.*"

"Attribution, sixteenth-century dead white poet. Do you know my shock in Poetry 101 to discover your pearls of wisdom were all cribbed?"

"Just standing on the shoulders of giants, rag mop." They laughed together. A creak came from behind the lime-green tiles of her bathroom wall. Every night before her shower, this scrabbling of a rat, the furtive sounds of another hidden life.

"No more wolf-baiting," she promised as Patrick vanished. She hummed as she undressed, and stepped singing under the water.

Alex sang out, her shower drummed, the plumbing throbbed, and Strav, listening from five inches away in the adjacent hotel room, thought he might go insane. Tonight she was mutilating *'S wonderful, 's marvelous, you should care for me*, one of his Brit grandfather's favorites. And what would his grandfather have said about his sitting here night after night, strung tight as a bow, waiting for the screeching turn of her faucet? A shower was a banal ritual: the body must be fed, be clothed, be washed. But every night his rational mind abandoned him to the naked places the water ran, her lifted arm, her hands gliding over her breasts, soaping between her legs, spreading open her private folds. One punch to the rotting wall panel, and he could reach through and grab her. His grandfather would not have believed it. Strav could barely credit it himself, even sitting there.

'S awful nice, 's paradise—

In the strict pecking order of TaskForce, Alex was in the dilapidated west wing of the Peace and Love. The concierge took his request for the west wing as evidence of the Wolf Khan's spartan tastes. In truth, the exterior corridors and stairway let him avoid elevators. A lift was too much like a cell, and set off the constriction in his chest. He soon noticed the row of rooms backing to Alex's unit was closed for renovation.

An easy lie to the concierge gained him the master key code to all rooms. He had entered room 23, the unit behind Alex's, on a compulsion to be close, intending a single visit. But room 23 gave more than he bargained for—exposed framing and pipes that conducted sound from her room. Every evening she carried on a long one-sided conversation. He could not make out her words, but she wasn't talking with Eric—that bull elephant rumble would carry through a phone. And her tone carried the immediacy of another person physically in the room. But his questions washed away once she entered the shower.

'S what I love to see—

It was her fault for smelling of jasmine, some conditioner or damn thing women used on their hair, the same night jasmine as on the Kommandant's deck, dooming him to relive that cycle of exhilaration-agitation-devastation over and over. He had found her after that reception. "We will both apologize," he told her through gritted teeth; they had danced with their words across the trellis, rebuilt a small world of faith. "Come, we know each other too well for this."

"Are you insane?" she had hissed back. "We don't know each other at all."

He could not forgive her erasure of that faith. She never did return his jacket, and he would never ask.

You've made my life so glamorous—

A giant cockroach crawled from the framing and wiggled crooked antennae at him. It seemed to Strav, sporadic Buddhist that he was, the roach might rate his next incarnation. It would be a relief, compared to the human complications of a perpetually inconvenient erection, the time spent trapped behind conference tables and strategically placed folders, the alarming mind-body disconnect he had thought was buried with the suffering indignities of high school. This was the fierce desire straight out of *Paradise Lost*; old Satan had nothing on him. He had no defense against her jokes about his sexual inadequacy, the gleeful pranks that ripped his manhood to shreds. For a woman who claimed they didn't know each other, she knew exactly how to drive him nuts.

The cockroach scurried for cover as Strav sprang to his feet. Alex had taken the affinity he felt with Prince Hal and turned him into the ass of *Midsummer's Night Dream*. Yes, there was the obsession and jealousy, *lovers and madmen have such seething brains, such shaping fantasies*, yes, *the lunatic, the lover, and the poet are of imagination all compact, one sees more devils than vast hell can hold.*

Hell was Alex with Eric, Eric with Alex. Did Eric know what he had? Earlier that week, he and Eric had been shooting hoops. "Doesn't Alex remind you of The Bat?" Eric asked fondly.

"Hell no!" Strav had choked, startled from a vivid daydream of Alex giving him a blowjob in the shower. "What a disgusting thing to say!"

Eric gave him a look of *who are you?* and readied his shot.

"Are you going to marry her, anda?" The question had burst out of him like some horror movie alien. Eric launched an air ball. "Slow down, bud. Alex is just a kid."

Naturally, Eric saw her that way, a slim body, pretty but not seductive, clever but not worldly. Aunt Tita would dismiss her as having narrow hips for childbearing. There was a curious quality to Alex's swings from dreaminess to scathing wit, the practical jokes and uneasy relationship with gravity, as if whatever trauma happened at age sixteen had left her frozen in time.

You can't blame me for feeling amorous, she sang. But he did blame her; he wanted to not want her, for the eyes to stop judging him, for Croatia to have never happened, for her to suffer like he was suffering—out, canker blossom; out, witch. Forget a psychiatrist; he needed counterspells to drive her away, before it was too late.

Strav pressed his forehead to the wall panel. He'd had a vision, that morning at the temple, of holding her underwater by her throat. The blood-rush thrill of it scared him to death.

Strav ran down the stairway and hit the Provna at a dead sprint. The black vultures followed along, circling unseen in the night.

7

Suzanne decided the War College outing would be a fine drill for Commission unity, but Strav and Alex were delayed at the Viceroy Palace, so the punctual Burtons went on ahead. Yuri Bulgakov had commanded the deadliest artillery battalion along the Sino DMZ, but a man so forgettable in appearance seemed better suited for the shadows as an intelligence agent. He was spare in build and expression, with receding silver-blonde hair, a long thin nose supporting steel spectacles, a touch of Tatar fold to his eyes. He did not blink. Bulgakov had been a geologist before the War, and his speech seemed measured in geological time, thoughtful phrases separated by epochal pauses. Suzanne bet it drove his faculty crazy.

Yet hearing Bulgakov give orders to his War College cadets about the brewing riot, Suzanne saw calm, understated authority, incisive decision-making, and a rare ability to listen.

At the moment, anything worth hearing was being drowned out by the crowd in Chekhov Plaza, the three-block square fronting the War College campus. The forecasted storm had ignored the weatherman, and impromptu Independence rallies were mushrooming across Prosperity. Suzanne and Eric watched from Bulgakov's office as students rigged a bamboo gallows. White banners rippled with slogans of "Independence Now!" and "Asylum Hacker for President!"

"Where are they?" Suzanne murmured to Eric. Signals were jammed for security, and Strav and Alex were an hour late. Cadets in jungle fatigues paced the crowd, trying to keep the peace. Black-helmeted Solidarity MPs, their mesh equipment vests heavy with firearms and walkie-talkies, set crowd control barriers and orange police tape around the Chekhov perimeter.

A line of black balloons broke free of the gallows, to nod in the wind like weightless severed heads. A straw effigy of the Viceroy was hoisted in a noose. Excited students batted at the stuffed suit as if it held candy.

"If the Authority loses jurisdiction," Eric asked Bulgakov, "how do you fill the security vacuum?"

"Nepal to retain defense and foreign affairs, new Common-wealth to have domestic law enforcement," said Bulgakov in his strong Russian accent. The swallowed consonants gave his speech the sound of lapping water. "The Joint Military to commit stabiliza-tion force of five thousand. The challenge is to contain the Mafias. Solidarity uses them for the dirty tricks." Eric's skeptical frown was returned with a placid gaze. "Da, da, Solidarity fosters instability to justify continued control."

"And 'Asylum Hacker for President?'" asked Suzanne.

"Gallows humor," said Bulgakov. He had the tranquil composure of a tortoise. "For many here, the refusés in the Netcast are separated family. They remember the kindertransports."

Suzanne stiffened, and checked for implied criticism. The kindertransports had smuggled children out of the Federation for several years following the Treaty, until the g-screens made it impossible to hide them. The children were returned, with scenes of screaming families that still rose in Suzanne's worst dreams. But Bulgakov's face remained serene. Suzanne wondered if it was possible for him to be outraged or shocked. Perhaps nothing surprised him anymore.

"Still, many here supported the removals," said Bulgakov. "New immigrants often have the harshest views on illegal immi-gration. And no people comprehend the threat of the Regime better than we do in the Protectorate." He pulled out his desk chair for Eric. "Please to sit."

Eric's exhaustion tremor had returned, and his clasped hands did little to conceal it. Bulgakov quietly suggested he and the Kommandant fetch coffee. Eric was asleep face down on Bulgakov's desk before they reached the door.

Suzanne and Bulgakov kicked through the litter of hamburger wrappings in the deserted ground-floor Commissary. They sat in the open-loft eating area overlooking the lobby and sipped coffee acidic enough to have been served in a beaker.

"I almost lost him," she said, and could not continue.

Bulgakov put his hand over hers, his worn khaki uniform cuff meeting her blue and gold. "My son, my Mikhail, is lieutenant. On the eastern border."

They sat quietly, a shared silence that spoke of the worry and pride and sacrifices that never seemed to end. Outside in the Plaza, the MPs formed a blockade of plastic shields. Students banged on the shields with fists.

"Young idiots," said Bulgakov. In the same calm tone, he added, "Tomorrow is performance *New World Symphony*." Pause. "Dvořák." Pause. "In E minor."

The man had led platoons in the War and spoke for millions of dispossessed, yet the simple question was apparently beyond him. "Colonel, are you asking me out?"

The spread of his grateful smile held surprising appeal. Suzanne scanned the crowd to buy time. While not clear fraternization, dating a lower rank military officer was a bad look. And she was returning to San Francisco in a few days. He did not seem like quick fling material.

She was relieved to see Strav and Alex headed their way across the Plaza, Strav's panther glide and Alex's bouncing pogo-step an unmistakable juxtaposition. With her high-bobbing ponytail and garish book bag, Alex was in her element. Her excitement made Suzanne yearn for her own college days, the career dreams and animal energy and conviction that everything that happened to you was of tremendous import to the universe.

The lobby doors opened, and Alex's and Strav's voices carried to the cafeteria loft. "The Minister," said Strav, "is an irrelevant pedagogue whose speech is unfettered by his ignorance."

"So?" said Alex. "Even a blind pig occasionally finds an acorn. His transportation bond will build Commonwealth infrastructure. You are intentionally obtuse."

"You are unconscionably naive. Domestic product here is zero. Fifty percent indigent. The Protectorate is a freak historical accident and an unsustainable abomination."

Suzanne cringed and was about to call down, but the twinkle in Bulgakov's eye said he was enjoying the high-toned boxing match.

"Stop harping on domestic product," said Alex. "That standard always undervalues—uh-oh!" The lobby reverberated with the shattering sounds of an unfortunate encounter with glassware. Suzanne and Bulgakov ran to the rail overlooking the lobby. Alex was on her hands and knees, collecting the remains of a pyramid of coffee mugs. "—undervalues household production. Did you even read my brief?"

"I tried," said Strav. "I was stymied by your hackneyed language and clichés."

"*Clichés?*" said Alex from the floor. Her affront suggested a hard uppercut had connected. "At least I don't count on my fingers, you—"

"*Alex!*" Eric stepped to the loft rail next to Bulgakov. Alex popped to her feet, her upturned face an instant beacon of virtue.

Bulgakov stared down at Alex's revealed features. The force of his reaction—a double take of recognition, disbelief verging on horror—was nothing Suzanne could have imagined from the man beyond surprises.

"I see you know our Alex," Suzanne said.

"Nyet," Bulgakov replied, serenity returned.

Am I crazy? Suzanne wondered. Alex bounded up the stairs. "Great to meet you, sir!" she cried, pumping Bulgakov's hand. "I'm a big fan, took all your e-classes."

"Ah. Perhaps I saw you in a chat room," said Bulgakov, with an exculpatory glance at Suzanne. "So, Alex, *what are you doing here?*"

"I'm here because of you," she said, and Bulgakov went blank. "Your writings on Independence led to this Commission. You are responsible for all of us!"

"Excuse her," Strav said. "We are in no way your responsibility."

"I didn't mean—" Alex went crimson and changed to stiff formality. "My father was with the Red Cross. Dr. Patrick Tashen. He opened the clinic in Abad." She searched Bulgakov's face. "He would *really* want to know I was here."

"Abad," Bulgakov said. "Was that the Medevac crash a few years ago?"

"Nineteen months ago."

There was pained silence. "I meant no disrespect," Bulgakov said gently. "I did not have the honor of knowing your father. Let me express the Protectorate's gratitude and condolences."

Alex nodded, her eyes glistening. A cadet spoke in Bulgakov's ear. Bulgakov explained he had been summoned by the Authority. Suzanne avoided the question in his eyes as they parted.

The celebratory air of the Chekhov was replaced by electric tension. Their car waited on the far side of the Chekhov. They were midway across the Plaza, moving at Eric's asthmatic lumber, when the MPs set a g-screen checkpoint. No exceptions.

Alex went last. The MP waited until Eric and Strav moved on before giving Alex a blatant ogle in addition to the swab. The screener flashed green, the MP waved Alex through, and Suzanne watched in surprise as Alex walked blindly in the wrong direction. When Suzanne caught up, Alex was sitting on the ground, hugging herself and shivering despite the heat.

Suzanne checked her for a seizure. Alex returned a sweet smile of such piercing misery that Suzanne put her arms around her. Whatever triggered the breakdown, Suzanne understood the cure. They sat quietly, a huddled island in the flowing crowd.

Alex's insatiable curiosity soon returned, with her head swiveling to each passing sight. The girl was part meerkat, Suzanne decided.

"Did the colonel ask you out?" Alex asked.

"None of your scheming beeswax."

"Ta-*da*!" Alex cried, jumping up to pantomime Cupid drawing a bow. Her elbow smacked a young monk. He had a pale shaved head, endearingly protruding ears, and carried two heavy gallon-size plastic milk jugs. Clear liquid sloshed up and soaked Alex's sleeve. The monk bowed his forgiveness for Alex's trespass and continued to a bench. He settled into the lotus position, milk jugs at his knee, and draped a white INDEPENDENCE banner across his saffron robe.

Alex sniffed her wet sleeve and wrinkled her nose. "Gasoline?"

A crowd formed about the monk as a theater-in-the-round. Suzanne caught the glint of a cigarette lighter. The monk's lips moved in silent prayer.

Suzanne felt the return of her battlefield perception, cool, quick judgments and ready command. Her hand went by reflex to her sidearm, and found nothing there. "Alex. Go find and wait with the boys." When Alex wavered, she added a cold, "That's an order, Tashen." Alex slipped through the crowd.

The students pressed forward. Their phones rose like a field of eyestalks, set to record a man burning to death.

Sometimes there was a benefit to middle-aged invisibility. No one stopped Suzanne as she poured the gasoline down a storm drain. She poured neatly, a bench scientist's habit, with time to ponder if risking your skin to save a stranger intent on suicide bespoke a glitch in your own genes.

"You've no right!" someone yelled, the stirring of a crowd deprived of entertainment. Young men blocked her attempt to leave. "Independence!" shouted a bearded student. His thick neck above his yellow War College T-shirt was corded with fury. "Fuck the Allied Nations!" He picked up a bottle and drew back to throw it at her.

"Stand down," said Suzanne, hands-on-hips. "You know better. You should be ashamed."

His arm lowered, and for a moment the crowd was ashamed, or at least flummoxed. She would never know, because Strav charged past her in a blur of speed and attacked the student with a whipping motion that left the student screaming with a broken wrist. "Eric, stop him!" Suzanne yelled as Eric plowed through the crowd like a juggernaut. Eric dragged Strav off, but another protester swung at Strav's unprotected face. Eric slammed the man hard enough to bowl over the students behind him. The crowd rushed Suzanne. Alex jumped in front of her, brandishing the broken bottle as a weapon. "Everyone stop!" screamed Suzanne, astonished they should be the match strike to set the place afire.

Deafening semiautomatic gunfire cracked through the commotion. Yuri Bulgakov stood with a short-barrel rifle pointed in the air. He edged over and handed Suzanne his service pistol. She pulled Alex to Eric and Strav, and stood cover in front of the three young people, her gun extended.

Yuri said something in Russian. Perhaps the word was "shame," because the young men began to disperse with their eyes downcast. The monk sat unscathed, murmuring prayers, his eyes closed against the vagaries of the world.

Alex had cut her palm on the glass. Suzanne applied pressure. Eric put an arm over Strav's shoulder and quietly talked him down.

Bulgakov exhaled deeply, pinching the bridge of his nose, and not until that smallest of gestures did Suzanne realize he had been uncertain of the outcome. Strange, how that gesture made her own path more certain. The future would never hold the thrill of wide-open possibility again; she'd known the world too long and well for that. She would not guess where this might lead. A beginning was a gift, and enough for now.

"Let's go," she told her family. And in front of them, and the arriving MPs, and anyone else who cared to listen, she said, "Yes, Colonel Bulgakov. I would love to hear the *New World* with you."

8

The g-screen and mob had left Alex badly shaken, and she wanted to trail after Eric or the Kommandant all day. But her wily setup had worked too well. The Kommandant had disappeared, spending nights at Colonel Bulgakov's and days at the War College planning her eighth Institute. Meanwhile, the attack in Chekhov turned Eric's eagle eye to his brother. Whenever Alex visited Eric's office, Envoy Beki was there working. Evenings, she and Eric used to stroll the koi pond, the giant carp spying on them with baleful bubble eyes. Now the soft twilights were cut by the *bonk-bonk* echo of a basketball.

The evening one-on-ones were a resurrection of ritual between brothers, and Alex understood she was not welcome. Each night she stood at her window, her neck craned to view the sport court, watching with a fluid mix of resentment, gladness, envy, and yearning. She had to acknowledge the sessions worked wonders for Eric's recovery, each game rowdier than the last. That night, Eric moved about with the deliberation of a crafty bull, guarding his basket and energy, while Strav dribbled and feinted around him, talking continuous smack. Strav kept hitting jump shots, celebrating each basket with an in-your-face rooster strut. Eric finally blocked his layup, stole the ball with a mighty swat, and stuffed it, to pound his chest jungle style as Strav lay mock-dead on the court.

Alex pressed herself to the window screen, wanting to share the moment.

"Focus on your search," said Patrick. He was in the blue scrubs he'd worn as pajamas in Plainview. He opened the *Bulfinch* to an antique mappa mundi, each mythical beast representing a contact on her list. The Prosperity creatures were on their backs with *X*'s for eyes. Only the beasts of Abad remained.

Alex went back to the window. "Eric is worried about his brother," said Patrick. "You should be too, after he snapped that student's arm like it was deadwood. The bad angel is winning."

Cicadas rasped their little jawbone music. A moth beat its frantic wings against the screen. Alex shut the blinds to end the moth's distress. She crawled under the bed, managed a sideways hit from the Russian Prince bottle, and retrieved the gun.

"Put it away!" ordered Patrick. She had charmed the sergeant at arms into issuing the pistol, sans permit, by sharing pictures of the nickel-plated Browning next to the Frank Lloyd Wright cutlery set in the Museum of Modern Art's design collection.

"This Beretta's a special issue," the sergeant had confided, "a 100FS polymer semiautomatic with a sound suppressor for concealed carry." Another beauty, they had agreed.

"I need it, Poppa. The Envoy calls Abad a crime-ridden malignancy posing as a war zone. I need to be like the Kommandant." She flexed the Band-Aid on her palm, a souvenir of the Chekhov. "Broken bottles make a limited statement. We're talking a whole new can of Texas whoop-ass."

A creak behind the shower wall announced the rat's nightly arrival.

"You can't learn to shoot from a book," said Patrick.

"Then maybe you should have taught me some self-defense along with the Herodotus." His pained answer was interrupted by a message from Eric, who wanted their stroll. The gun went under the bed, the *Bulfinch* closed, and the night was forgiven all hurts.

Alex's showerless departure was a torment that sent Strav flying from room 23 in a hornets' cloud of frustration, *lovers and madmen have such seething brains*. He ran at hard pace, four miles of the Provna going black-white-black-white under the streetlamps. His eyes stung with salt, his muscles cramped, and still his thoughts raced ahead.

Every effort to drive the witch away proved futile. Yet she had to go, for both their sakes. Something had been released inside him at Chekhov. The new nightmares did not require Freudian translation. Sometimes he was on top of her, and she wanted him. More often she cried and fought. Last night, her face was beneath the pond's surface, her eyes wide and unblinking, her hair floating in a black cloud, his hands still on her throat. He had jolted awake in sheets soaked with sweat, unable to tell whether it had actually happened.

His nights and days were bleeding into each other. The question was no longer whether he was capable of monstrosities but whether he could keep from doing them.

The rain started in earnest, releasing a heavy metallic scent and rattling like gunfire off parked cars. A black limo with the Viceroy's flags cruised by and stopped. The rear window rolled down. Strav shaded his eyes against the downpour sluicing over his face.

"Eh, mate," came an Aussie voice in the limo. "Isn't this taking that macho Wolfie crap a bit over the top?"

Strav grinned and allowed that perhaps it was. The voice belonged to Rob Blakely, Authority Communications attaché, a human scarecrow with spiky yellow hair, a raucous laugh, and the gift of making you feel as if you were the most amusing person in the world. Rob drank as much as he laughed, which explained his career spiral down from International.

Rob waved a bottle of champagne. "Welcome to Prosperity, mate. East of West Bumfuck and north of nowhere. Here, Atlanta wants to meet you." Strav waited with equanimity. The endorphins had kicked in, and he was a prince once more, clothed in rain and glory.

A woman stepped out with an umbrella, and the rain turned to the roar of the Valkyries. Atlanta was the most magnificent woman Strav had ever seen, an amber-haired Brunhilde with a sequined top in place of breastplates. Strav stood a chunk over six feet and was still looking up at her. Grand shoulders and breasts, a narrow clipped waist, hips to make Aunt Tita swoon in approval. Strav bowed. She appraised him with a feline gaze that measured his exact place on the food chain.

"Atlanta is a criminal prosecutor, here to speed up our renditions," said Rob. "Was on the US crew team, weren't you, love? Never understood how you know where you're going, sitting backward like that."

"Join us, Envoy," Atlanta said, a husky-voiced command.

"I'm hardly dressed."

Her answer was a lazy smile that should have left him steaming in his running shoes. Flattering as it was to be deemed worthy, his body recoiled. It was beyond unfair; the only woman who aroused him was the one he could not have.

Part of his brain ripped along in an ice-cold strategy. "An Olympian!" he could hear his anda say. "Hot *damn*." Suzanne believed that Eric was attracted to the golden lioness types who resembled his mother, a psychological theory that made Strav too queasy to discuss. Whatever the root, Atlanta was guaranteed to make Eric go brain-dead.

Here presented a battle plan that, in the style of Sun Tzǔ, made use of his enemy's weak points. He knew Alex's own self-control was stretched sheer as gossamer. He heard the clinking of bottles in her room at night, the layer of caution peeled back in her speech.

Out, canker blossom. Out, witch.

"I regret a commitment," said Strav. "But my Commission is hosting a dinner tomorrow night. I invite you both. We need your expertise and"—an even bigger lie—"the wine is quite good. I promise a scintillating mix of business and pleasure."

The monsoon escalated that night, and Alex was awake for every gust, thanks to a surprise assignment from the Envoy. Each Thursday a delegation hosted a banquet to present their work. Tomorrow was their Commission's turn, and the Envoy named her the speaker. It appeared a conciliatory gesture, bound to please Eric. Yet the crash preparation left her sleep-deprived and cranky, as if by design.

The morning brought a new assignment, to crisscross Prosperity with a security escort and survey the religious and civic leaders on Guizi Control policy. Each person she interviewed used the casual language of pulpits and campaigns: guizis were mutants, walking bio-bombs; death to the Asylum Hacker. Any few such comments would have been a normal day. In multitude, they were electric zaps to hypersensitized skin, each one ratcheting up the bar of anxiety.

The last interview was at the Regional Quarantine Complex. Alex's driver sped along cliff-hanging roads, his hand glued to the horn, swerving around landslides and wayward cows. The rain fell as an upturned ocean, turning the car into a steamy bathysphere. Alex rubbed a circle in the fogged window, hoping for sea serpents and monsters of the deep, and saw high walls topped with great mats of barbed wire. Snipers appeared as wraiths high in a misty watchtower.

The Complex Admin was a flint-eyed woman who had lost both legs in the War. She triple-checked Alex's ID, grumbling about young people with high clearance. The first building, the Admin explained, housed people with uncertain infectious agents. The five stories of solid concrete were marked by narrow bands of windows. At each window, hands reached out, palms up, to feel the rain. A tritone siren wailed, and the hands retracted like the closing of a giant sea anemone.

The next building had no windows. "Our Maximum Security Facility," said the Admin. After the heavy skies, the facility was fluorescent-bright, the air a sinus-burning disinfectant. The vault door opened with the sound of a muffled drill.

The cavernous space was lined with bars and metal walkways. Each cell held multiple men in orange jumpsuits. The catcalls started with hoots and jeers, then rose to a roar to dissolve metal—a feeding-time-at-the-lion-house din that jacked Alex to an instinctive fight-or-flight alarm. The Admin continued to an unmarked elevator with one button. Down.

"The Guizi Chambers require special authorization," said the Admin. "I'll have to call Solidarity. But this Chamber hasn't operated in years."

"Excuse me. The what?"

The Admin wheeled about. "Guizi Chambers. For research on the g-marker. Plus certain medical experiments not permitted on Allied citizens. Shall I call Solidarity?"

Alex thought of the vodka waiting under her bed, any trick to numb this day. "No thank you," she said. "I've seen enough."

When Alex entered the banquet room that evening, Strav saw she was already looped. She looked like she had dressed in a dark closet, her schoolgirl blouse untucked, her blue hair bow at a cockeyed angle. She cut through the milling guests and straight to the bar. Phase One of his battle plan, the anti-guizi tour, had left her even more disturbed than he'd anticipated.

Brilliant.

Phase Two was Eric and Atlanta, impossible to miss. Atlanta wore a black sheath dress, her skyscraper stiletto heels an arresting claim of power on a woman already taller than most men. Eric typically stooped when speaking to the average-sized world, but tonight he stood at full stature, his chest out, his eyes narrowed in excitement. Either of them alone attracted attention, but combined they exerted a gravitational pull on everyone around them.

The room was an excess of good-luck red, the crimson wallpaper, carpet, and table linens giving the effect of a giant bloodbath. The name cards had been placed at Strav's request. Atlanta and Eric were at one table, while Alex would be with him, forced to watch the leonine foreplay.

Buzzed and jealous, Alex would be primed for Phase Three. Why the guizi subject stripped her defenses was a mystery that did not concern him. He needed a wound to jab until she lashed out against him. The uglier, the better. Eric would never tolerate a public attack, and would send her packing this very night. And he, Strav, would be free of her spell before anything terrible happened.

Alex gave Eric a shy wave, but he was not looking for her. Her hurt was so naked that Strav supposed he would have been moved to pity if still capable of such things. He called in his small artillery—a gel-spiked Rob Blakely—to provide Alex with a drinking buddy.

"Ain't you a peach!" said Rob, filling her glass. "So, Wolfie." Rob gave Strav a waggish smile and pointed at Atlanta. "So you were pimping for Eric last night! You dog, you."

Alex twitched, and Strav silently cursed his loose cannon.

Eric, the official host, welcomed the guests with a "Sit." Alex took the podium, to the disappointment of those expecting the Wolf Khan. Strav had to admit that she did well for being tanked and competing with the salad course. Even the vicarious experience of standing before an audience had him in a cold sweat. His career was over, carrion for vultures.

"And now," Alex concluded, "a special toast to our own mighty Wolf Khan." Strav saw the glittering smile, and a voice in his head yelled, *Incoming! Incoming!*

"Congratulations, Envoy, on your recent marriage. May you be blessed with many little Naadam champions. Long life to you and your bride."

Before the cheers started, Strav sat as dumbfounded as everyone else. "Way to keep it on the down-low!" cried Rob. And down-low was the point, its privacy the only thing that made his marriage predicament bearable. However Alex had gained the knowledge, outing his marriage was genius retribution.

"Biggest decision of a bloke's life," said Rob. "Who to share it with." Strav's predicament gained an awful new twist. How had he contracted his life to a simple woman he barely knew?

Alex sat down to her chicken vindaloo and gave Strav a smile to draw blood. The other table guests, a delegation of Scientists for Peace, competed to pump Strav's hand.

"Hunky Wolf Khan newlywed," said Rob. "Instant sex symbol to a billion little Chinese girls." There was a less certain round of congratulations. "I can set you up, mate. Media, marketing, product placement."

"He's obvious cartoon material," said Alex. "You could mass-merchandise a line of Strav Beki action figures."

"That face," said Rob, examining Strav with a tipsy publicist's eye. "That *body*! I say, bag those goodies while you're hot."

"This is most disrespectful, amen," said Dr. Goro Vito, a neurologist from International. He had a shaved bullet head, the chest thrust of a bantam fighter, and a bolo tie clasped with St. George and the Dragon.

Strav raised his hand in a noble-seeming request for tolerance. Let the witch have her laugh. Time for Phase Three.

"Tell us about your project," Strav prompted Rob.

"I'm jazzing up Solidarity's anti-guizi campaign," said Rob. "Wolfie here is helping."

Alex's smile flickered. She drained her glass.

"Check out the poster," Rob said, extending his screen for the table. "It's a Mongolian icon." Everyone startled at the bug-eyed demon with a red-and-black snake torso and multiple heads of flaming hair. The banner read, GUIZIS KILL. REMAIN VIGILANT.

"It's Lord Yama," said Strav. Nothing could be more fun than showing her that ridiculous poster. "Ancient deity of death and judge of souls."

"Nailed the motif," enthused Rob. "Bonfires, burning things to avoid contagion."

"Such ignorance," sniffed Dr. Vito. "A bonfire can atomize infectious particles and increase risk, amen."

"You're posting this—this—monstrosity in the Protectorate?" asked Alex.

"No." Rob filled her glass. "International web blitz. Won't be able to escape it."

"You can't. The Envoy sent me on a tour today, and if you saw what I—"

Strav watched comprehension dawn on her. He felt a dark shock of power; this was revenge as a drug, and just as addicting.

"Don't you consult for Solidarity, Doctor?" asked Strav, moving in his heavy artillery.

"It's not public," said Dr. Vito, and hesitated. "But since we're all TaskForce—the ability to wipe unwanted memories remains the Holy Grail. We don't have an effective treatment for post-traumatic conditions, which can be cruelly debilitating. Those memories are held in neurological connections scattered in the brain. Laser ablation holds great promise. We stimulate the memories, detect the magnetic signals produced by the electrical activity of the cells, and excise them. Highly experimental, but interesting results on our subjects."

"The Holy Grail," whispered Strav. Oh, to be freed of Croatia, *canst thou not minister to a mind diseased, pluck from the memory a rooted sorrow, raze out the written troubles of the brain, and with some sweet oblivious antidote cleanse the stuff'd bosom of that perilous stuff which weighs upon the heart—*

He had not been aware he was speaking aloud. Rob and the scientists regarded him with concern. An awkward moment, if Alex had not been too distracted with her pain to notice his.

"Interesting results," she repeated. "You mean side effects?"

"Asphyxia," Dr. Vito answered baldly. "And confabulations. The brain abhors a vacuum."

"Must be difficult to get the subjects' consent. Unless Solidarity provides the subjects?" She held her trembling glass for Rob to refill. He hesitated, so she poured her own. "Non-citizens from Guizi Chambers, perhaps, with no rights. Isn't that abusive?"

"Abusive?" said Strav. "You impugn the entities entrusted with our protection." Their volume was up, the entire room listening. There were a dozen Solidarity officers, and her words were the kind that ended careers, or worse. The goal was to send her home, not to destroy her life. But the dark exhilaration swept Strav along.

"I detect a conspiracy theory," he said. "Could you explain your position to a suicidal veteran or a catatonic child? You sound more concerned about guizis than people."

"Guizis are people!" She was on her feet, blazing beyond judgment or restraint. "People demonized in *your* fucking poster, you jackass, you monster, you—"

"Enough." The command turned every head to where Eric stood at his table.

Alex started, as if from a dream. She took in the guests' appalled faces; even Atlanta had lost her amused ennui. Alex's eyes went to Strav in a mute appeal for help. He held her gaze, raised his fork, and took a deliberate mouthful of dinner.

"You are an evil man." Her voice was flat, carrying the unworldly aura of an oracle. The skin pricked on the back of Strav's neck, and a strange weight settled on the room. "Evil. You deserve every terrible thing that has happened to you."

"You." Eric pointed at Alex. "On me."

She followed him out, and the red lacquer doors shut behind them. It was a short-lived privacy, as a waiter propped the door ajar to bring dessert. Eric and Alex were around the corner in the hallway, unseen but no longer unheard.

"You're done," said Eric. "First flight out of here tomorrow. Don't let me see you again."

Done. No more mornings brooding over her, afternoons taunting her, evenings in room 23. No more marking the hours by their next encounter. The pyrrhic victory should have given him great satisfaction. But Strav could think only of waking up tomorrow with no idea how to fill the day.

"He's trying to ruin us, can't you see?" Alex said in a quivering voice. "He's a remora, a parasite feeding on you. How can you love him?"

Evil, she'd called him. He could see jackass. But evil? Was there any universe where he deserved what had happened to him?

"Why?" Rob asked Strav, like a man co-opted into murder. "Why did you do that?"

It was a good question. It occurred to Strav that he had landed in the wrong play, and Prince Hal had turned into Iago. He had never liked *Othello*. Everything revolved around Iago's vicious stratagems against two people in love, without credible motivation. But perhaps the cruelty had risen from events outside of the play. An evil inflicted begat more evil, simple as that, and it was enough to destroy something simply because you could not possess it. So there was no answer, just a reality as heartbreaking as a false friend.

Strav walked out and shut the doors against the prying audience.

"Please, Eric." Alex's defiance had dissolved to some desperate realization. "I need my visa. I have to get to Abad. I am begging you." Judging from her muffled cry, Eric shoved her away, perhaps harder than intended. Her footsteps resounded as she ran down the long hall.

Strav turned the corner. Eric stood slumped, his features haggard, and Strav had a disturbing vision of his anda in old age.

"You all right, bud?" asked Eric, and he gave Strav a reassuring shake by the scruff of the neck as from school days. Strav nodded, dumb with love and guilt; if he could have died for Eric in that moment, he would have swallowed any poison, taken any bullet.

"Okay then," said Eric, and headed back to the banquet. He was the host, his responsibility. By the time Eric reached the doors, he was an officer in full once more, drawn up to the same grave dignity as at his court-martial.

Strav stood in awe—no army could have dragged him back to that room. Eric paused for a single deep breath and squared his shoulders before entering.

At first it was a great drunk—the cathartic master-of-doom fury that Alex had never allowed herself before. What did it matter that her body understood a different reality and she could not stop crying? Five hits from the Russian Prince bottle and she was in her DON'T MESS WITH TEXAS nightie, jamming clothes into her duffel. The bus for Abad left in an hour. It would serve Eric right if she were murdered on the way. He would cry at her funeral and see the snake for what he was.

Bag packed, she pulled out the Beretta. The ammo case held three magazines preloaded with ten rounds. The manual said to shove the magazine into the gun shaft. She did, and gave the bottom an empowering smack. Come for the guizi! There was the creak from the bathroom—the rat in her shower wall, same time every night. Time to die, rat, die.

The safety lever tipped with a finger. She pulled back on the slide, the action harder than expected. Chamber loaded. Alex closed one eye, which made the room spin, and sighted down the barrel to the green tile wall in the shower. Even through the blur of tears and vodka, she had to laugh—as if she could kill a poor rat!

"Don't play with that," said Patrick, stomping his Plainview pitchfork. Alex released the magazine from the gun and dropped the empty weapon.

"You were right," she said. "The bastard was dangerous. No more visa. No search. Probably no more TaskForce ID. I'm sorry." Sorry for letting Patrick down, for losing Eric, for too many lost dreams to count. Alex curled up on the floor. Her tears built to great racking sobs, until her stomach muscles hurt and she could not breathe.

A mosquito whined in her ear, and her hip bone ached. In truth, it was not very comfortable, even drunk as a pledge, to lie on a wooden floor in your underwear. Alex had a hazy thought about mosquitoes and drug-resistant malaria. She grabbed the empty gun to club the mosquito—finally, something she could bear killing. The gun fired with a dull thud and a horse kick.

Alex scrambled to the bed in a fright, and examined the unfathomable weapon. Right, once the slide was pulled, the cartridge remained in the chamber even after the ammo magazine was removed. That sound suppressor really worked. "Your lucky day," she told the mosquito, which hovered blithely unharmed. But the shower was a mess of green tile shards, a hole blown through the rat's wall.

"And that's how tragedies happen," said Patrick.

"Put the gun down," added the Envoy. "Everything is going to be fine."

Alex blinked hard, but the Envoy image remained, wearing suit pants, an unbuttoned dress shirt, and an expression of uncontained terror she would have paid dearly to see in real life.

"I know," she told the Envoy hallucination. "The gun had to go off in Act II. Or is it Scene II? I think I'll just kill myself now." She put the gun to her temple. He froze.

"That's not funny," Patrick scolded.

"Sure it is," Alex said. She took a pull on the vodka and turned the gun on the Envoy apparition. Perversely, the pointed gun released him, and he stepped closer. This had the makings of a great game, and she played it repeatedly: gun to her own head and he stopped, gun on him and he kept coming—pretty brave stuff for a drunken epileptic figment. Finally, he came too close; she could see the rapid pulse under his jaw, the circles of sweat in his armpits, his stomach muscles contoured like a relief map. Shiny keloid scars ran through his dark triangle of chest hair. The intimate detail was alarming, the solid physicality a whole new level of crazy.

"I'm not dressed," she said, indignant. "Get lost. Poof."

"No worries," said the Envoy, the low, rich voice as soothing as a lullaby. "I have four sisters, eighteen female cousins." The voice was hypnotizing, some Diplomat's trick, and Alex got sleepy. He took the gun from her hand.

"It's not loaded," she said with a giant yawn.

Strav sat on the bed next to Alex, and his hands started trembling, then his shoulders, right down to his feet. He pulled her head against his chest and held tight.

"Can't breathe," came her muffled protest. She worked one arm free and waved the vodka bottle, a suggestion that he needed it more than she did. Strav agreed, but the bottle was empty. "*O churl*," he muttered, "*drunk all, and left no friendly drop to help me after?*"

Alex grinned up from his chest-cave. "Did ya really think I'd kill myself over you?"

Thinking had nothing to do with it. Strav remembered entering room 23, peeling down in the sweltering darkness, listening to her wrenching sobs and thinking he'd go insane. Then *crack*, a concussive whistle, and light spilling from a hole in the wall two inches from his left ear. Then he was here, which meant he had sprinted down two hallways with his shirttails flying, and used the master key code to open her locked door. Alex was not sprawled with her brains blown out. He need not follow her with the next bullet. Eric need not find their joint tomb. It would take a while to sink in.

"Whaddabout the rat?" Alex asked in alarm. She told him about the rustling in the wall every night, the poor rat trying to feed its family. "I think I killed it," she said, and began crying again.

"Don't worry," Strav told her, eyeing the shattered tile. "I guarantee the rat in the wall escaped without a scratch. Which is more than he deserves."

They rested, quiet and entwined. Strav became aware of the expanse of skin on tear-slicked skin, the jasmine of her hair rising through the vodka fumes.

"The Guizi Chamber," Alex complained. "Hooorible. You *weaponized* what I told you on the deck. Prick. Howdya like it if I did that to you?"

Strav blanched, taking her point. A word that his amnesia was a lie and he had withheld evidence meant a reopened case and perjury investigation. She could have destroyed him and had provocation. Yet she had held his words close.

Alex was saying something about guizis, then stopped as if interrupted by someone. "He's not *real*," she told the presence. "It can't hurt."

Strav looked to where Alex addressed her words; there was nothing but air. Yet her face was animated, and she spoke with the cadence he heard every night through the wall. "Alex," he said carefully, "whom are we talking to here?"

She wiped her nose on Strav's shirt. "Remember you called me 'convict spawn,' in front of everyone? Well, meet the convict. *Dr. Patrick Tashen.* Don't know why my father stands up for you. Says you hath a good and a bad angel attending on you."

Strav's dismay penetrated her haze.

"My father's right there. Big guy with the pitchfork?"

Strav swallowed hard. "I often talk to my grandfather in my head. I loved him very—"

"Right there!" She stood and swayed.

"Now that I know where to look," said Strav, squinting desperately at the air. "He's—"

Alex gagged, went white, and a gurgle started. "I hate throwing up," Alex wailed as Strav dragged her to the toilet. The mess went in her hair and Strav's sleeves; it was surprisingly warm.

"Poetic justice," Strav muttered. He ran the shower and propped her inside. She kept sliding down the remaining wall, so he took a breath, removed his shoes and slacks, and stepped in.

It was not how he had envisaged them together in a shower. He had never washed long hair before, and found it a surprising upper body workout. The hair clog in the drain could have stuffed a pillow. "Don't Mess with Texas" became a transparent second skin, leaving Strav nearly as useless as Alex. He kept up a running monologue about The Bat, knowing he would horsewhip any man he'd found like this with his sister. At least Alex was too far gone for embarrassment, taking a loopy delight in every soap bubble.

"Look!" Alex cried as a bubble perched atop the straining, helpless hard-on in Strav's briefs. She made a drunken grab like it was a joystick. Strav slapped her hand away. "Knock it off!" he said, light-headed. "Focus!"

By the time Strav toweled them off, Alex was boneless and dozing. He plopped her on the bed and began to pull off her damp nightie—there wasn't much left to the imagination anyway—but was stopped by a palpable sense of an irate father with a pitchfork.

"I wasn't going to *do* anything," Strav protested out loud, his face going red. Damned if he wasn't as crazy as Alex. Still, it was reassuring to know he was above violating a helpless woman. Perhaps the good attending angel had some fight left.

Strav checked her disaster of a closet for a dry blanket. And found instead, folded with the care due a precious keepsake, the suit jacket a nomad had thrown over a trellis to keep her warm. Strange, how a few threads of wool, and faith, could move him to tears. He put the jacket on and flexed his shoulders, like an angel stirring great wings.

He sat on the bed. "We're a pair, you and me," Strav told her. "Proud members of the society for the internally maimed."

A slurry grin. "We're *super* proud." She curled up to sleep against his leg.

Strav tucked her in, killed a mosquito, gathered the gun and bottles, and unpacked her duffel. He now understood the nature of the talisman. He was meant to protect her. It did not matter if they fought, or if he had to stand dying inside as he watched her with his brother. His fate might rank as a cruel cosmic joke, but he was armed with purpose again, a reason for the struggle.

He kissed her forehead when he left, and felt around him a wary approval. The dead were very close tonight, and Strav welcomed them.

9

Strav, Eric, and Alex were each quiet at breakfast the next morning, there seeming to be no safe topic of conversation. Strav had not slept a wink, and wore his recovered suit jacket and lucky red silk jacquard power tie as an energy supplement. Eric's grumpy face and bottomless cup of coffee made public that he, too, had been up all night, and although the astonishing joint apology had restored his usual appetite, he would not reward bad behavior. Alex, in contrast, looked like she'd been on the wrong side of a bar brawl, her face puffy, eyes bloodshot, hair sticking out at angles only possible when slept on wet.

Rain slammed in waves against the window. Alex grabbed her head, then gagged at a waft of Sterno and sausage. Strav flipped his tie over his shoulder, just in case. He'd had to enter her room again to shake her awake. "How do you get in here?" Alex had moaned. His reply, that he poured under her door as black smoke, had not seemed to surprise her.

"I've got a new room," Strav told Eric. "The Dynasty Suite in the Conference Center."

"Way over there?" asked Eric. "What was wrong with the west wing?"

"Rats in the wall," answered Strav, enjoying Alex's blush. She stumbled to the breakfast buffet, her hands out as if on a pitching deck. Strav watched over the brim of his coffee, considering how to monitor her drinking without room 23. His new quarters safely distanced him from that nightly siren call. The concierge had insisted the Wolf Khan take the Conference Center penthouse for visiting heads of state. The view was uplifting, the linens a heavenly thousand-thread count, and the confines of the lift provided rigorous exercise in self-discipline. It was the perfect place for his resurrection as Alex Tashen's guardian angel.

"You must see it, anda," Strav said. "It's styled between Versailles and a honeymoon suite on the Vegas strip."

"Ceiling mirrors?" asked Eric, brightening.

"Yes," said Strav with a sigh. It was depressing to observe himself alone in the great bed from so many angles. But he, too, was soon lost in visions of bodies bouncing and thrusting in an infinite regression of reflective glass.

"There's an in-room jacuzzi," said Strav, wresting their disheveled thoughts back in order. "The doctor said steam is good for your lungs, anda. You must use it."

"Will do. What's your key code?"

"Othello. Two *l*'s in that."

Alex returned with pastries. She kept a chocolate croissant, gave Eric a bear claw, and tentatively slid an English scone to Strav's plate. It was the smallest and largest of gestures, an offering from ancient times delivered on modern china. Although he was not hungry, and the scone tasted like papier-mâché, Strav finished every bite.

Eric called the briefing. The local news was as unsettled as the day—landslides, riots, and manifestos. Alex expressed concern that the northern territories might make unilateral declarations of Independence and the paramilitaries fight over borders. "It's biased intelligence here," she said. "I need to go to Abad."

"Nope," said Eric.

Alex turned to Strav in an unlikely appeal. "I need to go up north, for the Sustained Population Bill. My report is incomplete and—"

"On the contrary, the report is quite thorough," said Strav. "Far superior to your usual economic hyperbole."

That stopped Alex like a glass wall. "You mean—you *liked* it?"

"*Like* is such a strong word. I found it well written. A roundelay of symbolism, fact, and emotion in a few concise pages."

"You carry a lot of literary baggage," she said in a tone of some sympathy.

"Moi? I prefer to think of myself as a veritable cornucopia of pithy aphorisms."

Strav and Alex stared at each other, the tenuous cease-fire tilting this way and that, and the corners of their mouths twitched upward, guarded, breaking into full-on matching grins of general devilment and appreciation. Eric's craggy face lit up with hope of peace and tranquility.

"But your conclusion is dead wrong," Strav added. The smiles vanished.

Eric trudged to his office, Alex and Strav trailing behind with yellow umbrellas. The Sustained Population Bill contained abortion provisions, perfect fodder for a family civil war.

"A requirement of paternal consent?" Alex shouted over the squall. "That's too *liberal*?"

"The Bill follows Chinese law." Strav steered her from a puddle.

"With no exceptions for hardship cases! What if women are afraid of the father, or denied consent? They turn to black-market abortions."

"Stop following me," Eric told them. "Go away."

"Government may protect a father's right to his unborn children," insisted Strav.

"The Bill is a capitulation to the Russian Orthodoxy," said Alex, as they dripped across the lobby. "What about the Buddhists here?" Eric groaned a *no, don't get him started,* but too late to avoid a slow elevator lecture on Buddhist theology.

The life process of sentient beings, Strav informed Alex, began at conception, when a being's consciousness entered the fertilized egg. The fetus had feelings, perceptions, and karmic formations, which is why Buddhists considered abortion a moral crime and explained the pro-natalist laws.

"Dead wrong," said Alex as the doors groaned open.

Strav blocked her exit with his umbrella. "You presume to teach me about Buddhism?" he asked incredulously.

"No, about life. China had a one-child policy and the highest abortion rate in the world. Then workforce and gender gaps loosened the rules. Then Guizi Flu, and an imperative to rebuild population and power base. It's an economic incentive, nothing moral about it."

"Go. Away." Eric blocked his office door. Strav and Alex pushed through and took over his couch, leaving Eric in apparent calculation of how hard he could crack their heads together without doing actual damage.

Strav threw the Population Bill on the wall screen. But when he looked back to Alex, she was sitting with her chin tucked to her collar, her face slack and vacant, hands drawn into claws.

"Is this a game?" Strav snapped fingers in her face. "It is not very attractive."

Eric was there in two steps. "Alex, baby, look at me." Eric wiped a line of spittle from her mouth, rubbed her back and hands. "C'mon, bug, you with me?" A count of thirty and her muscles relaxed, her body sinking. She turned a dull gaze to Eric's voice. "There's my girl. You gonna throw up?" A bleary headshake. Eric ran a hand under her seat, and told her all good, nice and dry. Her head fell against his shoulder, and her eyes closed in infinite exhaustion.

Strav stood frozen, terrified that the monster had done something to her.

"Just a little seizure, bud," said Eric. "No one's fault. Don't worry. I got her."

The *Argo* rose and fell on the swells of a gunmetal ocean. The shining bird skimmed ahead on the crest of the waves, a free glide on a sun-warmed breeze that smelled strongly of shaving cream. The bird winked at Alex with its clever bright eye. A man's voice rumbled from the depths, more felt than heard. Alex awoke to a Cubist world of isolated shapes that turned into a cohesive picture: Eric on his velvet couch, her draped atop him like a human throw, rising and falling with his breathing.

"How's the big ticker?" she whispered.

"Ticker's good." He stroked her hair. "You've been out awhile."

"A seizure?" Embarrassment brought her awake. "Did anyone see?"

"That neurologist Dr. Vito came. He was super-pumped to see a toxin-induced epileptogenesis. And Strav. He's seen worse."

Alex groaned at that unwitting truth. Last night spewing on the Envoy's fancy shirt, now seizing and drooling. "You sure no one else, no photos, it gets everywhere—"

"No. I'd fix it, anyway. Like the Legion." With some stubborn extraction, Alex learned that forensic footage from the explosion scene had included images of her convulsing and exposed. Eric had erased the footage.

He acted as if the fix were as simple as shaving, but Alex knew better. That was evidence in a terrorist investigation. No alteration of even a fleeting image was allowed for personal reasons. She kissed his shoulder, moved by his professional compromise on her behalf.

"Let me work." Eric turned back to a revolving 3D tangle of purple-and-yellow skeins on the wall screen. The furrow between his eyebrows deepened with concentration. Alex slid her hand between the brass buttons of his shirt, thinking of Patrick's cardiology book — the delicate flaying of pale outer skin, pearly connective tissue and pink-blue muscle, arches of white bone and glistening pump. It was wrong for such a massive house to depend on that fist-sized motor.

She hooked a leg over his, and a consuming ache spread through her body. Her focus shifted to his groin, on high alert for signs of stirring.

"Nope," said Eric without breaking his gaze. "Think of something else."

Alex looked at the curving scabbards on the wall, a fruit bowl of bananas, a paperweight iron cannon, the campanile outside the window.

"It's no good," she said mournfully. "Everything looks like a penis."

Eric harrumphed, but everything *did* look phallic these days. She would have thought the ticking clock of Netcast #2 would deaden her sex drive, but she woke every night with her hips rocking, sheets jammed up her nightgown, her days antsy with frustration. Perhaps this was a soldier's urgency before a battle, an animal imperative to pass on your genes before you disappeared.

"I can't help it," she said. "It's evolutionary."

"Council report, October twenty-seven. Sex, October twenty-eight."

"That's four weeks and six days. How can you—" A vision came of the statuesque woman at the banquet last night. Alex sat up with a stiff elbow to Eric's gut. "I'll go. You probably have a date with Miss Akron."

"You mean Atlanta?"

"I'm not good for you anyway," she said, the weight of that truth pressing her small and flat. She rolled off him. Eric grabbed her hand, her seriousness sinking in.

"I will wait," he said. "I don't want anyone else."

The weight lifted from Alex on a song of what-if. What if she found Patrick and stopped the Netcast? What if Patrick found a gene edit to knock out the g-marker, instead of masking it?

Eric kissed her, a true kiss of promise and longing. They glanced at the locked door. He lifted her skirt to kiss the sensitive stretches of her inner thigh, playing with her.

"No sex," Eric warned. "Will this make you happy?"

"Not happy," she gasped as he moved higher, marveling at whatever bizarre male calculus he used to avoid calling this sex. "But definitely less miserable."

Over the next days, Eric cranked up a tarnished sense of duty and fulfilled Handel's Directive to hack Solidarity's Asylum Netcast Investigation. There was a rational basis, he told himself, beyond his selfish desire for reinstatement. The Nations faced a bully Regime with next-gen biowarfare stock in its pocket. The Hacker endangered the Peace. While he saw no evidence for the renegade claim, Solidarity's refusal to share breakthrough tech tools and data was a power play that compromised the hunt.

Still, helping a politician eviscerate a rival felt ugly, a sense of lifting a rock to watch the dark wriggly things go crazy. Handel might want to lynch Solidarity for its ambition, but Eric could not fault Jacob's methodology. No one was more difficult to apprehend than a lone hacker motivated by a specific political cause and agenda.

The Asylum Netcast itself was a *Last Supper*–level masterpiece program, protected by a chaos jungle of impenetrable AI cyber immune systems. Solidarity's Hallows virus, developed to geotag the Hacker, was an impressive feat of engineering that found and exploited a vulnerability in the Netcast immune system. Eric's intuition said—maybe. Great programs had definitive personalities, and the Asylum Netcast spoke with a wry confidence.

Chaos was different from randomness. A truly random universe had no logic, or cause and effect. Chaos was like life, complicated, but an ordered system. His strength was pulling the patterns from chaos, finding the order lurking within apparent disorder.

Family life, at least, showed a hopeful pattern. Strav and Alex debated everything—God forbid it was the only way they could get along—but Eric wondered if Strav believed some of his own crap. His brother was hyper-traditional but could also dig into his favorite role as devil's advocate. And the debates were punctuated with those full-on matching grins. Eric drank in those moments with a happiness strangely close to grief; God, they were both beautiful when they smiled.

Afternoons, Eric took regular jacuzzi breaks in Strav's Dynasty Suite. The steam eased his lungs and relaxed his mind. Thanks to Alex's outing the Wolf Khan's marriage, the suite was an ever-increasing obstacle course of wedding gifts, gold-foil boxes, and red silk lovebirds that multiplied to infinite flocks in the myriad mirrors. Strav ignored the gifts, but Eric enjoyed peeking beneath the wrappings like so much women's clothing; what people thought Strav and his bride would do with an electric waffle iron on the steppe, Eric could not imagine.

On a professional level, though, his imagination was on overdrive. The deeper he probed the genius chaos of the Asylum Netcast program, the more skeptical he became of Solidarity's geotag. One afternoon he dozed off in the jacuzzi, with a head of tangled data. When he awoke, the answer was in his brain, a gift from dreamland.

Solidarity had not discovered a vulnerability in the Netcast program. Rather, the Hacker had thrown out a fantastic bit of misinformation, and Solidarity had swallowed it whole. Eric didn't know how to trap the Hacker—not yet. But neither did Solidarity.

A Level-Five Directive could not be shared, even with Strav, but Eric needed his anda's political insight. Handel and Suzanne would certainly forbid his informing Solidarity of the correctable defect in the Hallows' geotag. That felt like sabotage, and it was not faceless. Jacob Kotas's career rode on the Netcast investigation.

He let Strav badger him into a dawn patrol run, hoping Strav's notion of an easy convalescent pace wouldn't kill him. Strav's pre-occupation, though, was a match for Eric's own—in his brother's case, the need to justify his role in that butt-ugly demon poster.

Electric billboards glowed through the drizzle, advertising the lottery and competing church services. Trucks rumbled and donkey carts clopped along piled with woven baskets. Eric clopped along too—jog a block, walk a block, stop to hyperventilate.

"The anti-guizi campaign is legitimate diplomatic strategy," said Strav, jogging backward so Eric wouldn't miss a word. "The Nations are at constant risk of reversion to tribalism and civil war. Focusing attention on an external threat helps prevent that." He checked the monitor on Eric's armband and slapped Eric's gut. "*Chu*, anda, *chu!* Think of the energy stored in that blubber."

Eric peered down in chagrin. "I thought I'd dropped a few pounds."

"Yes, from your chest to your waist. Good lord, did you work out at all while I was gone?"

The answer was no, he'd caught up on his sleep and waited for Strav to bully him back into shape, like always. Still, he thought Strav could show a bit of mercy, considering his grisly near-death in the Legion. "About Solidarity—"

"Exactly!" cried Strav. "Alex says their vilification of outsiders is an honored autocratic tradition used to deny the significance of the local politics and reduce underlying conflicts to a meaningless phrase like 'tribalism.' I find that a gross oversimplification."

"Do you," said Eric, considering a meeting of his elbow and Strav's thick skull. He looked up for a crackly breath. Every billboard along the Provna had gone dark.

"You should take her to Abad," Strav said.

"About Solidarity—huh? Christ, not you too. What the fuck is it with that place?"

"Her father died in those mountains. She needs closure. Grief does strange things to a mind."

Why can't people say what they mean? thought Eric. "I can't go. About Solidarity—"

"Professional upgrade required." Strav jogged circles around him while shadowboxing. "Alex's clothes look plucked from the lost and found. That satchel! An abomination in madras." Strav threw in a few jumping jacks. "I would ask Suzanne to take her shopping, but I don't trust her sense of propriety. Alex is very modest."

It seemed to Eric that the Envoy used the wrong word for once. "Modest" hardly described how Alex pressed against him, her body a compressed spring of need. She came like a shot; he'd never seen anything like it. "Men ask about her," continued Strav. "And I hear there's a wealthy Italian boyfriend in the wings. You should not be careless with her."

"Careless?" Yet Eric took the point. Alex was a prize, and the world a great circling of males in rut, ready to lock antlers and flash bank accounts. His thoughts swung to Atlanta, and the temptations that made life rich, and the fact that he had not been properly laid in weeks. Atlanta had asked him to lunch that afternoon. He'd keep it professional, talk criminal justice and such. He was not careless.

Eric checked for alerts to explain the empty billboards. Nothing. He pocketed his phone and misgivings. "Don't you upgrade Alex," he told Strav. "This isn't that pig play."

"That would be *Pygmalion*. Shaw."

"I like her the way she is."

"You treat her like a child. *Everyone* treats her like a child. She is not. She needs to be taken seriously to advance her career. You can't understand. The Burtons are ruling class. But appearances matter for people like us."

Eric's head reared back in surprise and hurt.

The Provna reached its morning boil of traffic and diesel fumes. Strav rubbed his face hard enough to take off skin. The odd belligerence passed like a rain shadow.

"Forgive me, anda." His lost smile pierced Eric through. "Been off my game, eh what?"

Eric replied with a solid cuff to the head that Strav barely ducked. They straightened to a change on the Provna—workmen crossing themselves, old women in kerchiefs tapping their foreheads and spitting over their shoulders. Each billboard was alive with the thirty-foot Mongol fire demon, its crimson skin rippling beneath multiple heads of orange flame. *Guizis Kill. Remain Vigilant. Solidarity.*

Strav stared in disbelief, as if he had summoned a minor spirit and a Kraken appeared instead. The brothers jogged back to the Compound in silence, the red demon eyes tracking them.

Alex knew the Kommandant was flying back to San Francisco that day, so she was surprised by the mystery order to meet in front of the Compound. The sight of the demon billboards hit Alex like the physical violation of a g-screen, the sick spin of panic and a need to run.

The Kommandant's sharp "Fall in!" helped Alex regain her composure. She followed for a forced march up the Provna. Street urchins darted about them like guppies, hawking freshly printed guizi demon T-shirts. Alex ventured a "What about Colonel Bulgakov?" The Kommandant shut her down with a coy smile.

The march ended at the Pushkin Boutique, a high-end shop painted like a green-and-yellow Russian Easter egg. They had passed the shop on previous outings, and the Kommandant must have observed her yearning glances at the sky-blue gown in the window, because minutes later a saleswoman with a sporadically Italian accent led them to a spacious dressing room, bearing the gown in her arms like a Pietà with Christ's body.

Alex touched the silk with one careful finger. The fabric was as fine as if woven by Arachne herself. The gown cost three paychecks, a backless slip designed to look falling off. "Where would I wear it?" asked Alex, scandalized. "How can you wear a bra?"

"What is wrong with your generation?" said the Kommandant. "You're as Victorian as Strav. See, the color looks dyed to your eyes. My mother said if you don't get it, you won't have it when you need it. You never know until you try it on."

The gown slipped over Alex's skin in a cool breeze of silk, and hope—the billboards weren't forever, and Eric was bound to relent on Abad. Alex shook out her ponytail, and her dark hair fell over bare shoulders. A strange woman stood in the mirror, flaunting her sensuality at some future party, another imagined world.

"Oh, to be twenty-three," Suzanne said with a sigh. "You have no idea how fast it goes." Suzanne paid for the dress over Alex's startled objections. "Shut it, Tashen. But keep it between us."

They walked back in the muted light of a tropical storm. Alex's head was swimming; even the waterproof dress bag was the most beautiful thing she'd ever owned.

"In the Chekhov," said Alex. "You were so brave."

Suzanne shrugged. "People say that, but you just do what's needed to get through that day. It's clearer when it's for someone you love. You'll see, when you have kids of your own."

She means Eric's kids, thought Alex. Eric wanted his own someday. That gift was beyond her. The third corollary to the rule was no pregnancy.

As Patrick explained it, her gene therapy only worked in cells that divided, like blood, saliva, and skin. Not egg cells in ovaries. The g-marker would be detectable in fetal cells circulating in her blood, and traced to her. Her gene therapy was no fix. The virulent delivery vector would kill a fetus or infant. Even if she avoided prenatal testing, or giving birth in a medical facility, she had no Plainview in which to hide a child.

The corollary had seemed like a distant abstraction. Who wanted to bring a child into this miserable world anyway? But Eric made the abstraction concrete. "I can't have children" was no excuse when she would have to refuse a request for infertility testing.

"I don't—want—children," said Alex, testing it out. How was that fair to Eric?

"No kids?" said Suzanne. "What, you going to be one of those crazy cat ladies?"

Alex looked up at the demon billboard. "Will it never stop raining?" she asked the sky, already grieving her loss. She found a flip smile for the Kommandant.

"Thank you for the dress, but no." Alex passed the bag to Suzanne. "Everything stains silk, and we both know I'll just ruin it."

Suzanne cocked her head to study the problem. "You won't." She passed the bag back to Alex. "I have faith in that pretty dress. It's a lot tougher than it looks. See you back in SF."

Alex watched until Suzanne's cab was out of view, left clutching the bag like a life vest.

The Commission was scheduled for a meeting with the Drug Czar at the Viceroy's Palace that afternoon, but Eric returned late from a lunch to announce that an important call had come up, and Strav and Alex were to go without him. Eric hustled them to the sentry gate, ordered Strav to call on the way back, chucked Alex under the chin as if she were ten years old, and walked off checking his shave.

"What did he have for lunch today?" wondered Alex.

"Am I my brother's keeper?" snapped Strav. The misery of his day had him twisting by a single glistening tendon. Typically a High Council Commission Report was handed off to a Council Speaker for the formal appearance at the Assembly in International. But today brought a gold-embossed Notice of Appearance naming him the Speaker, his Wolf Khan fame having gained him that wholly unwanted honor. In four weeks, he would stand at a podium before the Delegates, thousands of eyes in the gallery, and the thought was like having his tongue ripped out by the bloody roots. He doubted he could tolerate even a handful of stares at the Drug Czar meeting.

"Must you bring that abominable satchel?" he asked Alex. "This is not a Texas hoedown." Her screw-you smile brought Strav some satisfaction; she couldn't hate him any more than he hated himself at the moment.

An arriving cab disgorged a passenger. "Peach!" cried Rob Blakely, hugging Alex. "Envoy!" he added warily, as if Strav might go Evil Incarnate on him again. Rob explained he was here for the Viceroy's Rotary speech in the Conference Center. "Afraid it's my last gig. Had a few Kingfishers and gave the Viceroy the wrong brief. He gave the Sunni speech to the Shiites." Rob bent down to rescue a drowning worm from a puddle. "Still, the Viceroy's a great man, eh."

"He's a pedagogue acting in expiation of his own incompetence," said Strav.

Rob shook his damp-straw head in admiration. "What a voice!"

"An empty vessel makes the greatest sound," Alex sweetly agreed.

"Viceroy loves you, Wolfie. Busted my nuts for not getting a pic of you together." Rob headed off like a whipped dog dragging a chain. "Hooroo. Wish me luck on my next post."

"Wait!" cried Alex. "What if the Envoy introduces his pal the Viceroy? Tells a few bow-and-arrow stories, poses for that pic. Would it save your job?"

Rob snapped out an Irish jig. "He'd knight me! Thankee, mate, you're a rock."

"No." Strav thought his expression impenetrable but saw Alex pick up his flash of alarm.

"We have time before the Drug Czar," said Alex.

"No."

"No?" Her scorn was a delicate stiletto thrust. "Where are your big words, Envoy? Or do you only do criticism? Sorry, Rob, bit of a coward play here. Some people are all hat and no cattle."

Strav was striding back into the Compound before she finished, the word *coward* exploding in his head. He could master himself for a few Rotarians.

The Conference Center building was stacked high on the back slope of the Compound. The guards in the lobby bowed to Strav as they passed the private elevator to his penthouse Dynasty Suite. "You lucky wanker!" cheered Blakely. He led them onward to the Hall of the Illustrious Fallen. The carved bronze doors had a beehive hum.

The doors opened to a chandeliered ballroom. The hum was the swarm of five hundred guests milling around white damask tables. Strav staggered as if the floor dropped, and Alex grabbed him.

"Envoy?" Alex asked Strav in dread, trying to keep his arm as the Viceroy's entourage led him away. His reluctance to speak had made for fine mocking, but the game was no longer fun. He was sweating profusely, his face the ash of the concrete walls, his ballroom grace turned jerky mechanical motion. The Viceroy, an older Chinese National with dyed, jet-black hair, escorted the Wolf Khan to the stage podium, his hand on the tall shoulder as if guiding a favorite son.

A boom of applause rolled around the room, and a hush of anticipation.

"Just a few words," Alex whispered at the back of the Hall. But Strav looked like he'd seen Medusa. The audience craned in their seats. Wild thoughts came to her about how to extricate him from his petrified grip of the podium. Shouting "Fire!" would get her carted out by security. Any moment, the snickers would start, open laughter, derision.

She needed a disruption sufficiently credible; if she were ever to suffer another seizure, this would be the time. Yet she could no more summon one up than an earthquake or a tornado. The audience buzzed with an ugly new hum, a first low jeer. What was one more scam in a lifetime of accomplished fraud? Alex dropped to her knees and pitched forward . . . and realized she was never conscious to know what her body did in a real seizure—grunts or grimaces, flailing or rigidity? The situation called for a showstopper grand mal, but she heard those involved painful head-banging. She settled for flopping about like a hooked salmon and making gurgling noises.

The effect was dramatic, people shouting, "Is there a doctor in the house?" She squinted through her eyelashes to see a woman holding a silver cross over her, as for an exorcism. Cold tile against her back told her that her blouse had pulled up, her skirt too, and there was nothing she could do about it. Someone grabbed her head, shouting she had swallowed her tongue, and strange hands touched her, pushing her into a genuine panic. Then the Envoy's deep voice roared for everyone to back off. It was amazing how fast he got to her; he must have left footprints on the snow-white tabletops. He wrapped his arms around her, a straitjacket of damp body heat, and Alex went into a limp collapse that required no acting.

The MPs formed a phalanx to give them privacy. Strav held her upright in case she vomited. Alex had forgotten he'd watched Eric handle her during a seizure. So she reposed in appropriate post-fit stupor, peeking between Strav's arms and enjoying the fuss.

"She will sleep now," Strav coldly told the Viceroy, who hovered at a distance to avoid possible contagion. Strav turned to Rob. "Find Dr. Vito. Bring him to my suite upstairs."

Rob flew from the Hall like Mercury in tasseled loafers. Alex almost flew after him. Pretending to sleep on the Envoy's pillow would be awkward beyond acting. Strav picked her up. The MPs parted the enthralled crowd, phones flashing to record the souvenir moment.

Strav carried Alex from the Hall, his mind and body turned to a single singing arrow of guardian purpose. Her squirming protests in the elevator barely registered. He could have carried twenty of her.

The hall to his suite was hung with lithographs of the Battle of Trafalgar. The sword-raised boarding parties watched Strav sail into his own engagement, trying to keep Alex aloft while punching O-t-h-e-l-l-o into the keypad. The door would not open.

"I'm much better!" Alex yelled at him.

"The doctor will judge." Strav punched in the master key code from room 23. The door swung open. He charged headlong through the foyer of painted water lilies and gold-foil wedding presents, moving so fast that not until the end of the partition did he register the thrum of jacuzzi jets he had not left on, the puddles and wet bath sheets, the oversized khaki uniform and boxers that were not his, the lacy black bra and garter belt that were definitely not his.

Then came the epiphany that the jammed lock was a cyber do-not-disturb sign, and the owner of the uniform was using the spa for more than his damaged lungs, so that by the time Strav hurtled into the spacious bed area of angled mirrors, he was already leaning back in a fruitless effort to stop, like a horse in a four-legged skid before the cliff.

Atlanta faced them on the gold brocade bedspread, straddling a splayed pair of tree-trunk legs, her skin slick and rosy from the jacuzzi. A man's red silk jacquard tie fell between her heavy swinging breasts, pointing to an unashamedly luxuriant blonde bush poised mid-pump. The sight was so surreal—*his* room! *his* lucky red power tie!—that Strav's brain went AWOL again, this time to plant firmly between those breasts, even as a deeper recess of his mind mourned that he could never, ever wear that tie again.

The kaleidoscope of mirrors showed Atlanta riding Eric backward, with Eric palming her butt cheeks. Eric peered up, his face strained against a sensation too familiar to Strav, of an ejaculation about to happen that cannot possibly be stopped. There was a moment of silent tableau.

Strav caught his own reflection with Alex in his arms, the picture of an eager bridegroom crossing the threshold. "It's not what it looks like," Strav blurted.

Atlanta regarded Strav with a cool smile. "Lose the suit and join us, Envoy." She turned her consideration to Alex, who dangled from Strav's arms with her eyes and mouth in perfect astonished O's. "Blue eyes can join us too."

"No!" cried Eric and Strav in unison. Strav swung back to the door, and Alex threw an elbow that clattered his teeth. She struggled down and confronted Eric.

Atlanta looked at Alex with more respect, and gave a gracious shrug that sent her breasts in a tremulous sway around the tie. She dismounted, leaving Eric's erection on display, and strolled back to sit on the edge of the jacuzzi.

"Nice digs, Wolfie!" came a cheery halloo from the alcove, the afternoon gaining the surreal quality of a Bosch painting. Blakely entered with Dr. Vito and the MPs in tow.

"Oh, gawd!" gasped Rob, looking past Atlanta's nakedness to Eric's rampant spectacle. Dr. Vito took in the room with an outraged "What is wrong with you people!" and was knocked aside by the thrilled MPs. Eric flung a towel to Atlanta. Strav rushed the MPs as if to frighten back wolves, roaring, "Out! Everyone out!"

When the commotion died down, Alex was gone.

The afternoon rain settled into a steady drone that pitted the koi pond. Alex sat on the open-air stairway in back of the Peace and Love. By the time Strav found her, her first wave of emotion was spent, and she had stopped crying. Strav sat beside her, and they watched the water gush from a broken rainspout.

"It's my fault," said Strav. "You must know I set him up with Atlanta."

"I do know. You are a total water moccasin. But this is not your fault."

"Don't worry," said Strav. "This kind of thing doesn't mean anything to Eric."

"Shouldn't it, Mr. Family Values?"

Strav appeared transfixed by the gurgling spout. "Eric loves you."

"In his way. But I'm an idiot too." She finally understood Patrick's warning about attachments and the unique power of desire to lure you off the map of your goals. "I forgot why I came here. It's not for Eric. And we're not lovers."

"You mean you two never—"

"Oh, no, we never had *sex*," she said with a bitter smile. "Just ask him." Her anger was revelatory, liberating. "Atlanta is perfect for him. She's magnificent. Can you imagine ever being that comfortable in your own body?"

"*Bien dans sa peau.* No. I cannot."

"That confidence, that pride—do you think she gives a hoot what anyone thinks? What I would give to be like her! Choosing your own life, making your own rules. And what they were doing in bed—I didn't even know you could do it like that. Have you ever done it like that?"

"Not yet," Strav said reverently, and he blushed so dark that Alex let out a whoop, laughing until she fell off the step.

"Poor Eric!" she gasped, crying with laughter until the hurt and betrayal returned. Strav's hot blush spread to her, and they sat quietly, ashamed of what they had seen.

An ambulance wailed from the Provna, the sound of someone's life taking a bad turn. Strav jolted to his feet. "Bloody hell!" he exclaimed. "You've yet to see the doctor."

"Doctor?" Alex said distantly, checking her phone for the bus schedule to Abad. An overnight express departed at eight. She would leave her phone in her room, be untraceable for a while. A pity about her gun, but she could hardly ask the Envoy to return it. He'd worry she might shoot Eric. It was tempting. "A doctor? What for?"

"For the reason we went to my suite! You just suffered a terrible seizure."

She scoffed, distracted. "You saw me after a seizure. Would I be walking around—" She caught her blunder, and Strav's rising horror. "Oh, *that* seizure!" she exclaimed. "My new meds are formulated for faster recovery, really kicks those neurotransmitters—"

"You faked the seizure." Strav walked from the overhang to stand gobsmacked in the rain, his suddenly defenseless face telling her every thought: How could he have bought such a perfectly timed salvation from his mortifying breakdown at the podium? The only miracle was that she'd subjected herself to such public humiliation—for him.

"I—I—don't know what to say," said Stav.

"Well, that alone makes it worthwhile," said Alex, only half joking. "Listen, Envoy, I need privacy tonight. I'm okay, I won't drink. Tell Eric to respect my space. No visits, no calls."

She climbed the stairs up to her floor. Strav called her to the balcony, and he bowed to her in timeless pledge, his hand spread wide over his heart.

It lodged in Alex's heart, this beautiful man in the rain. She leaned over the rail, gathering every detail of shadow and light, locking the image so no one could take it away.

"I'll see you tomorrow, Envoy," she lied.

10

Suzanne Burton had a rule. She slept on bad news before acting. So when she awoke her first morning back in San Francisco to the gossip-rag headline about the Wolf Khan's noble rescue of an epileptic girl resulting in a certain super-endowed Director being caught in coitus interruptus, Eric gained a day of reprieve before Suzanne burned his red ears off with a call.

The headline led to an unwelcome call for Suzanne too. "Saw about your Eric. Dying this Friday. Come. Katrin."

Commander Katrin Bar-Illan had been dying for twenty-five years, she and Ari both among the millions of long-suffering victims of dirty bombs during the War. Suzanne and Katrin had attended West Point together, disliking and respecting each other as two combative personalities will. Katrin had taken Suzanne's transfer to Allied Service as a sign of weakness and personal affront. They had scarcely spoken in twenty years.

Katrin was at the Armed Forces Convalescent Center in Colorado Springs, a final station for progressive atrophy and dementia. Suzanne's plane touched down in the turbulence of a premature winter storm in the mountains. She drove to the Air Force base, her headlights drilling bright tunnels of snowflakes in the night.

"We look like hell," cackled Katrin as Suzanne entered the hospital room. "I'm cursed. What's your excuse?"

Suzanne tried to translate the gnarled figure in the bed into the tall, bold cadet with black sweeping eyebrows. One wanted to believe that old friends carried a mental picture from your prime years together, and despite the ravages of disease or time that startled you in the mirror each morning, they saw you as the person you still felt inside. But Suzanne saw nothing of Katrin in that hospital bed.

"I smell like shit," said Katrin. "Kick out the dog. It's the devil." She plucked at her blanket with her bird-claw hand. Suzanne opened the door for the imaginary animal. Katrin gave the high-pitched titter of a crazy woman. The overheated room smelled crazy, too, a mix of antiseptic, cloying sweet freesias, and yes, shit.

"I follow the news," said Katrin. "Nothing else to do. Troops staging in the Caucuses. Breach of Treaty. When I was your Eric's age, I thought liberal humanism was the natural evolution of things and we'd be walking around with chips in our heads."

Suzanne threw the stinking flowers into the trash.

Another cackle. "I believed if I willed it hard enough, I would never grow old. These young nurses don't think this could ever be them. I tell them, just wait. Bitches. Cunts."

Suzanne felt a hard whap of her own mortality, a terrifying preview of how a few dying gray cells could destroy one's dignity. Katrin rambled in agitation about her troops digging mass graves in icy Federation ground. The children had frozen huddled together in a classroom, their eyelashes coated white with frost, their little fingers and noses a meal for the rats. She used a flamethrower on those rats, and they screamed like children. Did Suzanne know that each snowflake was a dead soul? She wanted to die where it was warm, and instead the fuckers sent her where it snowed in every season.

Suzanne started to call the nurse.

"Your family made the news," said Katrin in abrupt lucidity. "Saw the photo from Prosperity. The nurses loved it."

Katrin called up the wall screen. To Suzanne's relief, the image was not a porn shot of Eric with the attorney but rather a few links earlier in that chain of events: Strav, handsome and stalwart in his trim-cut suit, carrying the stricken Alex from the Hall. The tag read, "Wolf Khan's Valiant Mission of Mercy."

Suzanne studied the burning intensity of Strav's face, the fainting helplessness of the girl in his arms. The scene was hopelessly feudal and regressive, but she supposed that set the nurses aflutter. "That's our Strav. Always one for the grand gesture."

"Not *him*," Katrin said in contempt. She pointed. "*Her.*"

Suzanne, taken aback, looked closer. The bright blue eyes showed more sprightly curiosity than expected in her dire condition—another Alex escapade, bound to bring a headache.

"She cursed me," said Katrin. "In the Riga Safe Area. It was snowing hard. Very cold, very white. The witch cursed me when we let the Regime troops march in. Can't forget those eyes, can you? Tell her, Burton. Tell her to lift the curse."

Suzanne looked for the imaginary dog, anything to distract from the descent to crazy. "Riga was twenty-five years ago, Katrin. She'd be our age now. Alex is twenty-three. Born in Texas."

Katrin enlarged the photo in confusion. "Must be the witch's daughter. Looks just like her. Genes do funny things." She counted on knobby fingers. "Baby must have come after the Fall. Maybe they got it out on one of those kindertransports, before your g-screens shut them down." Katrin gave her a cunning smile.

"I know it was you, Burton. With your fancy science degrees. You designed the g-screens. For Handel's Treaty. You always were his creature."

A nurse changed Katrin's IV. The outdoor floodlights illuminated the swirl of white flakes against black glass. Suzanne watched them, her stomach in an icy knot. After the Treaty, Pieter had asked for her help enforcing the Return provision. The task was difficult. Human populations were too mixed for security screening by racial or ethnic traits to be very useful. And the Federate population had people from every corner of the earth. Suzanne had realized that the g-marker from the Regime's failed cancer inoculation was unique—a modernly acquired bit of genetic sequence carried only by people from a specific geopolitical region. It was an ugly confluence of politics and science—a harmless inadvertent branding of sorts, to be passed down in every generation.

She had taken advantage of that branding. The first g-screens for the marker were meant for limited use at the border stations. She never dreamed the program would exist a quarter century later, having grown into a mass anti-guizi religion.

"There are no curses, Katrin. Alex has passed a lifetime of g-screens and my admission array. She's got some Nordic ancestry. She reminded you of someone in Riga. It's that Asylum Netcast preying on your mind. It's supposed to make us feel guilty, raise bad memories." New videos of families murdered in gulags were perfectly calculated to resurrect ghosts and haunt restless nights. They certainly haunted hers.

She had sacrificed her personal life and family's happiness for the great peace, and would die defending the Treaty. There was no compromise. But that Netcast hit a nerve.

The lights dimmed, visitor time over. "You will lie in the Guardians, Katrin. I promise."

The cackle returned. "The girl is a changeling, Burton. You so lofty, never could stand to do the dirty work. But the devil dog is yours now."

Fresh corn snow crunched beneath Suzanne's feet as she trudged to the parking lot. She was deeply depressed and anxious for a return to the real world. But rational thought was for another day. Suzanne sat a long time in the dark, freezing car, and watched the dead souls dance.

11

The monsoon season died spitefully the night of the jacuzzi debacle, with a convulsive gale. Throughout the Protectorate, the rivers rose and the earth fell, with landslides deep enough for the trees to stand vertical as they rode the roaring slopes like doomed surfers. Critical stretches of lifeblood highways were buried under fluid tons of mud, boulders, and splintered timber. Alex's overnight bus to Abad passed an hour ahead of a debris flow that spanned a small mountain and obliterated the only road to the province.

The following morning, back at the Peace and Love, an abashed and worried Eric forced open the door to her room. He found the phone she'd left as a decoy and a handwritten note of cool regret for the "grotesque invasion" of his and Atlanta's privacy, stating he owed the Envoy an apology and a new red tie, because "finding your best friend having sex in your bed with a woman dressed up in your clothes suggests a line of fantasy that is, face it, a little disturbing."

Prosperity's relief agencies mobilized in the slacking rain. Eric threw Strav's duffel bag in the back of a Corps of Engineers truck heading northwest to Abad. Eric had tracked Alex to Abad's medical clinic, and arranged a secure hotel. Strav was charged, once again, with fetching her. The two men stood awkwardly for once in each other's presence.

"Yesterday, in your room," said Eric, furiously rearranging ammo boxes and water filters into orderly stacks. "About Atlanta wearing your tie. It was just Atlanta getting off, right? Didn't want you thinking it was anything weird, you know, on my end—"

"Tie? What tie?" Strav looked ready to clap his hands over his ears and hum loudly. Alex had certainly planted the suggestion to stick the knife in Eric—oh, she was wicked good—but not even a desire to comfort his wretched, glowering anda could make any-thing about this line of conversation possible. Better for them to study the paper map Eric insisted he take, service being crap in the mountains.

"Don't get stupid if the road is blocked," said Eric. "I'll send a chopper." But that could take weeks. Disaster resources were spread thin over a vast region, and Abad was not in crisis. It was still plenty dangerous, and Strav and Alex were a heartburn marriage of the reckless and the oblivious. Eric kicked a Jeep tire that dared look underinflated. "Don't let her wander alone. Don't go out after dark. Don't—Jesus, bud. What should I say to her?"

Strav squinted at the silver dime of sun. "Perhaps the wisest course is to say nothing until we return. Remember, men of few words are the best men."

A hostler passed with a rank-smelling string of donkeys bound for the mountain passes, their loads covered with green tarps that reached the hoof. The line plodded into the mist like a bedraggled tent city on the move.

"This is a mistake, anda," said Strav in a surprise outburst. "If she is yours, you should go."

Eric shrugged unhappily, baffled by Strav's wild shifts of mood and advice. He had told Strav that Jacob Kotas was coming to Pros-perity in three days for a classified Solidarity meeting. The old Strav would have understood in a word this tear between heart and duty.

"Thank you," said Strav, startling Eric with a fierce embrace. "I'll protect her with my life."

And who, Eric wondered, *is going to protect you?* The motors gunned, the convoy rolled, and it took all of Eric's self-control not to run after his brother. "Nothing stupid!" Eric shouted, and forced his mind to the bigger problems of the world.

———————

The engineers looked at the collapsed bridge and the flooding river with uprooted trees and drowned cows, and told Strav he was crazy. Strav didn't disagree, but it was like warning a salmon about the rapids and bears upstream. The great mysteries of life were great because they did not belong to rational choice. It had taken two days of detours to reach the bridge, and what struck the engineers as thirty-one miles of impassable wild country ahead was to Strav nothing but homestretch. He cut his cargo pants to shorts, threw on a backpack of emergency supplies, and dove into the surging river. Twenty minutes later, he crawled to the opposite bank with just the map and wallet in his pocket, lacerated, bruised, and vomiting silted brown water.

The rest of the day, he scrabbled through rocky forested hills and picked up a logging road to Abad. The night was cold at this altitude, but the moon scudded in and out with enough light for him to jog to keep from freezing. There was something emancipating in this shivering test of flesh. He was one with the physical world, no more thoughts than a shard of metal drawn by a magnet.

Soggy dawn brought a buried stretch of road. His climb around set off volleys of slides, red clay staining the tattered remains of his clothes. By afternoon, the hills contained remnants of a past era— stone houses and prayer wheels. It felt so much like the Khanate that he shaped a thick branch as a club against guard dogs, an instinct that saved him a mauling and sent three big mongrels limping home.

Sunset settled in as a darkening curtain of sky. A final ridge, and the path trailed down through Abad's shantytown, ramshackle huts stuck like barnacles to the steep hillside. Smoke from kilns rose in acrid black plumes. Strav passed a yard with the small carcass of a curly-tailed dog roasting on a spit, its black tongue protruding and skin crisping over the charcoal fire. It wasn't exactly filet mignon, but he wasn't feeling very charitable toward dogs, and at some point meat was meat; the flood of gastric juices in his stomach reminded him that he had neither eaten nor slept in thirty-six hours. Instantly, he was shaky with exhaustion.

The People's Liberation Clinic was on the rough plank board- walk of the town square. The whitewashed walls glowed in the twilight. An elfin towheaded boy dashed along the clattering planks and yanked at Strav's unraveling shorts. "*Vohlk!*" he screamed. A hodgepodge of children came running, each in the same printed shirt.

WOLF KHAN, read the T-shirts. A silk screen of Strav's own face stared back at him, noble of countenance and a whole lot cleaner.

Strav knelt, and the children swarmed him like pigeons on a statue. Three little girls with matted hair sat on Strav's knee, cooing and stretching the skin of his face. Young boys hung on his back and gabbled questions in Russian.

A familiar voice yelled, "Vlad, you put that back!" Alex grabbed the towheaded boy and extracted Strav's wallet from the boy's pocket.

Strav jumped up too fast and stood swaying in front of Alex, the last sliver of his reserves gone, filthy, stinking, robbed, and happy beyond all reason.

"So, Envoy," Alex said straight-faced, her eyes dancing. "You're here to take care of me?"

"Absolutely," said Strav, and toppled over at her feet.

Eric thought his meeting with Jacob went well. He explained the minor trespass into Solidarity protocols was required by his Commission mandate to analyze regional security. He foresaw no further investigation. Case closed. They retired to the bar for the wind-down Scotch they always shared after joint sessions.

"I'm always amazed," said Jacob, "by your ability to inspire trust in your judgment and character. No one at the agency believed you would misappropriate Solidarity intelligence to undermine our mission."

Jacob's smile said that he wasn't buying it. Eric swallowed his Scotch and the insult. The dig was true. And debating the mission with Jacob was like debating the Resurrection with a bishop, a pointless joust against the rigor of unassailable faith. For Eric, this past year was more like sailing the Golden Gate—every rip current and gust trying to muscle you off-course, your steering a constant series of overcorrections. Let Handel and the Kommandant play politics. He had given them the Hallows. But he refused to sabotage

Solidarity by withholding the flaw he had discovered in their geotag. He would flag the error for Jacob, and achieve course correction.

They threw back an end-of-the-world Scotch and talked about the basketball team they coached for International's troubled youth. Jacob thought their A-16s could take the championship. Eric was touched by Jacob's faith that he'd be reinstated come November.

Eric said, "Got something for you. Let's walk."

"I met your Alex." Jacob settled back in the wingback chair, the "your Alex" drifting like bar smoke. "In San Francisco. I liked her. The twins loved her. Chocolate moose in Texas!" Jacob laughed. "Heard she ran off to Abad on you, eh?"

Eric was acutely aware Jacob was fishing, and his own foolish face was giving it away.

"My men think you're fucking Alex *and* that Atlanta woman. I told them, no, even you wouldn't risk a fraternization at your Tribunal. My bet is Alex trusted you, and you got caught with your dick in the wrong place. Again." Jacob raised a Scotch rocks to winning his bet. "Cheer up, eh? Alex will forgive you. Doesn't everyone?"

No, thought Eric. *Not everyone*. A few drunken minutes of shared flesh with Jacob's girlfriend ten years ago—he and Jacob had moved on, hadn't they? He had pulled Jacob through firefights, celebrated at his wedding, played with his twins.

"There's a complaint from your Commission banquet," said Jacob. "About Alex attacking our anti-guizi campaign. An impressive stream of subversion from that pretty mouth."

"Subversion?" Here was chaos theory made real, every bad choice and mistake spun into a flesh-and-blood web of consequence. Still, he could not believe Jacob would cross the firewall between professional and personal lives that kept family as sacred off-limits. "Subversion? You're shitting me. Alex is a twenty-three-year-old Academic. They'll say anything for effect."

"Ain't that the truth. But charges have been brought on less."

Eric leaned forward, and Jacob raised a conciliatory hand. "I'll bury the complaint. It would help if everyone keeps in their lane."

They walked out to the hazy afternoon. "You said you had something for me?" asked Jacob.

"Did I?" said Eric, with nowhere to go and everything to reconsider. "Don't remember."

Strav had envisioned his time in Abad with Alex as a golden glow of leisurely meals, dazzling conversation, and walks through sketchy Townships that provided multiple opportunities for him to perform small but thrilling feats of protection. Instead, this being real life, he was gripped with an intestinal bug from the filthy floodwater, gut-cramped with diarrhea, and never far from a toilet. On the plus side, Alex's run-in with a bad samosa had her in similar distress, the reality of low economies being *Giardia lamblia*, *E. coli*, and explosive bowels.

So the morning brought a different kind of bonding than Strav imagined, one of shared antibiotics and a gingerly walk to Fishtail Marketplace, their pockets stuffed with scratchy toilet paper, sprinting for an invariably disgusting bathroom every ten minutes and standing guard for each other in front of the broken doors.

The mission was to buy him clothes. When Strav awoke in his pine-paneled room in the Dragon Hotel, he found Alex had replaced his pile of rags with hospital scrub pants and a T-shirt. He had touched the outfit with a sense of the sacrosanct; no kindness was more fundamental than clothing another person, preserving their dignity against the jeering world. Then he saw the T-shirt had the Wolf Khan print of his face. Very funny. He wore it inside out.

They wandered market aisles of white lace, hand-loomed rugs, and red beef carcasses rimmed with flies. Sparrows swooped from corrugated iron roofing above old men playing chess and dominoes. Pigs nosed in vegetable peelings. The air was pungent with wet wool and charcoal fumes from braziers.

Strav hefted a leather-handled knife with a robust curved blade perfect for skinning game and slaughtering tough old goats. Alex inspected a line of Russian nesting dolls.

"See the workmanship?" she said. "The cottage industry here is primed for growth. There's hydroelectric energy to power low-impact manufacturing. Independence would allow a steady stream of private capitalization to fund transport infrastructure."

All she talked about was Independence, and all Strav heard was the despondency beneath her hyperkinetic enthusiasm. She wasn't pining over Eric. Those roles seemed reversed. Eric called her multiple times a day with unnecessary Commission questions, and Alex made him wait ten chimes before answering with a sigh. It was quite a novelty watching Eric learn to beg.

No, something had happened in the three days she was alone in Abad. Strav went easy on her, even when she insisted he buy a "perfect for export" billowing white Cossack shirt with embroidered collar and cuffs.

"Ya look a foocking swashbuggler" came a sneering child's voice below the market counter. Up popped Vlad, with a plastic toy warrior. Strav looked closer—damned if there weren't Strav Beki Wolf Khan action figures.

Alex cringed. "The cottage industry spot-turns on trends for international export—"

The boy pulled down the figure's pants and flexed the hip joints in an obscene pumping action. Strav saw his action figure was anatomically correct. In fact, the manufacturer had been quite generous.

The boy darted through a curtain of crispy ducks hanging by red webbed feet. Alex muttered an ominous "brace yourself" and led Strav through to the next aisle. Every inch was crammed with Wolf Khan tchotchkes—his face on bobblehead dolls, beer mugs, boxers, pennants. Strav's gut knotted. He bolted for the bathroom, with Alex right behind.

"Tell me about your feral little friends," said Strav as they hobbled out to the mist. Any topic other than those souvenirs shipping across the Nations.

"We met in Prosperity. The Odessa Mafia ships them around. The kids live here in the market. They are little sponges of information. They know everything that happens in town."

The gang followed them to a piroshki stall. Alex handed out the steaming buns in a daily ritual. The elfin boy dragged his piroshki across Strav's new shirt, leaving a greasy trail of malice. Strav wanted to administer a few thwacks with a Khanate birch stick, but he understood the kid. It took one green-eyed monster to recognize another.

A splatter of rain kicked the milky puddles, and Strav felt a pricking at the back of his neck, hunter instincts that had nothing to do with thieving children. He glanced about. Shopworkers took their lunch break, rheumy-eyed men slugged from bottles, miniskirted prostitutes leaned in doorways. Nothing unusual—just another manifestation of the watching eyes.

The afternoon was scut work at the People's Liberation Clinic. Abad bulged with families displaced by the floods, and the line stretched across the town square. It did not take a doctor to diagnose what ailed many of the children, with their listless gaze and dirty gym shorts that slipped below bloated bellies. The harried medical staff assigned Alex to patient intake.

"Come on, Envoy," said Alex. "I can use that translation service you call a brain." They moved down the line of Abad's ethnic smorgasbord. Strav spoke in the Jin dialect to an old farmer who wept to hear his native tongue. The younger people chatted in pidgin English, the new language of a new world that the elderly could not enter.

A mother with three children and an infant was called to the examining room. She thrust the infant at Alex, who took it as if being handed a live grenade. The infant screwed up his face and howled to beat a police siren. Strav looked at Alex with the baby held at arm's length, her face screwed up like the infant's.

"For God's sake." He took the infant and tucked him firmly under his arm like a football. The crying stopped. "Haven't you ever held a baby?"

"We didn't all spend our childhood protecting little sisters from wolves," she retorted. "Try growing up the only child on a penal ranch. See how much babysitting experience you get."

When the clinic closed at twilight, Strav and Alex swept and took the trash to the shed in the back. The yard was choked with weeds, but someone had once cared to build a wooden shrine. The platform was covered with shattered beer bottles, the horizontal on the Russian cross dangling like a broken arm.

"Oh," Alex said, a quiet exhalation. The base of the shrine was engraved with names and an inscription. *In Memory of the Founders of the People's Clinic/ Flown Home to God/ Never to Be Forgotten.* Patrick Tashen was top of the list.

Alex sank to sit in the wet grass.

Never could Strav recall feeling so useless. He pulled a scythe from the shed and cut the weeds around the shrine. *Don't know why my father stands up for you. Says you hath a good and a bad angel attending on you.* He nailed the fallen cross into place. Found and lit a stick of incense, bowed to offer his prayers. Alex stared through the spiral ribbon of fragrant smoke.

"Never forgotten." Her voice was a rustle of breeze. "Such a lie. He wrote to me from that window. The sky is blue as sapphire. The snow plumes stretch to the sun. The doctors swear they haven't seen him. No one remembers him. The aid workers come and go, they say."

Strav sat beside her, felt the wet of the grass wick through his pants. She had expected to find her father here. Not memories but the living, breathing man.

"Can a man completely disappear?" she said. "Where do I go now?"

A bat fell through the dying light as a streaking black star, criss-crossing with another, and another, until the sky was a rapturous threading of silent chase and prey.

"When we get home," said Strav, "we'll build your father a proper memorial. Then we'll have a place to visit him."

"Home?" Alex said blankly. "What home?"

Strav realized he had no idea; there was no place they belonged together.

But Alex was reacting to life around her again, a look of surprise at the wet ground. She touched Strav's hand and he stopped breathing.

"I'm glad you're here," she said. Strav looked up at a dark sky in motion, his fingers closing around hers.

And who, in their most magical thinking, would have imagined Abad as paradise? The earth remained moody and dangerous, new landslides swallowing any small progress on the roads. Not that Strav was counting days or anything else. The severed roads had severed time. His Abad existed in the floating realm between Heaven and Earth, the obligations of past and future hanging as distant as the mists that hid the mountains.

"I need you two back," Eric told Strav, with an unexplained urgency that increased with every nightly call. Strav did not want to think on his anda's worries. He had to manage his own complex evasions, particularly why he and Alex were still in Abad after Eric had arranged space for them on two different Chinook cargo choppers.

With the first chopper, Strav claimed to have missed Eric's message in time to reach the landing site. Missing the second chopper required the more active deceit of paying the driver to have the car break down, a common enough occurrence with every vehicle in Abad held together with duct tape. Alex remained in the dark about the missed evacuations. Eric did not want to provoke her with an order to return, relying on Strav's persuasive arts; Strav, in turn, had a thousand burning reasons to never mention a helicopter. Still, it was hard to discount Eric's nightly admonishment to keep Alex close, and report anything unusual.

What, wondered Strav, constituted unusual in Abad? The Dragon Hotel was a block of fortress architecture overlooking a hillside slum, smoke-blackened walls set with tangles of barbed wire and fangs of broken glass. An archipelago of bonfires roared from kerosene drums in the alleys below Strav's window, each bright island gathering its own denizens. At one fire, men leaned toward the flames for warmth, their backs set in the same curve of despair. On the next block, a nightly bacchanal of laughter and cavorting bodies cast animal shadows on the walls. No one paid attention to the background staccato of automatic weapons unless the bursts got too close. Then the night held its breath before returning to business.

The calls from Eric were like the gunfire, sporadic reminders of the world beyond the firelight. The fact that Eric was incapable of doubting his brother's loyalty filled Strav with rage, both at Eric and himself. *Friendship is constant in all other things / Save in the office and affairs of love.* But was he really that inconstant friend, when Eric slept with another woman?

He that is robbed, not wanting what is stolen / Let him not know't, and he's not robbed at all.

And so his floating realm would return. He knew Alex was floating, too, that she felt close to her father here, that she was lost and hurting. Meet for breakfast, work in the clinic, debate Independence over dinner at Yuan's Noodle Shop. Nightfall, to the Dragon Bar with the blind balalaika player, existential discussions to music that took great pleasure in being glum. To their own rooms, their own beds, to keep talking all hours on their phones. No row of weeks or lined calendar; just a circle of day and night marked by a smile, a touch, a story. She needed stories, and he needed to tell them.

"Where do I go now?" she had asked. *Nowhere. Just be with me.*

Time listened, and stopped.

Morning. Vlad and gang pop up like marmots to follow Strav and Alex to the clinic. The urchin faces take names. Tiny Nadia drags her naked doll by the hair; Peter is nimble despite a wandering eye. Bin is the big, dim, smiling boy who scratches his blonde head raw; Ahmed eats alone because of a cleft palate. None are sure how old they are. The kids matter to Alex, so they matter to Strav. He keeps them in line with a soccer ball he carries like a Pied Piper, juggling the ball off his feet and head, for impromptu pickup games. Vlad alone is immune to Strav's charm, pulling sneak attacks that promise a brutal and rapid ascent through the criminal world.

Ahead on the boardwalk, a teenage boy and girl practice a foxtrot to a scratchy crooner recording of "Witchcraft." They bite their lower lips in concentration, not unaware of passerby attention but too engrossed to care. "Wish I could dance," Alex says dreamily, and Strav whirls her around to ready position, always ready to instruct.

"Do you know how to do *everything*?" Alex protests. "I didn't think the Three Manly Virtues included ballroom dancing."

"I am a multiplicity of virtues," he says. The piroshki vendor claps his doughy hands in one-two-three time that has nothing to do with the music. Strav glances at Vlad, draws a quick finger across his neck to indicate the skill set he will utilize if the boy throws that rock at him. The boy throws instead at a three-legged dog nosing in the gutter. The dog runs, the children give chase, and Alex tries to pull away. Strav stops the dance lesson, but his arm stays around her waist, their palms touching, eyes meeting with the click of magnets.

Midnight, apart in their own rooms, the light of the bonfires flicker through their windows. The light catches the flaking gold paint of the Russian icon on Strav's wall, a dark-eyed archangel glaring down at human frailty. Strav lies with his arms behind his head and his phone on audio, trying to focus on storytelling instead of the bed-bouncing Mormon missionary couple next door. Tonight's story is from *The Once and Future King*, Wart's lessons as a perch, a merlin, and an ant. "Wart pulls the sword from the stone. Do you know the first thing the new king does?"

Alex waits expectantly.

"He bursts into tears," Strav says.

"I would too. Think of leaving a magical childhood in the forest. There's nothing good about growing up." They are both silent, considering. "Keep going."

"Book Three, The Ill-Made Knight." Strav stops. Here begins Arthur's journey with Guinevere and dark Lancelot, who both love their king. The tale held certain parallels—triangles, more precisely—too painful to explore. Truly, there were only so many stories in the world.

"Are Lancelot's tournaments like Naadam?" she asks. "I wish I could go everywhere. Travel to the seven wonders of the world and add a thousand more."

"Why don't you?"

Silence, then a wistful "I wish I could see a Naadam."

"Maybe I'll bring a Naadam to you." Alex laughs, which sets his resolve. "I will bring you a Naadam."

"Fine, Envoy." Strav can visualize her yawn, her slim legs tensing and parting, the supple shift of her breasts, and he stiffens in a cruel state of agitation. It does not help that the missionaries' rhythmic *thump-thump* through the wall has sped to a frenzied crescendo.

"Who is banging there?" Alex asks in innocent indignation. Strav groans and rolls over. "Are you laughing, Envoy?"

"The name is Strav. Is there some speech impediment that prevents you from saying my name? Try it. *SSS-traaav*. Hiss like a snake, then open up the back of your throat as if gargling. It's a beautiful sound, done correctly."

"Fine, Envoy."

Gunfire cracks in the night. Strav does a countdown like for thunder after lightning. The answering gunfire spits *ra-ta-ta*.

"At least there's no crowds here," Alex says. "I hate crowds. There is a moment of transformation, when people turn into this huge animal. You can feel it breathing."

The party starts up again outside. Bottles smash to a drunken round of cheers.

"In my dreams," says Alex, "I can't even run. They are very bad dreams."

"It's okay." Strav watches the shadows outside caper and writhe. "I know about those."

The next day, they hike to the ridge above Abad, a picnic of yellow cheese and rock-hard baguette. Dark-bottomed clouds rest on the hills like an inverted ocean. Birch saplings shiver silver and white in the wind. Alex's arms fly like a symphony conductor as she lays out her plans for Abad. "Down there by the river, perfect for an agricultural trust. That knoll, for a green power plant. Wait until you see those mountains!"

Every day Alex tells him the mist will lift tomorrow, but Strav has stopped believing in the mountains. He sits on an orange poncho, using the baguette as a bat to send rock after rock sailing into home-run oblivion. It is immensely gratifying.

"This could be a tourist mecca, Envoy."

"The name is Strav. There's a real person beneath these dapper Diplomatic duds." His drawstring pants are plaid pajamas, his big toe pokes out from his running shoe, and the Cossack shirt is down to one sleeve, the other torn off by excited kids in a soccer game. He hasn't shaved since Prosperity, and the straight, dark stubble accents his jaw. His hair, already long from summer in the Khanate, has reached critical mass to fall in his eyes.

Alex grins and brushes his hair aside. Strav vibrates inside like a tuning fork but knows to keep it light, nothing to endanger this delicate new dance. He walks his fingers across the poncho like a determined three-legged bug, making her laugh, ending at the ragged tear in her skirt from her climbing a fence to pet a yak.

"I'm a mess," she allows with great pathos. The finger-bug bobs in agreement and strolls up her leg. Strav recites, deep and low: "*A sweet disorder in the dress / Kindles in clothes a wantonness . . . Do more bewitch me than when art / Is too precise in every part.*"

Their faces are close, their breath in shallow unison. Strav reaches for her and stops, sensing more than seeing a motion in the woods. "Maybe the gang?" Alex suggests. Strav isn't sure, which is just as well, because if he caught Vlad ruining the moment, he'd send his weasely little head bouncing down the hill like a soccer ball.

"But you love children," Alex teases, though there is trouble in her eyes. Strav does not understand how the inches between them turned into miles. She says, "You want children."

"Obviously," Strav says. "What man doesn't want a son?" His hastily added "Daughters too" brings only a distant smile. He cannot predict what sets off her spells. Yesterday, a g-screen by a Vice and Virtue Squad had left her spacey for hours. He'd had to reenact the entirety of *Macbeth*, complete with sword fights, to bring her back. "There are notable compensations for growing up," Strav says. "Namely, children. And the making of children."

"Not for me," she says from the ozone. "I'm fated to die a blighted virgin."

She catches the word too late. Strav understands that she has not slept with Eric—yet—but not even the Italian boyfriend? No, she has been waiting for him, fate in any language of the world. The internal tuning fork revs up to an open-throttle takeoff. "Holy Mother of God," he says, and bends as if gut-punched.

"I knew you'd be like this!" Alex shouts. She clubs him with the baguette. It actually hurts. "You are a Neanderthal! No, that's unfair, give a Neanderthal a shave and he'd fit perfectly in the modern world." Strav waves a hand, pleading for a minute to recover. "I'm just *technically* a virgin, Envoy. Nothing romantic about it. For a woman my age and background, it is a failure of intimacy. Maybe it's about fear. Maybe it's *tragic*!"

But her laughter wins out. "How old were you, your first time?" she asks.

"Seventeen. In a haystack. Poorly executed, but with great vigor."

She grins. They lie back to watch the roiling sky. "What about your wife, Envoy? The future mother of those sons. And daughters. Did you sleep together before the marriage?"

The floating realm shivers like the birch leaves. Strav watches a white bird soar above the dark valley, an illuminated speck outracing the coming rain.

"No," he answers. "Before would not be unusual. Mongol culture was never as strict as the Chinese overlay. And those are very dark, cold winters. But to not sleep together *after* your marriage—that's problematic."

"Don't," Alex whispers. "I didn't mean to pry."

"Croatia happened. The hostages. It changed everything."

"Don't." She stands and packs up. They've been here before, revealing secrets best left in the dark, and it brought nothing but pain. Still, Strav appreciates the irony; after a year of people begging him to remember his captivity, the first person he tries to tell refuses to listen.

"I know what I want to hear tonight." He hears her clinging to a world of bright, unspoiled picnics. "*All's Well That Ends Well.* Best title ever."

Strav bows his head to the nape of her neck. Breathes in the jasmine smell, the salt of her, feels the catch of her breath. There will be a story tonight, but told in one room, one bed.

Strav takes her by the hand and leads her downhill until she is pulled at a half run behind him. The Dragon Hotel comes into view, a last twenty feet to the entrance.

Their phones are off but buzz anyway with Eric's commanding overrides. Alex hesitates and breaks from Strav's hand. He can do nothing but watch. She reads Eric's text.

"*Another* helicopter?" she says. "How many times has Eric tried to get us out of here?"

And quick as thought, time starts again.

The heavy skies allowed no discernible sunset, but night came anyway. Strav had been running for two hours. The wind carried a frenzy of savage barking from the nightly prize dogfights. Garbage can fires sprouted in orange bloom along the alleyways. The flames reminded Strav of fires lit in front of a dead man's *ger* to drive away evil spirits. The magic did not work here; the twilight swirled with angry creatures, and Strav flew as one of them.

It would have been easier if she had yelled. Instead, she had looked around as if awoken, registering every ugly detail of Abad—the barbed wire, waterlogged trash. Him. "I can't be here," she had said in a panic. "There's nothing for me here."

Strav knew an animal in a trap. It set off his own panic, the familiar roar spiked with jealousy and hurt. He had told Alex to get inside the hotel. He'd been running ever since.

He made a final sprint up the shanties, and cogent thought resurfaced as pieces of shipwreck after a storm. The few men on the streets hurried to whatever shelter they called home. Abad turned into a no-man's-land come nightfall, left to the rule of gangs and beggar kings. Strav checked his phone, but service was down, the first blackout since arriving in Abad. Good, let her worry, the lying, conniving witch. Nothing for her here? There was *him*.

I'm conniving? he could almost hear her exclaim. *Total water moccasin.*

The ground bounced like a boat on a wave. Lanterns swayed, and roof tiles rattled to the ground. For a Himalayan earthquake, it was a mere peccadillo. Strav thought of Alex's delight in the daily tremors, her chatter about the ramming tectonic plates, and how everything that seemed immutable was riding on an orange-skin crust of earth. Even an earthquake was a joy with her.

He ran down to the Dragon, with the quake as cover for wounded male pride.

She had not checked in at the hotel.

Strav hit the gloaming streets again in a growing unease. She was probably at Patrick Tashen's shrine, downing the local Czarina vodka. He readied a choice lecture.

The clinic was shut and boarded, the shrine empty.

Now came the first tendrils of fear. Strav raced from the doctors' apartment to the few eateries. No one had seen her. He ran a wild course from can fire to fire. No one had seen a slim young woman, or was willing to admit it. He retraced their steps from the first day. The Fishtail Marketplace was now a silent hull. Empty meat hooks hung as inverse question marks, rats darting along the butcher blocks. Strav recalled who else lived in the market, the little sponges who knew everything that happened in Abad.

"Vlad!" he roared, spinning about. "Where is she?"

The children crept from beneath the counters. Strav went still as if on a hunt where any motion would scatter the game.

Vlad spat, releasing the others to speak. Ahmed raised a hand from his disfigured mouth. "She took a bottle to the shrine behind the clinic." Even half out of his mind, Strav felt a flare of vindication.

"Then the bad men took her," added little Nadia.

"Men?"

Nadia held up two fingers. "The two men who been watching you. Odessa."

Watching them: that sixth sense of being stalked, the men awaiting an opportunity he had graciously handed them. But now he understood the field, and had a flesh-and-blood enemy.

"Take me to them."

"I'm not afraid 'em fookers," Vlad boasted. He bolted from the market and Strav followed.

The lane twisted through a neighborhood of crumbling mud-brick row homes. A drunk husband screamed at his wife, the sound of poverty echoed behind many of the shuttered windows. They reached an empty square lit with can fires. Four twisting alleys branched from the corners of the square. Vlad scratched his head, suddenly uncertain. Strav had a sink of despair.

A stocky man with a bulldog face sat on a wooden crate by the alley across from them. He was peeling an apple with one of the leather-handled hunting knives from the Marketplace. The apple skin hung from the white flesh in a spiraling crimson ribbon, an unhurried artistic touch.

Vlad whispered that he didn't recognize the man. Strav was turning to another alley when the boy frantically tugged his shirt. The man was wiping his blade with a garish pink-and-green plaid cloth. It was Alex's madras book bag.

The night went still to Strav's eyes, a slowing of time and heightened sensation. He saw the fresh mud tracks where the crate had been pulled to guard the entrance, the practiced, methodical swiping motion of the lookout's calloused hands, the incline of his head to a cry from the alley.

Strav whispered instructions to Vlad. The boy was a natural. He howled when Strav dragged him into the square and smacked him, ran to escape, and fell weeping a few feet from the man on the crate. The man watched the domestic disturbance in amusement. Strav limped over to collect the kid, his empty hands raised in cringing apology. The man motioned to get lost, and Strav kicked him in the face hard enough to crash the man backward. In two steps and a pivot, Strav had the knife in hand, the man's head yanked back by the hair, and made a single blade slash across the corded throat to sever his trachea and esophagus to the spinal cord before the man could sound a warning. The man jerked still in a spreading pool of blood. His bowels loosened, and an outhouse stench filled the air.

Vlad watched frozen in shock. "Run home, boy," Strav said, low and harsh, and the child stumbled off like a broken marionette.

A search of the body provided no additional weapons. Strav edged along the alley's brick wall and peered into the alcove. Two men in the long black leather jackets of the region stood beneath a sputtering gas lamp. The first, a tall Asian man, measured liquid in a syringe, squirting out little jets to get the level just so. Farther in, a bald Slav with the pugnacious bulk of a bar bouncer was inspecting a bite mark in the soft meat of his hand. Alex sat curled against the far wall. Blood streamed from her nose and down her chest to where her blouse was torn open.

Strav made a slight movement to draw her glance. Their eyes met. She looked away to keep him in her peripheral view. Strav could not see past the lamp; he motioned with his fingers, *How many men?* She raised two fingers, followed by a warning of her fingers held as a gun.

The bouncer finished sucking his wounded hand. He unzipped his jeans and stood over Alex, rubbing himself. He pulled her up, and Strav lunged at a run from the shadows. The first man with the syringe turned in time for the hunting knife to slice across his eyes and lay open his astonished face. Strav kept running even as the bouncer swung his gun free from his jacket, pinning Alex back with his left arm and aiming point-blank at Strav's chest. But Alex was moving too, having grabbed a fallen roof tile when pulled to her feet, and in one wild swing connected with the man's mouth. The gun fired wide, and Strav had the split second he needed. He fell on the man with a howl, punching the knife into the man's exposed groin and ripping upward, punching again and again until the man was a lifeless slumping weight.

The other man crawled blind on the ground, making animal whimpers. Strav returned to him, nearly blind himself with rage, and kicked him savagely in the ribs and face, heaved him up and ran him headfirst like a battering ram into the brick wall. The man's skull broke with a liquid sound, gray matter showing through the bone.

Time shifted to rapid-fire bursts, fragmented images from an inner explosion that would not end. Alex pleaded for him to come away, but Strav kept returning for another slash or kick until she dragged him out to the square. Scavengers were fighting over the madras bag. The lookout's corpse was already stripped bare, an obscene sprawl of white limbs and crimson throat. Strav ran at them like a berserker and the scavengers fled.

The next moment, it seemed to Strav, he and Alex were in his room at the Dragon, Alex bolting the door, him pacing in a frenzy and kicking over the furniture. Madness that he could not stop yelling or release the knife. Alex's face and blouse had dried to a dark, sticky rust.

"I told you to get into the hotel!" he yelled. No one could survive this rage; his skull was going to burst like that man's against the wall. "Did you want them to take you?" He grabbed Alex and pushed her against the wall. "Is that it? Did you want them to fuck you?"

She went limp in his grasp, searching his mad, contorted face. "Strav?" she whispered. "Nomad?"

Something inside him broke. Nothing painful, for a change; he was just weightlessly detached, and it seemed natural to be observing the scene from a perspective several inches off the ceiling. Maybe this was death, his spirit joining his ancestors. But maybe not, because his body below still gripped Alex by the neck—him, yet not him, a Strav-shell in a ridiculous one-sleeved shirt, covered in other men's gore and seized in some catatonic state.

He knew Alex, though, would know her through any layers of grime and tears. Even floating detached, he did not want to leave her.

The knife dropped. The Strav-shell sank to his knees in a slow collapse, his dazed face buried against Alex's stomach, his arms wrapped in a death grip around her waist.

Watching from high up, Strav knew what Alex would do; bow her head over the shell of a man, raise a trembling hand to stroke the blood-caked hair. The room was finally quiet.

It felt all right for him to leave them there, in a hollowed little shelter of time, and to drift off to blissful nothing.

12

The curtains stirred in the breeze, and the room ballooned with rose-hued morning light. The light played around Strav's pillow and raised him to surface consciousness. He stretched in the happy realization that he had slept solidly through an entire night. Still, he had often experienced dreams of well-being in the hospital, only to wake to a very different reality. He felt cautiously along his body—limbs free of traction rods and wires, no IV's puncturing his arms, no surgical staples, no Foley catheter snaking up his penis, but rather the immense reassurance of a solid morning hard-on. He opened one eye. No swirl of pain and nausea. Yet it could be the hospital, seeing that pile of bloodied towels and clothes.

Strav bolted upright, the sheets in a whirlwind as he looked for Alex.

"I'm here," she said. "We're fine." The room righted, the barbed-wire balcony as familiar as his room in the Dragon. Alex sat in a straight-back chair by the open window, wearing his scrub pants and Naadam T-shirt, her face hidden by her hair. She had dragged the dresser in front of the bolted door. The hunting knife rested in her lap.

Now came bewildering memories, a howling kicking that seemed to belong to someone else. Strav covered his face. It was not possible she had been the one to stand guard while he slept in a warm bed; not possible that after what she had endured at the hands of strange men, he had subjected her to a maniac bloodbath, screamed at her, hurt her. He recalled that internal snap and out-of-body experience, terrifying in retrospect. He had watched Alex lead him to the shower, pull off their gore-splattered clothes, and wash them both. The water had run red, then pink. Then, that sleep of the dead.

"Like Lancelot," Alex said from the window. Their last story had been from *The Once and Future King*, where the knight had his breakdown, guilt and shame driving him to a rampaging madness. A psychotic break, Strav supposed, though no label could make that loss of control any less mortifying. "Did anyone see me, when I was mad?" had been Lancelot's question upon awakening, and Strav understood the exact sentiment.

"So, like Lancelot," Alex prodded from her distance. "Anyone else?"

"King Lear in the storm," Strav muttered reflexively. "Arguably Hamlet." A shadow smile from Alex. He realized she was confirming his core brain was intact, while pointing out that madness kept notable company.

The archangel regarded him from the wall, black eyes luminous with contempt. Strav checked beneath the covers and saw that she had left his briefs on, a nice reciprocity for the Peace and Love. His fantasies seemed destined to remain just that—together in a shower only when one of them was non compos mentis and about to pass out.

He wrapped the sheet around his waist and went to the window.

The valley of Abad stretched before them, red clay rooftops etched against an ice-blue sky, the morning sun turned to diamonds in pooled water. A somber dark forest rose beyond the town, its hilly foreground giving way to leaf-green mountains. And rearing as gods beyond the rim of those summits, the serrated range of rocky gray monsters, each capped in blinding white, the feathery streamers of ice crystal drifting from spear peak to Heaven.

"Ta-da," said Alex, a dreamy voice at odds with the tension of her body. Strav thought she might fly out the window if she were touched. He pulled up a chair.

"They were bright pink a minute ago," she said. "That's Annapurna. Eight thousand ninety-one meters, though they grow a few centimeters every year. There's Machapuchare, the Fishtail. Six thousand, nine hundred ninety-three meters. Patrick's plane is on the other side. Maybe that's the way to go. To sleep under the stars on the roof of the world."

They watched the rose tint fade, the sky shading from lapis rim to a sun-bleached blue.

"Eric is coming," she said.

The surge of resentment almost lifted Strav from his chair. As if Eric had the right to swoop in as savior. But, in truth, he had mucked things up in every conceivable way, and silenced three assailants instead of saving one for interrogation—Eric would have his hide for that.

"Let me see," he told Alex. She reluctantly pulled back her hair to show a purple swollen black eye. Strav could only guess at the damage beneath her clothes.

"Alex. Did they—did they hurt you?"

"Hurt me?" she said, a flare of sarcasm. "You mean did they fuck me like I wanted?"

Strav blanched and Alex began rocking. "I'm sorry," she whispered. "They were touching me. It was—disgusting. You stopped them before they could do anything else. I'm sorry I went to the shrine. It's my fault."

"You can't believe that." He reached for her, and she flinched. Strav knew what her exact next words would be.

"I don't want anyone to know," she said fiercely. "You can't understand."

"Nothing will ever excuse my actions or words," he said. "I don't expect you to forgive me. But I do understand."

Her rocking slowed.

"Certain things happened when I was a hostage. I've been lying to everyone about not remembering. But you know that."

"You don't have to say."

"I want to." Even so, the carefully constructed habit of silence was not easy to dismantle. He looked helplessly at her.

Alex dipped a hand into the beam of sunlight between their chairs. "Just tell me a story," she said quietly.

Strav could do that. "Once upon a time, there was a young Consul. He had his measure of flaws, and was accused of arrogance, but he loved his family very much and overall was a decent chap. He had an aptitude for languages. A gift, or so he thought.

"There was another young man named Chullun, born on one of the Mongolian forced settlements. He blew up a Han police station and fled to the black zone in the Krajina region of Croatia. There he joined one of the bandit groups that specialize in taking hostages for ransom.

"Chullun kidnapped a French team there in Croatia to research war crimes. The Consul never did learn which war, or what crimes— the region is an embarrassment of riches that way. Hostage negotiations are a career enhancer, and the hazard pay is a glittering hook. The Consul could speak to Chullun in Mongolian, the hostages in French, and Headquarters in Mandarin and English. Even in Diplomatic's Tower of Babel, that was a rare bird. He lobbied to be sent in."

Alex made the sound of protest she always did when someone in his stories was about to make a terrible mistake.

"The pickup and blindfolding went without incident. Later the Consul learned he had been held at a cement factory in Vukovar, with enough explosives to take out a hundred bridges. The hostages were dismayed by his youth. Five men and three women, anxious and dirty but not otherwise mistreated, held in a storage room with a bucket for a toilet and a few cotton mats. Marie Claire was a grad student who developed a shy crush on the Consul and worried whether her neighbor was feeding her cat. Antol's wife had cancer, and he was missing their fortieth anniversary. Jamal and Maryam were devout Muslims and distressed by the lack of privacy between the men and women. The Consul worked to establish the right gravitas as their leader. He felt he understood Chullun, who resembled his uncles, the big Naadam wrestlers. It's always a relief to speak your native tongue, like slipping into a warm bath. Chullun intended a phased release of the hostages, but the Consul boldly refused and demanded an entire group release.

"The supposed day of their release, Chullun led his six men into the room. He set a camera, explaining the event was live streaming to the people everywhere. He turned to his men and said in English, 'Who wants first to fuck the pretty Khanate boy?'

"The Consul said a polite, 'Excuse me?' He actually said that. It had to be a crude mistranslation. They laughed. The first one came at him."

Strav focused on his split, swollen knuckles from the alley, the tendons in his forearms rising in cords from clenched fists. "I can fight, you know." He walked to the bathroom, gagged and retched over the sink, but there was nothing to come up. He sat on the floor and pressed his clammy back to the cool tile wall. Alex slid down beside him, just as unsteady.

"The Consul got the first man in a neck-snap, but Chullun grabbed Marie Claire and jammed a gun in her mouth. The Consul released the man. The others tackled him. They held him down, and he went into a flat-out panic, he fought and would have kept fighting if they had shot every hostage. God help me, but it's true. They kicked out his teeth and cracked ribs, and cut off his clothes along with a fair amount of skin. Chullun told the hostages he would shoot anyone who did not watch. And it happened."

It happened. He had no other words in any language to express that pain, or absolute, impotent rage. He glanced uncertainly at Alex, because she held his life in her hands: if she shrank from him, showed any sign of revulsion or even pity, he would walk out of here with the knife and put an end to himself as he should have a year ago. But he saw only a fury to mirror his own. She laid her head on his bare shoulder.

So life went on. Now there was relief in the telling, irrational events placed in rational order, with him controlling the story instead of the other way around.

"Afterward, they tied him to a beam, crucifixion style, in front of the camera. They told the hostages they'd kill anyone who helped him. They left.

"One minute, you know exactly who you are. A blink later, you're hanging naked on a live stream, covered in your own vomit, blood, and shit. But after a while, you realize you cannot die of shame, however much you want to. He was bleeding everywhere and struggling to breathe. Hanging a man like that is a punishment we still use in the Khanate for horse thieves, a crushing weight on the chest and slow suffocation. Chullun left a stand at the Consul's feet positioned just out of reach. It took a day to lose consciousness."

"Would none of the hostages help him?" Alex asked, wild-eyed.

"They cried and prayed, but everyone wants to live. The Consul woke alone in an underground cell. Those eighteen shadow squares on the floor. He'd been given medical care. They needed him alive. He tried to focus on revenge, but he was losing it up here." Strav tapped his temple. "Chullun had chosen the worst thing that could happen to a man in their culture, since ancient times the ultimate violation to show defeat of an enemy. The stain even passes to the next generation. And every detail was on public view, every-one *knew*. He started seeing people in his cell, his parents, crowds staring, eyes everywhere."

Alex's nose was bleeding again, drops of crimson wicking into the white T-shirt. Strav tilted her head back and pinched her nose.

"Why?" she said, her bewilderment muffled under his hand. "Why would anyone want to destroy a human being like that?"

"Martyrs have their own logic. Chullun saw himself as a freedom fighter. The Consul, of all people, should have considered that Chullun might view him as a collaborator with Beijing. A symbol delivered from Heaven. Chullun said the live stream transformed a traitor's shaming into a worldwide entertainment that defied and humiliated the great powers. He said other rebels would flock to him."

"I am going to kill him," said Alex.

Strav judged the nosebleed stanched. "The Serbs did it for you. The police stumbled upon the factory and launched a rocket-propelled grenade. It hit the explosives. Everyone dead except for me, barely. Marie Claire never got to feed her cat. Antol's wife buried him first.

"It was not your fault."

"I'm a miracle of modern medicine." Strav brushed her fingers over the planes and bones of his face. "Reconstructed, with new teeth." He clacked them for her. "Rebuilt spine and pelvis. Such public concern over my virility. Though I'll confess to concern myself."

"You can't believe it was your fault."

"The memories returned later. But no one seemed to know what they did to me. Why? The witnesses were dead, but what about the camera, the live stream? I asked Eric if anything was missing from the report. Eric cannot lie to me. I read him like a book. But it feels as if people *know*. I could not live with the whispers, knowing no matter what you do or accomplish, people would always associate your name with one shameful thing. Maybe they do know, I can't breathe, can't—"

"No one knows. I searched for any gossip I could use against you, and there is nothing. Do you hear me?"

"I should have died with the hostages. Call it whatever you want; they died *because* of me." The walls pressed close, and Strav lurched to his feet.

"I'm glad they're dead," he burst out, and finally, it was said. "I am glad they are dead and cannot tell. What kind of man would be glad of that?"

Alex needed a final visit to Patrick's shrine. The pedestal was littered with fresh broken glass. Strav sat lifelessly and watched Alex copy his efforts from their first day, collecting the trash, lighting the incense. Alex was so tired that she tilted sideways as she moved. She gave up and sat with Strav. The cross's long shadow shrank with the climbing sun.

"Patrick wouldn't give a damn about a dirty shrine," she said in a burst of anger. "Life is for the living, Patrick always said. He'd care about the people in line for his clinic. About Vlad and the gang. About the families in the Quarantine Complex." She tossed a bottle at the cross. It missed by a yard. "You promised to build a memorial for my father, Envoy. I know what it needs to be."

Strav didn't have the spirit to ask.

The next bottle shattered on the granite. "Independence, Envoy. *That's* the memorial for Patrick Tashen."

Strav looked heavenward. What else had he promised her? A Naadam? The gift of flight? "I used to believe," he said, "that your inherent sense of self-worth and dignity could not be destroyed from the outside. The truth is you can be reduced to nothing. Alex, I've got nothing."

"Seems you still have your silver tongue."

"You must know I would do anything for you," Strav said more sharply. "But a majority Council vote would be a miracle for a Winston Churchill. I can't handle even a backroom caucus. Are you going to fake a seizure every time I give a speech?"

An unspoken *promise* settled through the stubborn silence. The bile rose in Strav's throat. "I know I should seek—help. I could talk to a psychiatrist—"

"A what?" Alex said in genuine horror. "Tell your private life to a total *stranger*? They are your secrets. *Yours.* No records, no one else's business!"

Strav watched the distant mountains swim through a lens of tears, overcome that she should understand. But of course she did, crazy damaged kindred soul; it was why they belonged together.

"We can treat this by ourselves," she declared, flushed with indignation on his behalf. Her words tumbled out, yes, they could learn the cognitive therapy, try the drugs the doctors had pushed on her after the Legion to "take the edge off"—doctors loved taking the edge off. "But here's the thing, Envoy. No one knows, but you cannot live paralyzed that someday they might. You were tortured by criminals. It is not who you are. Not what you are. It is not a fatal secret marked in your genes. Believe me, I know."

Strav wiped angrily at his eyes, unbelieving.

The last ringlet of incense smoke rose in drifting prayer, leaving a charred stalk and a tang of sandalwood. Alex's head cocked as when listening to her father's invisible counsel. She knelt and bowed three times to the shrine, duplicating Strav's show of respect, and repeated the three bows to Strav.

He straightened warily.

"You saved me last night," she said. "You killed three men. For me."

"Oh." A verbal shrug. "That."

"Oh, that. You'd be surprised how much time I've spent trying to figure you out." She was right; he was surprised. "You tell wonderful stories, a regular British invasion. But there's a story you never tell me, about your great-great-something ancestor from the other side of the world. *The Secret History.* It's crazy how clearly I see you in those pages. Blood really does tell."

Strav listened, every nerve in his body intent on her words.

"I know what happened to Genghis when he was a young man," she said. "It's your story. He was captured and enslaved. He, too, was tortured and humiliated. God knows what unspeakable things they did to break his spirit. But they just made him stronger. Strong enough to pull the tribes together and lead armies. He used that shame and anger. It gave him power. It made him a king."

She put her hand on Strav's chest, over the racing beat. "The heart of a warrior. You are going to change the world, Strav Beki."

Footsteps pattered on the deck, a child's voice calling, "Lady, lady, there's a big, big man coming." Alex quietly told Strav what to say to set their stories straight and went to stall Eric.

Alone, Strav lifted his face to the sun and let a billion pricks of light dance inside his eyelids. The sun's warmth channeled through the place she had touched him, flooding every dark corner; he was made of hard bright light, could touch any object and make it glow.

He knew that a few yards away, Eric was cradling Alex's bruised face in his hands. It was all right; a warrior could abide. If she wanted Independence, so be it. Already the mental gears were in motion, calculating his new currency as Wolf Khan, alliances and fissures, trades and bribes. It would be a fine thing to join the great game again.

Strav stood and brushed himself off as after a hard fall. It was time to reenter the world like a comet, prove to be the man she believed him to be. And Eric, his brother, his rival. Eric would come to accept that he and Alex were destined for each other. No more guilt or weakness. This was war at its most elemental—a scorched-earth campaign to win the only woman he would ever love, who loved him too and always would, whether she knew it or not.

Eric had asked Bulgakov to come to Abad. Together they pulled the yellow plastic from the scavenged bodies of the kidnappers, sending up a cloud of fat black flies. The three corpses lay piled like slaughtered livestock. Their wounds and mutilations ran beyond any self-defense. The gashed and crusted eyes stared up, still somehow expressing alarm. Eric stared back and wondered how well you really knew anyone, even your brother.

Yuri knelt, apparently immune to the knee-buckling stench, and gave a particularly Bulgakovian summation. "Our Wolf Khan is a very angry young man."

Eric could think of other phrases the press might use, starting with psychopath. The event had to be contained. The flies settled back to feast, and Eric was hit full impact with what he'd nearly lost last night. If the gun had been drawn a second faster, he would be watching the flies crawl over Strav and Alex. For a moment Eric saw red, a literal veil of crimson over his vision.

This was Jacob's doing.

Alex's account of the attack detailed the gun as specifically a Beretta 100FS polymer semiautomatic with a sound suppressor. It had skidded into the dark when Strav stabbed the man. "How did you recognize the gun?" Eric had asked, reeling at implications she could not understand. Alex explained how the sergeant at arms had issued her the same model.

She did not know that Beretta was special issue to Solidarity.

The gun was gone with the scavengers, but still linked a chain of coincidences. Strange that the attackers had stalked for days, had a syringe, that he couldn't source the blackout.

No Solidarity agent would carry an identifiable piece while undercover. But local operatives, used for dirty tricks, might make that sloppy mistake. Even in his most cynical moments, Eric never believed Solidarity would order harm to fellow TaskForce members. He had been criminally naive.

A sham mugging, a transdermal sedative for interrogation: Jacob wanted to see if Alex knew anything about Eric's incursion into Solidarity's programs. The sedative acted as an amnesic, the drugs quickly metabolized to leave no trace. The sexual assault on a pretty subject, even if not ordered, was so likely that Jacob might as well have held her down—a personal form of vengeance against him, Eric, that spoke of a genuine monster.

That must have been the plan, until Strav's arrival in Abad. A crime against an Academic like Alex would have justified increased Solidarity crackdowns. An attack on the celebrity Wolf Khan risked an unacceptable level of outrage and scrutiny. The operatives had been forced to wait.

Eric had no proof. He had three butchered thieves, circumstantial evidence, and the intuitive certainty of a pattern that had never proved him wrong.

Their helicopter lifted off into the sunset. The roar wrapped everyone in private thoughts, or dreams—Alex so dead asleep that Bulgakov kept a hand on her head to keep it from lolling with every pitch. Eric glanced at Strav. He always saw the boy in his brother's face, the unguarded affection and passing storms. Now that face was cold and closed to him. If the change didn't come off with the week's growth of beard, Jacob would have another charge to answer.

By the time they angled sharply over Abad's foothills, Eric knew his course. Get his family the hell out of the Protectorate, then burn Solidarity to the ground. Already he comprehended the strange, illicit thrill that Jacob must have felt, mixing private revenge with a greater good objective.

The Himalayas went pink, then gold, detaching from the dimming earth until the peaks hung suspended in deep night blue. The lights of Prosperity rose up to meet them one last time.

III. CITY ON THE PLAIN

13

The Allied Nations International Settlement was the very wonder that Alex had long desired, at the very worst possible time.

International was the farthest-flung satellite city in devastated Shanghai Province, built in a postwar blink and embedded like a chunk of gleaming crystal in the muddy farmland. Every structure proclaimed a romance with the past. Gold cathedral spires and silvery onion domes punctuated stone-fronted cottages. Families biked up the tree-lined Fifth Avenue to picnic in Central Park, watch shows on the Old Globe Stage and fly dragon kites on Mao's Great Lawn. Monumental bronzes of Alexander, Genghis, Charlemagne, and Ravana, each set with different racial features and the same heroic scowl, stood watch as the daily commute of the TaskForce brigades dispersed upward into TaskForce Headquarters Tower, one hundred stories of iridescent mirror glass and sky-bending soul of the Nations.

Alex's sense of dissonance was amplified by their whirlwind exodus from the Protectorate. One minute it was monsters and madness in Abad; the next minute she was wedged between Eric and Strav on a flight to Shanghai. They had been in International for a week now. Laser treatments had reduced her black eye to a faint yellow tinge, while her real troubles gathered speed.

Any uncertainty she'd felt about Patrick's existence was left behind in the floating realm. She had eighteen days left until Asylum Netcast #2. She could hope that one of the contacts she had made in

Prosperity was the real confidant, and that Patrick would still reach out to her. But hope, as her father said, was not a plan.

Her unexpected uproot to International could, with a fair amount of psychic effort, be seen as an opportunity. Patrick's location would be revealed by Solidarity's Hallows geotag. Now she had landed in Solidarity's mother ship. That presented a role of last resort: guizi spy.

Hup! said Patrick. His incarnation, gone missing in Abad, now wouldn't leave her alone. At the moment he was in his Aggie linebacker days, shoulder pads and helmet. *You are late.*

"Hurrying," she answered aloud—no one knew you were crazy when everyone wore an earphone. It was Treaty Day, and their Commission was required at Secretary Handel's noon address in the park. But there was no hurrying past a faux-jewel-encrusted Thai Grand Palace or, equally gawk-worthy, a seven-story Notre Dame listing dangerously in a sinkhole.

"This place is a Potemkin village on growth hormones," she marveled to Patrick. Recognizing another impostor was about the only advantage of being a perpetual outsider. International had been built so fast that, beneath the superficial gloss, the place was already falling apart. The fissures were visible in the population too. Each morning, thousands of sullen day workers commuted from the ring of refugee Townships to clean and repair the gleaming TaskForce Settlement. The War was not the first time a Euro refugee exodus had followed the frozen tracks to Shanghai, and probably not the last. But the Townships now burst with the second generation, three families to each tenement flat, and grew daily with the influx of Chinese peasants displaced by the inland famines. As with the Protectorates, the resentment turned to the TaskForce keepers.

Hup! Your Commission has honor seating with the Secretariat. You cannot be late. Alex trotted into the park as fast as her new pencil skirt and mid-heel patent pumps allowed. She had forgotten that Eric and Strav had called International home for seven years, somehow enjoying rich, stimulating lives without the benefit of Alex Tashen. Strav's life included a personal tailor. When Alex had checked into her Gasthaus studio the first night, a mean little man with a tape measure appeared, handling her body with the respect due a headless mannequin. The next day, she found her closet stocked with outfits of the finest weaves and silks, each altered to perfection.

The tailor refused to disclose the bill. The Wolf Khan, when confronted, suddenly spoke no English. *"Ah, mademoiselle, quel est ce bruit laid?"*

A crowd had backed up on the path as an MP pulled random folk for a security check. If tagged, this would mark her long dreaded tenth g-screen. *That's not how one-in-ten odds work*, reminded Patrick. His logic did not help; ten crossed the dark imagined border of her luck.

A flock of the park's famous white pigeons pecked on the lawn. Alex looped onto the green with a "Gaaah!" spooking up a wave of winged outrage into the crowd ahead. Even the helmeted MP ducked. When the feathers cleared, she had skirted the checkpoint.

Having fun? scolded Patrick. But how could she not, running through birds? *Get to high ground and scout out a safe route.*

International had been built on an alluvial plain and was as flat as a paper map, so high ground meant the sixty-foot viewing deck atop the Tomb of the Missing. The Tomb—or Pestiferous Eyesore, as Strav called it—was a faux-bombed, four-story rubble building constructed of precast aggregate boxes and water chutes that delivered a nasty déjà vu of the Legion. Alex edged up the slick walkway, her new pumps frictionless as skates.

The centerpiece of the Tomb was an obsidian infinity pool edged with glassy spills of water. Alex bent over the surface. The liquid reflected an inky shiver of her face, and through some holographic trick, the shadowed faces of the missing, dozens of faces, hundreds, thousands rising past each other to the surface, each on the verge of speaking before swallowed back by the dark.

Alex touched the surface, a spreading of silver ripples, and the faces disappeared.

She sat in a daze until roused by a school group. The childish laughter sounded of sky and freedom. Alex ran up the spiral staircase to the viewing platform. At the top was a geographer's delight. To the north, the opalescent promise of Headquarter Towers. To the west, the fleeting pleasures of Happy Valley Racetrack. To the south, faded blue housing blocks of the Townships. To the east, the rainbow canopy hustle of the Friendship Market. Beyond the visible realm, she could hear the hum of an ancient continent, the march of emperors and armies, cartwheels on Silk Roads and the clamor of settled places. She was the spinning compass at the center, where all things met and merged and fell away, and it was a fierce, precious wonder to be alive.

Hurry, there'll be security sweeps up here. How strange that Patrick's presence, proof of insanity by any book, was her vexing tether to reality. No checkpoints in sight, only preparations for His Honor's processional across the cobblestone expanse of St. Peter's Square to the Globe Stage. Eric was visible standing guard over their seats. It occurred to Alex that his monument size made him as freakish on the outside as she felt on the inside; perhaps that was part of her comfort with him. He'd barely spoken since Abad, trusting her to know every meaning piled in his silence. He was sorry, no more screwing around, their future settled. Alex was torn between wanting to jump into his arms, and conking the presumptuous lunkhead.

If you care for the lunkhead, said Patrick, *then cut him loose. The demon campaign is working.* Alex checked the news on her phone. Anti-guizi rallies were burgeoning in Townships around the Nations. Rallies, however, were perfect venues for multiple frustrations, and very hard to control. Many protest signs read, DEATH TO GUIZIS! on one side, and DEATH TO SOLIDARITY! on the other.

"That's just greedy," said Alex. "People should have to pick one."

People are perfectly capable of hating two paradoxical things at once. Well. That makes you and Solidarity rather strange bedfellows.

"Hard stop." Still, she had to consider that bedding the enemy was a high-risk, high-return investment for spies. "I'm just extrapolating," she replied to her father's scowl. "You're the one talking strange bedfellows."

"*Alas, the storm is come again,*" quoted a deep and embodied voice, and Alex pronged straight up like a startled antelope. It was Strav, come to fetch her again. "*My best way is to creep under his gabardine; there is no other shelter hereabouts: misery acquaints a man with strange bedfellows."* He held open his gabardine jacket for her to shelter under.

"No creeping!" warned Alex. She had told him they could only be friends, and he had sworn to honor her platonic decree. "Though you are plenty strange."

A smile touched his eyes, he grinned, and she was gone, no hope of coherent thought while her soul dipped and reeled in that beam. It seemed to Alex that beauty, like time and space, must have a place in Einstein's theory of relativity, because she distinctly remembered that the first time she had seen Strav, before his evil reptilian phase, she'd found him good-looking in a way she was not attracted to, maybe a one-glance face. Then he was standing in the rain, his hand over his heart, the same face mysteriously turned one-in-a-thousand handsome. Now he was an unearthly Adonis, every imperfection a new definition of symmetry, and she could not understand why people did not go slack-jawed as he passed and birds swoop in for a closer look.

"I'll tell *The Tempest* tonight," he said. "It has peril, Eros, and your requisite happy ending." He was a male Scheherazade, every story a thread to bind her. It was agony for her not to touch him now, to open the silk tie and white collar to the hollow of his neck, graze the plane of muscle beneath his shoulder blades, trace a finger down to the contour rising in his slacks, the physical proof of the effect she had on him. He wasn't ashamed—in his mind, they were already together. How he rationalized this possession with his love for Eric, she could not imagine. She thought that she had denial down to a fine art, but Strav was a veritable Leonardo, a Renaissance master of every color and nuance that denial could take.

"No story tonight," she said, knowing he was taking deep satisfaction in her torment. "You need to study."

Strav dismissed the plebeian concept, but she meant it. Independence required a two-thirds Council vote, which meant turning the China, America, and India blocs, plus corporate empire Yang Enterprise. As went Yang, so went Beijing, and the other votes would fall in.

Strav was working the small groups with his champagne wit, and appeared supremely confident. But tomorrow was a podium with hundreds of eyes, and she was sick with worry for him. Study was her charm for safekeeping.

"Pop quiz, Envoy. Consider my paper on 'Capital and Secrecy Jurisdictions to Circumvent Austerity Restrictions.' Which concept will appeal to Yang's oligarchic self-interest?" She watched his chin jut. "One word. Tax haven."

"That's two words," he huffed. "Possibly a compound adjective."

Her hand floated to touch his face. These accelerating swings from fear to drifting fantasy, guilt, desire, euphoria, despair—such extremes were not sustainable. One swing too high, and she would detonate, freed to a wisp of smoke.

Heavy boots clunked up the staircase. It was Patrick's predicted security sweep. A burly MP stepped into the glare and unhooked his g-screener. Alex's legs turned to rubber.

Strav gave a casual hitch adjustment to the front of his pants and turned with a glint. The MP stared, flipped his visor, and handed the g-screener to a dumbfounded Alex.

"Permission?" the MP asked, and crowded in for a selfie with the Wolf Khan.

Trumpet fanfare from the square announced the processional. Alex laid down the screener and escaped into the stairwell. The school group blocked the landing, so she ran to a green-lit emergency exit. The exit became a steep concrete ramp, slick from the waterfalls, and her leather-soled pumps turned to skis. She slid into a hard stop against the exit door.

The door popped open, and Alex kept going. Everything was an astonishment—the sunshine, that the exit should open to an unprotected ledge ten feet above the gravel path, that she could be teetering at that edge, her arms beating like the pigeons, trying to defy gravity. The stately procession of dignitaries filed below her. To Alex's disbelief, one was the Kommandant, who looked up in her worst ambush yet.

The Kommandant lunged to cover the one-armed patrician gentleman in the path of Alex's fall. Then Alex was tumbling through space, her greatest astonishment that somehow, single-handedly, she was about to take out the leader of the free world.

The news that evening read, "Catch a Falling Star!" and showed the secretary general with his one and a half arms outstretched to catch the young woman. In actuality, Pieter had been moving to protect his own silver head, and a second later, Suzanne and his guards blocked the worst impact. Still, Suzanne had to admit the snapshot presented an icon of selfless quick-witted courage, a priceless photo op beyond what any publicist could cook up and well worth the sprains and bruises.

Pieter was ebullient, his world returned to a place of keen political advantage where pretty girls rained from the sky when you needed them most.

"The picture of manly vigor," Ari ribbed from his hospital bed. The last reserves of Ari's strength and fat were gone, the bones showing as if to slice the yellow wrapper of his skin. Suzanne took his hand, grateful that here, at his end, he had been spared the grotesque dementia that Katrin suffered from the radiation poisoning. Suzanne felt like she was walking through a forest with the great trees falling around her, some uprooted in storms, but most gone quietly, eaten by disease.

Pieter stroked Ari's silver-stubbled cheek. Suzanne checked that the door was shut.

"We'll run it against the demon posters," said Pieter, captivated by his photo. Polls showed him losing his bid for reelection against the Solidarity Chief. Suzanne had faith. If the Burtons were oaks of the forest, cursed with rigid principle, Pieter was the palm swaying through storms.

Conversation turned to the reason that Suzanne was in International. Eric had called a face-to-face with her and Handel. "You were right about Solidarity," Eric had told them. "Give me my CyberIntel team. I will give you the Asylum Hacker. I will gut Solidarity. I'm the only one who can."

"Remarkable," said Ari. "In the meantime, Strav is making Independence the sexy new talking point. Solidarity may actually lose the Protectorate."

"That's why I put Alex on the Commission," said Suzanne, a fat bit of revisionism. "She promotes Yuri Bulgakov's model Commonwealth." They looked at Alex captured midair on the wall screen, the embodiment of *uh-oh*.

"*Sie ist ein schönes Mädchen*," Ari said to Pieter's "*Ja, ja*."

"Say what?" asked Suzanne. After thirty-five years, she still got miffed when the men lapsed into their mother tongue. "Sounds like you're cursing. But what doesn't in German?"

"That our Alex is a beautiful girl."

"Of course she's beautiful," said Suzanne. "She's young."

"Such eyes. You would never forget that face."

"Bah." She refused to contemplate Katrin's fantasy of the light-eyed witch in Riga, except in the small hours of night, when her own nightmares of prison camp pulled her from bed, the cold and hunger forever hooked in her bones. Katrin was right that genes did funny things. Suzanne was old enough to have met offspring with a striking resemblance to the parent she had known at that age, and knew firsthand that dizzying sense of time travel. And this singular face would have been etched in Katrin's mind by a traumatic event.

The thoughts of curses and changelings were made ridiculous by each rising sun. Even so, Suzanne did not need Alex's face on the screen of another overheated hospital room.

"Our Alex is an idealist," said Ari to Suzanne. "And Strav loves a prizefight. But when did you become a fan of Independence?"

"When I started sleeping with Bulgakov."

Pieter groaned, and took two of Ari's pain pills. "Do we know a Bulgakov?" he asked Ari.

"I think we awarded him a medal after the Treaty."

"No, that was Tarakov. A Distinguished Cross, in London."

"No, Tarakov was Beijing. Remember that freezing hotel? Maybe in Brussels."

Since this would continue until she ended it, Suzanne told them she was flying to Prosperity in a few hours. Pieter objected strenuously that they needed her here, while Ari gave her the thumbs-up behind Pieter's back. They moved on to the recent intelligence report on the Regime—assassination attempts on the Supreme Marshal, mass execution of dissidents, attacks by rebel warlords.

"What if," Suzanne said, thinking of Katrin, "we did push back on the Removal provision of the Treaty? The external pressure might weaken the Regime even more."

"*Gott behüte!*" Pieter exclaimed. "Are you on Ari's drugs?"

"She has a point," Ari said. Together, she and Ari had kept Pieter threading the fine line between confidence and megalomania. And what would happen when Ari was gone?

"A weakened Regime," said Pieter, "is exactly the Regime that will go to war, to reconsolidate their internal power base. Those rebel warlords are worse than the devil we know." He leaned forward with a Julius Caesar gleam. "The Supreme Marshal needs a symbol. Thanks to Eric, we can give him the Asylum Hacker."

"Eric is better than us," said Suzanne. "He thinks he's working to prevent a war. Not to prop up an unstable tyranny."

"Same thing, old girl."

They looked to Ari, but he was asleep, his mouth open, his featherweight caught in a web of tubing. "The Treaty *will* hold," Pieter said. His grief loosened his skin and sagged in dark pockets under his eyes. "And this"—he pointed a quivering finger at Ari's poisoned body—"this will not be visited upon another generation."

"*Gott behüte,*" said Ari, wiggling his toes. "But I'm not dead yet."

Suzanne left them alone to say their goodnights. She limped into the balmy Shanghai night, and realized she had expected snow.

Disgrace.

"What the fuck is it with you two?" thundered Eric in despair. "How could you not even fucking get down from the fucking Tomb without causing a fucking riot?"

"It was a design flaw," protested Alex. "An exit to *nowhere.*" She was still frightened, and not just for herself. In the confusion following her tumble, a bodyguard had pinned her to the ground. Eric tore him off her, Alex scrambled up Eric like a cat up a tree, and the hypercharged MPs had turned weapons on them. Despite

Eric's uniform and commanding voice, it was a precarious interval until Jacob Kotas ran to their rescue.

You can only do them harm. And they endangered her. Eric made her think of responsibility. Suzanne made her think of sacrifice. Strav kept her from thinking at all.

Therein lay another danger. Her body said that one of these final mornings, she would wake up with Strav in her bed. She could not bear that her legacy on this sometimes precious earth should be the destruction of the bond between brothers.

The *Bulfinch* that night seemed written in private code. Prometheus chained, vultures eating his liver. A virgin huntress stooping for a golden apple and losing the race. A bird winging alone through the deadly clashing blue rocks.

Rob Blakely answered her midnight call, his blade-sharp features backlit by disco lights.

"Tell me about Jacob Kotas," said Alex. "I met him and his twins in San Francisco. He helped me today, and I could tell Eric hated it. Aren't they friends?"

Rob's smile on her screen made Alex grateful for each scurrilous fiber of his heart. "Friends, considering everything," he said, and explained about Eric shagging Jacob's girlfriend back in the day. "For the smartest man in the world," Rob observed, "Eric Burton's got a bad case of the stupids." Alex had nothing to add to that. Rob's sunny face went crafty. "Maybe Eric's afraid of Jacob giving him a bit o' his own medicine with you. Imagine Jacob in the sack. I say bugger the man senseless."

"I may have to." She hung up.

Jacob Kotas, Solidarity Director of the Netcast Investigation. At some level, she had known this contingency since they met. Once the Hallows virus geotagged the Hacker's signal source, the manhunt could take hours, even days. If she was close enough to Jacob to spy the coordinates, she might yet tip off Patrick before the dragnet closed.

The percentages were laughable, but 1 percent odds were better than 0, and 100 percent that if/when she were caught, she would take Jacob down with her. His affair with a guizi would ruin him. It would be a small blow for the family in the Netcast, for the nameless ones in the Guizi Chambers.

An affair with Jacob would also drive away Eric and Strav. They would despise and be safe from her. One man, one elegant solution to a multifactorial problem.

There was a dark new border to cross here, a geography of no return. She wanted to believe there was another way.

The next morning, Strav and Eric waited on Alex for breakfast in the VA cafeteria. Both men had been up before dawn. Strav was training at the racetrack each morning; he knew only that Eric was running a CyberIntel control room, meaning a top-secret mission and a rottweiler growl if he asked. He did not blame Alex for hiding today, with "Catch a Falling Star!" the top headline news, and a titanic photo of Handel's catch supplanting the demon billboards. But Star Girl had to take food with her meds, and her blueberry waffles were getting cold.

Eric called her. "Alex Tashen, do not make me come over there."

Click. Eric turned to Strav with a mixed look of accusation and entreaty.

"Go on, anda," said Strav. "I've got her."

A brisk ten blocks later, Strav rapped on Alex's Gasthaus studio door. "What is this melodrama?" he said through the intercom. "Was someone drinking her potatoes last night?"

"No!" she answered to the scrape of a bottle being pushed under the bed.

Strav considered the door. Kicking it open might break an ankle or scuff his Italian shoes. That was why poetry existed, to coax open locked bedrooms. *"When, in disgrace with fortune—"*

"I'm never coming out!"

"So you have a glaring fifteen minutes of fame," Strav said testily. "You may have noticed my own brush with celebrity. There are benefits. Ambassadors ask you to tea. Long-lost relatives crawl out from the woodwork and contact you."

The door flew open, Alex wearing the ivory satin kimono from his wardrobe upgrade, and her hairy purple slippers with the googly eyes. She threw her arms around Strav. "Oh, thank you!"

Strav held her with an overflowing if confused heart. He saluted the white rumpled bed but did not go inside. When he did cross that threshold, he would not leave for a very long time. Her resistance was weakening. In a few more days, he would strike through with an unapologetic celebration of physical prowess, an extravagant pageant, a promise honored, and gifts laid at her feet.

"What are you plotting?" demanded Alex, pulling away.

"Moi? As if my poor brain has room with you cramming me for this speech. Get dressed. *Chu*, Dr. Tashen. *Chu*. I have a Committee to slay."

After the heated hubbub of Fifth Avenue, Headquarters Tower was the soaring, omnipotent cool of a cathedral. Alex tried to appear jaded and failed. A herd of apatosaurus could have roamed freely in the atrium. White walls flowed with the greens and violets of the Borealis. Strav had to drag her past a revolving globe the size of a hot-air balloon. Cloud masses floated about the globe surface, with red pops of real-time armed hostilities blistering the continents like smallpox. The world turned, the Nations illuminated day and night, the Federation in perpetual shadow.

Alex pushed aside her own shadow. Strav was right about fame. The Star Girl blitz was a pixelated godsend that Patrick would see wherever he was hiding. Her spy games and betrayals could wait in the dusk.

Strav's speech was to the Committee on Protectorates, an august body with the power to reject their Commission Report. Meeting Room A was a hundred-plush-seat theater cordoned off by green silk ropes. Committee members chatted while keeping an eye peeled for anyone more important.

"A bloody power-hungry bunch," Strav murmured to Alex. "Enough testosterone to put hair on a thousand chests. And that's just the women."

"Wait," she said, anxious for him, "where are your notes?" Strav's backroom dealings had focused on single-issue topics, like rare earth mining rights and soft political blackmail. But this speech required the comprehensive sweep of legal, humanitarian, and economic findings.

"Relax, Professor. I'm fine."

Which seemed hideously unfair, considering her palpitations. "The Yangs agreed to back Independence," said Strav. "We toasted your diabolical genius on the tax haven." To Alex's curious look, he added, "I have a particular friendship with Danny Yang, the son."

"A particular friendship?" she teased. "With a Beijing princeling? Does Eric approve?" Strav's shrug suggested some tension there. "I hear the princelings can be—eccentric."

"With that kind of money, one is not eccentric. One is eclectic." The members' attention shifted to the entry of a trim, debonair man in his thirties. One consequence of her time in Strav Beki World, it seemed to Alex, was her ability to recognize an expensive suit. The man bowed to Strav, then bowed at her. She reflexively returned a charmed smile.

"How do you know Danny Yang?" Strav asked, his eyes narrowed.

"I don't," she said, exasperated by his jealousy. "Must be my fifteen minutes of fame."

"You are not to associate with him."

"But he's so handsome," she said in her best smoky purr. "And rich, rich, insanely rich." As punishment, Strav deposited her with a clutch of mid-level staffers and went to greet Yang.

The staffers were from the Mayor of Shanghai's Office. The miles of refugee Townships warranted a keen interest in the Independence vote. The staffers' only concern, though, was the Mayor's wedding gift for the Wolf Khan. People constantly congratulated Strav on his marriage, and Alex understood she had nailed him into this box with her announcement in Prosperity.

"Perhaps French champagne," said the Director of Human Resources. She was a skinny forty, with a hard line of Cleopatra bangs. "But the Envoy's—special friends—report he consumes no alcohol." She glanced at Strav and Danny Yang standing in warm conversation, the distinguished Committee members trying to listen in. "Yang knows the Envoy's tastes. He'll gift an *er'mai* fit for a Khan."

"An er—what?"

"An *er'mai*. A mistress. A little wife."

Alex laughed at her. "You don't know the Envoy."

"I do." She spoke syrup-sweet as she would to a deficient child. "He'll have his first family back home and his *er'mai* in Shanghai's Gubei quarter, like all Chinese officials. The trendiest bars and shops, beautiful apartments for beautiful, expensive women. Gubei is owned by Yang Enterprises. The Mayor holds the management contracts. It's my business to know every little thing."

"Enough." She now knew exactly why Eric said that.

"Before he was injured, the Envoy spent countless hours enjoying the exquisite flowers on Gongzunch Street. It's beyond his pathetic means, but money hardly matters when Danny Yang shows a promising young Diplomat the finer things in life."

Alex had wondered how Strav gained his princely style, and now she knew—by being cultivated by a real prince. Given his current arousal levels, she could easily see Strav making a Gubei flower run every few hours. Well, fuck a yellow duck.

"Yes, the flowers give special consideration to rising stars, especially a handsome half-breed with an auspicious dragon birthmark on his *jibä*. They say he talks during the act, in several languages. Foreplay in English, French when he mounts, and when he gets riding hard, he calls out in his barbarian tongue—"

Alex kicked her ankle, a strike below public radar. The woman hopped off in a hiss of pain. Alex turned to the remaining staffer, a matronly woman with a pockmarked face. Her badge read, CHIEF APOTHECARY OF THE OFFICE OF DRUG LICENSING AND ENFORCEMENT.

"You don't need to kick me," said the apothecary. She seemed entertained. "The Envoy never used our private services."

"What services?"

"Confidential distribution of restricted pharmaceutical products."

It was one thing to study the economics of endemic corruption, and another to see it in well-oiled action. So the Mayor partnered with the Yangs in the lucrative sex and black-market drug trades. So the Envoy accepted favors in the form of high-class prostitutes. The only shocker here was her endless capacity to be shocked.

"Excuse my colleague," said the apothecary. "She is in a divorce and hates all men."

Alex could relate to that. "Mr. Virtue," she said bitterly. "Mr. Family Values."

"Remember where you are, *nǚhái.*" The rebuke was spoken with kindness. "Men have needs. If a young man is bound for an arranged marriage, straightforward business liaisons are more honorable than dating and misleading women. Once married, the *er'mai* contracts are accepted, almost expected. The wives ignore the contracts because they're preferable to the turmoil and emotional threat from an affair. The privileged classes always have their own rules."

The apothecary handed Alex a card. *F. Lawrence*, Friendship Market Dispensary. "We take care of our friends in TaskForce. If you need anything, rely on our discretion."

"Thank you," said Alex, "but I don't think there's a pill for my troubles."

An officious majordomo in a scarlet silk suit called the session. Alex filed in as Strav took the stage with a stiff, clumsy gait. Suddenly, only one trouble mattered.

"No, not now," breathed Alex. She watched him grip the podium, felt him try every breathing and visualization technique they had practiced to slow his slamming heart. This speech was the litmus test he set for himself. He *had* to give this speech.

Expectant silence turned to whispers. Danny Yang crossed his elegant legs in the front row. Alex flew across the room and took the seat beside him. Yang swiveled in pleasant surprise, and Alex leaned close with a suggestive "Hello there," and a hand on his arm. Strav twitched as if jabbed with a fork.

"Untenable!" Strav pronounced, and although he was glaring at her, the word surged through the theater as a wave up a shore, drawing back every person in its path. The audience sat rapt, and Alex's anxiety turned to wonder at how he did that.

"Untenable," Strav repeated, lit as the archangel bearing the Word. "I speak of the looming crisis that is the Nepali Protectorate. The Protectorate, once a symbol of hope amid war and chaos, has turned our own people into destitute foreigners, citizens of the Allied Nations but not of the plot of land beneath their feet. Today I am honored to present this learned Committee with our report. The resulting story is not what we had anticipated. It is a tale of paramilitaries along the subtropical plain ready to fight for nationhood. Of increasingly militant separatists mixing with criminal elements in the mountain provinces. Of a brave center holding true to the promise of a homeland despite hardship and humiliation. It is also the story of opportunistic agencies benefiting from disorder."

Alex nodded, close to tears, and Strav returned the barest wink to let her know he was just warming up. And he was, like a racehorse given its head to run. For the next thirty minutes, he spoke without notes, in seamless paragraphs, until even the majordomo bobbed in agreement with the model plan for an Independent Commonwealth.

There was great art in making the difficult look effortless. Alex relaxed into a beam of appreciation and pride.

The congratulatory handshaking took almost as long as the speech. "Pompous sycophants, every one of them," Strav said happily once they reached the Plaza steps. "I told you not to worry."

He was flying too high to remember how she had jump-started him with Danny Yang. "You were amazing, Envoy."

His cocky grin said, *Yes, I know.* "Tonight we celebrate!" He threw a triumphant samba slide along each limestone paver. "Sky's the limit! Anywhere you want."

"I know," she said, assuming a radiant innocence. "Take me to Gubei Flower District. I hear Gongzunch Street is the place for fun. I'd love to meet your special friends."

The samba ended with an abrupt missed step and off-balance collision with a flagpole. "Forget Gubei," said Strav. "Gubei is not for you."

"But I hear there's great clubs, and private parties—ohhh, am I being naive? Are we talking Texas cathouse? Degeneracy? The economic and physical exploitation of women? Forgive me, Envoy. I know how you condemn such things."

"Condemn as a rule," he answered cautiously, "but with some— compassion, as it were—for, say, young men who may have visited Gubei out of a compulsion to explore aspects of a foreign culture."

"There's a 'compulsion for culture' exception?" She needed to stop messing with him; his unaccustomed bumbling was turning her on, not a good thing. Alex guided Strav safely across the avenue. "I guess life makes all kinds of strange bedfellows."

Eric stuck his head into Meeting Room A during Strav's speech and, satisfied to see his brother doing his thing, returned to his control room on the fiftieth floor. Handel had chosen the code name Operation Daybreak, as a counter to Solidarity's Operation Hallows, and his CyberIntel Chief gave him his pick of talent. The windowless room was lined with workstations for the virologists, cryptologists, and tactical experts working out a deployment plan for the rapid reaction teams to converge on the Hacker by the anticipated Fall of Riga transmission. A holographic globe hovered at the room's center, strategic pins of colored lights winking like faulty bulbs on a Christmas tree.

The only person Eric took into complete confidence was Li Chow. The Forensics Director was a keen mind of sharp angles inside a doughy body, and the most decent man Eric knew. Chow agreed to investigate Solidarity for unsolved crimes of provocation against TaskForce interests, starting with the Legion bombing. He also agreed that Eric could reengineer the faulty Hallows geotag to embed imperceptibly in the Asylum Netcast program, giving CyberIntel the kill, Solidarity left holding its dick.

Not that Eric should. There could be no hint of personal ven- detta in a control room, said Chow, and cited Eric's raw anger as a prime example of why. Allowing Solidarity to proceed with its malformed Hallows virus carried serious risk. The most powerful programs were the ones most likely to go Godzilla. The Asylum Netcast's cyber immune system, when triggered, responded with unfamiliar forms of attacks. The result could be a virulent reaction of unforeseen magnitude, from disinformation in multiple systems, to electromagnetic disruptions in things remotely monitored, which was basically everything in the Nations.

"Stop," advised Chow. "Think. Don't let your temper cloud your judgment."

The advice stung. The Chief, though, a political animal, agreed with Eric. Any systems damage would be contained within the fail-safes of Solidarity's networks. Handel's orders were clear. Proceed.

Eric did. He thought he understood anger, the fire that flared and receded. But the attack in Abad brought a continual burn lodged hard against his sternum, like a small swallowed sun.

He broke out for dinner to celebrate Strav's Committee speech. Strav and Alex's debate over Mongolian or Texas barbeque would have lasted until breakfast if Eric had not exercised executive privilege for The Pig and Whistle. Chow came with his equally good-natured wife, while Bulgakov and Suzanne joined from Prosperity by screen. Dinner was a warm, lively glimpse of life if he won reinstatement—his family, friends, and career thriving, everything that mattered right here, in this moment, in his hands.

His next days were barricaded in his control room, catching a few hours' sleep on his office couch, minions scurrying for king-size chili nachos. In the wee hours, he finished the drawing of Alex's face he'd begun in Prosperity. He finally captured that elusive life essence, though the results surprised him—a wariness in her eyes that his drawing hand seemed to conjure up independently of his working brain. Regardless, the sketch had led to their first kiss, and would be his gift as long as she didn't hang the damn thing where anyone could see it. He turned to writing a card not dictated by Strav for a change. A dozen attempts produced "You excite my electrons." Eric groaned and erased. *Men of few words are the best men.*

A shrill alarm rocketed Eric to his screen. The second Asylum Netcast had been detected, seventeen days before expected, and his Daybreak program was not ready.

The grainy footage showed evenly spaced lines of men kneeling in an open field of brown stubble. The men were shirtless and emaciated, with shaved heads and jutting hip bones. Each man scraped weakly at a body-length trench in the ground beneath him.

Yet his team's frantic analytics showed that this was no premature Netcast. Remarkably, the footage had streamed from Solidarity's own files.

In effect, Solidarity got pantsed. They had been probing the Netcast program, which responded with a reverse bug that caused Solidarity's network to spew archived footage from its own database. It was a fantastically arrogant warning and taunt; Eric was reminded of his pitching days, a perfect high and inside fastball to brush back a batter crowding the plate.

He went to his office to suck down a pot of coffee. The starving men remained crouched in his mind. For the time being, he and the Asylum Hacker were on the same team, against Solidarity. He would be sorry when those lines crossed back and he did what was required.

Eric looked out at the lightening cityscape below. Every morning the view dawned the same yet found him in a stranger and stranger place.

14

The trim white home was typical of Directors' family housing, a Cape Cod style with a wink of blue wooden shutters and a bas-relief mallard on the mailbox. Alex stood on the sidewalk, oblivious to the joggers and baby strollers swerving around her, and clutched her candy bribes. The emerald lawn had a pink swing set and two pink bikes. "Waltz of the Snowflakes" roared from a window. It was nine o'clock on a Saturday morning, practically midday for five-year-old girls. Jacob had probably been up for hours.

Last night's Netcast scare had been the slap required to put aside her own childish things, the fantasy family and hope of a swoop-in rescue. It was time to glaze her heart and unite her warring selves. Ulysses had a wooden horse to enter Troy. She had two chocolate moose.

A luxuriant white cat shot out of the house, chased by two little blonde girls in pink spangled tutus, both screeching at the top of their lungs in Mandarin. They recognized Alex and ran over in delight.

"I threw up last night," said Lena importantly. "And I'm ten minutes older then Lia." Lena was taller than her twin, with a merry look of devilment that Alex suspected would age Jacob before his time; it was her own look, and had certainly aged Patrick.

"I threw up *two* times," claimed Lia, born to a life of catch-up. "From the top bunk. It went everywhere."

"Yeah, but mine was *blue*. From the pie. What'd ya bring us?"

Alex cringed. "Chocolate moose. Let's save 'em for when your tummies are better."

"We're already better!" Their nonstop chatter revealed that their ayah was out sick and had a scary glass eye, and Daddy was going to be their show-and-tell for kindergarten. The girls' happiness opened a flood of yearning for that priceless innocence again. Maybe five was the perfect age, before the inevitable boundaries between father and daughter were mapped—young enough to bathe together and get carried when tired, but old enough to share every breathless idea in your head.

"Lena, Lia!" came Jacob's voice over the deafening snowflake climax. "Breakfast!"

Alex tried to ring the doorbell, but the girls had her hands in vice grips. They pulled her to a white kitchen table set with plates of burnt toast. An odiferous pile of bedding lay in the doorway of a bathroom off the kitchen.

Jacob stood in an exhausted slouch profile in front of the toilet, chin to bare chest, as if asleep on his feet, one hand holding a scrub brush, the other holding down the front of his pajama bottoms as he pissed. His chiseled face was puffy, the golden hair matted with organic matter. He glanced up expecting his girls, to find a sight too nonsensical to register. The disconnect was shared by Alex, and the two stared blankly at each other until his stream of urine drifted to splatter off the tiles.

Everything broke at once, Jacob's shocked fumble with his pajamas, Alex yanked to the floor as the girls fell in laughing shrieks of "Daddy peed on the wall!"

"Sorry," Alex sputtered, but what apology could one offer for complete trespass of a man's home and dignity, with his daughters screaming in a kindergartner's heaven of potty humor. "I came to thank you for—" she began, and then she was off, whooping with laughter with the girls.

When she could meet Jacob's face, he was standing confounded with his scrub brush. Alex hiccuped and pinned a squirming girl beneath each arm.

"For God's sake, take a shower and go back to bed," she told Jacob. "We'll be in the Children's Park."

———

The chocolate moose got to pull the horn *hoo-hoo* on the miniature steam locomotive, and narrowly avoided death by nibbling goats in the petting zoo. The big event was to be the camel rides, but for some unexplained reason all twelve of the dromedaries were missing today.

The morning was a multifaceted education, starting with getting the twins dressed. Their dictatorial eye for style put Strav to shame—in their case, style equating with pink—and they expected Alex to do every zip and tug, holding their skinny arms up for pink undershirts and dresses. A classified Solidarity memo was on the screen in the family room, the oversight of a harried single parent cramming work around the edges. Alex did not dare open the memo. But there would be more.

The moose got their first ride on a carousel, as did Alex. The painted mounts picked up speed to the scratchy calliope music. Lena had a tiger, and Lia's big cat had a carp in its mouth. Typical of International, the gilded ride was a mechanical mess. Alex's rearing black stallion jammed stuck at the low point.

Jacob appeared in the watching ring of parents, wearing shorts and a white polo shirt. Her strategic challenge, Alex understood, was to restore an affronted male ego. She motioned to Jacob that she would jump off to meet him, and surreptitiously hooked the hem of her skirt on the saddle horn. Her dismount then left her in the intended tangle, exposing a length of leg that would have given Strav a small stroke, and in great need of a Brave Daddy Rescue before the twins.

The trick worked better and worse than she could have imagined. Released from her weight, her horse jerked to life and rose up the pole, lifting her skirt over her head, down again, then up, for a mortifying revolution past the startled onlookers. Jacob sprang aboard, choking with laughter. The girls cheered as he worked Alex free.

Lena said, "I like your underwear," which, yes, was pink.

The only good part, it seemed to Alex, about a reputation for outlandish mishap was how it banished any suspicion of an ulterior motive. Start a riot, tumble from a Tomb, flash the crowd, and no one ever asked the underlying *Why*? Certainly not Jacob, as they stepped to solid earth with her mission accomplished.

"Damn, girl," he said, laughing and wiping his eyes. "Is anything easy with you?"

"No," she said, still flushed a hot pink. "I'm naturally complex and difficult."

The girls floated past, yelling, "Watch me!" Alex and Jacob produced spot-on smiles and waves. "They're wonderful," said Alex, and meant it.

"They are indeed." Jacob tilted her face for a professional assessment of the residual black eye. "Heard about Abad. Bastards really got you, eh?"

"I'll survive." She meant that too.

"Any second thoughts about granting Independence to a crime-infested war zone? God, what will it take?"

That took her aback. "The goal is regional stability. Different approach, but we're on the same team. Right?"

A sigh. "Right. That's why I'm protecting you. Again, not easy."

When it became clear she had no idea what he meant, he added in surprise, "There's a subversion complaint about your comments in Prosperity. I told Eric I'd bury it, but for you to be careful. Didn't he tell you?"

"No." She didn't have to fake her anger, or wonder how to use it. "There's lots Eric doesn't tell me. I learned the hard way that you can't trust him."

His new assessment of her was as cool as a drop in air temperature. Some things you only recognized in their absence. Even blindfolded, she could locate Eric by the animal heat he radiated. Strav was a torch of restless energy. But from this golden man, she got only a Midas touch of pure metallic certainty.

The breeze carried a wisp of down from the duck pond to Jacob's chest. Alex stepped close to him and casually brushed the feather away.

"My banquet—tantrum—was not what I believe," she said. "I've published many papers praising Solidarity's work. I was drunk and arguing the opposite of whatever Strav said. It could have been how many angels dance on the head of a pin."

Jacob offered a wry smile. "Been there. Strav has that effect."

"I'd love to forget that night." Alex pushed the advantage with a mischievous smile. "Maybe I should try Dr. Vito's memory ablation."

"Hell, that's a classified trial. What else did he talk about? The organ transplants?" Alex flinched. "Good grief, girl, we don't cut up unwilling prisoners. I'm not Dr. Mengele, you know."

A vendor walked by with a bobbling mass of balloons that could have lifted a child into the sky. Jacob bought two pink balloons, glanced at Alex and bought a third.

"Why does Solidarity invest in that research?" she asked. "It's not g-screen tech."

"You forget the scope of our mission, eh? We are the defense to the Federation's biologic threats. Like guizis carrying engineered viruses. The risk is grossly underestimated by Handel's Secretariat." He tied the balloon to her wrist. "It's money well spent. War research spins out to broader civilian applications. You'd be surprised how much cutting-edge medicine originated with the basic science in our labs."

"I'm all about surprises."

"Okay. Since we're on the same team. We needed to know if the guizi genetic marker could be manipulated in vitro. The experiments led to insights on immune suppression and nerve growth, which we passed on to the Health Institutes. That led to the first effective therapy to regenerate nerves in the spinal cord after traumatic injury. Crush victims like Strav. He's one of thousands walking today, thanks to Solidarity."

The universe, it seemed to Alex, was like the carousel, a gaudy ride running on broken gears. There were always winners and losers, and that which ruined and crippled one life might save another. The twins shouted out, but she was back in Abad with Strav, Strav in his swashbuckler shirt playing soccer with the kids, Strav grinning as he juggled the ball from foot to knee to head while dodging ecstatic urchins, the easy freedom and celebration of his body.

"I'm glad for your research," Alex said softly. "Very glad."

They had great works in the pipeline, Jacob continued. Therapies for those with organ transplants, new arterial systems and targeted immune suppressors to free them of anti-rejection drugs. Clinical trials for pregnant women too ill to carry their baby to term, the same bold therapies for transplanted organs, allowing for fetal transplants to a surrogate. Alex listened with a new confused hatred she thought might soon feel normal.

"I'll be glad when it goes public," Jacob said. "My wife— ex-wife—almost miscarried with the twins. They are my everything, I can't imagine life—"

The girls swept by again with rosy, expectant faces. At the speed with which the world was shifting, Alex expected the girls to be older somehow this go-around, every sighting a compressed year, the waving child turned teen, turned woman, each change another little stone to the heart.

"There's a party tonight for my Chief," said Jacob. "Black tie. Would you like to go?" It wasn't a real question, because they both knew the answer was yes.

"*Сум байхгүй*," Uuganbayer told Strav. "No arrows."

Strav's father, Beki, might be fifteen hundred miles north on the steppe, but his guff-puncturing grunt lived close, in loco parentis, in Uuganbayer, revered Chief Trainer of the Happy Valley Race-track. Uuganbayer was a *mal-dor*, a keeper of livestock, from Inner Mongolia, a staunch traditionalist with steel-gray hair and even steelier squint that judged horses and men in an instant. He had been grunting at Strav since the wayward hybrid appeared in his stables seven years ago, hungry to ride his wildest horses.

Uuganbayer had let him scandalize the trainers and radicalize the School for Mounted Archery. After Croatia, he had tied Strav to the saddle like a child again until his strength returned. He let Strav train the prize colt Fast Talker—named in vexation after his rider—and race the horse in Naadam. He had never told Strav no. Until now.

Strav looked longingly at the goatskin quivers on the tack room floor. The arrows' steel tips were blunted for training, but with the great power of the laminate bows, a hit could be deadly. It was almost noon. The Saturday throngs in the park had gotten word of something potentially gruesome afoot and were streaming into the stands. It was one thing to shoot from horseback on a closed training track, quite another when an errant arrow could pierce some screaming fan.

The track village was a preservation site, a medieval scene of stone water troughs and thatched roof cottages. Uuganbayer stomped off, trailed by Strav and nine fellow riders. They were all superb mounted archers, hardened in the Townships and trained at the track, a mix of Hungarian, Japanese, Turk, Korean, Mongolian, and a thuggish trio of Kazakh brothers to keep things interesting. Each wore felt boots and deel coats bound with a peacock assortment of silk sashes to match the fletch of their arrows. They were keyed up beyond endurance, especially the Kazakhs, who had been borrowing or stealing—Strav declined to ask for details—everything needed to throw a spell of time and place.

Spectators anticipating the white fenced oval of track were met with yellow furling flags, jewel-colored silks over gates and arches, *ooves* of waist-high piled stones, blue rag prayer flags, horsehair lances stuck in the turf, stands of ceremonial swords and helmets polished to catch the noon sun. Taoist priests in black caps and magenta robes paced in chanting dignity, ringing bells and blessing the one Earth. Horses grazed as a free herd in the grass center, along with a dozen camels looking mighty baffled to be there.

The Kazakhs' pride were the mural panels of ancient warfare "borrowed" from a minister's collection. Mongols, Scythians, and samurais fired arrows from horseback, impaled and slashed to leave slimy trails of enemy viscera. Chain mail defenders poured boiling pots of tar from the ramparts. Armored warriors wheeled catapults and battering rams into position. Ten thousand archers lifted their bows as one.

Hurricanes of arrows blotted the sun, darkened the sky, tore through time with the scream of banshees, arrows, arrows everywhere.

"No arrows," said Uuganbayer.

And by extension, no vicious tricks. It was asking rival wolves to play nice. Besting the Wolf Khan meant instant fame. Each rider would go for the throat, which was why Strav had chosen them. "We'll be cautious as rabbits," swore Strav, and Uuganbayer cuffed him for lying. Strav could have ducked, but the old man was getting slow, and Strav would not dream of embarrassing him.

So he followed him through the familiar fertile smells of sweet hay, oiled leather, and manure. The readied tournament horses were waiting behind the track's high wall.

Strav cracked the gate open to see the stands. He had called Alex repeatedly that morning, telling her to come to the track at noon, center rail. Her noncommittal response over calliope music was not reassuring. "She'll be here," he murmured to Fast Talker. His teammates kept their sly faces blank, tending to cinches and stirrups. Of course this was about a woman: What other reason was there?

Fast Talker thumped his muzzle into Strav's shoulder for undivided attention, and Strav put his arms around that warm, solid neck. The other horses stomped in anticipation, tossing beribboned manes and jangling silver bridles.

"Where's your big white useless anda?" asked Uuganbayer, checking expertly beneath saddle blankets for hidden weapons. The mal-dor had great affection for that unlikely son of the Khanate. Eric had helped train Fast Talker, even though the high-strung colt, unwilling to share Strav's love, tried to take a chunk from Eric's arm whenever possible. Eric was a favorite on Saturday nights in the barn, where the staff gathered to drink and bet on wrestling matches. Eric had won the mal-dor many wagers over the years.

"Eric has to work," Strav answered curtly. He tightened the saddle straps holding his thick curved bow, the weapon reduced to an impotent bit of costume. "Arrows honor our ancestors. The combined event is true to the first tournaments."

The mal-dor's grunt was eloquent rebuttal. Mounted archery might be resurgent in many places, but the Khanate Elders held to standing archery. Strav was abasing his track with a Dirty Naadam, exchanging spiritual beauty and tradition for testosterone showmanship. The Wolf Khan's behavior would be emulated by legions of young fans. Worst of all, this obsession concerned an Outside girl. Strav needed to remember his duty to his family and people.

Strav checked the stands again. The haze was dissipating, and a traveling shaft of sunlight brushed the upper deck with new brilliance and dimension. Alex drifted down the center aisle, lost in a daydream, a pink balloon floating from her wrist.

"Wake up, sweetheart," Strav whispered, and the sun must have heard, because the shaft of light raced down the stands to stop in bright glory over Alex. She instinctively lifted her face in welcome, the dark waves of her hair dancing in the breeze, the thin stuff of her blouse and skirt suffused with light, as if glowing from inside. The light lifted Strav too, a rapture that took his breath away even as Alex returned to earth, curious about the murals and flags, priests and camels. Strav felt her delight, her dawning comprehension. He had promised to bring the Naadam to her.

Alex put her hands to her heart, transfixed, and Strav closed the gate in a kind of despair; it didn't seem normal, or even decent, to want someone this badly.

His team was staring at him, then looking every which way. Uuganbayer had the same squint as when assessing a sick or damaged animal, which Strav thought pretty well covered the situation.

The mal-dor muttered a few curses, and clapped his hands for a stable boy. "Fetch the arrows."

Strav held his bow of reverence for a long struggle with unseemly emotion. Not until the war horn sounded was the joy of the devil back and singing in his blood. He handed Fast Talker's reins to Uuganbayer as planned, then strode out on the track.

"You need to be his brains out there," he heard Uuganbayer tell Fast Talker, and the horse's snort of agreement.

The hush that fell over the stands extended to the Yang Clubhouse, where the rosewood bar and mirrored windows allowed International's elite to lay wagers in privacy. Eric stood, his nose to the glass, watching Alex watch Strav walk across the track; one of those days where everyone watched someone, a giant Möbius strip of observation, twisting back ad infinitum, and revealing strange properties.

After the all-nighter with the fake Netcast, Eric's brain had hit the wall. He needed his real bed, and to assure his abandoned family that, no, Alex, he had not been abducted by aliens. Her signal showed her circling on the carousel at the Children's Park, which made Eric laugh aloud, a new and alarming sound to his team. He had walked down the avenue, his mouth furry with coffee and his mind trailing numbers, and followed her signal into the stadium, to be startled by the bizarre fantasy showcase. Chow hailed him from the clubhouse and—

—the beginning/end of the Möbius. Alex in profile, a row beneath his box window. Strav advancing across the green and out of the warlord murals in a quilted tunic and scarlet sash, a quiver of red-fletched arrows over his shoulder.

Chow and the other high-tech warriors crowded to Eric, gleeful as boys peeing in the snow. "A Dirty Naadam?" they asked. *No way*, thought Eric. Strav would not have excluded him; Uuganbayer would never allow that degenerate Roller Derby of the equestrian world to defile his track. Yet there were the enemy dummies, mocked up in tunics. The scoreboard was blinking, the track set to the half-mile lap of the event, and Strav had his Lucifer rebel glint.

Strav stopped mid-track and bowed to Alex, fist to heart in the pledge of fealty. Despite the distance, they seemed to be touching, and the only two people there.

Eric's legs went unsteady. Sure, Strav had a special bond with Alex, protective as with Batgerel, *sister* being the operative word here. This was sleep deprivation, misinterpreting things, and he had to shake it off.

The gate opened, and Fast Talker trotted riderless to the track, his chestnut coat a lustrous satin, powerful flanks and regal arched neck. *Fucking show-off*, thought Eric with awe. Somehow, without him seeing it, the willful colt had matured to a fully realized racing machine. On an invisible signal, the stallion took off, coming out of the curve at a hard gallop. Strav stood with his back turned while the horse bore down on him.

The stadium erupted with warnings. Eric knew the years of training involved, and his gut still clenched. The horse was a coil in motion, and Eric saw each chunk of mud fly from the hooves, the tendons bunching chest to legs, metal stirrups swinging to the silver pommel. Alex screamed; the stands were a tumult. Then the horse was on him, and Strav disappeared.

The stadium exploded as Strav rose in the saddle, joined in the mad exhilaration of flight. The track gate swung wide, and nine riders lit out in a manic break, yelling, "*Chu! Chu!*" The speeding half-ton juggernauts fell in with Strav, and the race was on.

"Rules?" Eric answered the officers. "Rule, singular. First rider with fifteen kills to cross the finish line wins." He pointed at the five dummies set thirty paces back in the green at fifty paces apart. "An arrow in a tunic is a kill. One shot per dummy on each pass. Get fifteen kills, then a finish lap to ride like hell. Could be done in three passes. But it won't be."

"That's all?" demanded Chow.

Eric considered. "Not a rule, but it's bad form to shoot the other riders."

The problem with bad form became apparent as the clustered riders approached the first dummy. Each rider carried his quiver in his favored position—on the thigh, behind the saddle, or on his back, like Strav. The riders dropped their reins to draw arrows in their bows. Only the inside riders had clear shots, but a barrage of the whistle-signal arrows still shrieked through the air, missing other riders by inches before burying into the bodies of straw. Two heartbeats later, the arrows screamed for the second dummy, each rider timing his release to the stride of his horse, rising in the stirrups at the height of the horse's rise—a continuous fluid arc of arm to quiver to bow, that ended only as they streaked into the curve, five bristling dummies left behind.

The scoreboard flashed names and colors showing Strav and the Korean ahead, with five kills each. The riders hit the backstretch, the horses' necks extended to run, their tails streaming like the banners. Eric watched for the low-scoring riders to team up against the front-runners, and at his thought, the Japanese and Mongolian riders swerved hard to pinch off the Korean. The Korean's horse stumbled, clipped by back hooves, and the rider kept going in an aerial somersault that landed him in front of the next wave of horses. Those riders tried to clear him, but he was left screaming with a bloodied leg. Groomsmen rushed to carry him away—no one wanted to be caught on the backstretch behind the targets during the next shooting pass. Ahead, the Hungarian and Japanese riders attempted the same pinch maneuver against Strav. The Hungarian grabbed Strav's saddlecloth while the Japanese threw a punch at Strav's head. Strav did something that made the Hungarian double over in the saddle, and Fast Talker drove ahead.

The racers rounded the curve and drew their bows. Riders were at their most vulnerable when shooting, with no hands on their reins or horse, and Eric held his breath. The first pass had been straight-on shots at targets, but now that they were better spaced, the riders added long forward and approach shots, to Eric's eye a fine geometric rain of angles. Strav hit the first two dummies and was aiming at the third when the Turk kicked at Fast Talker's eyes. The horse shied and Strav lurched from the saddle, barely hanging onto the pommel for the endless curve; he finally swung his legs forward so his feet hit the speeding ground with a timed bounce that sprung him back into the saddle. The officers went nuts, banging their fists and spilling beer. But Eric saw Strav's bow lying in the dust.

Down the backstretch, two Kazakh brothers accidentally locked saddles and had a slugfest at twenty-five miles an hour, while the Hungarian and the Turk tried to scrape off the Japanese rider on the rail. Strav caught up with the Turk, faked a grab for the reins and went for the bow, hitting the Turk's face with the stolen weapon and toppling him to the green. The Turk staggered up, spitting loam, and gave the crowd a woozy grinning "Huzzah!" The crowd roared back. The new bow seemed to suit Strav fine, and he hit all five kills that pass.

By the fourth shooting pass, six riders were left and the horses were near exhaustion. The blue silk Kazakh needed two more kills, and Strav three. The saffron flag marking a finish lap was ready to fly, the crowds howling and stamping so that Eric thought the wooden stands might splinter. But the Kazakh trio closed ranks and created a flying wedge to prevent Strav from passing. Both Strav and the brother hit the first and second targets; his fifteen kills complete, the Kazakh took off like a missile for the finish lap, while his brothers tangled with Strav, disrupting his third and fourth shots.

The crowd was confused as Strav seemed to give up and accelerated past the fifth target without forcing his last chance. The two brothers fell back as Strav's position grew hopeless, and they had just raised their arms in victory when Strav stood in the stirrups, the fabric of his trousers whipping as in a gale, twisting around for a backward shot at the receding target. The arrow hit the tunic at a fraction of an angle, and stuck.

The rest was a ground-swallowing chase to pandemonium in the stands, Strav and the blue Kazakh each poured flat with their faces pressed into the manes, their bodies stretching and contracting as one with their animals. Fast Talker found a new velocity, and pulled a neck ahead to cross the finish line.

Stable boys poured screeching onto the track like antic monkeys. The clubhouse officers shouted and pounded each other's backs. Eric stood in a sweat, wondering if his galloping heart was excitement or another coronary. Fast Talker came to a walk with his flanks heaving. Strav leaned over the horse's neck and spoke in his ear. The other riders, even the injured, loped back and forth along the rail, saluting the screaming crowd and having the time of their lives.

Strav dismounted, his deel and face caked with dirt, his eyes on one face in the stands. Eric realized that while he had forgotten about Alex, Strav had not.

Strav vaulted the rail and sprinted up the aisle. Alex looked just as wild, but also singed with despair, and Eric understood a resistance finally breached. She was knocked over by the rushing crowd, her pink balloon turned buoy in a rough sea. Strav dove after her. From his vantage, Eric saw their kissing so hot and frantic it seemed he might get the full show right there.

In the rush of anger, Eric saw every manipulation laid bare: Strav provoking his fight with Alex at the banquet, exposing him with Atlanta, stalling in Abad, advising him not to speak his heart— *men of few words*, and a. He's trying to ruin us, Alex had warned him, but he had refused to listen, the backstabbing traitor with his beautiful smile and horses and words. Eric was going to kill him.

First, he had to get past Chow, who stood cross-armed in his way. The quiet courage of his stance deflated Eric's rage. He was conscious of his earthbound self, as heavy and lumbering as a bear, thick with inarticulate loss, a fool beyond all reckoning and deeply ashamed.

Eric headed up to the exits, looking back just once. Uuganbayer stood amid the celebration, watching him intently. The mal-dor raised a hand in greeting, and Eric turned his back.

15

Alex found the most exclusive beauty salon in International and told them she had to be drop-dead tonight, irresistible. They straightened her hair so it fell to her waist in a dark waterfall, gave her nail extensions, makeup, and a beaded clutch to go with the shimmering blue gown that Suzanne had bought her in Prosperity. It felt like a sin to use that gift tonight, but she'd get over it.

Still, it took three burning slugs from the AK-47 bottle before she owned the creature in her bathroom mirror—kohl-lined eyes and red lips, faux gemstone necklace between barely covered breasts, a flawless finish, as if the old Alex had been airbrushed away. Tonight she channeled Atlanta's spirit, that feline confidence and power of her sexuality. Alex remembered Atlanta paused mid-pump and full glory atop Eric. Alex mimicked the cool eyebrow arch in the mirror. Nailed it. Thank you, Eric Burton, for that invaluable education. Thank you, Patrick Tashen, for showing me how to walk away. Thank you, Strav Beki, your fake Naadam today an exemplar of emotional manipulation. Well, the list was long and her bottle short.

The thought of Strav threw her back to the racetrack, just hours ago, the sudden weight of his body on hers, the salt blood of his mouth, the violent craziness of their need for each other. "Tonight," he had whispered before mobbing fans pulled him away. She had stumbled out of the stadium and right into a g-screen.

For seven years she had managed her anger, a suppression so ingrained she had become inured to the effort required. But now she sliced off one head and two grew back, an accelerating revolt against—*everything*, the men who loved her only because they knew nothing about her, fathers who bailed on their daughters, emaciated men digging graves in the epitome of abject helplessness. Let the universe beat up and toy with her; it was her decision, her *choice* to never hurt like this again.

That meant evading Strav this night. She had called Danny Yang, and it soon seemed the princeling's very own idea for his particular friend, the Wolf Khan, to join an illustrious group of fans for an overnight cruise on his yacht on the Bund.

"You have to go," she had told Strav when he called with the frustrating news. "We need the Council votes. I'll see you tomorrow, Envoy."

Alex took another slug, and waited for Patrick's nightly appearance. But nothing, a non-corporeal vote of disgust. A final hit for courage, and she left for Jacob's party.

Strav called as her car entered the weeping willow drive of the northside estates. Alex checked that his signal was moving at six knots up the Huangpu River. She had hacked her own signal to show it fixed in her Gasthaus room. The trick wouldn't fool Eric for a nanosecond, but then Eric had clearly forgotten about her. Strav would never figure it out.

"Are you in bed yet?" Strav asked.

"Working on it." Her dress was so low in the back that her skin stuck to the car's plastic seat. "How's the yachting life?"

"It's the pleasure barge of Kublai Khan." He described the mahogany decks and brass fittings, the sweet brackish smell of the night breeze off the river. When they hung up, he sent a shot of the shore lights sliding in the dark, as lovely as dew on a spiderweb.

The car arrived at a Moroccan-style *riad* set in acres of woods. There was no avoiding a g-screen for a Solidarity event. She accepted the swab with reckless certainty. She passed.

Jacob greeted her in a white dress uniform with gold braid epaulets. He did a gratifying double take at her approach.

"My, my, Dr. Tashen," he said, his pleasure and arousal as bracing as another drink. "I do believe you are the most beautiful woman in International."

Whether it was true did not matter, because she believed it. The guests were gathered in the courtyard, the mosaic fountains strewn with rose petals, the two stories of internal balconies set with filigreed wooden screens. Women in sequined gowns kissed each other's proffered cheeks, their laughter weaving a tinkling pattern in the citrus-scented night. And wasn't Jacob eager to introduce her around? A beautiful woman on the arm was such invaluable currency for a man.

For the first time, she was the hunter, the room a field of prey, and she understood the thrill of the chase. Champagne with the Solidarity Chief, a thoughtful woman who sought her opinion as an Economics Fellow. Champagne with the gold mine of a Science Deputy, from Lubbock, of all places, in charge of new g-screen tech. The sense of gracing every room, entrancing men and women alike, bestowing the favor of a laugh or a smile. She realized she had not spilled a drink this night, nor broken a glass or tripped in her heels.

The less she cared, the more she was desired, and wasn't that the way of the world?

Jacob stepped away for a call. Alex chatted up an arms industrialist who reeked of gin and talked to her chest. His wife came to pry him away. "Nice that Jacob has female entertainment," she said, with a look that turned Alex's dress to cellophane. "He and his ex-wife were both war orphans, and she ended up in a resident psych ward. That family has suffered enough."

The couple left, but the sharp pinch remained. Alex looked for the next stranger to target. She spotted a flashy, half-naked young woman with glazed eyes and a politician's smile, a cheap piece of work held together with glitter glue. Alex nodded, and not until the nod was returned did she realize she was looking in a mirror.

Jacob appeared behind her and put his hands on her waist. This was moving too fast, but what was fast when your threescore and ten was measured in days. "Let's get some air," she said.

The lawn behind the house was strung with festive lights that stretched as a twinkling spiderweb in the dark. The lights seemed familiar, but she was too jazzed with champagne to remember. The wind was alive and a perfect body temperature. She spread her arms wide, and the wind streamed over the exposed tender skin of her sides like liquid velvet, the most sensual thing she had ever felt. Jacob exhaled sharply. She ran ahead through the back woods. The trail led to a guest bungalow, a four-poster bed visible through the window. The porch rail was entwined with night-blooming jasmine, the perfume thick enough to taste. Fireflies flickered in the sheltering branches by a picnic table.

"Back in Texas, I'd catch fireflies in jelly jars," she told Jacob when he caught up. "It was fun to watch beneath the sheets." She hadn't meant it as a line, but what the hell.

"I used to catch red lily beetles. An invasive species."

"The guizi of beetles! Excellent training for your career." Jacob opened the cottage door and pulled her close. His urgent stiffening pressed against her stomach, and she was excited too, maybe at her own daring, or because he was gorgeous and she was heated, who cared why, the anger needed release. They kissed, a man's warm mouth on hers. Flesh was turning out to be fairly interchangeable stuff.

A firefly sparked bright from the dark of the picnic table. The spark turned to struck match, and a cupped handful of light illuminated Strav's face. He was in a tuxedo, with his hair slicked back, a refined, silent figure contemplating the flame.

Alex broke away from Jacob and into a sense of free fall. She knew why the lights behind the manor looked familiar. They were the lights in the photo that Strav had sent, supposedly from the yacht. He had suspected her evasion from the start, and she had failed to consider that here in International, he had Diplomatic intelligence to outgame her. He got himself on the guest list too, and watched from the screened balcony to see how far she would go. Now he knew.

A gust of wind blew out the flame. "Bloody hell," said Strav, a circle back to where they had started—a dark deck, a lit match, first lies.

She knew his stillness was far more dangerous than any loud scene. But the champagne was spinning the moment from unbelievable to ludicrous. "New tux, Envoy? Love the satin lapels. You look quite the secret agent."

202 **EDGE OF THE KNOWN WORLD**

"And you look like the whore that you are."

Her eyes welled up as from a punch. "Shut your fucking trap, Beki," said Jacob—oh strange new world, that Jacob should be her defender. "Don't you get tired of playing Eric's honor guard? Come on, you want a piece of me?"

Strav came at Jacob with a coiled animal grace. Alex threw herself in front of Jacob. "Don't," she cried at Strav. "Think of his twins, they need their father."

Jacob made a scoffing noise that faded as he took in their faces.

Strav stopped with great effort. "I can understand why you want her," he told Jacob. "Sex with the spice of retribution, a chance to sabotage the Commission Report. But do you understand why she wants you?"

"You have no right," Alex said. "No right."

"Brilliant. I thought I'd met my match in guile, but I'm a mere piker compared to her. She's using us all. Here's the pattern. Your relationship starts with an apparent coincidence or fortuitous meeting. Then she employs some device that earns your trust and puts you in her debt. All the while, she is a thief, on the prowl for whatever she wants from you. When she gets it, she uses you to move on to bigger game. How did it play out with you, Jacob? Did she ingratiate herself with your family, come bearing gifts for the children?" Jacob's expression hardened, and Strav pressed in. "She used your girls? Now that's low. The question is, why would she target a Director in Solidarity? Can't say I know. But then, it isn't my home and career."

Lies, Alex wanted to say, but it was like looking in that mirror— her, and yet not her. Jacob gave her a look she could not read—regret? admiration?—and he walked away, taking with him any last chance of warning Patrick.

"I think you just killed me," she told Strav in a daze.

"It would take a stake through the heart to kill you. Whore."

The threads of reality stretched thin and taut. "Whore. There's an insult, coming from the hypocrite famous for freeloading off his oligarch's prostitutes. Think I don't know about the sex games? What language you yell when you come? Everyone knows."

He turned a nauseous pale. "I would have been faithful to you. I'm not like Eric."

"No, you are nothing like Eric. Nothing like my father. They are good men."

"Your father?" It was a twisted smile. "Your father isn't anything. You think he is alive. I've known it since Abad. But I checked every record. He was on that plane. He's a pile of desiccated skin and bone on a mountainside."

Alex felt a snap in her head; had she once comforted this man with talk of his bloodlines to the Khan? Those were also the generals who razed cities, watched in pitiless calm as every woman and child was butchered. Maybe blood really did tell.

"Your father did things to you, didn't he?" said Strav. "He made you a whore, and then he died. You will always be alone."

"Stop." The disconnect was speeding up now; she put her hands to her head.

"It's because of Chullun," Strav said.

"What?" She looked up; his eyes were crazy with pain.

"What they did to me in Croatia. That's why you don't want me."

The last threads snapped. "You *know* that's not true!" she screamed. "You *know* that I want you! But what I *need* is for you to be my friend, God, no one has ever needed a friend more, I begged you, but no, it's about the big conquest. You can't even imagine I have reasons that have nothing to do with you. No, blame Chullun because it's all about your suffering, everything else is a footnote to the Great Strav Beki Story. Everything!"

The last word was a pure animal howl. She tore at her hair; no one could feel this rage and self-loathing and not burst into flame.

"You make me sick," she said, swaying on her feet. "You are Narcissus, the most selfish, vain, egotistical person I ever met. A year ago, you wanted your wife, your *wife*, and now she is some embarrassing peasant to you. Eric? Eric loves you more than anyone has the right to be loved, he would do *anything* for you, and you try to steal the woman he loves. And me? You think strutting around a racetrack in front of your adoring fans is about *me*? The truth is, you would use me to heal those psychic wounds, until one day you'd remember your precious family honor, your wife and parents, and the sister counting on you to get her out. And then, because you have to get everything you want, you would make me your *er'mai*, and I would get to watch you come and go home to your family and your *children* until you left me for your next obsession. No thank you, if I'm going to be a whore, I'll do it on my terms. *My choice*."

Not that she had any choices left. She heard her own rapid shallow breath, but from a growing distance, a curious numb retreat that felt like—nothing. She studied her hands and could have snapped off each finger as if it were dead with frostbite. Wonderful nothing.

She turned her study to Strav. He looked like a map she had folded up wrong. And she wondered that he had ever moved her to passion, or grief, or anything.

"You are dead to me, understand?" she said. One goal had been to protect him by severing their connection; in that, at least, the night was a raging success. "Come near me again, and I'll tell Eric how his beloved brother has been trying to fuck me."

She walked out the willow drive, toward the bejeweled ribbon of the avenue. The night wind whipped the long branches and snaked her hair about her face. The voices whispered, calling. Alex followed. When nothing mattered anymore, the future held no terrors. Finally, she was free.

16

The noise was insistent, *bang*, a white marble hand on the Legion floor, *bang*, the gavel at his court-martial, *bang*, dredging him from the sludge layer of sleep. Eric opened an eye. He had gone from the stadium to his apartment and crashed face down in bed. The clock said 1:00 a.m., which explained his stiff neck and the drool crust on his pillow. *Bang, bang* on his door. Eric opened it to sway murderously over a terrified aide.

There had been a bombing, in International. And he had slept through it.

Eric found Chow at the site. The car bomb had sheared off the four-story face of the VA Building, exposing the mangled honeycomb of offices and restaurants. Helicopters roared overhead and sliced the darkness with searchlights. Rescue workers clambered with search dogs and infrareds. The larger destruction didn't register as much as the details. A billboard melted to a glistening skin. A weeping man surrounded by yellow petals. Everything smelled of coffee.

"It's the same pattern as the Legion," Eric told Chow—a cultural hub, a bomb timed to minimize casualties and maximize insecurity. "It's another false-flag attack by Solidarity to stop the Independence vote."

Chow reached a calming, beefy hand to Eric's shoulder, and told him to check on Alex—she'd been walking up the avenue when the bomb went off, and helped the first responders with triage before disappearing.

Eric checked Alex's signal. Her location showed at the Gasthaus, but the coordinates were blatantly hacked. He followed the corrected reading through the dark trails of the park and into the Tomb of the Missing. The air was chill in the dim concrete maze, the din of waterfalls replacing the sirens. A blue dress lay as a tropical splash on the slick passageway. Eric started running.

He stopped at the Memory Pool, the hair standing up on the back of his neck.

Alex sat waist-deep in the black water, her knees drawn up to her chest. The bleaching fluorescent light showed that she was blue with cold. The holographic images of shadowed faces swarmed and schooled and touched off her naked body like silvered fish, slipping below the inky surface and rising anew in their countless numbers.

"You found me," she said, her words thick and slow.

"I'll always find you, bug."

"No," she said. "You won't."

Eric and Alex moved as a unit about his kitchen, Eric in his boxers, frying eggs, Alex in his terry robe that dragged behind her like a train. The darkness outside lightened to a purplish stain. He had wrapped her in his shirt and commandeered a car to his apartment, stripped them both and held her close beneath thick covers, her skin like an ice burn, her nipples little rocks against his chest, until he was sweating rivers and she was back up to 98.6. Yet even with her recovery, Eric felt like she was missing.

He kissed her as a test. Ran a hand around her bum, everything that two weeks ago had reduced her to quivering ecstasy. Now she was fine letting him do whatever. He tied her robe back up. She buttered his rye toast.

"I was at the racetrack yesterday," he said. "Saw Strav's show. You and him."

"Oh." She fixed him with great solemn eyes. "I am sorry. It was a heat-of-the-moment thing. A one-time mistake."

"Not for him. How long has the motherfucker been after you?"

"Nothing happened, or ever will. We fought at a party last night and we said things. Unforgivable things. He'll never even talk to me again."

"Strav not talk? Maybe when he's dead." Even then, Eric wouldn't bet on it. He took in the smudged eye makeup that made her look like a lemur. "A party?"

"A Solidarity party. Strav caught me kissing Jacob Kotas."

"Not. Funny." But her eyes were empty; this was a face that was never going to tease or laugh again. "Jacob?" Eric said in disbelief. "*Why?*"

"Why? Why did you do Atlanta?" Eric grimaced. "No," she continued, "you don't think about that. Such an amazing capacity to compartmentalize. The rest of us are not so lucky." She matched a red fingernail to the crimson tablecloth. "Because I was angry at you, because I was flattered, because I needed to derail things with Strav, because I drank too much and things got out of hand."

He sensed the truth, if not the whole truth. This was his fault too, for leaving Jacob the open move. At least he had one jigger of satisfaction: oh, what brute justice for Strav.

"Listen up, bug. Jacob is dangerous. The muggers in Abad were Solidarity agents. That's all I can tell you now."

"How could he—? He *likes* me."

"You talked about evil once. That's what it looks like." She followed him into the bathroom and sat on the toilet lid to watch him shower. He dried off, cleared the mirror with the flat of his fist, squeezed a dollop of cinnamon toothpaste on his toothbrush and handed it to Alex. He shaved, she brushed, and Eric was caught by the surreal intimacy of the scene—as if they were any normal couple, doing normal morning routines, talking this and that about the coming day.

"I'm leaving," she said. "I took a field research post in the Alemão."

Eric paused his razor, unsure of his hand. The Alemão was an RDZ, Remote Disaster Zone. They made Abad look like the petting zoo. "And us?"

"I can't be with anyone. I'm not free."

"Jesus Christ, bug. You mean there's *another* guy?"

That got a ghost of a smile. "That's all I can tell you now." Damn little he could say to that. "Now you listen up, Eric Burton. This is not Strav's fault."

He scraped too fast and sliced his chin, a crimson bud diffusing pink through the white lather. Alex sighed. "Strav and I met at the Kommandant's, before we knew who the other was. He fixated on me—no, on the *idea* of me. I represented what he lost in Croatia. He tried everything to fight it. To drive me off, to make you send me away, to be a brother. Then Abad—happened."

Memories of Strav's behavior rose in an uncomfortable shift of perspective. What had seemed like stratagems of betrayal now read as self-defense, even cries for help: Strav's initial cruelty to Alex, setting her up at the banquet, begging him, Eric, to go to Abad—*This is a mistake, anda. If she is yours, you should go.* And he had responded by throwing Strav after her time and time again, so he could focus on his career.

"You've been in denial too, Eric. Deep down you knew Strav was in self-destruct. I'm leaving. He'll go back to his wife and have a dozen children and think of me as a momentary insanity. Forgive him. He would forgive you anything."

Eric stuck tissue on his cut. His face in the steamy mirror looked like one of the Easter Island heads. "I don't know him anymore."

"You want the Strav from before Croatia. He's not."

"Enough!" He nearly punched the mirror. "Nothing to do with Croatia. He doesn't remember it."

"He remembers everything."

Eric numbly wiped down the sink. He laid out a fresh uniform, then sat on the bed, his head in his hands. Just when you thought your heart could not break any more, there it went.

"Strav told me in Abad," she said. She sat beside him. "He's ashamed, Eric. So ashamed. And platitudes about survivor's guilt and victimhood don't help, because he's not wrong. He's supposed to be this wunderkind diplomat. Instead, he got played by an uneducated thug, and missed an opportunity to get hostages released. We may not see him as a tool of the Beijing overlords subjugating the minority regions, but he understands those who think a public gang rape and crucifixion are exactly what he deserves. It's all mixed up in his head. But if it went public, it's his sanity, his career, his life. You saved him, Eric."

Eric missed a breath. "Don't worry," she said. "Strav has no idea about the cover-up."

Sirens raced by in post-terror frenzy. "How can you know?"

"I grew up in a penal clinic," she reminded him. "The body bears witness, my father said. I knew the doctors would never miss the earlier bone fractures and gut injuries of a prisoner brutalized like that. Yet the medical chart describes all trauma as secondary to the explosion. I thought about how you hacked the images from the Legion, to protect me. You were at Strav's hospital in Croatia. You must have convinced the head doctor that news of a rape would be too sensational to control—why save him in surgery to kill him with that?"

She held up Eric's shirt, got his arms in the sleeves. "You altered the records. The investigation closed, and Strav didn't remember, a blessing. So you could forget, too. Until the video surfaced. That's the problem with cover-ups. You have to keep covering."

Eric looked at her in mute flummox. Her eerie detachment was a boon.

"Chullun told Strav he was live streaming the abuse," she said. "The streaming part was a lie, to break him. But the blinking camera light was real. Chullun must have been recording for later use." She buttoned Eric's cuffs. "I checked the case evidence log. A camera with encrypted memory was found in the Croatia debris six weeks after the explosion. The file was downloaded to Forensics, maybe evidence to reopen the case. But when they cracked the encryption, the memory had been erased. Yup. You. It cost you, though. What went wrong?"

He appreciated her handing him a direct proof to finish. The logic gave him a voice. "Chow called me when the file came in. I told him I had to see it before anyone else. He violated policy and gave me the access codes. That's a friend. I watched the recording. I couldn't—" He could not describe the sense of being there with Strav but powerless to fight or help his brother. He was made accomplice by his own passive witness, a torture in its own right.

"It should have been a quick erase," he said. "But I was too shook, kept fucking it up. One of the Forensics officers logged in. In three minutes, he would see my breach, and game over. So I went old school. Ran down to his office and knocked the crap out of him." Considering his state of mind, it was pure luck he hadn't killed the poor bastard. "Went back with my three minutes. Finished and sealed it up."

Sealed it, straightened his immaculate desk, and waited for security to arrive. Eric had anticipated the court-martial. He could have never anticipated an Independence crusade, or a Solidarity vendetta, or a heart broken in two different ways.

Alex stroked his tie like it needed comfort. "Oh, Eric. What a choice to face."

"No, bug. The tough choices are where you don't have enough information. I had everything I needed."

"Thank you." He understood her speaking for Strav, who would never know.

"Wasn't just me," said Eric, thinking of the complicit silence of the doctors, and Chow, and the others who must have known or suspected. He still couldn't believe it worked—conspiracies, especially kind ones, so rarely did.

"Do you love him?" he asked.

The ghost smile returned. "It's *Strav*. How long did *you* resist him?" Not long, Eric had to admit. "I love you too," she added, a simple fact.

He took her back to the Gasthaus and tucked her into bed. Alex's eyes followed him with the question of forgiveness. The answer remained no. Strav had suffered greatly, but that served to reveal a man's underlying character. He was done.

Eric's control room was waiting for him, a world that obeyed the laws of physics and where every question had an answer that was ultimately right or wrong. He moved from station to station with his team, tweaking Netcast displays and immune simulations.

He soon had an elegant solution to an entanglement that was blocking his geotag. Instead of the pleasure due, the achievement brought steely satisfaction, and nothing he cared to share. Here was the truth he had known when he was very young: that people came and went, and it didn't matter, because you lived deep inside the space of your own thoughts. He had forgotten how to be alone.

So he would learn again. The problem was in the pit of his stomach, an angry gnawing that was either hunger or desolation. He opted for hunger. He sent his freaky genius teenage coder to fetch a double cheeseburger and monster fries, bring it back hot or die. She returned instead with a parchment sealed with melted red wax and Uuganbayer's signature Chinggis stamp.

His team was enthralled, the paper missive emanating an authority that obliterated any screen. Eric crumpled the parchment and made a three-pointer to the trash. The note waited while remnants of his pride wrestled with the respect due the old mal-dor. It was not a fair fight.

The note was written in Cyrillic, but Eric need not have spent half his life struggling with Mongolian to translate the five words. *Come. He is your brother.*

17

It was late afternoon, but the Happy Valley Racetrack had the bleary anticlimax of a nasty morning after. The lurid battle paintings were gone, banners stripped from the sky, enemy dummies turned into piles of straw. Eric cut across the green with cold military bearing. The prayer flag stood lifeless in its cairn, no wind horse to carry the mantras and blessings. Eric made a reflex obeisance before he could stop himself.

Uuganbayer was in the stables checking Fast Talker's front knees. The stallion pricked up his ears at Eric's approach, shifting his weight from ankle to ankle as delicately as a ballerina. Eric stopped a careful distance from the big square teeth inside that velvet muzzle. Fast Talker responded by lifting his tail to dump a steaming load.

Uuganbayer pointed to where, only yesterday, Alex stood in the stands. "Your woman?"

Eric said nothing. Uuganbayer grunted, and Eric had an uncomfortable insight about brothers and lovers being the oldest story in the book.

"Come," ordered Uuganbayer. They led the horse through the bustling village, the muck and straw clumping on Eric's good shoes. Stable boys pushed carts of debris from last night's carouse in the barn. From the clink of glass in the burlap sacks, it must have been a doozy.

They tied Fast Talker to the stone water trough outside the barn. The horse slurped noisily, getting a good snort and spray of cold water in Eric's face. Two blacksmiths stood watch at the doors like guards of the Sultan's treasure. Inside, the sun spilled as honey through the warped planks and knotholes, lighting the airborne particles of sweet-smelling straw.

Uuganbayer stopped at a loose bale of hay. "Oh Lordy," said Eric.

Strav lay asleep in the hay, naked but for a horsehair blanket thrown over his middle. His knuckles were split and bruised, his filthy face puffy and tracked with tears, a bottle of rotgut Chinggis whiskey cradled to his chest. Eric hadn't thought anything could be more pathetic than Alex shivering in the Memory Pool, yet once again Strav had succeeded in the art of one-upmanship.

Strav's bottle was down to the dregs, a feat for a guy who never touched a beer. Eric dropped to Strav's side in a fright to check for breathing.

Did the anda think him a murderer? Uuganbayer demanded. Of course he'd watered down the bottle before giving it to Strav.

Eric sat back in relief. He didn't want Strav dead—just hungover enough to wish he were. Judging from the bright stack of silver dollars on the floor, the Wolf Khan had been deadly in the wager matches the night before. Eric could imagine the grappling, straining bodies by lantern light, the roaring, red-faced crowd, Strav swilling and staggering until Uuganbayer called it a night. Uuganbayer must have stayed to clean Strav up after the invariable mess—judging from the stink, probably had to burn those clothes—and to protect Strav from shame.

None of which was his concern anymore. "Strav can call me tomorrow."

"No. He can't." Uuganbayer tossed him Strav's phone to read. Strav had submitted his resignation from TaskForce last night, a respectful letter written while sober. He'd also purchased a train ticket to the Khanate border, departing this evening.

It was a one-way ticket in every sense. The moment Strav crossed the border with his visa revoked, the tenuous passage between worlds closed for good. Strav would never get out again, and he, Eric, would never get in.

Eric looked up at the right angles of the rafters, the long fading spokes of light. It was possible for him to break with Strav, knowing it would never last. It was not possible that Strav would leave *him*.

The sunbeam on Strav's torso highlighted the sheen of surgical scars, the results of Eric's conferences with people in white coats who had held no clear answers. The doctors had thrown him the owner's manual to Strav's broken body, a frantic page-flipping education in the mandible, genitourinary structures, thoracic vertebrae—he knew more about Strav's machine than his own. Eric thought of the deal he had made with God, or the devil, for his brother's life. Now he wondered if his bill was yet paid, and the nature of the debt still due.

On a silent count, Eric heaved Strav up, bare-assed as he was, each of Eric's sadly unconditioned muscles screaming against the 185-pound deadweight in his arms. He carried Strav out past the shocked palace guards and threw him like an anchor into the cold water trough. Strav came up in a flailing wave, coughing and saucer-eyed.

"Wake the hell up," Eric told him. "You are such a fucking idiot."

Eric shot baskets in the hoop below the hayloft while waiting for Strav to emerge from Uuganbayer's cottage. He went at the rim with fury, a maelstrom of hay coating his hair and sifting down his collar. By the time Strav appeared, freshly showered and in a blue work shirt and jeans, Eric was a dripping, itching mess. He passed the ball to Strav.

Strav let the ball roll away. He had small broken blood vessels under his eyes from vomiting but otherwise looked fine. Whatever Uuganbayer's hangover cure was, Eric wanted some. The problem was the stillness in Strav's eyes; no sign of embarrassment, or grief, or any other expression, like seeing the stars snuffed out in a blazing night sky. Eric realized he'd seen the same flat affect and apathy in Alex today. It was as eerie as dealing with twins.

"What the hell, bud?" said Eric. Strav thought him a terrible liar, but Croatia had provided Eric a crash course in the art. A good lie, like a sketch, was a matter of drawing the eye and mind to where they already wanted to go. He and Strav were both prime examples, Eric supposed, of seeing what you want to believe.

"It's hard to explain," said Strav.

"That's my line," said Eric. "Try using your words."

"Everyone who said I would fail on the Outside was correct. You are the finest man I know. I never deserved you as my anda." Strav bowed his respect. "Forgive my cowardice. I did not know how to say goodbye. But I will be on that train."

The last of Eric's denial disappeared, replaced by a train speeding north. He would never ride the ocean of summer grasses again, or tease The Bat. His name would remind Strav of a life achieved, then lost, of dreams pulled out by the roots. The silence between them would stretch through the decades and bury them as strangers.

"I won't be with the family either," said Strav, as if that might ease the incalculable loss. "I'm toxic. I'll winter alone." Eric's confusion gained a color of panic. Only outcasts wintered on the steppe alone, a minus-forty-degree death sentence for all but the luckiest and most experienced hunters. Strav had not done a steppe winter since he was twelve.

The track was shutting down, the horses calling to each other as they threaded the rutted paths to their stables. But Eric was in an unknown land. The one constant in his life was Strav, the Strav who swung back at every punch the predatory universe could throw a man. For Strav to give up meant there were no fixed stars, no magnet pull to bring him home.

"Alex can handle my Council speech," Strav was saying. "But you must take care of her."

"I've got Alex covered."

"Do you now?" said Strav. "Then you are aware that she is a raging alcoholic. She hides the vodka bottle under her bed, but check her closet too. Look for guns while you're at it. She sees and talks to ghosts. Don't let on, just keep her safe while she's distracted. She refuses to believe that her father died. Our Commission was her ticket to Asia to search for him. Let it play out, then build a memorial to show he is remembered. Gershwin in the shower means she's happy. She needs a story to get to sleep at night, preferably from the classics. And she doesn't want you to know she's a virgin. Be gentle, and don't embarrass her."

Eric remained open-mouthed while Strav handed him his watch and phone, artifacts of a world he could not take where he was going. "Be well, my brother," Strav said quietly. "Ride easy."

Fast Talker kicked in his stall as Strav passed without stopping. The horse whinnied after him, a piercing trumpet of hurt that jolted Eric to clarity. He had all the information he needed.

He caught up with Strav on the green. "The VA got bombed while you were shit-faced last night. Don't know why, but Alex was there."

Strav leached of color and swayed. Eric sat him down on the cairn of rocks. "She's okay. But she's not. She requested a transfer to Alemão. Yeah, you heard me. You two fought last night. What could you have said to get her so whacked?"

"I called her a whore, and accused her of incest with her father."

"Oh. That might do it."

A warm evening breeze lifted the rags of prayer flag like bird wings. Strav covered his face and groaned, a deep gut-wrenching summation of the unspeakable year, and his shoulders racked and heaved as he wept. Eric sat with an arm around him until the worst of the storm passed.

"Alex is a challenge," said Eric. A twitch of work shirt showed that Strav was listening. "She may spend time in la-la land, but Alex takes care of Alex. Or did, until you broke her. I thought you were crazy in love with her."

Strav gave him a sidelong look of terror and fell off the cairn.

"Jesus, bud, you think I didn't know? You've been an open book since San Francisco." Eric figured these to be the most ridiculous words uttered since mankind invented speech, a transparent salvage of pride, yet Strav looked at him with nothing but guilt-ridden amazement. *Oh, come on!* Eric wanted to shout. But the mind went where it already wanted to go.

"Sure, I knew about you two," said Eric. "Why else would I have screwed around with Atlanta? Or sent you to Abad? Like I'm that stupid."

"But—you love her."

"Yeah, I love The Bat too. Told you Alex reminds me of her. I don't want Alex ending up in an Alemão landfill. You need to fix this."

Strav circled the cairn clockwise by habit, furiously drying his face. "Alex needs a reason to stay." Faster circling, a feverish glow. "Oh, anda, would that I were that reason!"

It was like watching the ignition point of a fusion reaction, and a thousand suns back online. Eric sat back to admire his best hack ever.

"But my marriage," said Strav. "Beijing. The Elders. How can I make this work?"

"You can't," Eric said in complete honesty.

"I will find a way," Strav declared.

Eric lay on the green long after Strav sped off to cancel his resignation. The grass hued emerald in the last rays of sun. Uuganbayer brought out Fast Talker with the colts, a sign of respect, and night fell in appreciative silence.

Eric had made his choice, re-upped with the devil, and now it was up to Strav. Whatever pain might result was a problem for another day. The mal-dor hummed and oiled a saddle; the horses grazed free. Eric squinted the stadium lights into stars, and it was any fine night on the steppe.

18

Alex sat on her studio's balcony, watching the stars come out over the dark ocean of the park. When the city went to sleep, she took paper and pencil to write a letter.

Hi Poppa,

I need to tell you how things ended, but I haven't seen you since the bad night. So I'm taking a page, so to speak, from the Confession you wrote in your lab notebooks. I don't have invisible ink, but erasure is secured by a single match. A paper letter! What a great system. Someone should have invented it a long time ago.

Remember when I broke my arm doing Icarus off the roof? You numbed my arm, and the pain went away. That's what my brain feels like, a relieved nothing bliss. I can think straight for the first time in seven years. The Alemão is perfect. When your Netcast comes, I'll be far away from everyone I've tainted. And I'll go out as an intrepid researcher in an RDZ instead of a lab rat in a you-know-what Chamber.

We always wanted to see the Amazon, right? Especially those amazing fish that live in puddles in the rainforest canopy, a hundred feet off the dark forest floor. Ain't nature grand?

Enough hem and haw. Just tell a story.

Once upon a time a few hours ago, a young postdoc received a summons to the Secretariat. She knew it was Strav getting creative. The postdoc refused to leave her room, and had Gasthaus security deny him entry to the building. The summons forced her out. The Secretariat Office is a gloomy museum of Prussian antiques and tapestries. His Honor, the Majordomo, Eric, and Strav were there. They stared at her feet. She had forgotten about her fluffy purple slippers.

Eric and Strav exchanged a meaningful look. The postdoc figured that Eric had used something to keep Strav here. She now understood that the something was a someone. Oh, Eric.

The Majordomo spoke about how the VA bombing affirmed Solidarity's position against Independence, blah-de-blah. The postdoc had no time for idiot speechifying, so she nailed him with hard data projections on the violence should Independence be denied. "Cancel the vote," she told them, "and it's a total goat rodeo."

She and Eric were dismissed, with Strav held back to explain about goat rodeos.

"I know you love your brother," the postdoc told Eric, like explaining things to a giant man-child. "But you can't just give me to him. It doesn't work that way."

Eric was still cogitating a response in the atrium. I pulled out your Bulfinch. I told Eric that you called it the thinking man's bible. It was a gift, for Eric to read to his child someday.

Eric bowed his head. From the postdoc's angle, the humongous globe rested on his weary shoulder. She did not like that. She checked his big ticker.

"Take care of yourself," she said. "And be careful. When Solidarity catches the Hacker, Jacob will become very powerful."

The ticker jacked up, and Eric trusted her with another secret. "The Hacker is smarter than Solidarity," he said. "Jacob's not catching anyone. Jacob is coming down."

Hear that, Poppa? Solidarity won't catch you. Or me.

The postdoc wandered blindly up the avenue. There were demon billboards, and lines for ice cream, but all I saw were those amazing fish in the sunlit rainforest canopy, caught high between Heaven and Earth. There is no way to explain their improbable adaptation, or survival, yet they are up there swimming.

It seems Strav was following close, because he knocked over a bike messenger who called me a bad word. Strav asked, very courtly, if he could see me safe to my room. Fine.

Some joker had hit every button in the elevator, so it was a long ride to the seventeenth floor. My flight for the Alemão left in seven hours. Alternatively, a fall from my balcony would take 3.8 seconds, impact velocity 84 mph, likely on my face. I decided to stick with the RDZ.

Strav waited as long as he could stand it. "I've spoken with Eric," he said. "Incredible, but he knew about us all along!"

"That Eric," I said. "You just can't put anything over him."

Strav came close. Even sweating, he smelled good.

"Winter on the steppe is very hard," he said. "Everyone fears the zud, the prolonged snows when animals and people starve. Spring comes with the joss, the warm wind. As a boy, I would ride out and stand up in the saddle to greet it. It smells of fertile soil and green plants. In days the ground is covered with blooms and grasses, and the land comes alive again. That's what you are. My joss."

I wished I hadn't heard what Eric said about the Hacker. I felt possibility, a chance of life in the canopy, and that brought fear again. I was afraid of being afraid.

"You could be happy enough with Eric," Strav said. "As I could be with another woman. There are likely many other people we could be happy enough with, and life would certainly be easier. But this is not a question of degrees of happiness, or being easy. We were intertwined before this life, and will be after it."

My hand floated to his face. "I have nothing to offer you," he said. "Croatia cripples me in ways I don't understand. I can't marry you until the other license is dissolved, and if Beijing or the Elders want to be spiteful, which they will, that may take years. But I promise you this. You are the only woman I will ever love. The only woman I will ever touch. I will find a path for us, and a way to give our children a name. We will grow old together, and our memories will be honored by our children's children and their children."

He had me until the end. Until the children, the golden years of birthdays and anniversaries I cannot give, the generations that can never be born.

My hand dropped, the confusion died. I was back in nothing bliss. Solidarity will miss with Netcast #2, but there will be more. G-screen tech will advance. Strav might be right about us being intertwined, belonging together beyond time. I suspect it is true.

It is also true that it does not matter.

"I am sorry," I said, and set him free. "I wish you well. Truly. But I don't love you."

He absorbed that. He bowed. He left.

End of story, Poppa.

I am sorry. I am sorry. He left. I am very tired. Did you know the pre-Columbian Amazon had temple cities with millions of people? I'll look for ruins, but the rainforest reclaims things very fast. Fight it all you want. Knock yourself out. The dark forest always wins.

I'm out, Poppa. I needed you to know that I really did try. That I miss you more than a letter can say. The last thing to go, I guess, is this wanting to say goodbye.

Go with God, Poppa. Goodbye.

Alex lit the match, and the letter curled and smoldered before popping into beautiful orange gulps of flame that she dropped into an empty flowerpot. The pages produced surprising heat and smelled of roasted marshmallows.

She carried the pot to the balcony rail overlooking the park. The ashes were powder to the touch. She fed handfuls to the wind, like a scattering at sea.

The night took the offering and sent her to bed.

19

I *don't love you.*

One a.m. in the secluded park behind the Gasthaus, the first chill, moonless night of autumn. Strav studied the pinprick constellations as he flexed and stretched in his black track pants and shirt—gym-rat ninja, he supposed—bouncing on the balls of his feet in preparation for a stealth ascent under cover of darkness. It was the glorious sky of Asian steppe and Texas plains, black oceans teeming with phosphorescent creatures.

He enjoyed Alex's what-if rambles about the reaches of space, alien worlds, and parallel existences. He enjoyed Eric's valiant lectures about the predictive science of cosmic inflation, galactic collisions, and antimatter balances that created suns. But he knew what the stars were about. These dots were dead imitations, no imagery, no poetry, no grace. They belonged to a universe out of rhythm, a vindictive place without music.

I don't love you.

In his battle strategy, the Gasthaus loomed as a vertical challenge. He was locked from all entrances; even if the desk buzzed him in, he could only pound on the door she would not open until he was dragged away, with no chance to fix the hopelessness inside her. He had felt the same way before she brought him back to life, her smile a defibrillator to the heart. Now it was his turn.

Strav sighted up the dark column of wrought-iron balconies to Alex's room on the seventeenth floor. Earlier reconnaissance showed a curved metal support brace under each deck. He now made a running jump beneath the first-story balcony and grabbed the brace. It creaked but held his hanging weight. A chin up, some hand-over-hand, and he clambered over the handrail to the deck. Reaching the second-story balcony required him to stand on the rail and make a twelve-inch vertical jump for the next brace. If he missed, he'd ricochet like a pinball down the channel of balconies. He balanced and leapt.

Fifteen stories to go.

His hands blistered, muscles screamed—amazing that no one woke up at his clatter. Here was the pleasure of pure concentration required by a physical task, the faith when the mind turns off and trusts the body. No future, no past, no doubts. Balance and leap.

A final grab, and he pitched over Alex's rail. He waited for his breathing to regulate and his arms to stop shaking. With his face pressed to the sliding glass door, he made out her contour on the white bed. Their lives seemed to pivot on balconies or decks; fitting, he supposed, for two people always on the outside, always looking in.

Strav took off his running shoes and dropped them into the void over the rail. Socks next, balled up and lobbed through the air. T-shirt over his head. The cloth fluttered on an updraft, a black dream-bird. His track pants made a *V* as they fell. Briefs off and over the rail. The air was cool knives against his skin. Faith, that Alex would understand what he was about: a scarred and desecrated man stripped of all pride and defense, at her mercy; faith that they could trust each other, and that great loss and great joy could coexist. His reflection in the glass looked carved of silver moonstone. He placed his hands over his genitals, because they looked out of place, detachable somehow. How simple life would be. Hands away, a man in full once more.

He rapped lightly on the locked sliding door. No motion from inside. But outside came a pulsing thrum—the dragonfly of a SWAT helicopter tilting over the park, a suggestion that the Tarzan-ninja thing may not have gone unmarked. The police snipers aboard would have the VA bombing fresh in mind.

Merde. A naked bloody corpse on Alex's balcony was not the high drama he had in mind. Strav pounded the glass to wake the dead.

Light burst from inside the room and pinned him in harsh illumination. Alex came shakily from the bed, her eyes blown wide open from deep dream. Strav could see through her nightgown to the dark triangle at the apex of her legs, the points of her breasts. Her hands made a supplicating gesture for him to stay calm, an effort at comical odds with the terror on her face. Terror, Strav realized with no little astonishment, because she thought he was going to jump.

Not that he was above pulling such a fantastic ploy—he really should have thought of it—but he never so much wanted to enter a building in his life. He pointed at the search beam slicing the night, tapped his chest, and watched the light go on in Alex's brain as it had in the room. She yanked the lock open and Strav hurtled inside, carrying her beneath him to the safety of the floor as the beam ran across the empty balcony and moved on.

"You do love me," Strav told her. "Say it."

She looked like a bird that had hit the glass, stunned and wild-eyed. He couldn't believe the warmth of her skin on his; he'd never felt anything more alive.

"What if you had fallen?" She was gulping air, beside herself. "It'd be eighty miles an hour. What if you'd been shot? Shot! The city is on red alert, are you insane?"

"Say it."

Her tears arrived in a helpless flood. "I can't. I can't be afraid anymore."

"You are the cleverest, bravest fighter I know. You will not give up now. You will rise up, and we will face the world together. Say it."

"I love you." She was still crying, but with a breathless catch of excitement, her hands wandering the seams where their bodies pressed together. Strav sensed he was being distracted from the intended pledges and troths, but no help for it as her fingers traced up from the straining muscles in his thigh to reach the only part of his body that, to Strav's disbelief, was not rigid and responding. Weeks of walking around in a constant state of arousal, hard as a rail at every painfully inconvenient moment, and now, with everything he desired here in his arms—nothing.

They both looked down. "You have got to be kidding me," said Strav.

A gurgling laugh came through the tears, and she kissed his eyes, his nose, his chin, covering his face with butterfly kisses and laughter, a joyous flurry that lifted the last bar of shame. He pulled off her nightgown and warmed each of her breasts with his mouth, softly at first, then sucking harder, greedy as an infant. Alex cried out as if falling, and her excitement set off an explosion in his core; the problem flipped from uncooperative flesh to the full-blown opposite of not coming on the spot, the entire universe concentrated in his need to be deep and moving inside her.

He pried away her eager hands; this was going to be slow, be perfect. "Not yet," he said, gathering her up to carry to the bed. "We have a long way to go."

"No! Now, now, right now for God's sake, before anything else happens!"

Strav wasn't about to argue, either with her or with fate. He drove between her legs, past her stifled cry and into the tight warmth of her body. And held there, knowing that the slightest motion would put him over the edge, that he could live a thousand lives, travel a thousand worlds, and nothing, nothing would ever feel this good again.

Strav stayed awake long after they went to bed, with Alex asleep on his shoulder. He played idly with her hair, spreading it over his chest as a blessing, and watched the night through the balcony window. The constellations had shifted, and everything had changed, rotating in harmony, as to music. Strav knew that stars were going nova, and galaxies colliding, and that someday the universe would collapse on itself and end. But from this window, for this single, shining moment, everything just danced.

20

In the final week's run-up to the Council Independence vote, Suzanne and Yuri took discretely separate flights to International. Suzanne drove to the cottage she kept by the park. She did not know that Alex and Strav were waiting in her kitchen for a surprise welcome. Alex and Strav did not know Suzanne's flight was early. Suzanne got a surprise, all right.

"The good news is that Strav's reproductive surgeries were a thumping success," Suzanne later told Yuri. "The bad news is that we can never eat on that counter."

After the panic of zippers and undies, Strav had sworn to Suzanne that Eric knew about the relationship and gave his blessing. Alex's quiet told Suzanne that the truth was not so simple. Eric, for his part, refused to leave his secret Daybreak Operation, perhaps to avoid his cousin's dissecting looks. Which left Suzanne uncertain whom to be happy for, to ache for, or be mad at.

Suzanne stressed to the new couple that they could not go public. Adultery between TaskForce officers was a serious violation of the morals clause, and Strav's marriage was a bubbling La Brea tar pit. Alex complied, with a public show of disinterest so convincing that Suzanne wondered if she wanted a brake on the relationship. The problem was Strav, normally the most polished of dissemblers. Whenever Alex was in the room, Strav could not keep his eyes off her. Suzanne swore she could see his pupils become vertical slits and his powerful tail sway, feel his chesty vibration to warn off rivals. Suzanne could only remind him about La Brea, and those saber-toothed skulls on display, and for God's sake to get a grip on the whole intemperate romance thing.

Not that she had the right to lecture. It was springtime in autumn, and age and experience offered no immunity. Sunday morning, Suzanne and Yuri strolled through Friendship Market with their hands touching. Antique vendors in Wolf Khan T-shirts chanted, "Very old, very old," over identical faux merchandise. The apothecary stalls were a sensory riot of ginseng root, bogus tiger bone aphrodisiacs, and neon powders. Perhaps the afternoon breeze always dispersed the charcoal smog. Or perhaps the blue sky was just for lovers.

"Who could believe?" said Yuri. For Strav had stepped up with blazing potential realized to secure the China and India bloc votes needed for Independence. If the majority of the thirty-five Delegates held true for five days until Friday's session, Colonel Bulgakov would realize the dream he never thought he'd see in his lifetime.

Springtime ended with a call from Pieter. "Are you with your young man?" Pieter asked.

Suzanne looked at Yuri. Blondes didn't weather well, and his lined face showed every rough insult of his fifty-three years. "Maybe."

"Good," said Pieter. "We need him for a funeral."

They met the Secretariat cavalcade at the green-glazed wall that had once blocked the Settlement's view of an embryonic refugee Township. Now, the Township's wooden shanties reared above the levee, making Suzanne think of an amoeba engulfing its food particle. The funeral was for the Township night workers killed in the VA explosion. Pieter was to speak. Bringing a famous face of the Independence movement to the funeral made fine political theater.

"Welcome to the family chessboard," Suzanne told Yuri.

The cavalcade was a limo and single MP escort car. No one could contest Pieter's personal courage, which drove Suzanne and his security detail to ulcers. An armada did not show goodwill, Pieter insisted. While the limo could take a small nuke, he often got out to walk among his flock.

The cars rolled through the crimson Shinto-style Heavenly Gate checkpoint and onto the Township's dirt roads. Old folks gossiped in steaming communal kitchens. Children filled water buckets at spigots by the neighborhood toilets. Teenagers gathered beneath the animated demon poster billboards, drinking beer and imitating the jerk-jerk monster dance moves.

"People cheered when we opened this refuge," said Pieter. "Now, to quote a critic, we are too content with the grandeur of our mission to perceive our status as mass jailers."

"I am honored you read my work, sir," said Yuri.

They arrived at a Pentecostal church papered with Independence posters and death portraits of the workers. The overflow crowd turned with hostile curiosity. Faces squashed against the glass, peering into the elegant viewing case. Suzanne and Yuri glanced at each other in a communion of minds.

"Abort," Suzanne instructed the drivers of both cars. "Proceed slowly. No fire."

A man in a Yankees cap yelled, "Shit-eating TaskForce dogs!" and smeared brown goo on the window. It was actual shit, realized Suzanne, and how did they get it so fast? The chant rose, "TaskForce dogs," and the exit became a seething human forest.

The limo interior brightened as they picked up speed, and people fell away. A show-off teen with a pale horsey face jogged alongside Pieter's window. The teen put a handgun to the bullet-proof glass and waved at the crowd. The MP leaned from the escort car with his rifle, deaf to Suzanne's shout to stand down, and the window turned a spray of red.

Come Monday, Strav really did leave for a two-night Huangpu River cruise with Yang and the Beijing moguls. Alex urged him to go, for the reason they could discuss: to seal the Independence vote that Friday. Strav went for the reason they could not discuss: to lay the political groundwork for his divorce. Two nights apart seemed unbearable, but he was not about to bring Alex. The yacht was the ultimate power men's club, men with an eye for beautiful things and a way of getting what they wanted. If he could not claim what was his, he could not defend what was his. No yacht cabal for Dr. Tashen.

Instead, he took Alex for a nighttime gallop on Fast Talker, holding her in front of him for a pounding hurricane with her hair streaming and Alex thrilled out of her mind, followed by another vigorous pounding in bed, ensuring a double dose of saddle sore to remind her of him with every step.

"That was not very subtle," Alex gasped afterward, spread-eagle and incapacitated.

"Subtlety is for the weak."

Alex hobbled through the next few days, forced by Strav's absence to confront a different tender problem. How could she bear to leave him?

She had not understood that love was so like a seizure. One moment high-functioning, the next moment an electrical storm in the brain that short-circuited time, with the world moved ahead like a skip in a song. He didn't even need to be present. A certain tempo of footsteps, a similar line of a firm jaw or square knot of yellow tie, the pregnant heaviness in the air before a rain, lyrical music or a British accent, and she was levitating in flashbacks of excruciating pleasure and tension; the sounds he made, his unhurried explorations of her every secret place, that breath-catching border between excitement and shame.

If she tried to focus at a meeting, she saw the way he closed his eyes and threw his head back before he climaxed, the euphoric release in his face. In line at the cafeteria, she was watching him sleep, his hand marking the steady rise and fall of his chest, a sheet slung over his thighs—her favorite time, when she could study him as long as her heart desired, trace every shadowed contour of his face and body, from the sweet hollow of his temple to the thick hair around his relaxed sex. All her imaginings had underestimated the power of this physical bond, a trusting abandon of your body to another, the joy of a man reaching for you even in his sleep.

Yet even the most electric love, she learned, was no panacea. He still suffered violent nightmares and needed her in sight to give a speech. If the demons jumped in bed for a hijack, the results were anyone's guess. But things always worked out at each morning's light, him spooned against her, inside her and moving before they were truly awake.

Something was healing within her too—an inner balance gained, days passed without a fall, gliding through crowds like a silver twisting fish. The vodka bottle went untouched. She studied herself in the mirror with great interest. So this was life when you paid attention, keen to a world full of wonder.

It was everything Patrick had warned her against, and she finally understood why.

The Commission would disband with Friday's vote. Saturday, the anniversary of the Fall of Riga, would bring Asylum Netcast #2. Patrick was safe, for the time being, but the g-screens were proliferating. Despite an offer of her dream Fellowship in International's Institute, she needed to return to San Francisco, that foggy g-screen sanctuary that offered less professional opportunity for her and absolutely nothing for a career Diplomat. There was no explaining that move to Strav.

Better to embrace her old friend denial one more time, and focus on the passage of Independence—a debt she owed the kids in Abad, and proof to herself that the world could change.

That change required shoring up their tenuous eighteen Delegate majority. Wednesday morning brought a call from Rob Blakely, who was mining for useful gossip regarding the vote.

"There's a replacement Italian Delegate arriving today," Rob told her. "The old fart is being recalled to Rome. Something about a child prostitute."

The old fart was abstaining on Independence, so here was a chance to turn a vote. "What's the new Delegate's credentials?" she asked.

"A doctorate in Global Security, but mostly being the old fart's nephew. Stark-naked nepotism, my favorite kind. You following, peach? Because he follows you. Calls you his *fuggitivo di amore*."

Sly finger drumroll. "Give it up for Dr. Michelangelo Giancarlo Valenti. Bloke looks like he knows his hair product."

The bloke did, indeed. Alex burst out laughing—Michelangelo, who had started her quest by leaking High Council intel between kisses and bottles of Umbria. She had not thought of him since climbing down his fire escape, eight weeks and a billion years ago.

"Texas!" Michelangelo answered her call. "I was to surprise you! Sì, lunch!" Strav would hate it, but better to ask forgiveness than permission. The Yangs' yacht had just docked on the Bund, and the limo ride back on the crowded highway would take at least five hours. When Strav returned to her that evening, she could present a vote gained on her own.

The Imperial Café was an opulence of garlanded columns and hostesses in killer-tight satin cheongsam. They took a table on the second floor. "How you have changed!" Michelangelo declared, and it seemed to Alex that he was a measure of her change. She swirled his excellent wine, and wondered back to the lonely, unworldly girl who had not known how to use him.

She knew now. They laid bets on the honorees for the Black and White Gala, the annual award extravaganza that opened the Assembly session, and she segued to politics. By the time the crispy duck arrived, Delegate Valenti was nearly persuaded on Independence. They were interrupted by diners oohing about "Aston Volante." Michelangelo hurried to the window overlooking the street.

Alex snuck a call to Strav. "I have news, nomad! I can't wait to see you."

"You don't have to, sweetheart. Look out the window."

Impossible, thought Alex. A screaming banshee could not have driven from Shanghai that fast. "*Love like a shadow flies when substance love pursues*," said Strav into his phone, vaulting from a stunner of a scarlet convertible she could only hope he had not stolen. He was windblown, wearing sunglasses and an open-necked shirt.

"Oh," breathed a woman next to Alex, "doesn't he look fine."

"An orangutan would look fine in that car," Alex said darkly. Men on the street clustered around the Aston like children to an ice cream cart. Strav grinned up at her, immensely pleased with himself. *"Pursuing that that flies, and flying what pursues—"* he began, until Michelangelo put his arm around her.

The sunglasses came off.

Alex flagged the hostess. "Could you bring another place setting? And please remove all the knives."

"A pleasure, Envoy," said Michelangelo, when Strav appeared at their table. "I heard about your Committee speech. It's hard to believe you are as good as they say."

Strav bowed. "I appreciate the compliment and acknowledge the nuance."

"Sit, eat. Alex tells me you are recently married. Congratulations. I should be so lucky." He squeezed Alex's hand. "And you, *mi bella*, with no boyfriend."

Alex flashed Strav a look that morphed from warning to pleading and back again. "The Delegate is reconsidering Italy's abstention," she told Strav. "He understands a failed vote would unleash violence in Townships along the Mediterranean."

"Sì, sì, so, Envoy, I understand you won an important tournament in your country, in—martial arts?"

"A critical vote!" cried Alex, hastily serving the duck. Blood plum sauce splattered everywhere. "The vote is so very close!"

"Martial arts are so popular here," said Michelangelo. "Everyone wearing T-shirts with that iconic face from the old movies. You look like him, Envoy."

"Because it *is* the Envoy," said Alex through a painful rictus of a smile. "Those are Wolf Khan T-shirts. Manufactured in the scenic Protectorate hinterlands—"

"Where are the knives?" Strav asked Alex.

"—more scenic than the Alps! A huge new market for Italian wine and exports."

"You must show me, *mi bella*. Why could I never get you on a plane? Ah, Envoy, I am envious of your travel with her."

"Not envious," said Strav. "Jealous. Jealousy involves fear of losing a desired one. Envy is directly between two people, with a fixation on social status, which is first cousin to shame, or loss of that status, which brings us to schadenfreude, my personal favorite, the pleasure of watching your rivals brought low. Really low. Just crushed."

Michelangelo stopped swirling his wine.

"But we digress," said Strav. "You would abstain on the Independence vote, Delegate. I would be honored to hear your reasoning."

"National policy, to be honest."

"An interesting phrase, 'to be honest.' Does it imply that in the normal course you are not totally ingenuous?"

"Don't play with your food," Alex told Strav. She did not mean the crispy duck.

"Abstention is based in neutrality," said Michelangelo, a slow flush rising above his dark trim of beard. "Neutrality is highly advisable for a nation as small as ours."

"A brave stance. Neutrality is so often construed as cowardice, a pretext for avoiding tough moral choices. Now, some may argue that neutrality is a tool of mere endemic greed, a position taken for financial gain. That requires a certain moral myopia, but is not really the same as cowardice. Either way, cowardice or greed, it's a fine thing that your nation does not care what anyone thinks of it."

"Yes," Michelangelo sputtered. "I mean, no."

"There we have it, a burst of polysyllabic exactitude from a perspicacious mind. The speed, the wit, the repartee!"

"What was that?" Michelangelo exclaimed.

"A verbal orgasm," muttered Alex.

"The duck is very tender," said Strav, tucking in. "Falls right off the bone. Really, a knife would be overkill. *Aggettivo delizioso.*"

Strav paid for the lunches, eaten and not, and found Alex by the Aston. The high cirrus clouds appeared as stress fractures in the blue dome.

"All you had to do was be civil to him," she said.

"Which I might have, if he didn't live on Planet Buffoon."

She looked at him like something that crawled out of Kafka, speaking in mandible clicks. "He was always kind to me. And if we drop one Delegate, *one*, we lose the vote."

"You told Valenti you don't have a boyfriend."

"We are not public! And you are not the boss of me."

"I have no idea what I am to you. But I do have a boss, and a dinner with him tonight. Perhaps I'll call you tomorrow." He roared off in the suddenly ridiculous car.

The problem with achieving your heart's desire, it seemed to Strav, was the necessity of keeping it. His time on the yacht had been professional triumph, and personal failure regarding his divorce. Two days of despairing, starving for Alex, then expected to watch like a eunuch as that cretin Valenti mentally undressed her, spread her silken thighs and mounted up.

Valenti, he knew, stood as a symbol for the true conflict—Alex's refusal to discuss their future, an evasive tour de force of misdirects and intimate diversions. Once, in his office, Strav had pressed her about her transfer to International. She had closed his door, unzipped him, and slid under his desk. Left him brainless, answerless, and an hour later passed him in the lobby like a stranger. She made love like every time was their last, and that concerned him too.

Strav left the Aston for the Yangs' valet and stalked to Headquarters, surprised that people didn't sizzle and combust as he passed. Let her hide behind the adultery rules. Let her suffer in silence awaiting his call.

A fine resolution, except that his feet were carrying him to the Gasthaus like runaway horses to the stable. Alex insisted he always take the back service elevator for privacy. The seventeen-story ride now brought the usual Pavlovian arousal. He strode into her studio, ready with ultimatums, and was greeted by the sound of a running shower and soprano, "The Man I Love," letting him know she had not just predicted but timed his arrival to the minute. He followed the trail of pink bra and zebra-striped panties—serious fashion regression in his absence—to the steamy bathroom. The shower door was open to assure his view.

"Big and strong," she sang, her eyes closed, water pouring over her in glossy sheets. Her left hand lathered her breasts, her nipples swollen and rosy in the hot water, her right hand moving a washcloth between her legs. The washcloth found a rhythm, and Strav heard a raw animal noise that probably came from him. He tore off his suit jacket so fast that both arms got caught backward in the sleeves, leaving him in a crazed tangle, and Alex laughing too hard to be much help. She worked one of his arms free, and he lunged fully clothed under the water. He entered her standing up, his pants to his knees. They swayed as she wrapped her legs around his hips, finding each other's mouths, then nothing but cries and hoarse whispers and a frenzied drumming that rattled the tile wall.

The world continued its slow roll through space, and the Gasthaus rolled with it. Strav had come three times, the last a dry, straining spasm that put him in a Zen state of one with the bed. Alex lay between his legs, visiting the auspicious dragon birthmark. She nuzzled his spent and rubbery penis, repeatedly propping it upright with her nose to watch the endlessly fascinating topple-over.

"Come to the dinner with me," Strav said lazily, stroking her hair. He thought about his wet clothes. He kept an extra suit in her closet, but he'd squish in those shoes all night. Life would be infinitely easier once she rented an apartment in his building. "Did you sign the lease?"

Her body peeled from him like a delicate membrane. Strav realized that, once again, he had been adroitly manipulated away from a confrontation.

"I can't break my lease in San Francisco," Alex said. "And the rent here is astronomical." Any talk of his subsidizing her rent ventured onto the treacherous ice of the *er'mai* topic. In humiliating fact, he could barely support himself on a junior Diplomat's salary, much less a second apartment. Never before had he so craved money, or understood how the need could bring men to murder and war.

"The money is details," Strav said. "It is all details. You know I will find a way."

She sat with her legs bent like the Danes' Little Mermaid and gazed out the window. "Patrick wanted to live across the Golden

Gate," she said, lost on a sun-kissed California coast. "The North Bay is like a nature preserve. Redwood groves and red-tailed hawks, mountain lions. He said seals bob up to follow as you walk the beach. The tide pools have giant orange starfish and sea anemones that close on your fingers. It was so close, yet I never got to see it."

Strav's throat tightened, a dread rising to the conviction that she was going to leave him. This had to be how the ancient ones felt watching an eclipse swallow the sun. "I'll buy us a ranch there someday. I promise."

"Someday." She kissed him, and her eyes were huge with reflective tears. "We're happy right now, aren't we?"

"Happy?" Strav choked. "I creep to your room like a thief. I play the deaf-mute while men touch you. Happy? It will kill me. I don't care anymore about the rules, or if it causes earthquakes and black holes. If you really loved me, neither would you."

"Let's focus on Friday's vote. Please, nomad."

"Until the vote. Then everything changes."

Handel ordered Eric to make a guest appearance at the Black and White Gala that Thursday night, for appearance's sake, and nothing else could have chiseled Eric from his control room. His Operation Daybreak was ready, as was Jacob's faulty Hallows program. Eric's last qualms about the risk had disappeared into the usual anticipation of the kill, an almost sexual tension.

The Black and White was held downstairs in the atrium. After the green glow of his workstations, the transformed lobby hit Eric like a Snow Queen's blizzard—suspended sails of rippling white silk, pearly white oyster shells on hills of ice, long white dresses and crisp dress whites. Handel climbed atop a fake snowdrift to announce the annual awards. Eric focused on Jacob, who had ventured from his own control room. Jacob appeared confident, though Eric detected a distinct metal fatigue in his smile. They nodded at each other, cold acknowledgment of their upcoming race.

"Lastly," said Handel, "the high honor of our night. The Star of Valor goes to Dr. Alexandra Tashen and Director Eric Burton!"

Eric turned with a belligerent "huh?" The giant screen behind Handel's munificent smile read, *For Conspicuous Gallantry in the Legion of Honor.*

Delegate Valenti presented the medals. He stood on a chair to pin the Star on Eric's chest, a good-natured jest that brought waves of laughter and broke the stiff formality of the night. On Alex's turn, the giant screen lit up with the Falling Star publicity shot of Handel catching her at the Tomb. The crowd roared, Handel waved, and Alex went scorched red. It occurred to Eric that the great man was also a real jackass. Valenti triple-kissed Alex's cheeks to another roar. Alex wore a modest, full-skirted white gown that was certainly picked by Strav, a choice that now backfired by creating the vision of a flushed bride enduring raunchy toasts on her wedding night.

Alex must have sworn Strav to keep his distance, because Eric spied his brother standing rigid among the cheering Diplomats, wearing the cold face that meant borderline apoplectic inside. His anda's suffering filled Eric with an unfamiliar mordant satisfaction.

You can't just give me to him, Alex had said. But the alternative had been to lose them both, forever. Which did not make it fair, or quell the inner voice that said he should have fought to keep her. Strav probably had a word for this emotion, for his obsessive flipping through Alex's *Bulfinch* each night, for Hercules clearing years of shit from the King's stables only to be poisoned by the person he most trusted.

The band struck up a pulsing Japanese electro-beat, and everyone under forty rushed the dance floor. Alex hid against Eric.

"I'm proud of you, bug," he told her. "Get out there and show the bastards."

Reassured, she did. Eric grabbed a seltzer instead of the Scotch rocks he craved and went to watch with Suzanne. The gyrating dancers heated the air, and the party gained a manic overdrive. The turn on stage had anointed Alex the belle of the ball, and she hopped and bopped with great energy and zero rhythm, surrounded by admirers and as incandescent as a woman in love. Valenti claimed Alex on the next song, but was overrun by rivals.

"It's like sperm wriggling around an ovum," marveled Suzanne.

Secretary Handel signaled for the band to cut the hideous racket already. Musicians rearranged like a child's transformer toy into a stringed orchestra and launched into the upbeat chords of Handel's favorite Strauss waltz. The dance floor emptied as for a Hazmat drill.

"Hoo-boy," said Suzanne, an eye on Strav. "Get out the old medicine kit. The saber-tooth is about to get stupid."

Alex's gurgling laugh rose above an enchanted flight of strings. Valenti led her to the center of the empty dance floor. The Delegate whispered in her ear, lingered to smell her hair, and Strav went after them like a guided missile. He reached the open dance floor, and Alex flashed him a don't-test-me look that would have sent any sane man running. Strav did not pause, or even deign to acknowledge Valenti's existence. He put his left hand behind his back, his right arm extended to Alex with his palm up, a hopelessly old-world declaration and demand. Strav waited.

Everyone waited. The conductor's stalled baton stopped the music. Eric saw it dawn on Strav that he had driven top speed off a very high cliff. Alex let a fuming Valenti pull her away. Guests craned to see Strav left alone on the polished floor, his arm out-stretched as in a one-sided duel.

Valenti looked back and laughed.

Big mistake, Eric could have told him. Alex shoved Valenti and returned to take Strav's hand. Strav remained frozen a few beats behind the rescue, so she moved him into waltz position, her head held high as a queen. "The Blue Danube" swelled in a one-two-three-one, and Strav recovered to spin her into the music.

Just a dance, but there was no misunderstanding the way that Strav held her or the language of their bodies. They danced lost in each other, the bride and groom of every first dance, and Alex looked graceful in his arms.

No way Strav deserves her, thought Eric. Still, he had to give the devil his due, and he remembered why he loved his impossible brother even when he could not stand him. Other couples streamed onto the dance floor, joining the joyful swing for a soaring, enrap-tured moment where the world was a wedding of youth and beauty, and anything seemed possible.

"Oh no," said Suzanne. She handed Eric her phone to read. Eric let the beautiful dancers fly by, and waited for the music to end.

Eric stood apart as Suzanne gathered Alex and Strav to a quiet corner of the Gala for the bad news. The Independence vote had been canceled. The Committee on Trusts cited the VA bombing and security threats, but Eric heard the real story: Solidarity had broken through and scored a point.

"This will not stand, anda," Strav said furiously. "I swear the Council will hear our report before your Tribunal." Eric recalled that their little Independence Commission had been created for his benefit. The notion seemed impossibly quaint.

The atrium sound system gave a sharp ship-whistle that stopped the party dead. The giant screen lit to a flickering blue Allied Media Service logo, giving the white atrium a ghostly underwater quality. *No*, thought Eric. *It's too early.* Text flashed on the screen.

Asylum Netcast #2. Occasion: The Fall of Riga Safe Area, twenty-fifth anniversary

Eric sprinted through the guests to the elevator, Jacob on his heels. Not that it mattered—in the Dark Net universe, their race was long over. When Eric reached his control room, the panels were a chaos of random digits, an electrical storm of misfiring pathways. The holograph of branching skeins dissolved in cascades of green and peacock blue. His team worked frantically to save Daybreak results and isolate and quarantine the contaminated matrices.

His virologist's best guess was beyond Eric's worst nightmare. Instead of slipping past the Asylum Netcast's immune system, the flaw in Solidarity's Hallows virus—the flaw he'd allowed—had caused the virus to mutate, now with a mix of Asylum program code. The hybrid result was a virulent new cyber-virus out in the wild. It was tearing like a pandemic through the networks, triggering an autoimmune response that had the Nations' Net attacking its own pathways.

Headquarters' lights dimmed and flared, fire alarms whooped on and off. Across the Nations, Eric knew, power grids and networks were failing, cars crashing, police screens blanked. Soon fires would be burning, candles and bonfires and buildings. Perhaps cities.

Eric needed air, needed to see for himself. Jacob was already on the observation deck when Eric arrived. Together they watched in stunned wonder as, far below, the lights of International unraveled line by line into darkness.

21

Alex appreciated that technology was not her friend, but never so much as the day it died. The Gala had turned into an all-nighter at Headquarters with everyone working damage control. When she stumbled outside, the sun was rising on a world slapped back in time—power out, screens frozen, and, gift beyond all gifts, the g-screen devices corrupted and inoperable. Eric's prediction about the Asylum Hacker was proved gloriously correct. Not only had Patrick outwitted Solidarity, but he had exacted this Yahweh-like vengeance, smiting the godless ones who would destroy his Word. Alex wanted to hand flowers to MPs and dance on stalled trollies. Today, she was a garden-variety illegal from any other stretch of the globe—any stretch of history—able to pass on nothing more than a forged ID and a bravado story. It felt positively romantic.

The morning was a scorcher with winds cooked on the inland furnace plains, air that made the hair stand up with static electricity and negative ions. Corrupted security systems blocked access to hundreds of hotels and apartments. Bleary TaskForce officers in black-and-white formal wear wandered as homeless gentry. Alex was locked out from the Gasthaus and her meds.

Rumor said the Medical Center was open for emergency supplies. Today, a hospital held no terror; generators might keep the lights on, but the downed cyber meant no blood work. She could safely stock up on her meds, and inhalers for Eric.

Strav was still at Headquarters. Alex hailed an enterprising vendor selling sticky notes and crayons at a buck a pop. She scribbled a note to Strav: *Gone to Neuro Clinic!* She added it to the pink and yellow squares flapping like manic butterflies on the Gasthaus wall.

Alex's romanticism dimmed as she walked the avenue. For the rest of the world, the wholesale slaughter of instant communications was as disorienting as sudden blindness. Older people trembled to relive the deadly blackouts of the War. At every corner, anxious crowds gathered to shortwave radios that blared fact and fiction at equal volume—systems failures across three continents, a flu virus that ate human brains, runs on banks, guizi invasions. The Allied Media broadcasts assured that everything was under control.

Nothing belied the official assurances more than the exodus on Fifth Avenue, which was gridlocked with the cars of TaskForce elite sending their families to secure compounds far from the volatile Township. Little Lia and Lena Kotas stuck out golden heads from their ayah's sedan. Alex picked up her white skirt and ran to them. They told her they were going on a 'cation without Daddy, was she mad at them, why didn't she come over anymore? Alex gave them kisses and promised to do the merry-go-round soon. The car rolled on, leaving Alex bereft and guilt-ridden. She could only imagine how Jacob must have felt watching that car pull away.

What was good for her, it seemed, was flat-out lousy for the rest of civilization. Alex recalled what Strav had said: Maybe not my fault, but still *because* of me.

The Medical Center lobby was empty except for the Kommandant, who sat in one of the scattered wheelchairs in wrinkled dress whites, drinking coffee and smoking a cigarette.

"Are you all right?" asked Alex cautiously.

"All-time stupid question." The Kommandant explained she was working from the Chief of Staff's hospital room upstairs, just taking a break from the end of days. Alex told her about the meds, and gained an unwanted guide to Neurology down the hall.

Strav had found her pink sticky note and beat her there. His sweat-spiked hair and angry sprawl in the waiting room chair spoke of abject and unaccustomed failure.

"You look rode hard and put away wet," said Alex, thinking how anxious she had been about him giving the Council speech. Somehow the world was having the panic attack instead.

"The Committee gave a riveting display of ineptitude," said Strav, tearing open his bow tie and tux collar. "The Nations are hanging on the radio. An announcement reinstating the Independence vote would remove the worst provocation to violence. Bloody fools will burn on the funeral pyre of their own egos."

The sleepless night caught up. The three of them yawned hugely at the same time and laughed a little. Alex felt scuzzy inside and out, with a great longing for mint toothpaste and a shower. A plastic stay in the gown stuck her in the breast; her white satin pumps rubbed her little toes raw. She wanted to curl naked against Strav on cool sheets and sleep for days.

The nurse was an imposing older woman in a hijab. Alex took inhalers to give Eric, while the nurse looked for a physician to approve her meds. The radio on the counter blared that martial law had been declared for International. The Friendship Market was to close at noon, Township curfew at sunset. Violators would be fired upon without warning. The Joint Military was at red alert and calling up a million reserves to active duty.

Alex registered the Kommandant's bleak face. With Allied defenses down, the Nations were utterly vulnerable to attack. Colonel Bulgakov would ship out today, as would multitudes of frightened teenage recruits. Alex finally comprehended the speeding catastrophe of nightfall.

Patrick was no nihilist. He would end the blackout if he could. Perhaps it was time to consider that he was beyond reach, maybe trapped somewhere, and that her map of the world had changed. TaskForce Security Ops was working desperately to end the cyber-rampage and save lives. Would it help them to know the Asylum Netcast origin? She did not have the tech savvy to even guess.

But Eric did. She could say: *Eric, you know how you hacked systems to protect your family? I have a long story for you. You are not going to like it.*

Telling Eric was the choice that would upend her life, and likely his too. But it was Eric's voice telling her that this was no longer about her and hers.

"Alex Tashen, amen." A short doctor stepped from behind the large nurse. "My favorite toxin-induced epileptogenesis." He glanced at Strav with frosty moral judgment. "I saw how you two danced at the Gala last night. Unexpected, considering our last encounter."

Polish accent, shaved head, bolo tie clasp with St. George and the Dragon. It was Dr. Vito, from the Prosperity banquet fight where she'd announced Strav's marriage—a grand slam of a night, rounding the bases from heated to auto-destruct.

"More medicine, less commentary," said Suzanne. "Give her the damn blister pack."

"It is not candy to hand out," said Vito, his chest puffing. "It's a powerful drug." He pried Alex's eyelid and shot a penlight in her pupil. Did she suffer confusion or hallucinations?

No, claimed Alex. Yes, claimed Strav.

Vito pointed her to an examination room. Suzanne accompanied her. "Family only," ordered the nurse, accustomed to thwarting important people.

"I'm her medical guardian," said Suzanne. "Fuck off."

"And I'm her . . ." Strav's voice trailed away. The nurse pointed him to the reception like a truant to detention.

The changing room felt like a lockup, with vertical window blinds for bars. Dr. Vito laid out an unnerving row of vials in the adjacent examination room. The paper gown, always an exercise in humiliation, added to her sense of exposure as Vito poked and tapped.

"But systems are down," Alex protested as he pierced her inner elbow for a blood draw. It hurt more than it should have. "The machines can't do an analysis, right?"

"True, without the Net, the machines cannot talk to each other. But one performs as a stand-alone. I'll run the standard battery of blood work. Your drug can cause serious liver damage without monitoring." He shot a castigating look at the medical guardian. "You should know that, *Dr.* Burton. Why hasn't she been seen?"

"I'm a molecular biologist," said Suzanne. "And she's a swamp of irrationality."

Vito left with the blood vials. "Typical God complex," muttered Suzanne. "They go to medical school when they're not smart enough for real science."

Alex peeked at the waiting room. Strav had switched to beautiful boy mode and was chatting up the nurse, a charm fest designed to get him into the exam room. Dr. Vito abruptly called the nurse to the lab. Something detected, something shocking. The what-if in Alex's head went to a shrill of terror.

Dr. Vito returned, looking somber. "Is the problem related to my liver?" Alex asked. He nodded, and Alex almost floated off the table with relief.

The doctor addressed the medical guardian. "She was treated with a seizure drug that stimulates liver enzymes, and can degrade certain hormones. Drugs that induce the cytochrome P450 system can aggravate the effect. Did she have recent antibiotics?"

"Abad," said Suzanne. "Antibiotics in Abad. Oh, hell. But the initial drug—didn't anyone warn of interactions?"

Vito's chest puffed larger. "She was triaged after the bombing in San Francisco. Not the drug of choice, but reasonable in crisis circumstances."

"What are you arguing about?" said Alex, bewildered. "Am I dying?"

The glares disappeared. "Much the opposite, child," said Dr. Vito. "You're pregnant."

Alex would have laughed, but he was so solemn it felt rude. "That's not possible. I've been on birth control for years. Mostly wishful thinking, but—"

"The bad news is that your anti-seizure medication degraded the estrogen. The antibiotic finished it. Your HCG shows an early pregnancy. About two weeks."

"Not possible," she said, even as the back of her mind did the math. Two weeks from Strav on her balcony, Strav in the starlight, in her bed.

"The good news is, the seizure meds are not associated with congenital defects," continued Vito. "Next blood work, we'll get fetal DNA for routine genetic testing. You are statistically prime for a healthy baby, amen."

The bile rose, the room tunneled, and Alex ran to the sink to vomit. She heard Dr. Vito say morning sickness, and the Kommandant tell him to shut it.

"Alex, honey," said Suzanne, rubbing her back. "Calm down. It's not the end of the world."

But yes, it actually was. "I can't be pregnant," she told Vito. "You have to get rid of it!"

The insect hum of the generator filled the startled silence. "This is not my fault," said Alex. "Please, help me."

"This is not *its* fault either," said Dr. Vito. "*It* did not ask to be created out of an adulterous affair." He touched St. George for patience. "This is why the law makes you slow down. Termination requires counseling. And the father's consent."

She need not have argued pro-natalist laws with Strav to know his response. Even if she explained the guizi truth, endangering his life, too, he would still try to find a way. "I don't know who the father is."

"That might surprise the young man pacing out there. The prenatal tests establish paternity, you realize."

"It's none of your damn business," Suzanne told Vito. "*It* is a ball of cells, barely implanted. What about Dire Exception? It's two fricking pills."

"Dire Exception requires rape or incest. Again, the tests establish paternity."

"So don't report the pregnancy," said Suzanne, and Alex almost hugged her.

"Even were I willing to risk the criminal penalties," said Vito, "which I am not, the results are recorded. The pregnancy will be tracked." He sighed, ragged and unexpected, and his hand stole back to St. George. "Listen, Alex. I understand more than you think. Terrible things happened during the War, to my own family. Pregnancies that were difficult to accept. But God has a plan."

Suzanne was ablaze. "Of all the self-righteous, irrelevant, unprofessional—"

"It's okay," said Alex. She rinsed the sick from her mouth. Think, *think*, fetal cells slipping into the wild ride of her blood, each one a little g-marker bomb. With systems down, finding a more permissive jurisdiction was a moot question. If the world did fall to chaos, she could lose any chance to terminate in time.

Think. She recalled Strav's Committee speech, the staffers schooling her about Gubei flowers and black-market drugs. The Chief Apothecary had offered the dispensary in Friendship Market. *Anything* she needed. Two pills, and she could claim a miscarriage.

"Sleep on it," advised Dr. Vito. *"Wisely and slow, they stumble that run fast."*

"I will." The Market closed at noon; she'd have to run the whole way. "But you can't tell Strav. Don't let him bamboozle it out of the nurse either!"

"We respect patient confidentiality," said Dr. Vito over Suzanne's "Bah!" of derision. "Now, about your meds. Yes, you may get dressed first."

Once in the changing room, Alex dressed in silent frenzy, the stubborn pearl buttons fighting her with every loop. Her satin skirt seemed to fluoresce. She would be a beacon of TaskForce white when she needed invisibility. The nurse's chador hung in the closet like a sleeping shade. The fabric smelled of cloves, and enveloped her.

The changing room window was easily pried open for a body-length drop to the clinic lawn. The sun was almost straight overhead.

"She seems unusually fearful," Dr. Vito told Suzanne as they waited for Alex to emerge. "Even for a girl in trouble. Does she know of some syndrome or genetic condition that runs in the family?"

"Shhhh," said Suzanne. "She'll hear. And, no. I've seen her Institute records, familial history to genetic arrays. She's so perfect it's boring." Yet Suzanne, too, was disturbed by Alex's outburst. Distress was to be expected, anxiety, maybe even shame, as silly as that was. But Alex's entire body had expressed raw, visceral fear.

The ascending wail of a curfew siren pierced the clinic. Suzanne blinked hard to banish tears. Yuri had departed to the eastern front, and God knew when they would see each other again. It seemed symbolic that even news that should bring great joy, of a child conceived by two people in love, brought pain and fear instead.

And yet—how irrepressible of life to seek out the little mechanical failure, to find the crevice in stone.

Suzanne picked up a vial of Alex's blood. It winked like a ruby when held to the light.

"Would the stand-alone let me recreate Alex's genomic array?" Suzanne asked. "It might reassure her." Calming Alex was a plausible excuse. In truth, Katrin's changeling rant had rooted in her own dreams, a fertile soil of guilt and regrets, until Suzanne wondered if dementia was contagious: a nightly swirl of curses, black dogs, and falling snow, always culminating in a singular blue-eyed face.

She needed her nights back. Alex's Institute genetic arrays were seven years old, and diagnostics had improved. A new array would prove nothing missed, nothing hidden, and clear Katrin's poison from her mind.

"Do you have Alex's consent for a new array?" Dr. Vito asked.

"Now you worry about her rights?" But his point remained. Was lack of patient consent an ethical transgression, if merely updating a previous array? Before she could answer, Alex's prediction came true. Strav burst in like a human exclamation mark, wild with the expectant news, the bamboozled nurse in hot pursuit.

The vial felt right in Suzanne's hand, weightless as an act of love.

Out of nowhere, it seemed to Strav, the avenue teemed with pregnant women. Suzanne had propelled him from the empty changing room, stunned and mortified, with orders to take a walk, soldier. Strav wandered past round-bellied women in saris, moms with toddlers and the curve of a sibling on the way, businesswomen in tented silk blouses. They were everywhere, Madonna hands draped atop protruding stomachs, a spontaneous bloom of expectant women and none of them his.

The Settlement was out in a flood force, a turmoil to mirror his own. Riot police ripped down INDEPENDENCE NOW and DEATH TO TASKFORCE posters featuring the teen Township martyr killed by Handel's guard. Street screens were frozen on Solidarity's guizi demon, a reminder of disease and chaos. The War always stirred as fire under the ashes, ready to flare, but still: How could life have twisted so fast?

Even men with beer guts looked pregnant.

He understood the accusation in Alex's flight. Pushing Beijing for his divorce risked his work visa. Strav imagined himself as a black-market laborer mucking stables, an embarrassment to his son. College! How would he pay for college? As an unwed mother, Alex would lose her teaching post. No, she was too clever for that; she would marry that twit Valenti, adding Delegate's wife to her CV. His firstborn was going to be named Giorgio and speak with his hands.

Another scenario appeared, more disturbing because it was real. Alex would do what they all did in crisis, and go to Eric. Eric would take her back. His son would know him as a pathetic figure skulking around the family's happiness, always outside looking in.

The pain in Strav's stomach clawed to his chest, and bent him hands to knees in front of an antique bookstore. A short, fifty-something woman with curly blonde hair was padlocking the door. "Oy!" she said, pushing up reading glasses to examine him. "What's the matter, boychik?"

"I'm pregnant," Strav blurted.

A fine-drawn eyebrow went up. "Mazel tov. I'm guessing this is your first?"

"Yes it is!" exclaimed Strav, astonished by her clairvoyance.

"So. Boy or girl?"

Strav started to say boy, and stopped. Maybe a girl, God, a little girl! Instantly, he was bone-crushed with a new stampede of emotions, a fierce and tender protectiveness that nearly dropped him.

"*Meshuga,*" muttered the woman. The glasses pushed higher to read the fine print of his sorry solo state. "So, a situation." A nod from Strav. "She got spooked, run off on you?" Double nod. "News flash, boychik. It's not about you anymore. Maybe she got reasons nothing to do with you."

She patted Strav's cheek hard enough to be both blessing and command, and Strav had an awed flash of his good angel in readers.

"Think, boychik. Sometimes the reason is hiding in plain sight. Go back. *Run.*" She vanished into the flow of the sidewalk.

Strav's head cleared; such was the power of a kindness from a stranger, celestial or not. And why was Suzanne so eager to boot him from the clinic? Strav ran back until he was threading pedestrians like slalom poles—*you can't even imagine I have reasons that have nothing to do with you*—Alex's flight from that window not about marriage, or pride, but the secret reason behind her every flight and evasion—*marked as different, marked in your genes*—and him always too inflamed to listen, to understand that the black dots wheeling high overhead had never been for him.

Seconds later, and Strav would have missed Suzanne shutting herself in a clinic lab. He pushed inside to a mystery of glass shelving, centrifuges, and a black box labeled *i-scan*. Suzanne's hands shook, and although the room was hard science, Strav would have sworn she'd seen a ghost.

"Leave," Suzanne told him. "That's an order." She tried to block his view of a monitor. Flashing red letters read, ANOMALY DETECTED. Strav moved her aside, but he already knew the name on the report.

"Oh, Strav, forgive me," said Suzanne, a heartsick admission. "I did not know."

22

Eric assured Strav and Suzanne that his CyberIntel secure room was scoured by anti-surveillance tech, and it was safe to speak freely. He soon realized he was wrong. Suzanne's story required the absolute privacy found only in deep space or the grave. Eric pressed his palms against his eyes until he saw flashing points of color. Maybe he was asleep, would bolt awake thinking damn, that was a bad one.

"I want the exact sequence of events," he said. Professionalism was his handle to maintain control. Alex, Alex, lit-up smile and hand on his ticker. For all the recent lessons in betrayal, he lacked the imaginative capacity for a gutting like this.

Suzanne, too, maintained stiff military order. When the blood sample had shown positive for the Federation g-marker, she explained, she pulled the culprit segment of genome and confirmed the snippet of viral DNA. But it was only in one cell. The second sample found altered amino acids, a sign of genetic tampering, and another positive cell. If the pattern held true, then some fraction of Alex's cells contained the g-marker. That made no sense, because the marker was germ line inherited—meaning in every cell, or none at all.

Suzanne's theory, an ephemeral mix of training and intuition, was a gene therapy that knocked out the markers. It was not completely efficient, and left the g-marker in a few cells.

"That's why she hates any tests," said Eric. It was the second time today he'd been forced to admire a feat of technological brilliance from the wrong side. "But she panicked and ran *before* the array. Why?"

"She can pass the handheld screeners because field-based diagnostic tools still run partial genome sequencing. It's a compromise to get quick turnaround readout and portability. But an array through a central lab is a different animal. It sequences the whole genome off more reliable tissue types, measures orders of magnitude precision and detail."

"Answer. The. Question."

"She is pregnant," said Strav. He wore his cold face, but Eric saw the shifts of defiance, guilt, and irrepressible masculine pride.

That pride pushed Eric to the edge. But for Strav, there would be no array, no impossible choices already streaming to the black hole of his heart.

"The g-marker test results are still isolated in the lab machine," Suzanne told Eric. "I tried to erase the result, but the program blocks me. When systems come back online, the detection will set off a thousand guizi-alarms. I need you to stop it from transmitting."

"You ask me to commit treason?" His cousin looked as if he had shot her. "The Nations' defense has crashed. We may already be at war. And you want me to destroy evidence that Regime spies can pass the g-screens and infiltrate our highest ranks?"

Strav made a harsh sound, and Suzanne held him back. "Alex must be found," said Suzanne. "We need her to study the gene therapy and the systems breach. But the circumstantial evidence is refusé—"

"Let's calculate the odds," said Eric. "She takes the extraordinary risk of applying for TaskForce. Talks her way onto a Security Ops Commission. Disappears to Abad, a terrorist hub. She's on-site at the Legion and VA explosions. She targets Jacob, and the next Netcast destroys our Net. When her cover is blown by the pregnancy, she runs. They always have an exit strategy." In retrospect, a dozen incidents could have been staged to gain his trust. What had he confided in her, carelessly allowed access to? The shame was staggering, unbearable.

"I'm not asking you to alter the results," Suzanne said. "Only to buy me time."

"Time, to do what?" But for once, there were no hands-on-hips, and no answer. Best case, Alex was an innocent actor—which still meant thousands of bad actors could be passing with the same gene therapy. Worst case, Alex was a mole, a saboteur, or even the human bioweapon Jacob feared. If Suzanne went to Handel, a refusé might turn pawn in the Treaty game. If she erased the results, a spy might walk. If she did nothing, Solidarity scored a guizi.

The test of great leadership, Suzanne had taught him, was the ability to make decisions when faced with incomplete information. To see the powerful Kommandant paralyzed with indecision was nearly as shocking as the g-marker revelation.

Strav stepped forward in a bodily drawing of battle lines. "Alex is no spy. But even if true, it is irrelevant. She is my wife, your sister. She carries my child, your niece or nephew."

Eric gripped the table to keep from hitting him. "She's not your wife, and it's not a child."

"She is family, anda. *Mea familia curo primum.*"

"And let the rest of the world burn," said Eric bitterly.

"If the guizi news goes public," said Suzanne, "it will be beyond anyone's ability to control. If Alex isn't lynched on the spot, she will *have* to be returned to the Regime. What happens to young women? A few years as a sex slave before the bullet? What about the baby?"

Strav went pale to his lips. "She hurt you, anda. You seek revenge. But this—our bond—I call on it. I will beg. I will kneel, whatever you need. As you love me, brother. As you love me."

The insult to Eric's integrity was a final kick between the legs. "What haven't I done for you?" Eric yelled, choking on every sacrifice that Strav refused to see, his career, the woman he loved. Now the devil demanded the ultimate price—his most profound convictions and native responsibility, that essential sense of self that passed for a soul.

"Thank you, anda," Strav said hoarsely, hearing only a promise. The mind went where it already wanted to go. "I will find her."

"Try the Tomb. That's where I found her last time you fucked her over." It was sheer spite, a strange new sensation. He had to leave before he hurt someone. "You two wait here."

"You are stopping the transmission on my orders," Suzanne told Eric at the door. "You are covered."

She was wrong, Eric knew. A Director should have already issued a Code Red, stat. For the first time, Suzanne Burton was compromised, and he needed to substitute his judgment for hers. Eric felt the generational flip as sudden and disorienting as a magnetic pole reversal.

Eric went to his office and let loose, yelling curses and overturning his heavy desk, to stand panting in the hot sun through the window. A plume of smoke rose above the Township, curved to an arc by the winds—the black smoke of a newborn fire, yet untouched by water.

Despite Suzanne and Strav's faith in his prowess, he had no magic to hack the clinic with the Net down. He might get caught, Alex detected anyway, and he, Suzanne, and Strav held guilty on conspiracy to commit treason. Inaction held its own dangers. Delay gave a spy time to escape. And when the arrays did transmit, the conspiracy would be revealed. Capital punishment would be a relief at the moment, but he had to think of his family.

He had one move. If he acted in his Security Ops capacity to apprehend Alex, there was no conspiracy. It kept Strav and Suzanne safe. It was also the right thing to do.

Strav would always invoke the god of absolute family loyalty. Suzanne had somehow broken over fear of an individual injustice. But he remained the thinking man for the Nations' voiceless billions. He had justified a series of personal compromises this year, cover-ups, Handel's dirty work, the vendetta with Jacob, in an ever-accelerating slide from what he knew best. Now he stood at the border of one of Alex's weird old maps, places ruled by myth and monster, where any behavior could be justified by the law of necessity. Alex had been living there for a long time. Not him—that was a border he would not cross.

Eric summoned his exhausted team. He told the agents to secure the Neuro Clinic. The geeks were to grab any functional communication devices in Security Ops emergency stores, and connect to backup radio systems and cable lines. They were to post a

Code Red Fugitive Warrant. Subject: Alex Tashen. Designation: Witness, Classified Investigation, flight alert. If apprehended, she was to be transferred to Director Burton's custody, and his alone.

Jacob would sniff out the vague warrant like a bloodhound, but there was nothing to prevent it. Eric steeled whatever wasn't yet numb inside and went to confront his family.

Their note informed Eric that Suzanne had returned to the command post, and Strav had gone to the Tomb. Eric cursed himself—he should have known it would take manacles to keep Strav from his search, especially after his dig. Now he needed to recover Strav himself, before the firestorm came bearing down on them.

His uber-elite cyber team were arguing over the dusty haul from emergency stores, flummoxed by walkie-talkies, electric type-writers, and a fax machine trailing a Gordian knot of cords. His freaky-smart cryptologist thought the fax could circulate a warrant with the fugitive's image. But with systems down, they could not access a photo. Did Director Burton have a likeness of the fugitive?

Eric found his sketchbook beneath the overturned desk. He touched Alex's face, traced the smile that didn't match the wistful eyes. Strange how the artist's hand could depict a secret without being able to name it. He felt like the portrait should cry out in protest, dissolve and run through his fingers like sand. Eric ripped out the page.

23

The conflagration in the Township made mockery of curfew orders, turning Central Park from civilized haven to refugee center. Eric cut through the bedlam of the Great Lawn. Park rangers in neon vests directed families to drop cloth tents. Children darted about with their tongues out to catch the flakes of white ash. The smoke and chemical particulate gnawed into Eric's protesting lungs. Wheelbarrows loaded with hysterical caged chickens added feathers and dust to the mix. It was a piss-poor time to discover he left his inhaler behind.

Eric's Director badge had cut him through the roadblocks, possibly ahead of Strav's hopeless search. How to convince him that Alex belonged to a distant land, and she had run home?

The scene in the square was a daylight rave with young men swilling Snowflake Beer, a long-necked bottle known for making excellent Molotov cocktails. The giant stage screen was frozen on the flame-haired demon, its curled tongue and crimson eyes fueling the air of macabre festival. INDEPENDENCE NOW and DIE TASKFORCE SHITHEADS posters emblazoned every structure except the Tomb, which was faced with bamboo scaffolding for repair of Star Girl's infamous exit to nowhere. Looters strolled about with a wealth of construction tools.

The Tomb's inner sanctuary provided respite from the broiler heat, but no sign of Strav. The Memory Pool where Alex once shivered was now a water fight. A hooded figure in a black chador sat in a corner with her head bowed, white shoes in her lap, a perfectly sketched study in faceless despair. Eric looked away to avoid violating religious modesty.

Back into daylight. Waves of heat shimmered off the titanium rubble sculpture. People flowed into the square as in response to inaudible drums, the friction of bodies creating a restless kindling of excitement. Eric's walkie-talkie beeped with a call from his team, but the signal distortion produced the same crackling protest as his lungs.

A tremor in the crowd made Eric turn around. Ten steps away, a looter aimed a large-gauge nail gun at his head.

In that pop-flash moment, Eric saw that the gunman's narrow face spoke a relation to the Township martyr, perhaps a brother; more importantly, he and the gunman were two points of a right triangle, the third being the woman in the chador, who whizzed one of her white shoes at the gunman. It clipped the man's ear, and she readied her other shoe. There was a surreal standoff between orange nail gun and white satin pump. Eric ran the man over like a freight train.

The gunman crawled off to jeers from the crowds. The woman bounded to Eric. Her hood fell back, and by some freak optical twist she was Alex, *his* Alex, her face fierce with triumph.

"Ta-da!" she cried, waving her shoe. "It was like Clara and the Rat King!"

"You could have gotten shot!" Eric yelled.

"He wouldn't shoot me," Alex retorted, though Eric could tell from her trembling hands she had been maybe 50 percent certain, tops. Alex banged the shoe on Eric's chest, leaving dusty scallops across his whites. "You're the one stomping around like the Abominable Snowman. Is 'Die TaskForce Shitheads' too subtle for you?"

"I'm Security Ops!" His lungs felt like they were being cauterized, but he could not stop yelling. "It's what I *do*! But you—you're pregnant!"

The fierce light left her, and her eyes welled with tears. "I am so sorry, Eric."

He made a gruff sound. It was strange enough to have her apologize for getting knocked up by his brother, and stranger still that the apology brought consolation.

"I thought I could get rid—take care of it before Strav found out," she said. "But the apothecary closed."

"Jesus, bug."

"It's the Labyrinth." The falling ash clung to her hair like burnt snow. "Every turn is wrong, and I can't see a way out. I can't do this alone anymore."

The burn in Eric's lungs turned all-consuming. He folded, wheezing, to his knees, seeing only a pattern in flux. Alex was not on the run; her distant land was right here.

They sat pressed together in the shade of a rubble sculpture. Eric drew on the inhaler that miraculously appeared from Alex's chador, marking a loop around the Möbius and back to where they started in the Legion.

"It's a long story," said Alex. "You are not going to like it." She started hyperventilating. Eric handed her his inhaler, figuring it couldn't hurt her. She sucked on the inhaler like a scuba diver run out of air.

"Tough story, huh," said Eric. "Try starting at the end."

She took a hit of courage from the inhaler. "My father is the Asylum Hacker."

Since nothing about that sentence computed, Eric took the inhaler away as punishment until she got serious.

"I am serious! Not my biological father, whoever that is. I mean Patrick, you know, the great mind? I joined the Commission to stop him before he got caught, simple in and out, but I had been alone for so long, and—oh, Eric, I've made such a muddle of things. Rule one is to never tell, for everyone's sake. But, the Net crash! Will the Hacker information help?"

Eric recalled what Strav said about her grief. "Your father is gone, bug. Even if alive, he couldn't program the Asylum—" Eric stopped, snagged on the memory of Patrick Tashen's old CV, the wasted promise of a genius bioengineer.

"My father can do *anything*," said Alex. "He created a gene therapy that everyone says is impossible, just for me. He did it solo in our Plainview Clinic. Took him sixteen years, but still. Are you ready? Because this gets worse."

A new pattern shot into Eric's brain, predicting what she was about to say, and explaining the personal motive of the Asylum Hacker. And no, it could not get worse. Eric yanked Alex to her feet. Every second measured against the need to get her to a safe house, where he could figure out what in fucking hell to do next.

"But I haven't finished!" She slapped indignantly at his hands. "I've waited seven years to tell someone, Eric. Have a heart!"

Eric kissed her like he used to, to shut her up, and he tried the walkie again. He dared not move her until he called in the warrant retraction. Until then, any MP could grab her. Maybe he could hide her in a witness protection program. Secrecy was their only chance.

The walkie gave nothing but static. "There's better signal on the viewing deck," Alex suggested. "Top of the world."

Eric shoved her into an installation of toppled pillars. Girl and chador blended into the crosshatch of light and shadow. "Wait. Here." She held her questions, and promised.

Eric climbed the scaffolding ladder to the viewing deck, fighting an Orpheus urge to look back. For all the entertainment they had provided lately, he figured the crowd on Olympus owed them a few minutes more.

Top of the world, a blare of heat and sun, and Eric saw that he figured wrong.

"Just beat you here," said Jacob, a tall blaze of dress whites and golden hair. The revelers on the deck eyed the two officers. Jacob raised his gun overhead—the familiar Beretta model—and the deck emptied.

"Remember that drawing class we took for the nude models?" Jacob asked. He held up a fax copy of the warrant, squinted a critique at Alex's portrait. "Your style hasn't changed. Still need to work on your mouth."

He motioned Eric to the rail with the gun and patted him down. Close up, Jacob wasn't in much better shape than he—a sour, sweat-pitted uniform, hair plastered to his head and neck, the misery of the Net crash lodged in his bloodshot eyes.

"Wasting your time," said Eric. He counted a dozen Solidarity MPs scouring the crowd below, though not near the rubble sculptures. "Alex is long gone."

"Agreed. We won't see her again. No, I'm here same as you. To find Strav."

Incredible, but Eric had forgotten that original errand. "He was sighted in the park," said Jacob. "He's looking for her, eh? Sad. Still—tell me his pain doesn't give you satisfaction. Your best friend fucking your woman and all. Tell me that betrayal hasn't steered your choices."

Eric's silence spoke for him. Jacob holstered the gun in a wary truce—a kind of cosmic equilibrium achieved, and the two of them finally even.

"Your warrant hit us like a nuke," said Jacob. "Last night at the Gala, Alex was our rodeo princess. What happened? My men started at the Gasthaus. They found her note about going to the Neuro Clinic. Damn lucky break. We beat you there. We got Dr. Vito. Got the array."

Jacob wanted to hash details, and Eric had no time for details. Promise or not, Alex would come looking for him soon. "It's my case," said Eric. "You have no jurisdiction."

Jacob smiled, a twisted grimace that didn't seem wired to the perfect symmetry of his face. "Jurisdiction is the *only* thing I still have. We're both finished, why shit each other? We built our careers defending something good, and holy, yet we brought darkness to the kingdom. What intelligence did she get from you? She took my girls to the carousel, I told her about Solidarity research, and—" It was a moment before Jacob could continue. "I know the Kommandant and Strav went to you. Hell, I could hear that ugly comedown like I was there."

"A warrant was issued. You can't charge them."

"Well played. I still need to question Strav. But he's a victim too. Imagine never knowing what happened to your kid." Jacob shuddered and put a hand on Eric's shoulder. "Family is tough. I appreciate what it cost you to call the warrant. I thought you forgot the Oath. But you did right."

Eric stood mute, caught on the grist that Jacob should be the person to understand. "Damn it, Eric," said Jacob in wonder, almost reverence. "Didn't she take us for a ride?"

Across the square, someone threw a smoldering Molotov at the giant screen. It exploded with a concussive flash, some mechanism jarred loose, and the flame-haired demon resumed its six-armed dance through roils of pitch smoke. The crowd gave a cannon roar and began prancing and jerking in imitation. Another Molotov exploded by a huddle of park rangers. "Burn the pigs!" a woman screamed. "Burn!" The rangers turned in a rout, stripping off orange vests as they ran.

Eric and Jacob stared aghast at the screen. "Holy mother," Eric said. "Can you turn it off?"

"I don't know how."

A young man approached the Tomb, his intent pace through the havoc making him an easy mark. "Eyes on Beki," Jacob said into his walkie. "Black tux, fifty meters dead ahead." To Eric's relief, Strav's trajectory was along the border of the rubble sculptures — not a direct threat to Alex's hiding place, but no room for variables. Jacob's hand grazed his holster, a reminder for Eric to behave, but Eric was several moves ahead. He had exactly one play to remove Jacob, so that he could return to Alex. He needed to stand here, verging on heatstroke and clammy as a heart attack, and let them take Strav.

"On target, *suh*!" responded an anxious cadet in a uniquely shrill voice that could have been heard back in Alabama. Eric saw the same beach-boy beauty as Jacob at that age, one more loop the loop in the ever-accelerating dislocation of time and space.

The crowd threw bottles that bounced off the MPs' helmets and flak jackets. Strav slowed as two drunks in his path traded shoves, then swings with stolen hammers; it was a human truth that the tools made to build and create also made great weapons. What were the chances, wondered Eric, of a drunken encounter at that precise location? The universe turned on such meaningless events. Strav took a detour through the sculptures.

The rest unfolded with dreamlike inevitability. Strav gave a cry that Eric could feel, if not hear, and disappeared in the shadowed pillars.

"What the—" exclaimed Jacob. Eric could play out the reunion below, Strav's *no time to explain, we have to move*; Alex's *I can't, Eric said to wait—*

Eric? Eric is here? Where? Alex stepped from the pillars and pointed up, an unsuspecting arrow straight to where he and Jacob stood shoulder to shoulder, targeting her location.

There was no denying it looked bad, so bad that the moment rose through Eric in a bubble of morbid absurdity—an endless crisscrossing of astonished sight lines between Jacob and Alex and Strav, each of whom struck Eric as remarkably slow on the uptake for once. The sight lines shifted to him, Alex questioning, Strav in savage judgment.

It's not like that, Eric wanted to protest. But he had thrown the bones and invited this fate when he issued the warrant.

The cadet burst around the pillars. He fixed his rifle on Strav and motioned for the girl in the chador to step away. Jacob raised his walkie-talkie, and Eric punched him with everything he had.

The force spun Jacob over the rail onto the scaffolding. Eric went after him with a crash that sent a shower of bamboo poles raining on the crowd below. Jacob landed a vicious kick to Eric's groin. When Eric's vision cleared, Jacob was shouting into the handset, "Forget Beki, get the girl! She's the fugitive, alive, alive, we need her to talk!" Eric went for the Beretta and they grappled, neither able to gain the advantage, until noise from the crowd brought them to a panting stalemate. Strav and Alex had their hands raised at the center point of six electrified MPs.

Game over, yet not quite, as Strav began shouting to the sullen onlookers. Though Eric could not catch the words over the rising calls of approval, he understood that Strav was making the speech of his life—an exhortation to violence, to rise and defy the oppressors, the thunder of all magicians trying to summon the dark.

People poured across the square as if sucked toward a vortex. The relentless pressure of bodies pushed the MPs into an indefensible ring, unable to shoot without endangering each other or the priceless prisoner. An MP fired a round into the sky. An oceanic swell raced through the crowd toward the noise. The wave rose, and the crowd crashed down on the MPs.

The rifles were wrenched from the MPs and turned to bloody clubs. Strav pulled Alex after him into a stumbling run. The cheering crowd parted for them as the Red Sea, the stolen rifles strafing the sky in ear-splitting celebration.

"Where does he think he's going?" yelled Jacob. And even knowing there was no escape, Eric felt a visceral thrill at their flight.

"Guizi!" The cadet with the piercing voice stood howling from atop a bench in a spectacular show of misplaced courage. "She's a real guizi! Guizi, guizi, stop her!"

A new shudder raced through the crowd, a turn of baleful interest in the young couple it had just freed. Eric and Jacob jumped up, their own fight eclipsed, both roaring, "*No! No!*" at the cadet, like stomping on the lit fuse to a bomb.

Quiet. The two men held their breath and gauged the tipping point of the crowd. A few arms raised to join the herky-jerky demon dance. More arms, the chant accelerating through the square. *Burn. Burn.* The passage in front of Strav and Alex closed in a pincer.

Men grabbed Alex and pulled her from Strav. Her fingers slid one by one through Strav's desperate grip, and she disappeared into the boil of the crowd.

Eric and Jacob bolted down the ladder, a joint insanity to enter the mob, and no hesitation. Someone threw a hammer and Jacob went down. Eric kept going.

The center of the square was an impenetrable thicket of bodies. A struggling figure appeared above the sea of heads—Alex in the black chador, thrashing and kicking as the hands passed her along. Down again, then tossed skyward like an orca's broken plaything, her dark hair weightless in the wind, her gown a slash of TaskForce white.

The mob roar at that revelation drove Eric directly into the wall of flesh, throwing people bodily from his path. A clearing appeared ahead—Strav swinging a crowbar like a crazed samurai, hacking an indiscriminate path through the crowd. Men and women screamed and tried to escape.

"Where?" yelled Eric, and Strav, gasping and wild-eyed, pointed to a gang dragging Alex up the stage by her hair. Her face and white gown were bloodied and she was unconscious, her hands contracted in seizure. The gang leader strutted for the crowd, feeding on the noise and frenzy. It was the man with the nail gun whom Alex had humiliated not twenty minutes ago, back when the world was sane. The man upended a sack of looted tools and pointed at the demon's blaze of hair. He picked up a welding torch.

The crowd was so tightly packed in front of the stage that no one could move from Strav's swinging bar. More people poured in behind them. In seconds, Eric and Strav were immobilized as if encased in concrete.

The gang on stage held Alex's limp form upright and poured a paint can of clear liquid over her head. The torch ignited in a streak of orange flame. Strav screamed something that didn't sound remotely human, straining forward as in a straitjacket. *This is not real*, thought Eric, *Strav is not watching this, such things do not happen in bright daylight, a bad dream, time to wake the fuck up.* Alex's hair caught on fire.

The thunder of the crowd was in Eric's body, a sense of his heart actually exploding in his chest. The leader abruptly folded, surprise on his face and a hand to his gut.

A figure was halfway across the stage before Eric comprehended it was Jacob, Jacob white and gold, firing the gun. Jacob threw himself over Alex and smothered the flames with his body.

The gang fell on Jacob with a fury, a hammering fall of metal and boots. The thunder in Eric's head turned real, as a camo Joint Military attack helicopter angled in over the park.

The chopper lowered in tightening circles, showing a turret of guns at the sliding doors. The crowd began a backward surge from the square. Great percussions of heat-stoked air beat down from the blur of rotor blades, whipping people's clothes.

The cough of machine gun fire cut a straight line through the crowd in front of the stage, where the press of bodies provided no room to even cover one's head. The dead and injured could not fall. Then pandemonium, the surge turned stampede. People screamed as they slipped and struggled to stay upright; to lose your footing was to die. A second burst of gunfire, and a teen in front of Eric collapsed, crimson bubbles foaming at a neat hole in his throat. Strav charged toward the stage and Eric tackled him, slamming him face down and immobilizing him in a wrestling hold. A third strafing of machine gun fire raced toward them and veered away at the last second, Eric's white TaskForce uniform turned from target to shield.

The gunfire stopped, but Eric did not let go. Snipers still leaned from the chopper, covering any motion toward the stage. The chopper settled down. Two soldiers with combat packs raced up the stage. They rolled Jacob off Alex with surprising gentleness. Jacob was dead. Alex seemed to be, too, but the soldiers checked for a pulse and quickly unfolded a stretcher.

Strav fought to rise and Eric tightened his grip. "Stay alive," Eric whispered. "For her." The soldiers threw Jacob a salute of respect and raced Alex's stretcher to the chopper. The snipers leaned back, and the chopper took off in a gale of dust.

Eric released Strav. He spat in Eric's face and staggered away through puddles of blood, the bodies sprawled as if fallen from the sky.

Eric limped heavily onto the stage. The air was seared with the smell of burning hair. Jacob's skull and jaw were caved in, but his upper features were oddly intact, his eyes wide open. It seemed he should blink at the light fall of ash. Eric took off his shirt and covered the ruined face, then sat to keep Jacob company. But he was tired, too tired even for that, so he lay down with him in the beating sun.

IV. THE SEA

24

On Thanksgiving Day, one month after the Netcrash riots that swept three continents, Suzanne held a secret funeral at the Allied Cemetery of the Guardians. The Guardians had been built over a Paleolithic burial site northwest of International, hallowed earth for thousands of years before the replica Taj Mahal Chapel gleamed on the plain. That far inland, the lull of warm autumn days could do a gymnast flip to plunging cold blasted down from Siberia. But Thanksgiving—a nonevent for all but bluesy US expats—arrived in a mild, pinkly translucent dawn.

Suzanne walked behind the undraped casket in a processional of one. Shiny crows pecked for bugs atop sun-warmed rises of loam. The neat lines of War Service tombstones extended to a seamless plain of wild rye grass and yellow poppies, directing the eye and mind to the cloudless sky and whatever immortality lay beyond. In contrast, the recent graves from the Netcrash riots looked raw and surprised, as if those laid to rest still couldn't believe it.

An hour later, with General Katrin Bar-Illan finally in the earth, the temperature had dropped fifty degrees and the ground crackled like glass underfoot. Hoarfrost branched in delicate crystalline stars across the polished tombstones, and a dusting of snow hid the fresh-turned earth. The dead could have been there forever.

"Very funny, Katrin," Suzanne told the unmarked grave. Pieter had asked her to keep Katrin's burial quiet, to avoid media or activist attention. Suzanne had no doubt the weather was Katrin's middle-finger response. The caretaker had loaned her a coat, an orange puffer jacket apparently reserved for people who talked to the dead and did not read weather reports. Her teeth still chattered, and every bone ached with cold.

"I've got a story to read you, Katrin. About the girl. Then we're done."

Katrin's crazy titter came up through the frozen earth: *Not done, the girl is yours, Kommandant, your student, your Institute, your watch.*

The wind slapped with an excited tang of snow and pines. The dead souls danced in a flurry. The only thing missing was the satanic black dog.

Damned if a dark form did not approach from the mists. *Come on*, thought Suzanne. If the ghoul thought she had any fight left in her, it had not been paying attention lately.

Suzanne unrolled her copy of the original handwritten pages, tied with black ribbon for a touch of funereal gravitas. Her reading glasses fogged in the bitter air. No matter. She carried the pages as a cross, knew the exact weight of every word. She pitched her voice for the restless dead.

Confession of Patrick Tashen

Welcome, future jury, to the Plainview Penal Ranch, north of old Lubbock and a thousand miles from nowhere. I'm a MD/PhD in computational biology, serving a seventeen-year sentence of medical labor. But I'm a father first. So I'll begin with—

A blast of north wind riffled the pages like an astonished speed-reading ghost. *You were right, Katrin*, thought Suzanne. *Genes do funny things.* Right about the blue-eyed woman in Riga. Right about her newborn on a kindertransport, landing deep in the heart of Texas. Right about the changeling. Maybe even right about getting cursed.

Suzanne picked up reading where the wind left off, on Alex's sixteenth birthday.

Every g-screen will be Russian roulette. She's tearing about the ranch in my Jeep, celebrating her Institute admission, out of her mind with the freedom ahead. What do I tell her now?

A blast of Jeep horn punctures my despair. The flock of chickens explode into brainless riot as Alex peels around the curve. She coasts to a long dainty stop, as if that was the only driving I could see. The Jeep is festooned with banners from the Alex Tashen Inmate Fan Club. "Kick Butt, Alex!" "Watch Out for Them Weirdos in California!"

The portion of my brain apparently reserved for hope begins to see things in the light of possibility. Someday, either the Regime will collapse or the Nations will come around on asylum. The therapy need only buy her the time until things change. Call it denial, but the San Francisco campus might be our razzle-dazzle play.

This Confession, though safe from electronic networks, is another roulette, a tremendous risk if discovered by the wrong eyes. Yet I can imagine a different politic, where this document might be evidence for asylum. How else to confirm Alex's story, if I am dead or unavailable? There is little chance anyone would believe that a lone scientist in Plainview created a gene edit declared impossible by every expert. Attached to this statement are sixteen years of lab notebooks that prove otherwise. Love and desperation do wonderfully focus the mind.

Tonight, I will tell her the truth and break both our hearts. After the tears, my daughter will never look at me the same. But right now, here she comes, bounding to me out of the dusty Jeep, her hair flying, face aglow with news to tell, a whirligig of skinny arms and legs. All I can think is—bless, child. May the world find you as beautiful as I do right now.

The wind quieted, and went still.

Suzanne turned to the crunch of gravel. She removed her reading glasses, and the canine ghoul morphed into a man in an eggplant version of her borrowed puffer coat.

"Hello, Yuri," said Suzanne.

The light was unkind and showed Yuri's age, his eyes rheumy with cold, dark eye bags to match the coat. They had not seen each other since his deployment, and she did not return his calls. Allied troops remained massed along the fronts, missiles programmed, tensions at combustion level. She would have been surprised to see him here, if she weren't so numb and empty.

"Tashen's Confession is a fitting eulogy for Katrin," said Yuri. It could have been a continuation of their last conversation before the crash, about pruning roses for spring. "He would be pleased."

"Would he?" Suzanne said. "Thousands dead in the Netcrash riots. His daughter in a coma. War and nuclear winter a beat away. I doubt this went down like Patrick Tashen wanted. Whoever released his Confession did so because the worst had happened."

Suzanne laid the Confession on Katrin's grave and weighted it with a stone. "I know it was you, Yuri," she said.

Weeks earlier, when Patrick Tashen's double-edged genius came to light, Suzanne had realized that the Asylum Netcasts had not been his most dangerous subversion. The Nations were equipped for high-tech assaults, and Eric's information about the Hacker helped reestablish critical system failures within days of the crash. Tashen himself evaded justice. The Netcasts were not proof of life; the cyberforensics showed that Tashen had written the Asylum code shortly before his doomed flight disintegrated in the avalanche, with each Netcast scheduled to automatically transmit. His daughter, it seemed, had been chasing a ghost.

No, the true subversion was Tashen's handwritten Confession—a zero-tech hack beyond any computer, and therefore infinitely harder to control.

Immediately after the attack in the square, Alex was flown to a

Black Site medical facility for terrorists. Within that secrecy, Handel could frame the story to suit an official narrative, spin the news, while Alex either conveniently expired in surgery or was quietly shipped to the Regime.

Instead, in a Mozart-level stroke of disruption, an anonymous delivery was made to the Academy of Sciences. The package contained sixteen years of lab notebooks, along with specifications for the light spectrum to read the invisible lines. The impact was like tossing chum to a school of great whites. The frenzied scientists confirmed Tashen's novel gene therapy, authenticated his Confession, and nearly bloodied each other in the rush to give interviews.

The commotion might yet have died, had Strav not obtained a copy of the Confession for Rob Blakely, that expert in feeding frenzies. Blakely knew it was critical to leverage the public's morbid fascination, if not their actual sympathy. Different times called for particular kinds of genius, and Blakely showed his.

STAR GIRL PREGNANT BY WOLF KHAN AND EXPOSED AS REFUSÉ!

The media went bananas. Vendors hawked copies of the Confession across the Nations. Blakely's finest stroke was the catch to the heart on the back of each copy: Eric's sketch of the girl with the wistful eyes, lifted from the Fugitive Warrant. SHE IS OURS.

The uproar forced Handel to bring Alex from the Black Site back into the public eye of International's Medical Center. The phrase "invisible freckle" entered the lexicon, as Rob fed the media sentimental pictures of the adorable toddler in a cowgirl onesie, the Institute graduate tossing her cap, the brave officer accepting the Valor. Even die-hard guizi conspiracy theorists were disturbed by the video of the mob attack on a pregnant woman.

The She Is Ours Campaign exploded.

In the meantime, TaskForce Special Intelligence looked for Alex's origin. Suzanne's account of Katrin's ravings led to a surviving soldier who confirmed Alex's resemblance to a singular blue-eyed woman in Riga camp. Two years after the Fall, when the

Regime disappeared the internees, a flight manifest showed that a cargo plane from the Swedish border made an unusual stop at Reese Air Force Base, six miles from Plainview. The dates aligned with the purported birth of Patrick Tashen's daughter.

The individuals involved in the kindertransport were beyond questioning, either dead or in the Federation. They each owned stories, Suzanne knew, of heroism, betrayal, and great sacrifice. But only one story had no ending.

Patrick Tashen had found his future jury—the public—and pled his case. The question remained: Who was the criminal accomplice responsible for the delivery of Tashen's Confession?

"How did you know?" Yuri asked Suzanne. He threw a handful of frozen dirt on Katrin's grave, and touched his forehead in Orthodox prayer.

The beady-eyed crows hopped in to judge her. "The Confession made me remember your shock when you first saw Alex in the Commissary. You denied knowing her, or her father, and I let it go. This time I did the research. The service records are probably hacked, but I found a photo in paper archives." A faded snapshot of two young soldiers playing chess in a primitive snow camp, the big swarthy one waiting on the blonde one with a look of wry affection. Suzanne had slipped the photo from the archives and burned it. "You and Tashen were comrades in the War. The data points suddenly fit. You're a good man, and a liar, and I was a fool."

That's love for you, said Katrin. *Turns the brain to chocolate pudding.* The Thanksgiving flurries lightened to drizzle. The puffer coats turned to heavy sponges.

"I had never met Alex," said Yuri, "but I watched her entire life, from a distance. After the War, I worked with kindertransport network in Protectorate. Word came from Nordic network, a newborn girl needing to go west, fast. Patrick was in Texas prison. He could have been one of the great scientists of our age. Instead, they locked him away. He lost everything. I gave Nordic network his situation. He was smuggled Alex. How he loved that child."

They walked shivering to the chapel. Suzanne wondered when she got too old for the cold. The Paleolithic folk did it right by expiring young, before hot flashes, cataracts, arthritic bones. She and Yuri were literally walking on bones, millennia of men, women, and children layered beneath their feet. The Guardian's neat rows were the barest new sprinkling.

Sprinkled to their right was the Viceroy of the Protectorate. Despite his famed ineptitude, he died protecting his staff. Sprinkled to the left, the Mayor of Shanghai, who abandoned his family to a mob. The smaller headstones of his wife and children lay apart, in permanent reproach.

Beyond them lay the inexplicable story of Jacob Kotas. His headstone was etched with the handprints of his twins, now wards of the State. The splay of fingers, delicate as buttercups, stole the very breath from the wind.

Eric had been proved correct about Solidarity's false-flag bombings of the Legion and VA. The Solidarity Chief claimed the attacks were orchestrated by an overzealous Jacob. Jacob, conveniently postmortem, could not defend his name or implicate his superiors. Even so, Solidarity was on its knees, its head on the block. Suzanne had insisted that Jacob lie among the Guardians. A time for healing, Pieter agreed, having gotten what he wanted.

Why, Jacob? Suzanne wanted to ask. Why the grotesque death protecting a guizi? To save a priceless witness? Some twisted kind of love?

You never know until you're there, said Jacob, and Katrin cawed with the crows.

"What is Dr. Vito's report on Alex?" asked Yuri.

"The good doctor is mindlessly consistent. This surgery, that drug. The pregnancy continues uncomplicated." She thought of Pieter's daily harangue: Uncomplicated? That's easy for Vito to say!

"Why are you here, Yuri?"

His answer was to reach for her hand. Suzanne pulled away. They had each helped bring the world to this chasm, and now stood on opposite sides.

She had told Pieter and Ari the unflinching truth about how, in a guilty panic, she had tried to erase Alex's g-marker detection from the lab machine, aiding and abetting a guizi. Pieter had protected her, as always, by having an investigator scrub the evidence of her crime from the machine. Ari, as always, wove a seamless cover story.

There was no cover for her pain. She had frozen in her most essential duty to the Nations, and left Eric to the soul-destroying dirty work. She could not support Strav's "She Is Ours" campaign — the great peace now hung on Alex's return. Her family had burst into shrapnel, severing the bonds that would have seen her through the twinning fears and humiliations of old age. To unclench her heart would kill her.

Yuri's hand dropped. "And Alex?"

"The Regime agreed to a January 1 deadline for her return. But she goes the moment she's cleared." It was a fraught and remarkable piece of peacekeeping, perhaps the finest of Pieter's career. "No sacrifice can change that. No one can fix this mess."

They reached the chapel and the eternal blue flame at the altar. "Is there no compromise?" Yuri asked quietly. "Compromise has no glory. Some people will always read it as defeat. But sometimes compromise is the tough stand."

Suzanne said goodbye, and left Yuri to what he believed.

25

The January 1 deadline for Alex's removal created a unique security conundrum. As December ticked down toward Christmas,
Suzanne watched Pieter's blood pressure tick up. Alex might not
be an intentional spy, but when handed back, the Regime would
mine the ex-TaskForce officer for any classified information she
possessed. Allied Special Intelligence refused to clear her for return
until she woke from the coma for them to interrogate first.

"Heal her up and wake her up!" Pieter ordered Dr. Vito. But
Alex, off tripping about in her private night sky, was only half
cooperating.

Her physical healing was remarkable, a pairing of extravagant
medicine and effortless youth. "She's a lucky girl," Pieter told
Suzanne, a patently absurd claim, yet true from a certain vantage.
Unknown to Alex's assailants, the varnish poured over her contained
fire retardants, and her burns were mostly first degree. Her stem
cells were isolated and sprayed back on with great success, healthy
skin and scalp growing like gangbusters. The cracked skull and
internal injuries were serious, but Jacob had cushioned the worst
blows. Critically, the medics had cooled her body to a protective
hypothermia within minutes of the attack, preventing permanent
brain damage.

The scramble for stimuli to speed neurological recovery
turned the hospital room into a slapstick ballet of music therapy
and bongos, jasmine perfume, projections of antique maps, live
newscasts, and, to the angst of the security detail, a flow of civilian

visitors. The psychology cannot be separated from cellular processes, insisted Dr. Vito. Familiar presences helped rewire the brain.
Rob Blakely brought gossip. Michelangelo Valenti brought policy.
Strav lay beside her with great care and whispered things that were
nobody else's business.

Eric had been reinstated at a low rank, not that he cared anymore. Suzanne never appreciated the psychological decimation of a
true shunning until Strav passed Eric each night without a flicker
of recognition. For the sleeping girl, though, Eric's presence was
bedside magic, producing the long, healthy brain waves the doctors
sought. Each night Eric settled in with a groan of leatherette reclining
chair and read aloud from the *Bulfinch*, the stories unspooling like
twine in the maze to guide her back from the dark.

No one could fix this mess, and yet—Suzanne felt the sea ice of
the old order grind and groan beneath her feet. Pieter struggled with
the heartburn of his Diplomatic protégé turned personal menace, as
Strav's canny leverage of the celebrity he once loathed kept Pieter in
check. Delay was a deportee's best friend, and Strav, riding high as
Wolf Khan, embraced every minute. Danny Yang hedged his family's
bets by bankrolling the campaign. Atlanta ran the legal strategists,
Blakely the media. Michelangelo sponsored an Extraordinary Asylum
Legislation, a courageous stance certain to cost him his Delegate seat.

"It's a fine thing not to care what anyone thinks," Valenti
dryly declared at the press conference, Strav wincing at his side.
"She Is Ours!"

"*Scheiße*," Pieter told Suzanne. They were in Ari's room field-
ing calls from equivocating Delegates. "Without that damnable
Confession, we would have quietly disposed of her."

"Maybe strangled in the high tower." Suzanne reflexively
looked for Ari, expecting him to chime in about the limits of the
"royal we." But Ari, like Alex, was adrift in unknowable dreams.
The two souls were crisscrossing in the dark, the youth rising back
to the light, the old vet sinking toward the Guardians, and Suzanne
wondered if the juxtaposition was making Pieter unhinged.

"Heal her up and wake her up!" Pieter vented to Dr. Vito.
"Whatever it takes!"

Alex began to speak from her deep winter sleep. As the true coma ebbed into a medically induced coma, the Special Investigators brought her to the prime twilight state for credibility assessments. The stretchy cap of electrodes, eye trackers, pupil readers, facial action codes, and infrared helped track neural impulses and unconscious physiological responses to carefully constructed questions. Her own body was the ultimate lie detector test.

The embryo spoke with a *whoosh-whoosh* on the sonogram screen, refusing to skip a beat or a cell division. Some doctors saw a tribute to their medical skills. The devout, like Dr. Vito, saw proof of mysterious ways. Suzanne saw that the toughest combatant Pieter ever faced was a squiggle the size of a sweet pea.

Christmas Day. Alex's room smelled of fresh-cut pine and looked like Santa's workshop. "It's ironic," Suzanne told Pieter as they stood over the sleeping girl. "This moral compunction to get her healthy enough to die of starvation or firing squad."

Pieter stroked Alex's cheek. "You think me heartless? I have daughters of my own. I also have the Regime's promise to take out Paris if she's not returned by New Year's Day."

"They should be thanking us." In a mordant twist, the Regime was blasting video of Alex's immolation across the Federation, stoking nationalistic frenzy over the torture of one of their own by the barbaric Allied Nations. "We've given them the greatest propaganda coup of all time."

"And we gain mutual Diplomatic Missions and export markets in the satellite states. My Joint Chiefs are happy. Beijing, Berlin, Washington, and Delhi are in a unison we could only dream. It is not just preventing apocalypse. It's an evolution in the peace."

Suzanne watched the sonogram.

"If I stop Alex's removal," said Pieter, "our coalition dissolves and my successor deports her anyway. No sane human being starts a war over one person."

"Two persons." Strav had established paternity of the fetus, then bootstrapped the claim into a Petition for Custody requiring

Alex's removal to be held in abeyance until after childbirth. The petition was denied. The court held the law crystal clear. The safety of the Nations could not be held hostage to gestation periods or custody claims. Under the Treaty, the child of a refusé was a refusé. The Regime claimed mother and child; it went when she went.

"There's no proof the Regime will harm her, or the baby," said Pieter.

"What do they say will happen to them?"

He paused, a small concession. "They say it's none of our business."

Three days to deadline, and Special Intelligence issued its report. The twilight credibility assessments confirmed the independent findings. Alex was as illegal as a dirty bomb, guilty of a thousand perjury and fraud offenses, but no spy. Her only knowledge was within her lowly TaskForce security clearance—a headful of diplomatic embarrassments, certainly, but nothing to imperil the Nations' defense. The Order on Removal was approved, pending medical release and Strav's latest maneuver: an expedited appeal entitled "Declaration of Khanate Citizenship of Unborn Child."

"I think sweet pea has you by the short hairs," said Suzanne, reading the appeal on Ari's hospital room screen.

"Strav did learn from the best," said Pieter. "Ja, how much sharper than a serpent's tooth."

"He's the prodigal son you two never had," said Ari.

"He doesn't guard his back," said Pieter. "It is the nature of prodigals to learn the hard way."

"How hard?" Suzanne asked warily.

Pieter nabbed her reading glasses and scrolled down. "Our Wolf Khan is calling on his tribe. Khanate law says a child fathered by a member of the Clans is a citizen of the Khanate at conception. Archaic trivia, except for an obscure clause in the Nations' Constitution that gives full faith and credit to such laws. Ergo, sweet pea is a citizen of the Nations. No. This stops now."

"How hard?" repeated Ari. There was scuffling outside the room.

"The prodigal just learned his visitation privileges with Alex are revoked," said Pieter. "Let him in."

Strav entered heated and off-kilter. He still bowed in engrained deference to his commander in chief. Suzanne saw the room through Strav's eyes—three gray-haired crones stirring their foul pot, double, double, toil and trouble.

"You can't keep me from her!" It was a rookie mistake to make the opening move, and they all knew it.

Pieter raised a conciliatory hand. "Dr. Vito's orders. Your presence is agitating her."

"That's a lie."

"May we speak freely, Envoy?" said Pieter, turning Suzanne and Ari into silent props among the green blinking monitors. "I have brought you to this veteran's room to see the face of a war you cannot remember. That millions suffered, as this good man still suffers, is an abstraction to you. You are young and in love. You would let the world burn for one person. I admire that. I even envy it. But I cannot allow it."

Suzanne saw Strav's flicker of apprehension; it was sinking in that the revoked visitation was a silky preliminary to a master class in power politics.

"I invited the Khanate Elders Council to comment on your appeal," said Pieter. "The High Court has adopted the Elders' statement." He threw a new page to the screen.

Appeal denied. The Court holds, to wit: The removal of the guizi Alex Tashen is of no concern to the Khanate people. Strav Beki's misconduct and adultery, however, is of great concern. Beki's private request for annulment is denied. His bastard mekin is no citizen under tribal law, and the Beki Clan disavows the child. The Elders apologize for Strav's shameful behavior, and demand he honor his vows or forfeit ancestral rights to the land.

Strav looked to Suzanne, his bewilderment a wrench in time to the ragged boy in her Kommandant's office, plucked from the steppe and his beloved home on her assurance of safe return. Suzanne was the first to look away.

"You can't win this one, Envoy," said Pieter. "Your only weapon is public outrage, and that's a fickle friend. By the next morning, people shake their heads and get another cup of coffee. You run out of shock value. It's a very, very old story."

It was a story wasted on Strav's back as he headed for the door. Pieter called sharply at the disrespect. Strav turned, and Suzanne saw a new face, of a warrior done wasting time.

"I thank you for the lesson," Strav said. "*The villainy you teach me I will execute, and it shall go hard but I will better the instruction.*"

They blinked at him. Strav translated for them with a hard smile. "Your reign is almost over, old man. I am going to destroy you. There will be no mercy or forgiveness."

The guards followed him out at a cautious distance.

"Speak freely," muttered Ari in the rattled silence. "Fabulous idea! Can't say you didn't ask for that." Ari's monitors reflected his agitation. Nurses came to shoo the visitors. Suzanne bent to tell Ari goodnight.

"If Pieter's wrong," Ari whispered, "and there is another way, promise to do whatever it takes. Someone has to fix this mess."

She kissed his forehead, *we'll see.* If she had known he was hours from a catastrophic stroke, she would have promised him anything.

December 30 was Armistice Observance, a natural overlay of year-end reflection and anticipation of vicious hangovers. Suzanne and Pieter made their annual commemoration trek to the Guardians. Light snow fell in a freezing vanilla haze, but this time Suzanne was armed with her wool greatcoat and the company of a thousand other living souls. Pieter lit joss sticks on the altar and led the crowd in the call and response: "*Fini la guerre. Fini la guerre.*" The chapel infused with tangy sandalwood. Families scattered to picnic with their dead.

Every young person Suzanne passed seemed to wear a sticker with the sketch of Alex's face. She Is Ours. *She's yours*, mocked Katrin with a malicious puff of wind. *Whatever it takes*, added Ari. Ari wasn't legally dead—Pieter could not bear to kill the life support—but Suzanne felt him already haunting her, joining company with Katrin and Jacob, the black dog and the blue-eyed mother. She needed a bigger bed to fit everyone in at night.

Katrin's gravesite was hard frost, the Confession still folded beneath the rock. A man hailed her, and Suzanne turned in senseless anticipation, expecting Yuri.

"Look, old girl!" Pieter broke through the invisible host. "We have the medical release! She goes tonight." His screen showed Alex sitting up in her hospital bed, giving the doctors loopy drugged grins. Eric knelt at her side. "You're naked," Alex warned Eric, which startled a laugh from everyone except Eric. He tucked her back in, and she returned to dreamland.

"An Armistice miracle," said Suzanne. Maybe Pieter really did rule by divine right.

"The Nations are saved, even Strav can't—" His screen flashed with a new filing: "Emergency Assembly Petition pursuant to Charter Section 310.54." The hearing was set for noon, January 1—an hour before the deadline.

Pieter let loose a guttural rant of *fickens* and *schießes*; sometimes the German meant exactly what it sounded like.

"Forget prodigal son." His English returned. "That boy is the scourge of God."

Strav's new loophole was a buried Charter provision defining refugees as "displaced human beings entitled to the same protections and respect as citizens of the Nations." The Petition argued that Alex, as a displaced human being, was entitled to Charter protections.

"A Hail Mary," said Suzanne, carried back to chill winter stands, the vertiginous soar of a spiral launch on a prayer. So the Assembly, faced with the unappetizing prospect of explaining why the Star of Valor recipient was not a human being, had set this extraordinary hearing—without informing Pieter.

The sea ice shifted and groaned, and the Assembly heard it too. The Wolf Khan had his world stage. Blakeley's press release promised scandalous revelations and personal secrets.

"Think of it as a tribute," said Suzanne. "To your fine lecture about shock value."

A birdcall of children pierced the haze. Suzanne had a horrible thought of dirt-encrusted babies rising up to sing in her ears, but it was real children; their laughter ran up and down the rows of the cemetery and chased the crows to flight.

"Let him have his show," said Pieter, his mad gleam returned. "Meet me at Ari's. We have a wolf to skin."

Suzanne wasn't about to rush. The crowds cleared, the day grew warm. The layered bones settled beneath her feet. Ancient hunter or farmer or traveler-through, each had looked up, like her, to wonder at the changeable sky; a flit of life, and back to the heavy earth. Suzanne felt their countless numbers, their great indifference and apparent peace. Whether comfort or oppression, she could not decide.

One day, none of this would matter. Perhaps nothing would transcend. Yet some moments had to stretch across time, forever alive in the present. Somewhere, a father watches his daughter bound from the dusty Jeep, her face aglow with news to tell, a whirligig of skinny arms and legs. *Bless, child*, he thinks. *May the world find you as beautiful as I do right now.*

26

The drugs are *great*. The white room blurs, and Alex laughs as she swings to the sky—

—back on her wooden swing in Plainview, the astronaut freedom at tippy-top, then backwards in gravity's grab. She has no intention of coming in for bedtime, but hears "*In ancient times there lived in Thessaly a king and queen*," and even knowing the voice is a lure, she is curious.

The door of their Quonset hut opens to the Legion's resplendent rotunda, and the mad party is rocking. The Thinker, covered in white powder, pumps his fist to the electro-beat. Dog-headed people in dress whites drink flutes of champagne served on mappa mundi napkins by winged cupids. Sea serpents spout and breach through the rippling mosaic floor, and snatch the occasional cherub. "Who abhors an empty space?" screams the poodle-head Majordomo. "We abhor an empty space!" the company howls back. It should be a blast, but her slinky blue dress keeps slipping off, the four-eyed men beginning to ogle and pinch. The galleries are a maze, but the voice returns, a thread to follow.

She finds Patrick in a longship made from tumbleweeds. He glances in reprove at her dress, which hardly seems fair, considering he is in a Greek tunic cut high on his hairy thigh, jade beads braided into his beard. A tiny wolf cub chases a snarling golden fleece about the deck. The cub has amber yellow eyes, and Alex can hear its excited heartbeat *whoosh-whoosh*. Patrick grabs the cub by the scruff and gets a wet lick on the nose. The fleece hops overboard in a snit.

"Someone has to fix this mess," says Patrick, pointing at her. She understands that he isn't dead, but is in no position to help. The fleece hunkers like a wolverine and bares gold spiked teeth. "Don't worry," says Patrick. "It's more afraid of you than you are of it."

The fleece scoots behind the marble Hercules. The embittered loneliness in the demi-god's pose brings Alex to tears. She presses her hand against the cool stone chest. Eric yawns and scratches his great alabaster balls.

"Well fuck a yellow duck," he says, looking around.

"You're naked," she warns, but the other milling statues don't notice. If he doesn't get a hard-on, they should be okay. She knows everyone, and, thank the gods, the rest are clothed. The Kommandant wears Hera's jewels and holds a grenade-like pomegranate, marking her as the patron goddess of childbirth. Her sour expression suggests it's a prank.

"Ja, ja," booms towering Zeus in an Austrian accent. "No sane human being starts a war over one person." Alex can't disagree, but Rob adjusts his Hermes cap and takes off on winged loafers to bomb His Honor with Confessions. Michelangelo throws back a skin of wine, paws the ground with his Pan hoof and headbutts Handel's knee. "My favorite toxin-induced epileptogenesis!" cries Vito Daedalus, brandishing a blueprint of her brain. Handel swats them away like mosquitoes.

The fleece slinks to the *Argo's* bow, which sports a magnificent blonde figurehead. The pair of globulous breasts threaten to front-capsize the ship. Eric pinks from scalp to toes, and there's the hard-on.

"Hey, blue eyes," Atlanta purrs to her. "I'm your lawyer. Want to touch 'em?"

Who wouldn't? She and Eric reach up together, but a furious cry rattles the glass ceiling, "*Chu! Chu!*" and a creature of the sky races earthward—Bellerophon, riding flat along Pegasus's streaming mane, refusing to pull back until, *kaboom*, they crash through the glass rotunda.

"Fucking show-off," mutters Eric, straining to hold up a broken column that would reduce horse and rider to goo. Strav dismounts, oblivious, while Fast Talker tries to take a chunk from Eric's bulging arm. Unlike the rest of the toga party, Strav is in a tuxedo. Zeus prepares a thunderbolt.

"Surrender!" Strav yells up at Handel. "I've got a speech!"

She knows about his speech, the Emergency Petition and New Year's deadline, which seems oddly specific for a dream.

"That's because everyone talks in front of you," sniffs Kommandant Hera. "The news is always on in your room, Blakely gossips with the nurses, Pieter strategizes without any understanding of conscious sedation. Hell, you have the best vantage in town."

Beyond the galleries comes music of the ocean—the bray of a foghorn, the *splosh* of piers, the thunder of distant breakers. A wave glides in, cold and sucking at her ankles. Chiron the centaur wades by, carrying elfin Vlad on his broad equine back. The Bulgakov-upper kisses the Kommandant and hands the child to Patrick on the *Argo*.

"Problem of the week," says Patrick, going Socratic on her. "Following trauma, the brain's cognitive machinery strains to reboot a computational model of subjective awareness. What then is the crucial difference between being asleep and waking up?"

That should be an easy ten points, but she's distracted by the swell of calliope music. "*Think*," Patrick says with urgency. He heaves on the halyard. The mainsail rises into a blinding sun. Apollo spirals in on a chariot of flame pulled by carousel horses. The sea hisses and boils as Jacob hands the twins to Bulgakov, each girl clutching a chocolate moose.

Jacob pulls her into the chariot and a scorching takeoff. "You owe my girls," says Jacob.

"I can raise them. Like Suzanne did Eric."

"And see how that worked out." They look down at Eric, naked and punching a winged horse. Still, Jacob's conviction that she is lousy parent material bothers her. Where does she fit in this pantheon? Loyal Psyche? Beautiful Aphrodite?

"Hint," Jacob says. "Deceitful, manipulative, destroys families, casts spells."

Medea the witch. Well fuck a yellow duck.

The gallery turns distant island in a white-capped sea. The horizon ends at a dun plain so featureless she thinks it's West Texas. Another look, and she shrinks in dread. No color, no light, a cartographic bane of nothing—the void beyond the imagined world, edge of the true unknown.

A monster gust heels the chariot like a sailboat in a squall. A black wall of hurricane speeds toward them, and it is a god killer. The sea serpents, no fools, escape to the open ocean, leaving foamy wakes in the maddened waters. Fear for herself turns to fear for those in the *Argo*.

"About time," mutters Jacob.

"The entrance of the sea," comes the voice, "was impeded by two rocky islands, crushing and grinding to atoms any object that might be caught between them." Two mountains of Legion-rubble smash together as the *Argo* tries to reach open ocean. The ship is trapped.

"*Think*, witch!" Jacob yells. "Remember the research you got me talking about, transplants, memory. You're the only one with all the pieces."

The chariot heels over, and she falls, flailing, until the thread of voice stops her like a bungee cord, a stomach-lurching *boing ba-boing* that leaves her wing-splayed like a bird, talons out, in the calm white eye of the storm.

The white turns hospital room, low lit for nighttime. Little flapping motions let her fly around the ceiling, which is extremely cool. Curled below in the bed is a caricature of herself, hair shorn, new skin pink as a hatchling. The squiggle on the natal sonogram makes a rapid-fire *whoosh-whoosh*, a wolfish little grin of a sound.

Sweet pea, ha! This one is going to make Genghis look like Mahatma Gandhi.

Eric is spilled over the recliner, reading aloud from the *Bulfinch*. "When the *Argo* reached the islands, they let go a dove, which took her way between the rocks." Eric's constant voice; she always knew it. The room is stripped of fantasy—that's real musky heat off Eric's uniform—but time is playing games. Strav scuffles with the guards, or maybe that's to come; Pieter Handel will stroke her bandaged face tomorrow, or last week. *Think*. The crucial difference between sleep and waking is the ability to distinguish between memories and current events—

—morning light through her room's barred window. It must be January 1, removal deadline, because a transport team of Marines lines the hallway. The Emergency Petition Hearing begins in an hour, a promise of blood sport, and the newscast on the wall screen is giving pregame coverage. To her astonishment, there are asylum rallies across the Nations. People wave SHE IS OURS signs with Eric's finished sketch of her face.

The newscast zooms to International's great domed Assembly Hall. Three blows on the ceremonial ram's horn announce the secretary general. An artfully placed shaft of light beatifies Handel's silver head. Delegates and speakers take plush seats. The cameras search for the one indispensable speaker. The hearing is about to start, and where is the Wolf Khan?

Alex flap-floats to her hospital window. Strav is on the lawn, gazing up at her room. *Oh, my love*, thinks Alex. He bows at her window, fist to his heart. And strides off for battle, no idea that she is winging along, joined to him sure as a hawk on a tether.

Once in the Assembly, she flies above the audience on thermals of body heat. Delegate Valenti presents the first and last Council action he will ever sponsor. Anything sounds great in an Italian accent, yet he could do a strip tease and no one would pay attention. His role is to cede his time to Strav.

Pieter Handel takes the podium. "There is no denying," says Handel in a tone of intimate conversation, "the emotional impact of brutal images. We are moved by the plight of an individual, and we share a special affection for this young woman who has suffered a great trauma. So let her be the face of the thousands of young people maimed or killed in the riots. Let them remind us that the Treaty is not a capitulation but for our benefit, to prevent an uncontrolled exodus from the Federation. The riots were triggered by a single guizi. Do the Nations have the security or stability to handle an onslaught of millions? The petitioner's own horrific experience is the strongest argument for compliance with the Treaty."

Alex feels the chaos in Strav's head. Handel is the best, and there is nothing he can do about it.

"The petitioner's return is not the gratuitous cruelty that some claim," says Handel. "It is simple ethics. It is unethical to permit the pathos of an individual to eclipse our larger obligations. It is unethical to negotiate over the heads of our constituency and place billions of people in peril of war or aggression." The Delegates' postures reflect their moods—a few are cross-armed, but most are leaning back as if on a chauffeured ride. Alex realizes that Strav could talk the planets into new orbits and still not change this vote. The result was fixed before they got here.

When Strav goes to the podium, she is in his head. She feels the crushing pressure, the eyes staring, the darkness obliterating coherent thought. Just as Alex thinks it is over, she sees an image form in his mind—of her, giving birth alone in a freezing barrack, the pain and terror of it, the weakening cries of a newborn and bleeding that will not stop.

Strav lifts his face. The words are a near stutter, but they come.

"I stand here—here in several capacities today. To plead as would any man for the life of his wife and child—for Alex is my wife, in the eyes of God, if not yet the law. I stand as a Diplomatic officer who proudly serves the Nations. And I stand as a witness to the experience of captivity. Many of you know I was taken prisoner during a hostage negotiation." The Majordomo raises the gavel to throw him off-stride. The cheap trick enrages Alex. But Strav's pulse steadies to a *whoosh-whoosh*, a wolfish little grin of a sound.

"I do not argue to overturn the Nations' policy on refusés, though, God forgive me, perhaps I should. I plead for an exception due to extenuating circumstances. Alex has but one homeland, to which she has given her love, loyalty, and service. Her offense is the wrong parents and a will to survive. Yet we offer her as a human sacrifice, not just to the Regime but to the fears and inculcated compliance that would turn this Assembly, turn us all, into willing procurers. Procurers for slavery, for murder, for torture.

"In many ways, Alex is a mirror for the rest of us. I hope that none of you ever have to live with the weight of a fatal secret, as she has, but we all have secrets. We all understand shame. Yet there are times when shame can force us, individually and as a people, to the right action. This is such a time, and so I will speak of shame, a condition with which I have some personal experience."

Alex flies from his mind in alarm. Strav is going to tell the Assembly, the world, what happened to him in Croatia.

Disaster. Yes, his story will feed the ravenous public appetite, light a torch on this fight, even empower other victims. But his sacrifice will not save her or the unborn child from the transport. It will not save his steppe family from eviction to a squalid settlement, or keep him from death or prison. What the story will do, unwittingly, is destroy everyone who kept his secret. Eric will be charged with destruction of evidence and conspiracy, along with Chow and the doctors.

She flies between Eric and the Kommandant, each sitting stiff-backed and apart. She beats invisible wings in their faces—don't let him speak!

"The experience I am about to relate," says Strav, "is to provide a measure for your vote. Know this: the shame I have lived with the past year would be nothing compared to the shame of belonging to an institution that could shrug at the politically expedient condemnation of a pregnant woman. Has this Assembly been rendered so toothless and ineffectual, so captive in its own right? There are always alternatives, if one has the will and motivation to search for them. Is it not the role of the Administration to present those options for your consideration? This once, can we not tell those who make the deals and decisions in the closed back rooms, tell them no, this time is different, you shame us, we will not condone the sacrifice of a young woman who has served and suffered for us, nor the life of her innocent child, so go back behind your closed doors and *find us another way.*"

The Envoy is back, holding even the skeptical Delegates at rapt attention. *What a creature you are*, thinks Alex through tears of pride and frustration—obdurate, soaring Bellerophon, doomed to defy the gods. And Zeus sent a gadfly to sting the winged horse so the rider plummeted to earth, left to wander crippled and blind. She would give anything to fix this.

The gavel cracks like a deal struck. The wind rises, carrying the taste of brine and the chorus from a trapped ship. *Think, witch.*

This Assembly cannot be real, for the simple reason that *she* is here flying around.

"*The dove took her way between the rocks, only losing some feathers of her tail. Jason and his men seized the favorable moment of the rebound, plied their oars with vigor, and passed safe through, though the islands closed behind them and grazed their stern.*"

The rocks grind open with a terrible noise. She must go first, and alone, for the others to reach safe waters. Her course is into the true unknown, and she is afraid.

"Wake up, bug," she hears. A diver's slow spinning rise from the deep, toward a silver curve of light and sound. The shapes magnify, painfully bright, and she is through.

Alex opened her eyes. The grinding noise was a heavy snore—Eric in the recliner, the *Bulfinch* open on his chest. The wall screen read December 31, 2:30 a.m. The New Year's Day Assembly, and Strav's speech, had yet to happen.

The sonogram display beside her bed showed a bitty critter that looked dredged from the vasty deep, stubby little limbs and a bright curve of spine. A green speck blipped in its middle, *whoosh-whoosh*, a wolfish little grin of a sound. Alex grinned back with the most curious feeling, like a piece of her own heart had skipped out to play.

"Aren't you the little troublemaker?" Alex said softly, and just like that, she fell in love.

She spent the rest of the night in calculation, her eyes on the blipping heart. Eric left at dawn. Feigning sleep when Eric kissed her goodbye was the hardest thing she had ever done. They needed to comfort each other, explain and forgive. But she would inevitably tell him her plan, and he would stop her. This is what it meant to go first, and alone.

Time to test out the body. She flopped her wasted chicken legs, stretched her pink drum skin, tried to find a place that didn't hurt.

"Welcome back, child," said Dr. Vito. He rubbed his shaved head, his face chalky with night-call exhaustion. "I know it hurts. They forced me to pull *all* the drugs yesterday." Alex understood why she was sharp-minded, her dreams so acute. Her brain had healed long ago, but Dr. Vito had kept her asleep to delay the removal.

Dr. Vito increased the magnification on the natal sonogram. "Meet my star patient. He's a fighter, like his mother." Dr. Vito touched his St. George. "Forgive me, Alex. I did not understand before. But there is always a greater plan. Some children are just meant to be born."

"I know," said Alex. "That is why you are going to do exactly what I tell you."

27

"A secret New Year's Eve summit tonight!" exclaimed Pieter, reading the card from Alex. "To discuss a 'mutually advantageous' plan? Who does she think she is, Franklin D. Roosevelt?"

"The joys of junior faculty," said Suzanne. "That's what they do."

"She wants you too, old girl."

Yours, she's yours. The ghosts were close and restless this final day of the year, playing expectant witness. Pieter's cover-up report on her detection of the g-marker had been issued that morning, clearing Kommandant Burton of any malfeasance, and commending her for running the genetic array. The ghosts were not buying her absolution.

"Do not underestimate Alex," Suzanne advised Pieter. The peace required Alex gone the minute after the hearing tomorrow. There was no upside to a clandestine visit.

But Alex's bait was irresistible, with a gleaming barb to set the hook—a twice-underlined "It is imperative that Envoy Beki not know of our meeting." Astute, wily girl, to reel in Pieter Handel. Suzanne was never so proud of her.

Security reported a stream of doctors and lawyers to Alex's hospital room all day, including the unflappable Ms. Atlanta. She looked flapped. "Don't go," Suzanne advised, but Pieter had moved beyond the constraint of her opinions. Suzanne understood that she had slid among the ghosts.

———

Alex had chosen to believe the secretary general would come, but his actual arrival seemed as miraculous as Zeus's shower of gold. The Kommandant was a different shock, a gaunt, diminished presence that snuffed any fantasy of Hera intervention. Handel took the recliner while Dr. Vito and Atlanta retreated to corners. Alex tried to emulate Handel's royal posture, but her new skin itched as if swarming with ants, and her back was killing her; whoever designed hospital beds needed to be shot. She waited for Atlanta to present the plan. The attorney's supreme cool made her seem like perfect counsel, but angst about her role now kept Atlanta as mute as the Kommandant.

So much for her power-women role models. Alex tried to push back her hair, but it was gone, a phantom limb, like His Honor's missing arm. She could see herself as they did, a buzz-cut fledgling in a pink paper gown, squawking to stay in the nest.

"Your Honor," said Alex. "Do you know American football?"

Handel glared at Suzanne. "Always, this football!"

"Every Sunday in Plainview we had pickup games. Gig 'em. If our team got trapped, my father tossed the rule book and called a razzle-dazzle." She saw Handel's skeptical noblesse. "You and I are trapped, Your Honor. You need to save your legacy. I need to save my family. Together, we can pull a razzle-dazzle. We'll both win."

"Thank you," said Handel with amusement, "but my legacy is in perfect health."

"Editorials in the premiere military and financial journals describe a fading world leader unable to capitalize on the turmoil in the Federation due to his blind obsession with an archaic Treaty. With due respect, sir, the money says the bloom is off your edelweiss."

"Alex!" said the Kommandant. Handel waved her off.

"The world is changing, Your Honor. My father kicked the door open with his Confession. Envoy Beki is about to drive a tank through it. I know the Petition hearing is rigged. You will win my removal. But Strav's *speech* will cost your coalition and election. By the end of tomorrow's Assembly, I'm a pregnant Mary and you're Hitler in the bunker."

Lawyer and doctor flinched in the background.

"You cannot know that," said Handel.

"You'd be surprised." Her flat certainty knocked the amusement from Handel's face.

Floodlights switched on outside the barred window, illuminating a chase of midnight snowflakes. "Go on," said Handel. "Razzle-dazzle me."

Alex started breathing again. "Simple as one, two, three, Your Honor. *One.* I consent to my removal, and leave before tomorrow's Assembly. That cancels the hearing, and the speech. *Two.* Before I go, Dr. Vito uses Solidarity research to secretly transplant my fetus to a surrogate. The Regime will believe I had a miscarriage. *Three.* When the child is born, he remains hidden safe in the Nations, in Strav's custody."

The confounded silence went on and on, as if His Honor and the Kommandant had stalled in a different time zone. *Come on, people*, Alex wanted to yell. *Keep up!*

"It's what Eric calls an elegant solution," she explained for the ossified minds. "I did not want to be pregnant. But this child is no longer a theory. In six months, he will take his first breath. It must be in a safe place. Solidarity has success with fetal transplantation. Jacob told me, when—well, he told me. The procedure gives the child better odds than where I'm going."

Everyone turned to Dr. Vito. "She's thirteen weeks, inside the window. The program has surrogates prepped for reproductive grafts. Yes, it can happen first thing tomorrow."

"Is this Envoy Beki's idea?" Handel asked, a baffled grope of a question. "He would sell you out for the child?"

"Never!" She was insulted on Strav's behalf. "It is *my* choice. Strav can't know until I'm gone, or he will stop it." She tried again. "This is multifactorial. For all the trouble Strav is causing you, he's still constrained by my presence. Send me and the child back, and you create a monster with nothing to lose. Strav *will* come after us. Every scenario ends terribly for Strav, for you, your Treaty, the Nations."

She let them catch up. "If you want to control Strav, you need a sword to hold over him. The Regime can't claim the child if they don't know he exists. Sure, the kid has my g-marker, but look how long my dad hid me, without resources. Make that secret conditional on Strav's good behavior—he makes trouble, you expose the child. This is his son. Strav will swallow any bitter pill to protect him."

Let the child save the father. If she knew both were safe, she could bear anything.

Alex looked to the Kommandant. She would understand that saving Strav meant saving Eric. But the Kommandant was lost in the flurries outside the window.

"The plan has one flaw," Alex acknowledged, a preemptive strike against what no one would say aloud. "Me. The Regime will interrogate me, and they will be efficient. That's why Dr. Vito is going to pull another trick from the Solidarity hat." *Yes, Jacob. I have all the pieces.*

"Memory ablation," explained Vito. "We excise her memory of the plan by lighting up the specific neurons and using convergent lasers. It's particularly effective with recent, unconsolidated memories. She'll basically lose a day—in effect, reawake from the coma, but no longer pregnant. She'll believe a miscarriage because she won't remember the transplant."

"*Gott bewahre,*" said Handel. A cloud settled over the room. "What happens if the lasers damage too much?"

Vito shrugged unhappily. "We are all a few gray cells from being a different person."

This was not an ethics debate Alex could allow with her skittish team. She turned on Vito. "You insisted on this child's right to be born, damn the consequences. Here they are. I missed the last three months of my life. What's one more day? You don't get to sign out."

Atlanta recovered a professional poise. "Dr. Tashen's mental competence is certified by a panel of psychoanalysts. Her consent provides you legal protection, Your Honor."

"I'm not exactly welcome here," Alex said helpfully. "They did try to burn me to death."

"I know," Handel said with a heaviness of spirit that took her by surprise.

"I'm not martyr material," she said in honesty. "I'm doing the math. The video of the lynching makes me a unique propaganda asset to the Regime. I intend to leverage that value. I spent the last seven years wondering about my biological parents. Now I have a mother who put me on a kindertransport. I need to look for my family." And so her search continued, transformed in scope and geography. "The only answers are over there."

The Kommandant remained fixed on a vision outside the dark glass. "Of course I'm scared," said Alex, to reach her. "I may end up in a gulag. But my chances are exponentially better if I'm not limited by being pregnant or caring for an infant. I believe the world will change. I believe that someday this kid will meet his grandparents. But now, for both our sakes, I have to go alone."

Handel nodded. The *whoosh* from the sonogram sped with Alex's excitement. The dream-wind shrieked, the waves veined with white, and the clashing rocks ground open.

"I have ancillary requests," she said, leaping on the momentum. "Each one provides you a strong secondary benefit." She listed them. Eric's Directorship reinstatement, for Security Ops loyalty. A settlement for the Kotas twins, for a clean slate with Solidarity. An annulment for Strav and safeguards for his Khanate family, another way to control the Wolf Khan. A new vote on Protectorate Independence, to consolidate the Asia base. Alex finished in a blaze and fell back exhausted, the map laid out complete.

Handel sighed in admiration. "From a hospital bed, in one day," he marveled. "If I had you in my Cabinet, the world might be a different place." He glanced at his watch.

Alex's soar of elation stalled, and reversed. What leverage had she on a god? Her hand moved by a strange new instinct to protect her belly.

Handel stood and bowed. "I will think on your proposal. Good luck to you, Alex Tashen." The Kommandant followed him out.

"That's youth for you," Pieter told Suzanne. "They dazzle and disappoint at the same time."

They headed across the hospital to visit Ari, not that Ari knew it anymore. The transport team of Marines scrambled up from their card games, jamming black berets over buzz cuts. Pieter waved them at ease.

"Well?" Suzanne asked in the privacy of Ari's room.

"Well what?" Pieter collapsed in the chair. The monitor lights gave a green tinge to the shadows under his eyes. "She gave a stunning performance. Fini."

Suzanne went to the window. The spill of light from the room made a snow globe in the night. She felt the seep of cold air on her wrists, heard the nameless things banging against the glass. Something was going to shatter.

"Alex is trying to do what her mother did," said Suzanne. "Give her child a chance. And she's right. Going alone gives her a better chance too."

Pieter stiffened in shock at an argument. Ari's bedside was holy ground, a family vigil of remembrance and past.

"Fetal transplants," said Pieter. "Memory ablation! If word got out, it would be perceived as a grotesque strong-arm tactic against a desperate mother. I would be the fini."

"Alex has found a way to fix this mess. It's a dangerous, no-glory compromise." As Yuri said: sometimes compromise is the tough stand. "You could turn it to your advantage. You always do."

"I tend to, don't I?" He kissed Ari's waxen forehead, gave a bitter exhale of grief. "Yet here we are. The reality is that Envoy Beki's stirring oratory will soon be forgotten, as will Alex. I will not risk the peace or my election."

Suzanne took Ari's limp hand. "He would want this, Pieter."

"Do not speak for him. I am not requesting your opinion."

"Pieter, you must do this."

"*Must?* Exactly who is going to make me?"

Outside in the night, Katrin is cursed by a blue-eyed woman. A father blesses his whirligig daughter; Ari whispers, *whatever it takes*. In a nearby hospital room, Alex awaits Pieter's verdict, her face a quicksilver of hope and despair. For what is having a child, at bottom, but an attempt to outwit death?

"I am going to make you," said Suzanne.

Pieter threw up his hands, as if inviting a witness to this farce. "You have no power over me."

The host gathered at the window, waiting on the schism between her mind and heart. *You never know until you're there.*

"You will do what Alex asks," said Suzanne, "or tomorrow I will confess to the Assembly how I tried to erase the guizi detection. And how you covered it up."

She would go to prison. Pieter would lose his election and career. Ari was already gone. Pieter would be left alone.

I will do it, thought Suzanne, watching Pieter reel. God help her, but she would do the dirty work. She was too old to wait for the world to change.

28

At sunrise, New Year's Day, the pieces came together. A secret surgical room was prepped. The Marines had an unmarked van ready for the ride to the Air Force base. Yet it seemed to Alex that her greatest feat was to shower on her own, though she did flood the bathroom and soak her hovering nurses.

Her nurses knew only that a procedure scheduled for seven in the morning required an empty stomach. They promised bacon and eggs when Alex came back up to her room. She could not tell them those eggs were going to get very cold, or thank them for their kindness. Nor could she stop obsessing over the salty bacon, a greasy, irrational craving. She didn't even like bacon.

Dr. Vito explained she would be awake for the brain mapping and ablation, since the brain lacked pain receptors. The fetal transplant, on her end at least, was a jiffy laparoscopic procedure. She would be wings to the sky long before the noon Assembly.

Alex studied her bare arms in the hospital gown, the long, light coastlines of new skin. The doctors promised the skin tones would soon blend. For now, she was a map of unknown places. The last point of departure was Strav.

She had insisted on a visit with him. The Kommandant called it her only stupid idea. If Strav learned of the plan, it would not matter that the vote was rigged, and they were out of time. He would try another loophole or blow something up, Handel would renege, and Alex would still be pregnant on that transport.

Alex had no clever answer. Strav would never forgive her this journey; her secrets translated as a lack of faith in him. Yet she had to make him understand.

Strav burst into the room, and Alex was struck by the time trick of her coma. He had been summoned from his furious pre-dawn ride, his face chapped from the cold and wind, his hair long enough to be tied back. For her, hours had passed since they spoke. For Strav, it was three hellish months. He stared at her and his face contorted, his eyes flooding with tears.

Guards watched on surveillance cams. She would not allow them to see Strav cry; she would not permit it. She rose precariously, placing her left hand behind her back, her right arm extended, palm up, a hopelessly archaic posture of demand.

Strav gave a sob of a laugh and took her in his arms for a gentle, shapeless waltz.

Her pain dissolved. He smelled of snow, sweat, leather, horses, sweet hay. He smelled like life. And after a few spins, like sex. Despite the voyeur guards, her hips moved against him and her breath went ragged.

"It's pregnancy hormones," said Strav, smug as when he'd been reading up. "Also, you must not eat sushi." He whispered intimate things that she hoped to God didn't get on record.

Alex pulled him to sit on the bed. She thought back to the night of a foggy deck, their talking in code, and how the words later sustained them.

"Listen, nomad. About the Petition. If it doesn't work, you'll need to trust me. Trust that I will be okay. An anarchic megapolitic like the Federation always presents opportunities, and I'm an asset to them now. I would send word to you as soon as I could. But that could be a long time, so you would get on with a busy, fulfilling life—"

He ignored her by grabbing a black marker and drawing on the white sheet.

"Nomad, please. I know you have a remarkable speech for this afternoon—"

"This afternoon," he said, not looking up, "I hit the Assembly with a metaphorical blowtorch and I take you home. Both of you."

A cottage floor plan was taking shape on the sheet. "Please, you can't win—"

"But I will!" He jumped up, shining and fierce. "Why do you think Handel restored my visitation rights? It's a conciliatory gesture, because he thinks the Assembly will grant the Petition. It's the only explanation."

Oh, my love, thought Alex, her cheeks burning. "There's always another explanation. We need to talk about Eric—"

Strav's face hardened with a ruthlessness that froze her. "We will not speak that name."

The sky streaked ivory, and sounds of a waking city came through the glass. Alex felt Strav's growing unease, the flutter of black wings he could not name. This could not be their parting. Sometimes denial was required to light your way through the dark. She handed Strav the marker and patted the sheet.

Five minutes later, the corrals were fenced and worms of smoke rose from the chimney. "It's north of the Golden Gate, where your father wanted," Strav said. "Danny Yang sold me the entire valley to the ocean. He holds the mortgage, an excellent rate." There was no mention of the purchase price of his soul. "The baby's room faces south, for the sun."

"The swing goes here." She drew in a cotton ball oak tree. "Are we sure about the sheep?"

"They're a tyke's first ride. Can be a bit rough on the parents." He pressed his ear against her little potbelly, and thumped it like a melon. "Hey there, little fella. Are you going to be rough on your parents?"

A knock at the door signaled time to go.

"Listen to me, nomad. After I turned sixteen and learned the truth, I always had one question. What if a man I loved learned I was a guizi? I did not believe that anyone could truly love me. You are a gift I can never repay. You make me stronger than I ever imagined. You give me faith in the future. Understand? Tell me you understand."

He pulled her to her feet and kissed her for a long time. "*Doubt thou the stars are fire*," he told her. "*Doubt that the sun doth move. Doubt truth to be a liar. But never doubt I love*. I'll see you tonight, sweetheart." Guards entered, and he was gone.

The loss hit her body before her mind, and her legs went out as if slide tackled. The nurses ran in scared and got her into bed. She rolled face down to muffle her sounds and screamed into the pillow until some dull worry came that the sheer physical violence of her grief might hurt the baby.

There had to be a guide to surviving the madness in her head. She thought of Eric's rational universe, what he had done for Strav. Suzanne, Patrick, her mother. Their stories were the same at heart. *It's clearer*, Suzanne said, *when it's for someone you love*. You make it through one day at a time.

An image came, of Strav scooping up a small, laughing boy, and setting him on the swing. The child flew high, crowing with excitement, and back to safe hands. It would do.

Vito looked ready to call it quits. Alex sat up, trembling and spent. A guard rolled a wheelchair to her. She pushed it away. This was her choice, an act of self-creation, and damned if she wouldn't begin on her own unsteady legs. What was a witch but a being of transformative power? She would be what she needed to be.

"Enough," said Alex. It was not so far to the door. Right foot swings into space, then the left. Such was the act of walking—you fall forward and catch yourself, each step a little act of faith. The body obeys, a miracle every time.

29

Eric figured Suzanne's messages would stop, but weeks turned into months, years, and messages kept coming, descriptions of research grants and summer fog, their new house in the valley, the aphids on her American Beauties. Eric knew that she and Bulgakov were tending more than roses. Beyond a numb pride in Alex's wickedly elegant solution, Eric felt—nothing.

His father stared back from the mirror each morning. *Quiet, boy, I am having greater thoughts.* His team at work was terrified of him. He slept a lot. He managed.

It took little effort to avoid old friends, and no effort to avoid Strav, who roved the Nations on a dark star rise through the Yang family business. Eric got that. He and Strav each needed their tools for the search. He needed his CyberIntel network. Strav needed wealth, great wealth, to access the shadow powers that bought and sold information and influence. The one time they passed in Headquarters, Strav looked through him like a dirty window. Eric had to check his own solid hands to see if he existed. He recalled the story of Genghis's anda, Jamukha. When Jamukha betrayed him, Genghis killed him slowly, without a drop of blood. Eric got that too.

The Regime claimed that Alex was well, and united with family, but refused to give proof. The Federation was in convulsions of assassination and coup, more dangerous and impenetrable than ever. Eric worried that Alex might be hungry or cold, because his mind rebelled against worse possibilities. Each day was a struggle against the truth that *not knowing* could be an end.

Three years after Alex's removal, Eric received an Uuganbayer-worthy note from Strav. *Come.* Eric crumpled the paper for a three-pointer. He was over needing anyone, and if Strav thought he'd come crawling, he could take a flying fuck in fantasy land.

The next day, Eric saw Strav and Alex across the avenue. Eric ran to them in such a fervor of anticipation that he knocked people over and caused a car crash. He grabbed the couple, and the resemblance ended—just youth, golden skin, and dark hair. The couple screamed for help, and Eric knew he was lost.

The Sunday fog cleared as Eric drove north over the Golden Gate Bridge. The old highway rolled along golden hills, a poke of green finger bay, dark sheaths of wooded ridge guarding the ocean. Red-tailed hawks rode the thermals, foxes stared, and Eric almost rolled the Jeep avoiding a flock of wild turkeys. Their outraged gaggles confirmed the trip was a monumental mistake.

"I'm returning a book," Eric explained at the Tennessee Valley sentry post. The road ended at a cottage with a stone chimney and a gnarled oak with a swing. The chestnut colt in the corral, teeth bared for a chance at his arm, looked sired by Fast Talker. A generation had done nothing to alter the disposition.

Suzanne came from the cottage. Eric gave a wary glance around. "He'll be back soon," said his cousin, hands-on-hips. Eric was spared her lecture by the serene arrival of Yuri Bulgakov, looking like a born rancher in patched overalls. A goblin screech came from a knoll of eucalyptus. A blonde teenage boy and two younger girls chased a toddler on a bleating sheep.

"Sasha Beki!" Suzanne yelled. "You leave poor Mutton alone!" The wild rumpus disappeared behind a barn.

"Sasha is nickname for Alexander," explained Yuri. "The records say he is orphan Strav adopted. But is getting, *da,* complicated."

The blonde teen, explained Suzanne, was Vlad, the pickpocket from Abad, now a Special Admissions at the Institute. Lena and Lia Kotas also attended school in the city.

"Hurry," screamed the girls. "Sasha's on the roof!" The adults ran to the barn. Eric had no explanation for the vertigo-inducing sight of the child standing like a weather vane fifteen feet above the gravel drive. Vlad was climbing a rainspout to reach him, while the twins yelled directions. Eric looked up at Sasha and understood the *da*-complication. No one could ever mistake his paternity. The beautiful boy perched atop the world was a glossy-haired copy of Strav.

The boy laughed, an infectious silvery gurgle, and Eric heard Alex in there even if he couldn't see her.

"Get down," Eric thundered, meaning for the child to wait on his bottom. Sasha gave him the heart attack grin that Eric knew too well, and obeyed by launching his little body in Eric's general direction. Eric rocketed into a diving football stretch of pure muscle memory. He caught and rolled with the child inches before the ground.

"Again!" demanded Sasha, to Eric's back-spasm groans.

Eric reclined on the playroom sofa with a melted ice pack. Center on the wall was a silver framed, wedding-style portrait of Strav and Alex dancing at the Black and White Gala. They looked absurdly young and happy. It was like contemplating light traveled from a distant star.

"Strav wants you to read this." Suzanne tossed Eric a manilla envelope instead of the pain pills he wanted. "Alex wrote him a letter right before the—procedure. She told Vito to wait three years to deliver it. She knew when you fools would be ready." Suzanne left him alone.

The letter was a few lines of hasty scrawl on hospital stationery. Eric felt Alex's hand on his chest—how's the big ticker?—and it struck him full force that they never got to say goodbye.

Eric was right to issue the warrant based on what he knew. He was the only one of us with the courage to do right. You left your brother bleeding in the dark. Forgive and return him to

your fire, if not for my sake, or because you miss him every day,
then for our son. He is a child of Eric's heart, too, and Eric will
protect him with his life.

Faith, nomad. You know I will find a way.

Eric replaced the letter, and he wept. He cried without restraint, the way Strav used to, body-shaking sobs for Alex, and Jacob, for the lost chances with his own parents, for the missing and the dead, the wounded left behind, and the idiot loneliness of it all.

The door opened. Sasha hopped over to him, wearing a pull-up and reversible Superman-Batman cape. "You gots a boo-boo?" the child demanded.

"Kinda," said Eric. He wiped his face on the cape and looked closer at Sasha's eyes. They weren't Strav's brown-and-gold flecked, or Alex's weird blue, but a yellow-streaked amber. Eric felt a touch of awe; the long arm of Genghis had reached out with this one.

"I gots a boo-boo too." Sasha showed a minuscule scab on his round tummy. Mutton had a boo-boo, too, and Lancelot the rooster, and every nameable animal in the valley, an extravagant flow of language for a child barely two, and not a syllable less than Eric expected of Strav's kid.

Eric pulled the *Bulfinch* from his bag. Sasha tried to lick the gold leaf. Eric took him in his lap, and they found a story to read.

When Strav looked in, Sasha was sprawled over Eric's chest, the child sinking and rising with each booming snore. Strav took in Eric's pasty face and bulging middle. Good lord, anda. Tomorrow they would run a mile and shoot some hoops. Take it slow. He glanced again at Eric's gut. Very slow.

Strav peeled the child off the sleeping mountain. He dressed Sasha and carried him past the freshly poured foundations for the new cottages and sport court.

"Did you make things change yet?" Sasha asked with a yawn. It was the explanation offered for his father's absences, and he asked it whenever Strav returned even from a grocery run.

"Working on it," said Strav. The fog billowed up the valley and shape-shifted the sky. The boy was warm and flushed from sleeping, and Strav held him close against the wind. Talker Too whinnied at their approach.

"Eric is the *best* horse guy," Sasha said. Strav started to retort that Uncle Eric couldn't ride a rocking horse, but he felt Alex shoot him a look: no jealousy. "Oh, fine," he said, and she laughed with a breeze on his face.

They cantered up the fire road that ran high along the cliffs edging the Pacific. Sasha sat in front of Strav, ecstatically gripping the coarse mane.

The change he promised his son was coming, seismic jolts large and small. Sasha needed to be raised here with blood family while his father was off waging war. Eric didn't know it yet, but he was about to be promoted to Chief of a new Security Ops West Division, headquartered in San Francisco. The Bat would soon arrive with a visa for medical school. The valley was destined for raucous years, filled with the pitter-patter of little Burton-Beki feet.

Rest while you can, anda, Strav thought with a grin.

There was no rest for him. He had an empire to bring down, a wife to win back, and a homeland to free. He was almost thirty; Genghis had torched half the world by then.

"*Chu!*" shouted Sasha, his arms out for flight. "*Chu!*" And they took the ridge at a gallop.

Strav pulled up at the peak. To the west, an unbounded gunmetal ocean merged into heavy skies. Back in the valley, the little house curled up and dreamed.

The colt pranced and fought to keep running. Sasha laughed, a trill of unconditional joy that filled Strav with wonder. He kissed his son's warm, silky head and turned the horse toward home.

ACKNOWLEDGMENTS

My heartfelt gratitude to the gifted teachers and contributors who gave this story a voice. Professors Mary Ann Koory and Lewis Buzbee shaped both author and manuscript. Suzy Vadori did an insightful edit. Brooke Warner, publisher, and Shannon Green made the novel a reality.

Jeff Appleman was my sage on immigration law, and Paula Goodman-Crews on ethics. Special thanks (and apologies) to Susan Birren, PhD, and Randy Taplitz, MD, for the science and medical premises. Daniel Taplitz, writer and filmmaker, was my guide for all things creative.

Ellie Smith and Natalie Venezia were brave early readers. Nancy Fish guided on publishing. Bonnie Ross, Suzanne Engelberg, Lisa and John Mathews, Becky Hlebasko, and Leslie Barry were generous sounding boards. Don Sr and Dolly Joseph gave "gig 'em" support. Iona Brindle, Dr. Kevin Nayar, Kelsey Harrington, Marissa Pittard, and Dr. Bruce Birren were a brain trust on subjects from academia to biotech and media.

Our found family in San Diego was an endless source of love, rowdiness, and encouragement for the novel. Thanks to Paula and Tom Crews, Natalie and Paul Sager, Rose and Dave Neagle, Joyce and Rob Cameron, Jen and Tom Turner, Kris and Matt Spathas, Joyce Maggiore and Guillermo Marrero.

I'm grateful to my brilliant siblings, Dan, Sue, and Ran, for literally everything. Our parents, Phyllis and Richard, blessed us with life lessons about creating art, and big thinking.

Above all, thanks to my explorer children, Kevin, Adam, and Jessie, each an inspiration beyond words. And Don, my husband and hero. You were always there when the page was blank.

ABOUT THE AUTHOR

SHERI T. JOSEPH graduated from UC Berkeley, earned a JD from UC Law San Francisco, and studied economics, geography, and creative writing. She serves as executive director of a nonprofit corporation that supports affordable housing for families, veterans, refugees, and vulnerable populations. She and her husband have three adventurous children, and live in Tiburon, California. *Edge of the Known World* is her debut novel.

Author photo © Theo Taplitz

Looking for your next great read?

We can help!

Visit www.gosparkpress.com/next-read
or scan the QR code below for a list
of our recommended titles.

SparkPress is an independent boutique publisher
delivering high-quality, entertaining, and engaging
content that enhances readers' lives, with a special
focus on commercial and genre fiction.